Published by: GladEye Press
Editors: Donovan Reves, GladEye Press
Beta Reader: Marissa Byfield
Interior Design: J.V. Bolkan
Cover Design: Iron Serif and Sharleen Nelson
ISBN-13: 978-1-951289-13-3 (trade)
ISBN-13: 978-1-951289-14-0 (hardcover)
ISBN-13: 978-1-951289-15-7 (e-book)
Library of Congress Control Number: 2024940753

Printed in the United States of America.
10 9 8 7 6 5 4 3 2 1
The body text is presented in Adobe Jenson Pro, 11 point for easy readability.

Footman of the Ether

Book Two of the Heartstone Series

JASON A. KILGORE
https://jason-kilgore.com/

GladEye Press
Springfield, OR

Dedication

For my dear friend, Jason Paul.

REGIONAL MAP

Taxia and Surrounding Lands

CHAPTER ONE

Caranamere

In all the worlds and all the dimensions Darilos Velar had known, Irikara was unmatched for its fine balance between scorching and freezing, chaos and order, blandness and flamboyance. Irikara was a world of contrasts and compromises, making it rich in energy. Little wonder the gods fought over it.

Does fighting over this world threaten that valuable balance, or does it accentuate it? He gave a wry smile. *Yes,* he decided, *it accentuates it. Peace, after all, is so very boring.*

He stood on a hilltop absorbing the sunny, late-autumn morning, just past sunrise. A light breeze, chill with the promise of winter, rustled the dry grass at his feet, yet the heat from the sun warmed his blond hair. Below him lay a valley adorned with changing oaks and elms. The vale seemed on fire with the vermilion and canary yellow of dying leaves, their host trees pulling away the life essence through each fragile petiole until all that was left was this brilliant display of sorrow.

In the center of the valley was situated the town of Caranamere, of the nation of Taxia. Its sleepy streets and somber stone buildings bespoke simplicity and harmony with the setting. A bell tower rang the hour, its deep toll echoing off the edifices of the Astronomer's Guild at the town's heart, then out to the surrounding hillsides and beyond into the bright cerulean sky. Two small children ran down the flagstone-paved main street playing "tag the orc." Goodwives fetched water from the town fountains. A baker pushed a small wagon filled with freshly baked loaves and called out for customers. Thin trails of smoke wafted over the town as townsfolk awoke to light hearth fires.

"How pastoral," Darilos muttered.

"Pastoral?" asked Apostle Agnon at his side—one of seven priests standing on the hilltop with Darilos. "Let us not wax poetic when destruction is at hand." The high priest of the Brotherhood of Blood, with his six disciples, were all dressed in the Brotherhood's crimson vestments. Darilos was not of the Brotherhood, and his garish red and orange traceried robe set him apart.

"Pastoral," Darilos repeated. "It's a shame we must disturb such simple beauty."

Agnon narrowed his eyes at Darilos. "You had better deliver on your promise. I've staked everything on this, Outlander."

Outlander, Darilos thought, a suitable alias he had given himself—one of many—for tasks like this. *An alias of an alias.*

Darilos followed Agnon's gaze off to his left. A massive, iron-reinforced oak chest sat on the hilltop with them, a long metal bar arcing over the chest like a giant handle. Even with the help of magic, it had taken all night for the disciples to lug the chest up the hillside on a strained wooden litter. Bright yellow light streamed through the chest's lid, so bright it defied the morning sun.

Strapped to the side of the chest was a long, slender sword—the Key of Otemus. The key featured a gleaming, silvery blade and a two-handed hilt, yet the blade was oddly carved with squared pits and curious projections. Darilos could just take the sword now, by force if he wanted to, but a contract had been made. He had to wait for the task to be completed. Contracts, oaths, and promises were perhaps the only things he held sacrosanct.

One of the disciples, a man with a cherubic face and eyes so blue they could only be described as ultramarine, stepped up to Agnon. "All is readied, Apostle."

"Thank you, Immolatos." Agnon then turned back to Darilos. The apostle's stark green eyes contrasted with his ashy, pock-marked face. "Your dragon is late! He was supposed to strike at dawn."

"Mordan does as he must, apostle," Darilos replied, but he sensed the dragon nearby. He didn't need to look. Its energy was blazed like a brilliant star on a hilltop behind them, to the west and behind a low hill. Evidence that he'd been infused with the power of the Triumvirate gods, so-called "terrestrial energy," which made up nearly all magical energy in the world of Irikara. But Darilos couldn't usually feel it unless it was very strong, since he was not of this world. He knew that the Triumvirate, the three gods who created the world of Irikara and now were imprisoned in it, would be reaching through the bars that morning, so to speak, endowing their energy into Mordan.

The Emerald Dragon had been there in the distance all morning, watching, calculating. *The Brotherhood priests can't feel it. Pitiful.*

"Why must we be so far away, Outlander? I can hardly see the Guild towers from this distance. It must be half a mile, at least!"

This peevish cultist whines like a child, Darilos thought. He didn't bother to answer Agnon. He could see farther than these humans. They would need every cubit they could spare during the spectacle to come.

Darilos felt the dragon's energy shift. Mordan was on the move, silently swooping down into the neighboring valley toward them and the town.

"Apostle, if you have doubts about continuing, now is your last chance to stop this," Darilos said.

"Of course I have no doubts!"

At that moment, the Emerald Dragon roared over the hilltop behind them, scattering the disciples. Agnon ducked and yelped in surprise. Treetops swayed with the cyclone from his wings. Darilos stood unfazed.

One of the largest of the twelve dragons, at around eighty yards in length including the tail, Mordan's body bulged with muscle, covered with scales gleaming like emeralds, and crisscrossed with scars. His back was armored with shining steel bars like a metallic exoskeleton of overlapping bones, with a skeletal metal helmet to match. He turned his broad head to look back for a signal. One-eyed from an ancient wound, with wide lateral horns like a water buffalo's and a mouth lined with serrated fangs, the dragon's visage was a glimpse into terror.

Darilos pointed down at the Guild compound—a sign that the mission was to proceed. The dragon roared again and swooped low over the town, gaining speed, then shot up past the resplendent hillsides to an incredible height, almost out of sight.

The bell tower rang out in chaotic tolling. Faint screams and shouts of villagers echoed into the sky. They knew the Emerald Dragon's reputation.

Darilos leaned forward. *This should prove interesting*, he thought.

Figures moved on the fortified walls of the Guild compound. The mages there harmonized their spell casting, creating a shimmering *Shield* spell, one of the strongest he'd seen, over the center of the buildings.

Darilos chuckled. A *Shield* spell would be little protection against the will of a dragon.

Apostle Agnon called his disciples to him, then brought forth a leather wineskin. Reciting a quick prayer, he poured out the blood of three virgin youths—two boys and a girl sacrificed just before they came up the hill—coating his right hand and the right hands of each of the disciples. The disciples knelt and bowed their heads, raising their bloodstained hands in the air.

"Oh, great Triumvirate," Agnon chanted, "to you we give the promise of the future. Take from us the shreds of our jaded past. Correct our ignorance. Deliver us to your great powers. See before us a symbol of our dedication to you!"

Darilos paid little attention to the mage's prayer, even as he felt the energy of the hill beneath him magnify, welling up from the core of the world.

The Triumvirate had come to bear witness. All three gods, creators of this world, Irikara, trapped in its energies by the Outer Gods.

Agnon finished his prayers and shouted, "They are here! We are in the presence of the Triumvirate!" The disciples each gave a hail of praise. Agnon searched the sky for the dragon. Darilos looked as well and found Mordan now but a speck in the blue.

The Emerald Dragon finally stopped his ascent, pausing a moment at the suffocative roof of the world. Then he shot downward toward the town, his descent reaching an astonishing speed.

"He'll kill himself!" Agnon gasped.

Darilos smirked. *He still underestimates the dragon!*

Mordan pulled in his wings and rolled himself into a tight ball. He barked a one-word spell. The syllable thundered across the sky. He burst into scintillating green flames and multiplied the speed of his descent to the point of blurring.

Mordan struck the Astronomer's Guild like a meteor.

A fireball of blinding white plasma exploded from the point of impact, instantly enveloping the town and shaking the valley. The wind and heat of the blast shot up and over the hillsides, leveling trees, hitting Darilos and the others with a massive wall of force that threw the others to the ground, temporarily deafening them with a grinding roar of destruction.

Darilos stood motionless. The heat radiated raw, magical energy. It swept through him, energized him, sent his senses into rapture. He laughed openly into the blast, feeling the heat sting the back of his throat. It was the most thrilling sensation he had felt in millennia.

The valley below was a hellfire. Smoke and dust exploded in a billowing cloud half a mile into the clear sky. Flames raged up hillsides in infernal tempests. The mages' *Shield* spell had no effect against such powerful magic, as the dragon's spell had been "renegade magic"—an incantation of immense power, forbidden by the Council of Mages. *Bombard*, Mordan had called this one, in his last message.

Darilos and the others were just out of range of the fires on their distant hilltop. The men were now struggling to their feet.

"Gods!" Agnon gasped. "Did he have to destroy the entire valley?"

Darilos turned and leered at the apostle. "My dear mage, what do you expect when you hire a dragon as mercenary?"

He glanced at the Key of Otemus, still strapped to the chest. "Now, apostle, my payment please."

Hardly taking his eyes off the destruction, Agnon gave a nod and gestured to one of his disciples, who unstrapped the sword from the chest and carried it to the apostle. Agnon unceremoniously handed it over to Darilos.

Darilos held it up, marveling at the lightness of the metal and the poetic nature of the valley's flames playing on the long, silvery, reflective blade.

The apostle raised an eyebrow. "I don't understand the significance of this weapon to you, Outlander. It is of valuable metal, some platinum alloy, but much of the treasure we brought is of greater value and power. It is magical only in its ability to remain sharp and untarnished."

Darilos stabbed the blade into the ground before him. "Its value to me is of no concern to you." He looked back at the destruction and pointed. "Behold!"

Seeming beyond possibility, a giant figure rose from the impact crater. Shadowy and warped to Darilos' sight by the heat and distance, Mordan winged up and over the smoke and dust.

"Your mercenary comes for his payment," Darilos proclaimed to Agnon.

The apostle waved his disciples away from the great chest. But Mordan was in no hurry. The soot-covered dragon orbited the valley a couple times before closing in on their hilltop. The dragon was visibly exhausted, but Darilos knew he was likely still powerful enough to give a good fight.

When the Emerald Dragon had flown near enough, Darilos hailed him and gestured at the chest. "Mordan, your payment is here."

But Mordan maintained a distance, circling the hillside. "We feel your energies now, Outlander." He spoke in Taxin, accented with the speech of the Northlands. "Or rather, the lack of them. You are not as you appear." He flew a bit closer and hovered in place for a moment, an act not easily performed for a dragon of his size, sending gusts from his wings. Darilos waited, amused at the game. Then Mordan's good eye opened wide with recognition. "Yes! We know you now! It has been a long time. Shall We state your true nature to your friends, so that they may fear you? Or perhaps we should order you to do our bidding, Footman?"

Darilos frowned. The dragon *would* go and ruin a good day, wouldn't he? "I would consider it a breach of contract, and gladly melt down the chest and your payment with a word. Go now with your reward and trouble me no longer."

Mordan stopped hovering and flew backward. "That sword before you—the Key of Otemus—yes, we recognize it. Is this your feeble payment as their middleman? You know it's useless to you. You cannot wield it, and the lock is long lost."

"It is of no concern to you, dragon."

Quickly gathering speed, Mordan circled the hilltop and gained altitude. "Hmm. Perhaps you have found that lock, then? Very well," he shouted. "We shall leave you to your fate and whatever fool's errand you embark on with that artifact."

Mordan shouted a spell. An explosion heaved up the hilltop, throwing the disciples off their feet again in a shower of soil and rock—propelling the Key of Otemus high into the air. Darilos stumbled sideways, trying to catch himself. Mordan caught the key midair and stabbed its blade through Darilos' torso, impaling him and throwing him to the ground. Darilos let out a bestial roar of pain, clutching at the weapon and arching his back.

In moments the dragon was gone, carrying the massive chest with his forefeet and disappearing, laughing, into the northern sky. Apostle Agnon crawled over to Darilos. "Outlander!" he yelled.

Darilos growled, sitting upright. He coughed out a strained chuckle as he watched the dragon's retreat. "Cheeky bastard," he muttered. Mordan had known perfectly well that the blade wouldn't kill him. Wrapping a hand around the handle of the key, he yanked the sword out of himself, emitting an inhuman bellow.

Agnon stood and stumbled back, drawing in a harsh breath. "By the three gods!"

Darilos winced as the bloodless wound closed. *It's pathetic how fragile human bodies are. Of all the forms I could have chosen!* He stood and stabbed the Key of Otemus into the ground once more.

Agnon gave Darilos a sidelong look, eyes wide, shaking his head. "How did you survive that wound? Outlander, why did the Emerald Dragon call you 'Footman?' Why would he think you should do his bidding, but then deal you what should have been a mortal blow?" He backed away from Darilos. "What *are* you?"

Darilos ignored him, scratching his chest through the cut robe where the wound had been. He looked down upon the burning valley and the crater at its heart. Nothing more than rubble remained of the institution of magic that had been the "Astronomer's Guild." Magic was illegal in Taxia, and yet this secret society and its annexes in other towns had its tendrils in every facet of this region, right up to the throne of Taxia's king. The Brotherhood of Blood had paid for a major political coup that would shake this part of the world, and, they thought, take care of a potentially powerful enemy of the Triumvirate. But using the Nexus, Darilos had seen enough of the future to know that the Guild could have gone either way in this fight.

There can be no neutrality in battles between the gods.

Darilos didn't care about all that. A minor loss for a greater gain. His mission was to find the Convergence, a mysterious object of such incredible power that its potential worried the Outer Gods. The mages of the Great Towers of Magic would investigate the destruction of Caranamere, and Darilos would use them to retrieve this powerful artifact. Whatever form this Convergence took, it would be the focal point for control of the world's magic. The Outer Gods knew it. *That* was why he was here. *That* was why he had traveled to the material world. *But does the Triumvirate know about the Convergence?* he wondered. The Key of Otemus seemed to mean nothing to the Brotherhood, so perhaps the Triumvirate they served didn't yet know.

And another notion remained at the forefront of his thoughts as he watched the conflagration spread up the mountainsides. A notion that kept him from rest, no matter where he had gone in the past few years.

The woman. That human mage he had seen at the Battle of the Tower of Light riding astride a griffin, at battle with the elves. She was the One who was always at the Nexus of futures in the Ether. She was the one he had foreseen before coming to this world, and then again, in person for a brief moment. The one named Torra Com Gidel. So rich in energy was she that it filled his senses just being near her for that brief moment. She would be the one he needed to implement his plan.

According to the scant information he could find about her, the burning valley below had been where she had been raised and learned the ways of magic. That certainly was no coincidence.

The Tower of Light would surely send the woman with their Expeditionary Mages. And he would be with her, at last.

Darilos trembled at the thought.

"Answer me, Outlander!" Apostle Agnon shouted. "What *are* you?"

Darilos shook off his thoughts. He had almost forgotten about the Brotherhood. "Something more formidable than the Emerald Dragon."

He looked again at the destruction below. "It is time for you and your disciples to leave," Darilos continued, his voice measured. "Our business is finished. Do not record it. Discuss it with no one. If you should see me again, do not reveal my role in this, no matter what the circumstances." He turned to look at the apostle and narrowed his eyes. "And do not stand in my way. Defy my demands and in your last moments you will find out exactly what I am."

The apostle scowled, but replied, "Whatever that sword may mean to you, you are still a hero to the Triumvirate. May the Triumvirate bless you for your assistance in their cause. But do not stand in our way, either!" He raised a bloody hand in salute, spared another look of horror at the destruction unleashed in the valley below them, then turned and fled down the hillside with his disciples.

Darilos gazed again on the flaming valley and mused on the contrast of the burning hell below against the blue heaven of the skies above. It was a fitting symbol for his methods, using the Triumvirate's followers to achieve the goals of the Outer Gods. Yet another compromise in a world of compromises.

Darilos smiled. What was he? If only the apostle knew! He looked back to make sure they had gone.

In exaltation of his true identity, Darilos dropped the masquerade. His human body disintegrated into ash. From its shell burst the giant, serpentine body of a demon. Sapphirine skin. Blue flames dancing. Slim amber wings jutting out like dagger blades. Talons that he held out to clack in the air in front of his long, rippled muzzle. He stretched to his full height, joints and tendons popping, muscles shaking. Enraptured, he roared into the burning valley like the thunder of its destruction. He was once again his true self …

He was Azartial.

Demon dragon.

Footman of the Ether.

CHAPTER TWO
Transmutation

Torra felt a change of energy ripple through the Tower of Light. It was subtle, a murmur in a great and ever-present symphony of forces constantly flowing from the depths of the world through the conduit that was the tower, then into the atmosphere above. She raised her cracking, diseased hand and placed it on the cool, bonerock surface of the nearest wall. The ripple was there, traveling up through the stone like a shiver on a cool spring night. She closed her eyes, let the Tower energies become her, let them seep into her mind, and in moments the bonerock warmed and melded with her energies, became almost pliable like milky white flesh, pulsing not with blood but with power, untamed power, rising like a geyser from the core of the world.

The ripple was familiar. An old friend she had lost. But she couldn't quite place it … and something was wrong.

"There you go again, stroking the walls."

Torra lost the ripple. Annoyed, she turned to face her tawny skinned tower mentor, Mistress Kai Ninga'ai, the master assigned by the Towermaster to teach her in the ways of advanced magic, though she was Torra's senior by less than a score of years. Kai's almond eyes sported her all-too-common smug look of having cracked a joke, but this only infuriated Torra more. Torra explained, "I felt a disturbance in the Tower energy."

With a graceful stride, Kai stepped past Torra into the room and ran her hand over the top of a gray granite block standing in the center of the room. "Funny. I don't remember that being the lesson you were to learn today. It's good I came to check on your studies." Kai's voice swung with the singsong rhythm of her Quisha accent. "You have not yet transmuted the stone." Her eyes sharpened. "Do not disobey!"

"But the Tower energy. Something has happened."

"It is not your concern, *apprentice*! Now return to your lesson. Focus! You lack focus!"

Torra tightened her lips, but she remained silent and stepped back to her spot in front of the stone, then knelt and closed her eyes.

"Now," Kai said. The anger that had been in her eyes only a moment before had now softened. "Place your mind in the stone. Let it expand and fill the block. Feel its structure."

Torra did as told. She closed her eyes, hands held over the granite block, and chanted, "*Taedium tenddori.*" She held a picture of the stone block in her mind and moved toward it, but her concentration wavered. The energies of the tower flowed all around her, through the floor and up the walls. Trying to feel the energy of the block was like trying to swim against the current of a raging river. Soon she had found an opening, an eddy in the current, and moved into it.

The ripple was there still, in the Tower energy, distracting her. She had to concentrate.

"Focus," Kai said. "I sense you in the block, but you waver. Let your mind expand into the block's form. Sense the dense areas. Feel the veins of minerals running through it."

Torra felt the block's presence, let her mind reach into it and sense its structure. "I feel it. There is a dense area on the far side."

"Yes. Good," Kai said. "Now go deeper. Feel the particles of the stone. Feel how their vibrations interact. Then use your mind to alter those vibrations. It is time for you to transmute the stone, just as I showed you. Change the granite to marble."

Torra strained to keep it all together, gritting her teeth. The stone was too large. The currents around her were too powerful. She felt herself slipping. It was too much for her level of experience.

"I have to pull out," Torra said. "Too much."

"Too late. Don't pull out. Transmute it now!" Kai snapped. "You could be trapped!"

Torra grimaced, felt her nose start to bleed. Suddenly the walls of the block seemed to fall inward onto her mind, pushing against her. She tried, but couldn't pull out. "I can't!" she screamed. Her head felt like it was being crushed. "The pain!"

Kai was shouting at her, but Torra could no longer hear. The energies engulfed her, pounded at her senses like ocean breakers.

Then a door opened in the back of her mind. The same "door" that opened and took control of her at the battle for the tower. In desperation she grabbed it, threw it wide. Deep energy gushed forth into her, then out to the stone.

There came a deafening crack. The floor shook. Kai screamed. Torra fell to her side, clutching her head. All fell silent.

The pain in her head subsided. *What have I done?* She opened her eyes.

Through the dusty air she saw that the stone had completely transmuted from gray granite to pure white marble, but it had also shattered into rubble. Shards had exploded outward in all directions, embedding into the walls and ceiling of the room. Torra's white robe was ripped in several places. She gasped, looking down at a bloody spot on her right arm, and another on her left thigh. Gritting her teeth, she pulled a shard from her leg.

By the stars! What have I done? she thought again, then looked around for Mistress Kai.

Kai moaned. She had crumpled to the floor. Blood dribbled down her right cheek from a laceration on her brow. Eyes alight with anger, she shouted, "You are a danger! You lack control, apprentice!"

"What do you expect? *Transmutation* is a skill for more experienced mages." But she knew it was a poor excuse. She was more advanced than her peers.

Kai stood, shaky and unsteady. A bloodstain was blooming like some macabre rose across the chest of her white robe. She pointed at Torra. "You have a great energy, Torra, but you will not control it."

"I can't."

"You *can*. You have. How else could you have defeated Peshiluud?"

Torra opened her mouth to speak, but couldn't find the words. At the Battle of the Tower of Light two years before, the spells had just come to her, found the right targets, annihilated the enemy. "I don't know."

She thought back to the feeling from the battle, the sense of vertigo as power rushed into her and expelled with such force she thought she would be torn apart. Visions of the battle flitted through her mind, like so many thousands of times since. The destruction of hundreds of mages and elves. The death of the ancient elvish leader, Peshiluud, pulled apart by invisible forces. The Gold Dragon, Ingal Jehai, releasing the Celestials into the world.

And the demon dragon, Azartial.

Torra shivered as she remembered the beast's eyes—intelligent, fiery, seething with alien energy. Deep wells of addictive power. *Such power!*

"Torra! Did you hear me?" Still bleeding, Kai stepped around the rubble to stand over Torra. Other mages had appeared in the doorway, peeping in to see what had exploded. "Control the energies. Allow just enough into you, then close it off."

Torra only shook her head.

Kai glanced up at the other mages, then looked back to Torra, a sneer spreading across Kai's face. "You are distracted—that is it! If you were not so frigid, maybe you would loosen up and let the energies come."

"You dare bring this up again!"

"What's the matter, apprentice? Strike a nerve? Will no man have you?"

Torra wanted to shout, *I don't need a man to be valid!* But she held her tongue. She didn't need to explain herself to this woman! "Leave my personal life out of this!"

"Casting magic *is* personal. It comes from your soul." Kai poked a finger into Torra's sternum. "But you would not know it, would you? You deny your own needs. You are as stiff and cold as a corpse."

Torra growled and stood to face her mistress. "At least I'm not a vamp like you, sleeping with any man who'd raise your robes and help you move up the Tower!"

"Look at you," Kai continued, ignoring Torra's gibe. "Diseased. Flaking skin. Smelly like rotten eggs. Dangerous. The Tower savior who cannot save herself."

How dare she use my disease against me! Torra shook with anger, then shouted, "*Raystonea!*" A bolus of light shot from her outstretched finger, narrowly missing Kai and hitting the bonerock wall.

Instantly Kai grabbed Torra's arm and cast a *Continuity* spell. "*Bene gontai!*" Kai shouted. Torra's *Beam* spell wouldn't stop. Kai's spell kept Torra's energy shooting from her, burning, etching a spastic line of cracks over the wall's surface as she struggled against Kai's iron grasp. Torra felt her energies flushing out of her through her finger.

"That is it!" Kai said, suddenly excited. "Feel the passion you poured into that spell. That is what you needed. Let it flow."

Torra fought to stop the spell, tried to cut the energy from her mind. But it wouldn't stop.

"Now reduce it," Kai said, urging.

"I can't!" The beam bounced up onto the ceiling, blasting off dust and bits of bonerock, then back down to the floor, smashing a small cask there. The water within boiled in the path of the beam before spilling out.

"Do not fight it. You cannot suddenly stop it outright. *Reduce* it, bit by bit."

Torra obeyed. Gradually, the beam became weaker and weaker until, at last, it disappeared. Kai loosened her grip. Torra yanked her arm free.

"You could have killed someone," Torra shouted.

"So could you, if what you did to the stone is any indication. You must learn control. You cannot just turn a powerful spell on and then turn it off. Manipulating energies at this level is not like casting a *Light* spell. It is a matter of degrees."

Torra understood. It was something she already knew from her studies, if only she could control herself.

The mages at the door were now jockeying for a better look, muttering and shaking their heads. "Go away!" Torra shouted, waving them off like flies, but they ignored her, whispering. She caught snippets of their gossip, "dangerous," "smelly bitch," " … should be thrown out … "

Finally, Kai shooed them away. "Give us some privacy!" she commanded, and they listened, moving away with obvious reluctance to stand in the corridor outside.

Torra glowered sidelong at Kai. "You shouldn't have said that about me."

"What? That you are frigid? I was trying to light your passion, apprentice, force you to anger so that you could conjure the energies for that spell. But, yes, you have developed a reputation." With a sardonic voice, she added, "Did you not know? Is it not obvious?"

She did know. The truth bit at her. Who could love her diseased body? Savior of the Tower, yes, in part, but rotting from the inside out from Brimstone Disease, or "demonskin" as some called it. It would take someone extraordinary to see past that afflicted shell to the being inside, the Torra Com Gidel that struggled to get out. She saw how the other mages looked at her, wrinkled their noses when she passed, muttered about "contamination," even though it was not contagious. None of them would do for a relationship. Medicines only took the edge off the disease, and the few clerics she had consulted had been of no use. Only the salve that herbalists had devised for her granted any level of relief.

All of a sudden, Kai tilted her head, her eyes going unfocused. Then Torra felt it too.

The Towermaster.

First came a prick at the mind, mildly painful, as the Towermaster melded the smallest portion of his sentience into hers. Then, from that small connection, waves of thought washed over her, urging her into sharing herself, pulling her mind into synchronicity.

Torra relaxed, let her mind be taken. It was an act of willpower that had to be learned.

Then the Towermaster spoke, though not in words—more like the thoughts made just before the mouth is impelled to move. Not the booming voice in her mind that she had imagined years ago, before she had joined the tower. No, gentler, almost apologetic. They were the whispers of a mentor, careful not to intrude on the more private corners of thought.

At first he sifted through her recent memory of her *Transmutation* spell, attempting to understand what had happened to his tower, but he quickly put that away.

Go to Taxia, he said. And in that thought a sense of urgency. She knew from his message, almost before the Towermaster communicated it, that the ripple she had felt originated in her homeland. On the heels of that thought was a brief emptiness, felt, as if from the heart, as when a loved one goes away; a mark that all communication—indeed, all flow of energy—had been lost from that region. *Travel with Mistress Kai. Be her guide to the land. Investigate the disruption with the Expeditionary Mages.* The thought shifted slightly, like a momentary frown: a reminder of her low rank in the tower and to obey the higher mages. *Be cautious. Dark forces rend the land.*

The Towermaster extricated himself from her mind, pulling away gently as if from an embrace. Torra supported herself on a nearby wall and rubbed her forehead. The experience always left her feeling dizzy, but she was getting used to it. Such communications were a mandatory part of how the tower worked, and were more common than she had once imagined, increasing in frequency the higher the rank of the mage.

Sometimes it was nothing more than a checkup, a "knock on the door" followed by a quick scan of the surface memory—his way of gauging the progress of her studies or the mood of the tower as a whole.

Torra wondered for probably the hundredth time what the Towermaster looked like. Was he as handsome as his voice (or, at least, the *thought* of his voice)? Only the most powerful masters had seen him in person.

She looked around. Mistress Kai was still in communication, her eyes closed with brows tensed. Clearly her message was more complex. Finally, with a sigh, Kai opened her eyes and took several deep breaths. Her pupils focused, and her eyes turned to look into Torra's.

"It seems the disturbance you sensed in the Tower energy was something after all. Are you ready to go home?"

Torra blinked in sudden realization. It had been two years since she left Taxia and the Astronomer's Guild—two years since joining the Gold Dragon, Ingal Jehai, in Peshilaree, then fighting the battle for the tower.

So much had happened. She was only twenty-four years old, and yet she'd already been part of a story that might one day be a legend.

What would her family think of her now? What about her friends? Her old suitor, Taenos? Would they hate her for openly practicing magic, an act illegal in Taxia? Taenos would. But others, like her mother, would be proud. And her aging, wizened master, Morikal, back at the Guild compound, certainly he would be.

"Home," she whispered.

The thought brought with it the earthy, creamy taste of hot salnac root soup with wild mushrooms, warm rye bread, and milk sweetened with covetberries fresh from the vine. The adoring smile of her mother, her dress sprinkled with flour from baking. The breeze through the oak trees of Caranamere. The rich, aged smell of the library of the Astronomer's Guild.

Kai straightened. "Clean this room and haul out the stone, then go and pack your things. We leave this afternoon, at Fifth Chime. Bring only what you can carry in your pack. You will need both arms and hands for the next step."

It dawned on Torra that she was being asked to investigate an important matter on behalf of the Towermaster. "Does this make me an Expeditionary Mage?" Torra asked.

Kai half turned, wiping at the cut on her face and smearing blood across her cheek. "Do not get cocky, *girl*. You are an apprentice, nothing more." Kai pushed past the snickering mages at the door and disappeared around the corner, the clack-clack of her boots echoing off the bonerock walls.

The mages turned back to stare at Torra, but she shot them a scolding look. With expressions that ranged from annoyance to fear, the mages turned and finally left Torra alone. The show was over.

She surveyed the room again, rubbing at the cut on her arm. "*Girl*, she calls me!" She stepped around the rubble to the far end of the room. The continuous bonerock walls of the tower thinned there to form a narrow, vertical window, so paper-thin as to be transparent. She forced her mind off the Towermaster's communication, a necessary thing to let the thoughts he planted in her sort themselves out. Otherwise they would annoyingly repeat in her dreams for days. "*Apprentice*, she calls me!" She shook with rage. She had been dubbed a "young master" at the Astronomer's Guild. But to be admitted to the Tower of Light, she was relabeled as an "apprentice" again, albeit on a "short ladder," as the Towermaster had put it, to getting promoted back to that status.

Her room was twenty floors up, far above any other building in the surrounding city of Taraman, but only about a fifth the way up the soaring Tower of Light. She gazed westward through the window, across the city and out onto the winding plain of the Alsanoos River. Though it was autumn, the sun still burned the vegetation, turning normally fertile fields into brown desiccation. Smoke wafted over the northwestern horizon, evidence of yet another forest fire in the timberlands there. This was the legacy of the Triumvirate's revenge on Ingal for not joining their conspiracy—a conspiracy to set themselves free to rule the world once more: constant environmental destruction of the White Lands Federation, an attempt to force Ingal into complying with their agenda. Faced with starvation and now fearing the tower after the battle, most citizens of the city of Taraman, around the tower, had moved into the devastated countryside, practicing subsistence farming, or fleeing to other towns in the Federation or south into Planistad. Torra didn't blame them.

People were dying in the hundreds from starvation and heat this summer and fall. Many more had died in the exceedingly cold winter before. The nation of Ocrin continued to threaten the western border. Elves still made sporadic attacks in the northern forest. Ingari tribesmen stalked the southern highlands. And, recently, Vinta pirates were raiding merchant ships in the Northron sea. The White Lands Federation was attacked from all sides.

It had been more than a year since Torra had visited Ingal and Rethuud at Palal Jehai, the palace of the Dragon of the Federation, but she kept in touch through messengers. He hid it well, but she knew the stress of the Federation's problems wore down the ancient dragon, exacerbating the mental issues spawned by his casting of the renegade spell at the battle for the tower.

As if in reminder of that fateful evening, two Celestials glided past the window, some fifty feet or so from the tower at her level. Their huge, angelic forms shone like stars, resplendent swords held at the ready. Their blank, eyeless faces turned outward, inexhaustibly watching for the enemy. They had hair of unruly blond curls, like those on a child, but their mouths gaped as if in a silent scream. Then they flew out of sight around the corner of the window. She never quite got used to seeing them. During the Battle of the Tower of Light, Ingal had opened the dimensional gate to allow them entry into the world. They'd been soundlessly guarding the tower ever since.

Torra turned back to the rubble in the middle of the room, then looked up to see tiny shards of marble embedded in the bonerock ceiling. Rock embedded in rock. It was a marvel she didn't kill herself and Kai when the block exploded. She had put far too much of her magical energy into it, at the end. Yet, despite herself, her initial shock at seeing it turned to a sort of conceit. She HAD transmuted the granite into pure white marble. It was a feat worthy of a master.

What would the Gold Dragon think of her lesson, she wondered?

She could almost hear his baritone chuckle.

CHAPTER THREE

A Surprise Visit

Ingal scowled. He raised a hefty forefoot to his face as if to wipe away his annoyance.

The Gold Dragon lay in the vast Audience Chamber of his palace, Palal Jehai. A few steps below his dais, all six viziers of the White Lands Federation, along with their generals, stood squabbling over matters of national defense and trade, their voices echoing off the vaulted dome of the chamber. Judging by the water clock to the side of the dais, this tedious audience had lasted three hours already.

"My lord, we must use our trade funds to fortify the Namistad border with Ocrin," shouted the Namistadi general, his voice gravelly. "Just last week we had another raid from Ocrin forces at Highwatch Gap."

"Yet it is to the north, at the entrance to Long March Valley, that their main attack force is focused," retorted the vizier of Alneri, Corin Declain, a young woman with broad shoulders who commanded armies with her badger-like demeanor. "We must concentrate our fortification efforts there."

"Alneri has already received the lion's share of our trade profits to rebuild Alneri castle, yet not a single stone has been laid," stated a third vizier, Entar Misaqi, representing the state of Aestistad. "It certainly doesn't help that you've taken some of those funds for your lavish statehouse."

"That was for security!" Vizier Declain responded. "Unlike you, our Lord Jehai didn't see fit to send his own guards to protect my estate."

It was no secret that Ingal had a closer tie to Misaqi than the others, and the favoritism was a source of awe and jealousy for them. Ingal had saved her life at the Keep of Casan two years before. She had been the only surviving vizier, a trauma that turned her hair white soon after. "It is time Aestistad receives its due for being the crux of our international trade," Misaqi said. "Aestistad's borders are no less secure against the elves. Do you forget the raid on our villages last month?"

"So what if you have a few squads of elves at your border?" Declain retorted. "*My* state is staring down an entire *army* of Ocrin soldiers! I've been to the front. I've seen fields turned red with blood, the young bodies of my men hacked to pieces. Have you? I have!"

Misaqi bristled at the comment. "And *you* haven't seen your soldiers *melted* by elvish acid spheres, their bodies dissolved right down to the bone! If all my priests weren't called away to your castle, maybe we wouldn't suffer that nightmare!"

Ingal could barely focus on their politics and feuds. He was exhausted from a night with little sleep, his eyes straining to stay open. These petulant viziers argued over how to spend what amounted to a trifle fund doled out from dwindling trade profits and how to allocate a shrinking population of fighting-aged men. Always, now, he had to choose who would be defended and who would not. It was enough that he had to lead the White Lands Federation during a time of war, against both the nation of Ocrin and the elves of Peshilaree, but the droughts and fires that plagued the land added to the discord of his life.

And then there was the "event" of that morning—that sudden mental slap in his face.

And it all came around to the Triumvirate gods.

The summer droughts and fires, the winter blizzards, the spring freezes were all their doing, his punishment for not joining them in their attempt to seize control of the world's magic. It was at the Triumvirate's behest that the elves fought the White Lands Federation.

And it was the Triumvirate who had invaded his mind that morning.

"Perhaps I should recall my clerics from the front!" Misaqi shouted at Declain. "Then perhaps you'd give me a little credit!"

"Here here!" yelled another vizier in support.

Declain pulled her sword and pointed it at Misaqi, an act forbidden in the dragon's audience hall. "You do that and you'll have *me* to contend with, you dragon's pet!"

"Enough!" Ingal shouted. He slammed a massive forefoot to the bonerock tiles of his dais. The boom reverberated throughout the dome of the Audience Chamber. Instantly the viziers and their generals fell silent. Ingal's ministers, who stood by him on the dais, fell to their knees and bowed. Declain sheathed her sword, seeming to only now realize she'd drawn it, and both she and Misaqi joined the others in acquiescence.

Ingal hadn't realized until that moment that he was standing on all fours with wings outspread.

"You squabble like griffins over fresh prey," he continued. He closed his eyes and took a deep breath. "Let us be civil." He paused to look each of the viziers in the eye. One by one, they bowed in acknowledgment of the Gold Dragon's control.

Ingal allowed himself to relax a bit, refolding his wings. He lay back down, trying to ignore the weakness of his left legs and his drooping, fluttering right eyelid—physical evidence of the coma he had suffered after the Battle of the Tower of Light—a coma that was the result of casting the renegade spell that won the battle. The symptoms manifested themselves most during times of emotion, as if to underscore the weakness of his mind.

"We have come to a decision," Ingal continued, using the "royal We" that all dragons use. "Thirty percent of trade profits will remain with Aestistad, to protect against attacks from Peshilaree, outfit the navy against northern raiders, and to help bolster trade along the Incense Road southward through Planistad. Our Federation needs the income and support of the Southern Nations, and with the war with Ocrin, trade routes to the west have become too disrupted to count on. Thirty percent will go to Alneri to help rebuild Alneri Keep and protect the border with Ocrin and Peshilaree, and thirty percent will go to Namistad to fortify their border with Ocrin. The remaining ten percent will be shared equally by the states of Homineri, Octunommed, and Oelistad, primarily to foster agricultural and mining needs for the war effort."

The viziers immediately began appealing for a change of percentages, each trying to pressure Ingal into giving more to their cause. The din of their objections resonated from the ceiling and irritated him like a sword to the forefoot. The stench of their stress-induced sweat overpowered his sense of smell.

Ingal gave a signal to his Minister of Audience, a tall, blonde woman named Asamaya Sa'Jehai, who bore the last name of one who had been birthed in the dragon's presence. She turned and announced, "Thus adjourns the audience. Bow to the Dragon of the Federation."

With obvious reluctance, the viziers and generals did as told and slowly filed out of the Audience Chamber through the main doors. As Ingal watched them, he noted in their eyes and faces how the horrors and troubles of the last few years had aged them. All except Vizier Misaqi had come in fresh to the job after their predecessors had been murdered by the traitor, General Tasami, in a failed attempt to gain independence for the state of Namistad, an act that had launched the war with Ocrin. Now the blood of untold youths saturated the soil along the western border, turning the headwaters of the Alsanoos as red as the Namistadi flag.

But the forces of Ocrin were no longer made up of only humankind. What Ingal knew from his spies, but the viziers had yet to discover, was that Ocrin was planning to unleash hordes of beasts bred in the foul warrens of the Doom Empress. He had to head it off—call a truce to the fighting before Ocrin had a chance to attack, or find a counterattack strong enough to defeat them. Federation troops had grown war-weary. But he had told no one of the beasts other than his closest advisers for fear of spreading panic amongst the viziers and their troops. Options were not yet exhausted.

Ingal's ministers and advisers turned and exited through the doors at the back of Ingal's dais. Soon he was left alone with only a handful of the Dragon Guard and his new, young chamberlain, Baliniq.

"My lord," Baliniq said, "may I prepare your sleeping chamber?"

Ingal sighed. The short, dark-haired youth was barely twenty-five years old, Vizier Misaqi's great nephew. Baliniq already understood how weak his dragon lord had become: even a simple meeting with the viziers was enough to tire Ingal. This new chamberlain was a far cry from the patient and sage Metharcus who had passed away two years ago. But given time, Ingal judged, the young man could come close to the same wisdom. *How short the human life*, he thought.

"No," Ingal replied without looking back. "We will not be taking our rest." It was more an act of defiance against his physical state than a statement to the chamberlain. "Leave us," he said, looking around to both his chamberlain and the palace guards. They all turned and exited.

Ingal was left alone in the vast chamber, his thoughts turning again to the way he had been violated that morning.

Then he smelled someone nearby, the faint, cinnamon scent of an elf. He tensed, ready to turn and attack.

"You know, they are whispering about you."

The words were in Peshilarn elvish and came from the doorway behind Ingal. He recognized the speaker immediately, relaxed, then smiled and turned, but he caught his breath at the sight of the speaker's wounds.

Rethuud leaned against the massive double doors in the informal way of elves everywhere. It had been two years since he had visited the Gold Dragon. Clearly, those years had not gone well. He wasn't looking up, but rather seemed more interested in using his thumb to polish the hilt of his battle-worn sword. The elf was as lean and strong as ever, but a long, dark green keloid scar stretched down his exposed left arm, a lightning strike running through the pale green of his skin, and the last three fingers were missing from his right hand. The wounds had healed, but they were jagged and rough, the result of field treatment without the benefit of Padgarun clerics, who served the enemy.

"Dear friend," Ingal said, replying in the same Peshilarn dialect, "It has been so long."

Rethuud looked up at Ingal. The elf's right cheek was puckered and melted, inflamed and dull red, and hair had failed to grow above the right ear. From the look of it, Ingal estimated

Rethuud had been hit with an acid sphere some time in the last few months. He was fortunate he still had his right eye. Ingal had heard the elf was wounded while fighting his countrymen in Peshilaree. He had no idea it was so severe.

"Your servants," Rethuud continued. "They gossip about you. Why do you allow such disobedience, Jehai?"

Ingal shook his head. "I know." He winced, realizing he had used the singular form *I* instead of *We*, another side effect of casting the renegade spell, reflecting his reduced mental state. "Something happened to us this morning."

Ingal heaved up onto his feet and lumbered over to the door, ignoring the weakness in his left legs, then onward toward his chambers. Rethuud took up pace beside him, limping slightly.

"How goes the campaign?" Ingal asked, referring to Rethuud's attempts to overthrow the Speaker of the Hall of Emeralds, the leader of the elvish nation of Peshilaree, and the Padgarun clerics, the spiritual leaders who had turned their nation into a weapon for the Triumvirate gods. Ingal already knew the answer. Highly conservative, few elves were willing to wage a civil war against their leaders, for it would mean a battle against the most basic tenets of their culture. Reduced to guerrilla tactics, Rethuud and his forces spent more time evading the enemy than attacking. It had been thus ever since the beginning, when they had traveled with Torra to the elvish lands and fought the resurrected elvish elders. She never fully trusted Rethuud, or any of the elves, with good reason, but Ingal saw a potential ally in Rethuud from the start.

Rethuud ignored Ingal's question. "They say you burst awake in your sleeping chamber, thrashed through the halls, shouted that the Triumvirate had taken your mind. Your servants say they ran from you, afraid for their lives. They later found you in the Egg Chamber scraping your claws across the floor." He paused a moment, eyeing the dragon. Ingal remained silent and kept walking. Rethuud continued, "You really must punish them for their impudence, Jehai. The Gold Dragon I know is a ruler with more control than this. Imagine if your viziers heard this sort of talk."

Ingal stopped with a huff. "You've made your point, Rethuud. Stop advising us on demeanor." He turned to glare at the elf, his eyelid fluttering again, and raised a massive digit to point at Rethuud. "And let us worry about our reputation with the viziers. You may be a graduate of the Dendarin Academy, but we have thousands of years of statesmanship beyond your experience!"

"Indeed," the elf said, returning the glare. "Then perhaps you can explain why you sent a courier to the Hall of Emeralds requesting a parley."

Ingal frowned, lowering his forefoot. "We wanted to confer with you first, Rethuud, but your whereabouts were unknown, and our envoys barely came back with their lives, unable to locate you. Our need was too great to take time to search you out before moving on this."

"Moving on what? A truce?" Rethuud's face tightened, his eyes narrowing. "In case you've forgotten, Jehai, I've lost hundreds of seasoned warriors in an effort to overthrow the speaker, and they are very, very difficult to replace. And now, at a time when we are finally making gains, you decide to call a truce? You know the Hall of Emeralds will never honor it! Their only concern is the Triumvirate."

"Calm yourself, Rethuud." Ingal continued down the corridor. "Think about it. Use that strategic mind of yours. The White Lands Federation is fighting a two-front war against the elves and Ocrin, pirates raid our shores, and our crops are failing due to climate changes wrought by the Triumvirate. And now …" He wanted to say what he was thinking, that the Triumvirate was on the move again, or that Ocrin-bred ogres would come raging over the western border in a few months. Trade along the Bronze Trail westward into Sofon was down to a trickle due to the war. "Now there are new concerns. We are forced to create a lull in the fighting, even if just a short reprieve. Call off your men, Rethuud. Return them to the White Lands. They need a respite. And with your supervision, perhaps some of our seasoned Alneri veterans could be trained to help you in the woods of Senosh'hori." Ingal made a show of studying Rethuud. "By the look of it, you could use some recuperation." Then he added, "And we have missed you."

Rethuud was silent as they continued walking through the wide corridors of Palal Jehai, pursing his lips as he thought, darkness haunting his eyes. "Perhaps you are correct," he finally replied. "Your forces and mine are both stretched thin. It is your harvest season, when your men are needed back home. And the elvish leadership seem to be … distracted, lately. But it will be no easy thing to restart the rebellion." He reached up with the remaining fingers of his right hand and rubbed at his melted cheek. "My warriors could use a rest. I will alert my forces," Rethuud continued, "but the word for withdrawal will not be given until a truce is called."

Ingal nodded, then he stopped and pointed a claw toward an adjoining corridor. "Find our chamberlain, Baliniq. Have him give you a room, then stay a while. We will need your counsel in the coming parley with the speaker."

Rethuud nodded. "And what of this 'happening' your servants speak of? I submit you are more in need of rest than I."

Ingal shook his massive head and snorted. "It's nothing. We had a bad dream, is all, and could not wake."

Rethuud flashed Ingal a somber sidelong look. "Let us hope you have better dreams tonight, Jehai, or we may all be fleeing your palace." Without waiting for the dragon's response, or bowing, the elf turned and limped away down the corridor.

Ingal did not watch him go. His thoughts had already gone back to that morning.

How his dreams had been interrupted, ripped away like silk in a gale. How the immense energies that had erupted through him when he cast the renegade spell, two years ago, suddenly were back, rolling through his mind like boiling oil.

How the energies pulled at him, urging him to follow, willing him to leave the palace and fly to some new horror unleashed in that moment.

In that paralyzing terror, a fist had closed around his mind, twisting it, forcing him to move his legs and plunge through the corridors of his palace.

Three voices were laughing at him, mocking him, burning through his consciousness.

And in those last few moments, as he had burst into the Egg Chamber, to the one place in the palace where he had once lain in perfect peace, the voices spoke as one:

Unleashed is our vengeance.

The Triumvirate had returned.

CHAPTER FOUR
Wayfaring

Torra preferred the blank, white, luminescent walls of her personal chamber to the clutter found in other mages' chambers. Using the *Rockform* spell taught to novice tower mages, she had embedded only two decorations into the walls: a small, woodcut likeness of her twenty-year-old brother, Nickos, and a framed icon of the Gold Dragon. Ingal's image was the sort typically displayed by those who worshiped him, wings raised with a forefoot lifted in blessing, though her purpose for displaying it wasn't in worship, but as a sentimental representation of his friendship. It was still a bewildering thought that a dragon could be her "friend."

Her chamber was cramped, with a small desk and chair set near the slit of a window, a narrow table with drawers, and a padded bunk. Both the desk and table were clean and empty on top, the writing implements and paper neatly tucked away. A small chest in the corner held her sparse wardrobe. Sometimes she felt more like a nun than a mage, living in such a confined space. Still, as she put the last items into her travel bag, she thought she might miss this place. It was, after all, her only escape from the curious and often disapproving eyes of the other mages—and Mistress Kai. Mages each had their own chambers, and it was an understood rule that no one trespassed or even looked inside without being invited.

She made her way down a short corridor, past the great helical stairway, to a wide balcony that circled the inner circumference of the tower at that level. Beyond the railing, an empty space rose to the very top of the tower, the ninety-eighth level, and fell twenty levels down to the foyer on the ground level. That empty space was called the "Column", through which the vast energies of the world shot up through the Heartstone and the tower into the atmosphere beyond. With any lighting duller than full sunlight, one could even see the energies as a pillar of light streaming upward.

Jutting out into the Column was a lift, a circular platform wide enough for eight people to stand together to be carried through the air to other floors. Swinging her pack and smiling to herself, Torra walked toward the lift. *I'm going home at last,* she thought, *and on an actual tower mission!* She stepped onto the lift and started to move her left hand over a silver orb attached to the railing but stopped as two older mages approached the lift and stepped aboard. Both had the sigils of Master rank on their robes. Standing side by side and facing Torra, they watched her, unblinking, as if examining her for faults.

"Take us to the fortieth level," the eldest commanded, his voice emanating from beneath a bushy gray beard.

Torra's brow tensed. "I cannot. I am not of high enough rank." Of course, the master already knew it. He had to know, for her rank of Apprentice was clearly designated by the yellow sigil embroidered on the collar of her white outer robe. There were ninety-eight levels, but no apprentice was allowed above the twenty-fifth without invitation by the Towermaster. This was a jab at her, she thought, an attempt to demean her and put her in her place. To some mages, she was the dragon's pet, the unwanted hero of the battle for the tower, accepted not on the merit of her magic, but as a reward for her actions on behalf of others, then promoted over other Novices to the rank of Apprentice. Perhaps even a spy for the Gold Dragon. So the rumors suggested.

And, of course, this master was making her operate the lift for him like some common servant. This was not the custom here, despite the difference in rank.

"Ah. Yes," the mage said snootily. "Move off the lift, then, so that we may proceed."

Torra tightened her jaw. The fifth chime would ring any minute now. Mistress Kai would be angry at her tardiness. But Tower etiquette demanded that the masters have their way over hers. "Of course," she grumbled, and stepped back to the balcony.

The other master wrinkled his face, snuffling, as Torra passed, and raised a hand to his nose. Torra wanted to shout, *You know who I am! You know my disease!* But she kept silent. It would do no good to quarrel with them.

The eldest mage placed a hand on the silver orb and with a lofty air while looking at her, stated, "Forty." The lift gently detached, the stone unmelding and separating from the balcony, and levitated upward and out of sight, carrying the men as if on a gentle updraft. Another lift from the floor below rose to take its place, but the minutes it took were more than Torra had time for.

Torra quickly stepped on and commanded the lift to descend to the ground level. But it had lowered no more than five floors when the fifth chime of the day sounded: a single, pleasant note that infiltrated every room of the tower. Each of the eight daily chimes had a different tone. This one designated midafternoon. Now she was late.

Torra's lift floated down past the massive bonerock Heartstone, at the center of the tower's lower floors. Running through the middle of the smooth, domed stone, from one side to the other, was a foot-wide crack that shone with a blinding light. This was damage wrought by the Triumvirate's elvish champion, Peshiluud. The tower was lucky this was all he had accomplished, but the uncontrolled release of even that amount of energy into the world was enough to give the Triumvirate unprecedented power—enough to grant greater magic to their minions.

To help rein in that energy, a ring of forty Tower mages encircled the Heartstone, arms raised, humming a continuous and slowly morphing tone in unison to "harmonize" their magical energies. The Correctors, whose song never ended, changed their harmony as necessary to counteract and balance the lost energy. As with spell casting, the making of sound triggered the magic centers in their mind to harness and utilize the world's energy. With every chime they were rotated with fresh singers, one by one, imperceptibly changing the guard, until relieved again by a third crew. Without their efforts, the ebb and flow of magical energy would make spells less predictable, more dangerous, and more likely to feed the energies of the Triumvirate. But they couldn't "heal" the Heartstone. No one could.

Down here, at ground level, mages of all ranks could be found. In fairer times, back before the battle for the tower, even the general public was occasionally allowed inside to gawk. Now it was restricted only to mages from the three Great Towers and other centers of magic, with the exception of special visitors like national and international leaders. Such a restriction was necessary to protect innocent lives in case of attack and to keep out spies who might serve Ocrin, the elves, or the Triumvirate.

On this level could be found low-ranking apprentices and novices milling about with high-ranking masters. These mages hearkened from nearly every corner of Irikara, differing widely in body features, skin color, religion, food choice, and language— although all speech was instantly translated within the tower walls. The diversity thrilled Torra, and thus she found herself down here often.

A massive recruitment effort had followed the Battle of the Tower of Light, in part to repopulate the tower, but also to bolster the number of sympathetic mages against what could well become a global battle against the Triumvirate. Torra was among those initial recruits, but far better trained than most. The majority were youths, from all over the world, who had had some basic training with local mages or who showed an innate and often unexplained ability, as she had as a young child. A group of a dozen or so of those recruits stood off to the left of Torra as she stepped off the lift.

The novices recognized Torra, pointing, whispering. But this wasn't the damaging gossip she usually faced. They rushed to her, followed her, a look of awe in their eyes. "Torra! Where are you off to?" "Torra, is it true you flew with the Gold Dragon?" "Mistress Com Gidel, are you truly from the school of Caranamere?" To them, she was the hero of the battle of the tower, not some upstart, diseased child. And to be fair, there were some masters who also regarded her this way, though they showed it less enthusiastically.

Torra answered as politely as humility would allow. "I'm traveling on a matter for the Towermaster." "Yes, I flew with Ingal Jehai." "I am not a mistress, yet. Please call me Torra. And, yes, I came from Caranamere, where I studied. We call that institute the Astronomer's Guild." In those fleeting moments, she appreciated the enormous attention lavished upon the Gold Dragon by his worshipers and had to remind herself about the value of humility.

Mistress Kai hated the attention on her apprentice, often screaming at the novices to mind their own business. Kai called their fandom a "ridiculous and small-minded distraction," but Torra knew there was an element of jealousy. Torra was far better known by them than her mistress.

Torra spotted Mistress Kai by the main doors and respectfully waved off the novices. Kai looked over at her. Instead of yelling at Torra for being late, Kai merely turned back to the opening, plucking at a leather strap at her belt. She had put away her white tower robes and donned a glossy brown leather suit for travel. Torra paused, wondering at her own stupidity. *Of course!* she thought. *Did I expect to run around in robes and sandals all the time?* She remembered back to her adventures in elvish Peshilaree years before and how her robes had been ripped and bloodied to the point of rags by the time it was over. *Well, too late now.* And she was visiting a center of magic, after all, where mage robes were the norm. But she had some travel clothes in her pack that she could change into, along with the healing salve for her skin disease, some salted pork, and a spell book to study. She put her pack over her shoulder and stepped toward Kai.

Home! Caranamere. After all these years! She couldn't wait to embrace her parents and her brother. Her mother would probably tear up and throw her arms around her. Her father would try to hide his emotions at first, but in private would tell her how much he missed her and then pull her close. And Nickos, he'd probably give her a playful punch on the shoulder and then crack some joke making fun of her magic, with a twinkle in his eye.

"It is time you learned a new spell," Kai said without turning to face Torra as Torra stepped close. "It is dangerous for an apprentice, but it is the most sensible manner for us to make this journey, since you are intimately familiar with the location we are traveling to."

"You're talking about *Wayfaring,*" Torra said. "I've seen it." She had witnessed Expeditionary Mages leave from this very spot many times, standing in groups of two or three, casting the spell, becoming obscured in a sudden fog, then disappearing in a point of light. "It is a way of instantaneous travel across great distances, like a rift spell."

"No, not a rift. Wayfaring is limited only to our plane of existence. Nor is it like a teleportation portal, which can transport only one person at a time and is too advanced for you to cast. Unfortunately, we don't have available to us any charmed device that could teleport us together." Kai turned to face Torra, her dark eyes set in a very somber face. "Wayfaring is exceptionally dangerous if you attempt to go where you have never been, for visualizing your location is crucial. We go today where you have been before, and I have not been there, so I must use you to guide us."

Torra nodded. "Very well." She reached into her pack and pulled out a short, black rod, then handed it to Kai. "You'll need this. It is a Rod of Translation. Since we are going to my homeland, I don't think I'll be needing it, but I doubt your Quishan will be understood by those who speak Taxin."

"I know very well what it is, thank you. And I have my own. Let's get under way." Kai tensed her brow. "As I cast this spell, you must harmonize on my incantation while concentrating on a location in Caranamere that you can recall with exceptional memory, one that has not likely changed in the time you have been gone. We call it a 'waypoint.' Do you have a location in mind?"

Torra closed her eyes and thought of the center courtyard in the Astronomer's Guild compound. There were plants in each of the corners, but the brick-laid center was always left open and uncluttered and was often used as a waypoint. "I have a location, at the center of the Astronomer's Guild."

Kai continued, "If I get distracted and lose my concentration on you, we will fly out of the magical current—the *gyre*—to our death." Kai was silent a moment, then added with a disquieting tone, "I have seen what happens to mages who fail to adequately visualize the waypoint. Places change. Things are moved. You could cast us into a wall, or some object, or even another person." A quick shudder ran through the mistress. "Do you understand the dangers, apprentice? Do not fail me. I am staking my life upon your *questionable* abilities."

Torra pulled in a shallow breath, then nodded. "Please cast the spell, Mistress."

"Very well." Kai muttered a quick curse in Quishan, then wrapped her arms around Torra. For a shocked moment Torra thought Kai was actually hugging her, until she remembered that other mages had done this for their *Wayfaring* spells. Kai's embrace was a bit too forced, wooden, holding her tight but touching as little as possible. Torra made herself relax and re-enter her concentration.

Mistress Kai began the incantation, and Torra saw the movement of energy in her mind's eye. She joined in where she could to strengthen the spell, "harmonizing" like the Corrector mages at the Heartstone, though being in a Tower of Magic made the spell all the easier. In moments she felt a surge of adrenaline as the air around her spun and grew cold. Kai raised her voice further, tightening her grip on Torra. Then came a thunderclap, and the world was on fire.

Torra's eyes fluttered open as every nerve burned. The space around them was a shuffling myriad of colors and shadows and a cacophony of loud, whipping wind, slaps, wails, or the rumble of rocks breaking.

"Concentrate on the waypoint!" Kai shouted in Torra's ear. "You must match your location with the world you see beyond us!"

Torra did as told. Around her she saw a phantom projection of the vision in her mind, a broad outline of the center courtyard.

But it did not match the world around them. The flashing environment "out there" was a rocky wasteland, tilting and shaking as her concentration ebbed and flowed.

"I can't get it to match."

"You have to!" Kai clutched at Torra's side. "I can't keep up the spell."

"It doesn't look the same."

"Then choose a new location! Some place away from the old one. Hurry!"

Torra desperately tried to think of a place other than the compound. Suddenly she remembered a hideaway up in a narrow ravine where as a child she would go with her brother, Nickos. Instantly, the environment changed, the rocky walls and thin stream of that ravine seeming to match her mental outline. The massive boulder where they would sun themselves after wading. The sheer outcrop where moss dripped year-round. "Now! It matches."

"Hold that vision!" Kai chanted the spell in reverse. As she did so, the whipping winds died down. The colors muted. The mental vision merged with an ever-clarifying world around them. The spell ended, and they were standing in the center of the thin gorge Torra had known, still clutching each other. Kai released Torra, then the mistress slumped to the ground, breathing heavily and closing her eyes.

It had taken only minutes to travel a distance that took Torra two months to travel by wagon, two years before.

Torra tried to step away, but her foot was trapped. Looking down she saw that the sole of her shoe was melded into the rocky floor of the ravine. She pulled her foot out and tugged on the shoe, but it wouldn't budge. She gave a quick laugh at what was surely a close call, but the moment of appreciation died away. The rocks and ravine were as she remembered, but woodsmoke filled the air. Looking up, she gasped, "What happened?"

"My spell worked. We're safe," Kai said without opening her eyes.

"No, not that. The ravine. It's been burned!" The walls of the ravine were covered in soot. The moss and ferns were withered. The fir trees that had once lined the top of the ravine were now blackened, shattered trunks. Wind howled through the hollow in a lament, blowing hot ash so heavily that she had to look through squinted eyes.

Torra climbed up the side of the ravine following the same footholds she and Nickos had used as children. Her heart pounded. Breath quickened. Something was very wrong! At the top she looked down the hillside into the town where she grew up. She caught her breath, eyes growing wide.

There was no thriving hamlet or wooded hill. Instead she saw before her, through thick smoke and blowing ash, a smoldering crater, buildings leveled to rubble, hillsides burning. It was utterly unrecognizable. *This can't be Caranamere!* she thought, *Did I wayfare us to the wrong place?*

Her mouth dropped, slack, devoid of the curses she wanted to utter. Instantly, her thoughts went to her family. Her mother. Her father. Nickos. Her Guild mentor, Master Morikal, and the other Guild mages. Her first love, Taenos. And all those villagers she had known since her childhood.

Torra fell to her knees, her hand going to her quivering lips.

"No," she said. "*No!* How? How could this happen?" And then, as the realization sunk in, she screamed.

CHAPTER FIVE
The Celestial Millwheel

Darilos felt a rising energy. Something raw. Like static electricity from the approach of a lightning storm, it pricked at his nerves and ran down his spine. This was magic, but not the power of the Triumvirate still pulsing around him. No, this was different. Personal. Suddenly the vague feeling grew stronger and coalesced. He could pinpoint it now. It formed somewhere up the hillside.

Even before he saw her, a white-robed figure peering over the devastation, he knew it was Torra. It was the same energy he had felt at the battle for the Tower of Light when, upon coming out of the dimensional portal, he had locked eyes with her, *felt* her as she commanded power that was far stronger than any other mage around her. Darilos heard her scream. He grasped Torra's despair. Even in her confusion and sadness, the pathos released a tantalizing leakage of that deep energy that welled up through her. He inhaled again the scorched air, seeking to pull Torra's essence into him.

His energies were celestial, as a being not of this world, and as such, he could not sense most terrestrial energy. He shouldn't have sensed hers, either. And yet, just as when he first made eye contact with her during the Battle of the Tower of Light, there was some unexplained bridge between them. Only when terrestrial spells were exceedingly strong, so-called "renegade spells" like the one that destroyed Caranamere or the one the elf lord used to attack the Tower of Light, could he feel the energy. Torra was like a walking renegade spell, hidden like an ember beneath wet leaves, ready to explode into a wildfire should conditions become combustible. That untapped power was intoxicating. He wanted it. He had craved it since he first experienced her, years ago.

And he would have it.

Darilos sat at the northern end of the ruined town where he had waited for hours, aside from taking care of some loose ends: a few witnesses to dispatch and a key to hide. Now disguised again in human form and dressed in the brown robes of the Astronomer's Guild, he had found a spot near the only real road in or out of the town, on the rubble of a collapsed mill, where he could get a decent view of the valley. A creek gurgled alongside where once it had powered the mill's wheel, a merry sound amid the destruction, even if its waters were blackened with ash and clogged with debris.

This mill had ground a part of the natural world to powder, day in and day out, he thought. *Now pressure of a different kind has reduced the building and its valley to rubble. Soon, the entire world will feel the pressure of gods and their magic.*

A charred body laid on the ground nearby, perhaps the miller, supine with one arm across his eyes and the other raised as if in worship of a sun that consumed him. There were bodies like this one all around the edges of the town, but there were none in the center. Those had been cremated instantly.

Since Caranamere's destruction, no one had come over the low pass into the valley save for a few peasant farmers and townspeople from surrounding communities. Their lamentations upon seeing the devastation had been entertaining. They had pulled their hair and wailed, occasionally slapping their own faces with some local custom of grief while chanting a prayer in the regional language, Taxin. *How useless their outbursts!* he thought. *Such expenditure of emotion, and for what? Their sorrows would not bring back the dead, enact revenge, or explain the nature of the town's annihilation for them.*

The peasants had no energies in their expressions, only selfish sorrows. But Torra's grief was different. She expelled raw power with her outbursts. He saw her, a flitting white robe against the carbonized background, stumbling down the distant hillside. Each sob released another bolus of that energy. Darilos consumed each one like an appetizer. It was intoxicating, and for a moment he wanted to drop his disguise and fly to her in demon form, confront her, demand her love and energy. Such a gross display of identity and purpose seemed right and truthful.

But no. As a servant to dragons and to gods, his was an existence of subtleties. He would bide his time, even here on Irikara. And from what he knew of human emotions, now was not a suitable time. A tricky thing, these emotions. Gods and dragons were not given to such displays of passion. Except for anger, that is—the universal emotion. *Anger* he knew very well.

It was godly anger and greed that started all of this.

But how would it end? Now that the deed was started, it was time to visit the Ether and check the Nexus.

Darilos closed his eyes and took several deep breaths. He focused on the moment of the bombardment, and then he found the bright spot of consciousness that was his guide to the dimensions. He let the spot expand until it took over his mind, then beyond, seeming to fill his consciousness with its brightness. His mind left his worldly body, projecting astrally into the space between dimensions, until it was in two places at once.

Nebulous fluorescent clouds consumed his vision: the "Ether", that thin fascia of energy that formed the connective tissue between dimensions and acted as a conduit for demons like himself. Then the Ether opened to him like folds of silk. He floated in the center of that universe, surrounded by an atmosphere full of luminescent flows of energy collapsing in on themselves, pouring into him and out of him, wrapping together and ripping apart. This flow of energy was the Nexus, and few entities had access to it. Even most gods were forbidden. These were representations of people and objects of magical power. In the moment of the town's destruction, many of those energy flows changed their paths, some colliding with his point, others joining with it. But would the new paths lead to the correct junction in the future—the one he wanted?

He scanned the thousands of flows that came to him. Here was the path of the Key of Otemus, arcing down from a point of near obscurity, sparkling with the magical energy imbued in it. There, apricot in color, was the path of the general from the Southlands, Lord Feng. His was a strong path, branching out in many directions. He was one to keep an eye on, for his energies were the sort that could change the outcome of the world. The path of the Brotherhood of Blood was here, too, wavering in intensity, a woven rope of individual life threads, each a different shade of red or brown. Their outcome was less distinct. No matter. He had gotten what he needed from them.

Darilos turned his attention to the shimmering, resolved cord that represented Torra. The other lines were fuzzy, wavering, or indistinct. But the human mage's line was highly resolved, flowing fast and tight like an arrow through the point where he now sat, electrified like lightning. Manipulating her futures was a dangerous game. With energy like that, any entity who linked their fate to hers was asking for peril. He felt the burning attention of many entities watching her, waiting for some coming moment, each wanting a finger in the icing. Only *he* was in the same plane as her, though, able to physically interact with her.

The Triumvirate was there, looming just beyond the mist. They knew *he* was here, too. Darilos turned to look down her path toward her future, but he could not see far enough to know if the Triumvirate's line would conjoin with hers.

Darilos concentrated harder, bringing into view his own blue-flaming Nexus pathway. It wasn't a natural fit. He was, after all, not a creature of her plane of existence. But right now it intersected her line at Caranamere's destruction. He used his mind to pull the line into hers, resistant as it was. The lines repelled each other, like two lodestones oriented wrongly, but he strained his magic center to force the line into order, massaging it, yet endangering other necessary points in his past and futures. He didn't care. None of those futures would matter if he failed.

He focused his mind on outcomes, asking of them what would happen if he deceived her, or if he revealed his identity. Should he work with her while posing as her equal, or force her to do his bidding, to find this convergence? In each case, the lines pulled closer together or pulled apart, but never joined. At times they sparked and popped, miniature ethereal explosions that represented true crisis points.

He growled. There had to be a way to make them join!

He *must* have her energies! He craved the orgasmic jolt he felt from her, when they first met at the Battle of the Tower of Light. The memory alone thrilled his senses, and he nearly lost his concentration on the Nexus.

Darilos found one place in the near future, at least, where things were promising. If he teased away one of the Brotherhood threads, the one for Apostle Agnon, he could nudge it just enough that Torra and he could come close to one another just after Torra and Agnon met. *Yes, just like that!* he thought. There were sparks, indicating a fight of some kind, and Torra's line wavered. Here Torra's life was in danger, but if she lived, Torra was more likely to follow his own thread. Darilos committed to it, wondering what moment of violence he was now creating.

He left the present and near future behind and followed her path backward in time. In moments he came to the point of the battle for the Tower of Light. There, touching in a moment of blinding white light, her line and his touched so very briefly. The moment their eyes met.

But her line was out of control there, frayed and wild.

And a third line traveled with hers at that point where they met—the line of influence from the Triumvirate—more of an encircling cord of energies than a line.

It was their energies that she had manipulated at the battle. They had *touched* her. But this was no surprise to him. He had seen it before in the Nexus lines, at the battle for the Tower of Light.

He sensed the Triumvirate gods laughing at him from beyond the mist. He ignored them.

Yes! he thought. *This is the answer I seek!* He returned to the present and reexamined the lines of the Nexus. If he wanted to be one with her energy, he would have to recreate that moment of convergence: his, hers, and the Triumvirate energies. Only a renegade spell could accomplish this. Not an easy task! Such powerful magic was forbidden on this world and exceedingly rare, with centuries in-between. Yet in two years it had happened four times: once when the Iron Dragon destroyed Alneri Keep, twice at the Battle of the Tower of Light, and then again here in Caranamere. So perhaps there was hope that another could be arranged soon.

Oh, if only he could have lured her here at the time of the destruction! If they were on an outer plane he could bring them back in time, but time was linear in Irikara's dimension.

Once he was one with her energy, he could control her magic. He could even possess her mind, if necessary, but spiritual possession of that nature could damage her. She was far more useful intact.

Darilos let his concentration lapse, and the Nexus faded away like a fog burned away by the sun. Once again his mind was entirely with his body in the Caranamere valley. But now wind whipped through the valley, feeding the fires and making fire tornadoes that danced up the hillsides, incinerating trees in their paths. Smoke, already heavy in the air, raced across the valley in diffuse clouds. Slowly, the wind died down again.

The solution to getting to Torra's energies was a harrowing one. He would need to join with her at a time of great power. Such a thing was impossible without gaining her trust. He would need to get close to her, emotionally, and there were only two emotions powerful enough to do that: Love and Anger.

Why not go for both? Anger was far easier, for what did he know of love? Still, perhaps he had seen enough to know that trust and attachment was the basis of love. Engineering such things shouldn't be so hard, right? Both could be used to garner vengeance: love for the victims who were close to her, and anger from their murder. And what of love between him and her? Seduction was a tricky thing. Power could seduce just as surely as a gentle touch or a kiss, from what he'd seen of humankind.

The thought of this challenge made him giddy with excitement. Finding the Convergence seemed mundane in comparison.

He looked across the valley and spied Torra moving slowly among the ruins, now, searching. He opened his mind and sensed her again. Her sorrow was suspended as she searched, and only a trickle of her intoxicating energy flowed to him.

Darilos looked down at the miller's corpse. "You were a human. When should I go to her?" he asked. The body only lay there, wisps of smoke still rising from the charred bits. "You may even have known her, eh? Did you sell her any flour in your pitifully short mortality?" A thought occurred to him. "Perhaps you were even related. An uncle? Cousin? Father, perhaps?" Darilos leaned toward the remains in mock interest. "Tell me, is she approachable?" The corpse didn't respond, its arm still outstretched. Darilos huffed a quick laugh and flicked a piece of rubble at the head. The burned face seemed to be frozen in a scowl. "I take it from your expression that you'd rather I keep my distance from her." He shook a finger at the corpse. "You're lucky I don't summon your spirit to tell me in person!"

Darilos stood, straightened his robe, and stepped toward the center of the town. He shot a mischievous glance back. "Thank you for your help, miller, but I think it's time to introduce myself to her, face to face. The celestial millwheel is coming back around."

CHAPTER SIX

Faces of the Dead

Torra stifled a gag response to the sulfurous stench of burnt hair and cremated bodies. She didn't know what she was looking for. Didn't know why. Through tear-blurred eyes, some animalistic part of her saw faces in every mound of debris. But there was nothing intact. No body parts. No books. No star charts. Nothing but unidentifiable remnants of stone and terra-cotta. She wanted to cry out, slap her face to feel the pain of those who had died, as her culture dictated, but the effort seemed insignificant in the face of disaster on such a vast scale.

She passed by the ruins of her parents' house. Only one wall remained standing. A scorched arm stuck out of the rubble there, burned down to the bones. She stared at it, disbelieving the reality her eyes presented. Father? Mother? Nickos? A complete stranger? The thought of her younger brother suffering this death was more than she could stand, and she fell to the ground in a fit of weeping.

Finally, she mustered her courage enough to approach. She moved bricks and stones. Sifted through the ash. Found bits of pottery. A melted pewter cup. Then, when she felt the tears were too much, she turned to move on but a glint caught her eye in the soot. Torra reached down, swept away debris, and found a copper bracelet, somehow left intact.

She gingerly picked it up, recognizing instantly that this was her mother's bracelet, given to her by Torra's father as a birthday present years ago.

Torra clutched it to her breast. A lone artifact of a life destroyed by magic.

When she was five, her family had come to Caranamere from Gidel so she could be trained in the ways of magic without fear of attack, for it was outlawed in Gidel as in most of the rest of Taxia. Now her family was dead, and where had she been? It was her fault that they even lived in Caranamere.

Half blind from tears, she slipped the bracelet on her wrist, feeling a moment of connection to her parents, then stumbled down into the crater where the Astronomer's Guild had once stood.

A voice snapped her out of the painful thought. "Torra!"

It was Mistress Kai, calling from the crater rim above and behind her.

"There's no one left! It's all gone!" Torra cried, and then turned to look upward at her mentor. She felt an inane smile stretch across her face. "Maybe some of them weren't here when it happened!" Her head was nodding, as if it had a will of its own trying to convince her.

She couldn't see enough through her tears to read Kai's face, but Kai remained silent, only tilting her head slightly and looking down in sadness. The mistress wasn't known to display gentle emotions, after all.

Torra turned back and ran farther down the crater where the Astronomer's Guild compound had been. Nothing was left beyond remnants of the foundation walls and rubble, but she moved forward, anyhow. Feeling an odd compulsion, she shoved a large stone off of some debris to look underneath. The stone went tumbling to the bottom of the crater.

She froze.

Beneath the stone was a dagger, its blade exposed and its hilt buried beneath blackened soil and debris. The charmed metal looked completely undamaged—glowing with a dim blue fluorescence even in sunlight. Carefully she dug around it until the entire dagger was revealed.

She knew this blade. This was the dagger that her old mentor, Lanos Morikal, always kept in his desk drawer. It had been passed down from mentor to mentor, and finally to him. On the rare occasions Morikal left the compound, he always kept it with him.

He had been here when the destruction occurred.

Torra picked up the dagger and held it in her sooty hand.

On her twentieth birthday, Master Morikal had offered the weapon to her as a present, but she had refused, seeing it as a token of violence. *Your intentions are honorable, Torra,* he had said to her in his deep and strong voice, *but we cannot always predict how the world sees us. As mages, we manipulate energies beyond the imagination of most laymen. Every spell changes the world in some small way, and we cannot always foresee the consequences. It is a great responsibility. Because of that, others will fear us, or try to use us. One way or another, you will be forced to defend yourself against them.*

Torra squeezed her eyes tight against another bout of tears.

Rocks fell, jarring Torra out of her thoughts. She jumped back. A figure loomed over her.

Torra held the dagger in front of her, stumbling backward, blinking rapidly. When her eyes cleared of tears, she saw before her a tall man in brown robes—the robes of the Astronomer's Guild. She lowered the blade.

He wasn't anyone she recognized from her time at the Guild. Someone new, from the last two years, apparently. His was pale skinned. His eyes were blue, a bright, deep azure, seeming to radiate with a power of their own under unruly blond bangs. His face and neck were thin, but the hang of his robes betrayed a muscular frame. She had never seen him before … yet there was something familiar about him. He watched her with intent eyes, seemingly indifferent to the waste around them, as if he had come here solely to meet her.

"What do you want?" she shouted, surprising herself with the outburst.

He didn't answer. The look on his face wasn't that of sadness, nor even sincerity.

She noticed something else. He and his robes were clean and intact. He clearly hadn't been here when the destruction occurred.

She opened her mouth to speak, but Kai beat her to it.

"You there! Identify yourself." Kai now stood only feet behind Torra, carrying both of their packs.

The man didn't take his eyes off of Torra. "I am Darilos Velar." His voice was silky, sliding through the air like an incantation.

"Tell us what happened here," Kai continued. "What do you know?"

A hint of a smile tugged at the corner of his mouth. Darilos finally blinked, the movement conscious and controlled, and then shifted his eyes to Kai. Torra felt as if she were released from a spell, allowing her shoulders to relax. Upon looking at Kai, Darilos' soft features hardened.

"My, aren't you demanding! Why should I know anything more than you?"

Kai's brows tightened. Torra saw the anger welling in her tower mentor's features.

"He wears the robes of the Astronomer's Guild," Torra said, tilting her head toward Kai, then looking back to Darilos. "And yet he is untouched."

"I was away, returning from the capital this morning. But I saw the explosion from the town of Gaes."

"Almost six leagues away," Torra muttered.

Torra's training allowed her to feel the signature of magic, but this man gave off none of that energy. "Are you a novice at the Guild?"

"No," he said, "I am an itinerant mage. First Astronomer Colnos Com Dimb bid me join only two months ago." A smile crept back into his lips.

"You lie," Kai said, pointing a finger. "You haven't the aura of a mage."

"And you haven't the manners of an ox."

Kai growled and made no effort to hide her suspicion. Darilos seemed not to notice, turning back to Torra.

Torra took a step forward, within touching distance of Darilos. Could his claim be true? She closed her eyes and concentrated on the energy around her. The ruins pulsed with the powerful residue of renegade magic. There was still a slender trace of the great channel of energy that had fed it from deep within the world. But before her, in the volume occupied by Darilos, was a void emptier than any normal air in the world. It was untouched, wholly alien to the energies of Irikara.

Torra opened her eyes to stare at the man.

Is Darilos Velar even of this world? she wondered. *What are you?* Torra wanted to ask. Torra knew she should tell Kai, but some inexorable force prevented her. Curiosity? No, something deeper. Something primal. She wanted to understand this before she spoke up. It seemed … familiar.

In his smooth and convincing voice, Darilos said to Torra, "I am your servant. Ask anything of me, and I will make it possible." He held out his hand for a handshake. Torra hesitated, then reached out to take it.

"Do not touch him!" Kai shouted and stepped between them. "We do not know him. For all we can tell, he had a hand in what happened here." Her eyes narrowed. "He may even have cast the very spell."

"I did not," Darilos said without looking at Kai. "But I will gladly help you search for whomever or whatever did. I may not have been with the Astronomer's Guild for long, but I felt a kinship to them. Besides, few could cast a spell of such power! I could not."

"It was a renegade spell," Torra said, cutting in. "I can feel it." She looked around the crater as if hunting for clues. "*Meteor*, perhaps? Or *Fulmination*? But both spell books were believed destroyed when they were cast."

"Why would casting them destroy them?" Kai asked.

"Both were acts of suicide," Darilos said. "The books were destroyed with the caster."

Torra was impressed. It had taken her weeks of searching the Tower of Light's library with special permission from the high masters to discover this information. How had he found it?

Darilos continued, "*Meteor* was cast by an insane mage who was angry at the townspeople who wanted to lynch him, deciding that if he was to die, they would *all* die together."

"And *Fulmination* was cast by a highly talented apprentice, enslaved by his master," Torra added, then muttered, "Both were murder-suicides."

The exchange created a palpable link between Torra and this stranger. But the moment disappeared almost as quickly as it came, for all around were reminders that renegade magic was not just an academic pursuit anymore, like it had been when she was at the Astronomer's Guild, or a shocking expulsion of energy, as it had been for her at the Battle of the Tower of Light.

Now it had destroyed all that had been dear to her.

Torra suddenly felt shame at her momentary excitement in discussing the topic. How could she think of anything right now other than horror? It was her duty to mourn.

Kai was trying to interrogate Darilos, but Torra paid no attention. She couldn't accept the destruction. She had to get out of there. She turned and headed back up to the rim. Her bare foot was bloody from stumbling on rubble. Her white robes, hands, and legs were grimy from soot. The exhaustion of emotion made her forward momentum seem leaden.

"Torra," Darilos called after her.

Have I told him my name? she thought.

"You keep your distance," she heard Kai command him. "She's my apprentice, and you are not what you seem."

"Torra," Darilos called out again. Torra didn't stop or turn around. "You'll want me with you. Together we can bring justice to those who destroyed this place. Torra!"

She moved forward because she had to. Each step up the crater was another moment of control she had over her life. But the faces of the dead seemed to hover in her mind, frozen in the moment of their last encounters with her; her parents and Nickos standing at the edge of town watching her wagon leave for the White Lands Federation, raising their hands in farewell; Morikal, calmly sitting beside his fireplace, nodding at her and tapping his pipe with gnarled, aged hands; and Taenos, her former suitor, standing with his militia guard, watching her with accusing eyes beneath the visor of his helm. Now they were gone. Murdered. For what?

She took her pack from Kai and placed the dagger in its pocket, but she stopped, sensing yet another disturbance in the magical energy of the land. She stood and turned, facing northward over the crater. She saw Darilos and Kai turn, too.

A party of three mages each walked out of shimmering, blue magic portals about a hundred feet away and dressed in the red robes of the Tower of Balance, immediately crying out in dismay. Two other mages in black robes, from the Tower of Darkness, were not much farther, walking toward them. Another one, dressed in the white robes of the Tower of Light, stepped out of a portal nearby, hand to his mouth and turning around to take in the devastation. These were Expeditionary Mages from the Great Towers, some of the greatest weavers of magic in all of Irikara and the ones that the Great Towers sent to investigate incidents like this one.

Torra turned away. She wanted nothing to do with them right now.

None of their magic could bring back the dead.

CHAPTER SEVEN
Osprey

Torra stumbled through the debris in a daze, searching for anything familiar, something that could tie together the blurred memories of her youth and the wreckage she saw around her. Here, an orange-painted wall, the only remnant of a bakery where she had bought bread as a girl. Over there, the shattered remains of a marble fountain where her cousins had gossiped on summer nights and teased passing boys. Dirty water now gushed over the fountain's broken, sharp chunks.

Torra passed a body with a shock of red hair still on its head. The bottom half of the body was missing. She recognized what was left of the face as the town constable, Toalbe. She turned away, but the horror of Toalbe's face had already etched itself into her brain—mouth wide in a scream frozen by fire and char, arm reaching out for help.

She passed by the remnants of the small home of Olos, the quiet, sturdy servant who drove her all the way to the White Lands Federation and the palace of the Gold Dragon, years ago, and then returned to Caranamere. Glancing through the charred doorway, she thought she saw a body bent over a burning beam. She averted her eyes.

Torra continued farther, half-running, climbing steadily up the side of the valley to the outskirts of town where there were fewer bodies, fewer reminders. The stately trees, so respected by the townspeople, had been felled in angles pointing away from the crater. Old pathways were obliterated. Still she climbed, coughing on ash. She had lost her remaining sandal somewhere, but she didn't care.

The scramble through fallen wood and blasted stone had skinned her knees and torn her robes. She climbed over obstacles, forced herself farther and farther up the hillside away from the horror of disaster. But despair followed her, assaulted her senses. She railed against it. Shouted. Cursed. Ran.

At last, she fell in exhaustion, heaving for breath, hands clawing through the still-warm ash and charcoal. She sobbed, lightheaded, the tears forming a paste in the grime of ash on her face. In despair, she slapped at her face, giving in to the ancient Taxin ritual, trying to feel the pain of her family and friends in those horrible final moments. But it wasn't enough. She slapped harder and harder, screaming, eyes closed, whipping her head and arms. Her screams were *their* screams. Her pain was *their* pain. Burning! Burning!

Suddenly someone grabbed her arm at the wrist. In her frenzy she hardly noticed, tried to force another slap. She felt herself pulled against a firm, masculine chest, held there with strong hands, cradled against him as she struggled to keep hitting herself.

"Shh, shh," he whispered. "There, now."

Torra sobbed, finally letting it out in bursts and gasps. She stopped fighting. She didn't care who he was. Didn't even look up. All she could see was the aftermath of destruction mixed with the memories she cherished. The embrace gave her a cocoon in which to envelop herself.

Slowly the sobbing lessened. The pain of her memories faded. Steadily she came back to her senses, stood, and wiped her eyes with the back of a grimy hand. She pulled away and finally looked up at his face.

Torra blinked in surprise, expecting to see Darilos, but this man was thin and sinewy with a stubbled face. He was around her age. His jet hair was singed, his clothes in burnt tatters, and he was covered in soot. The only possessions she could see were a scorched woodsman's axe and an amulet hanging from a silver chain at his neck. The amulet, a bronze sun symbolizing the god Okun, master of the Axinom pantheon of gods, had left an angry burn mark on the man's chest.

Torra and the man examined each other at arm's length, sharing a moment of joint survival. Then he gave an empathetic smile. "You're going to hurt yourself with all that slapping," he said with the slight drawl of a commoner from the countryside.

Torra looked down, suddenly ashamed of her excess of emotion. "I guess that's the point of it."

"It's all right. I think the dead will understand if you stop now," he said. "I'm Geron Tanithon, but my friends ... " He trailed off, catching himself and looking toward the ruins, then continued in a more somber tone, "You can call me Osprey."

She reached out a hand. "I'm Torra Com Gidel. I sort of remember you."

Instead of taking her hand, Osprey placed a hand on her shoulder and smiled again. "I know who you are. My papa and I sell wood to your family down by the Wainwright's place." His smile quickly faded and he lowered his arm. "We did ... before."

Though she barely remembered having met Osprey, she didn't feel quite so alone anymore. He was a living connection to all that was lost, a fellow survivor, a participator of common memories.

He looked toward the center of town. Torra followed his gaze. For a long while the two of them surveyed the destruction.

"It's all so unbelievable," Osprey said. "It is a mystery to me how the Gods could allow such a thing to happen."

"Which gods?" Torra muttered. It was said with finality and sarcasm, not meant to be answered.

But Osprey closed his eyes and stated with a solemn air, "And Okun spoke upon the dwellers of the world, 'Thou art but mine children, now, to whom I bequeath life. Take from this destruction and rebuild, for each ending is but a new commencement, a new chance to earn your key to the palace of the gods.'"

Torra recognized this as a quote from the *Holy Writ of Okun*, the most sacred text of the Axinom pantheon. An atheist, she closed her eyes in annoyance and said nothing. If there were gods, then they did nothing to save her family anyhow. She turned her attention back toward the center of town.

Torra saw other people moving amongst the rubble. She picked out the robed figures of the other mages from the Towers, clustered together near the crater. Kai was with them. Then Torra caught a movement of robes out of the corner of her eye.

Darilos stood by a collapsed house, facing her, some fifty yards away and downslope. He seemed emotionless, unmoving. His brown robes fluttered in the ashy breeze.

"A friend of yours?" Osprey asked.

No, she started to say, but it didn't seem right, somehow. "An acquaintance," she answered.

"Another wizard from the Guild? He wears the robes."

Unsure of the truth, and annoyed by his use of *wizard*, Torra didn't reply. She merely gestured for them to go back down the hillside toward the center. It seemed to her the right thing to do to bring him with her, and he came willingly, letting her lead the way.

Wizard, she thought, wincing inwardly at Osprey's colloquial term, used mainly by those who were ignorant of the realities of magic. Still, it was better than the curses thrown at mages in most rural villages where the law against magic was enforced.

Still standing by the shack, Darilos watched Torra intently as she approached, never taking his eyes off of her. She stopped several feet away from him. Osprey stopped a step behind her.

"You had me worried," Darilos said, his voice smooth. Torra started to explain, but he added, "Why did you run from me?"

Torra frowned. *Run from you?* she started to exclaim, but Osprey chose that moment to move forward to introduce himself.

"I don't remember you from the Astronomer's Guild, but then I'm no wizard. I'm Geron Tanithon, stranger, but you can call me … "

"Torra," Darilos said, ignoring Osprey and stepping closer to her. He gently squeezed her arm. "You and I need to work fast to find who did this."

Torra started to retort, when Osprey broke in again. "I know who did this."

Both Torra and Darilos immediately turned to the woodsman.

"I seen it all from the bluff." Osprey pointed with his axe at a cliff face on a distant hilltop.

Suddenly Torra couldn't breathe. Standing before her wasn't just a survivor, but a witness. "Wh … Who?" she gasped.

Osprey lowered his axe and leaned on it like a cane, his eyes glazing over. "It was a green dragon in silvery armor."

The Emerald Dragon, she thought. *Mordan.*

"But the beast weren't alone," Osprey said.

Torra heard a quick exhale from Darilos but didn't turn to look. Osprey continued, "There were people on another hilltop, people in robes. Couldn't tell if they was priests or wizards."

Did they hire Mordan? she wondered.

Darilos took Torra's hand. She pulled away from him, eyes still on Osprey. "What color were their robes?" she said. "Did they interact with the dragon? Did they direct him?"

"They was so far away. But—

"Stop," Darilos commanded. "You should wait to tell us when we are with the other mages."

"Just tell me," Torra said, turning back to Osprey, "did the robed ones interact with the Emerald Dragon?"

Osprey paused to think. "I was up there," he said, pointing toward a distant ridge. "The fire came so quick," Osprey said, walking toward the crater, with Darilos following. "I couldn't see from the brightness of it, and then the fire was upon me, blowing up the cliff. I jumped for the cover of some rocks … the dragon came out of the fire. By the time I found shelter, the beast was back with the robed ones. He attacked them, then flew off with a giant chest."

So that would be the dragon's payment, she thought. "What color were their robes?"

"Sort of dark red, maybe, like clay bricks? Except for one. He had many colors," Osprey continued. "And he didn't leave with the others."

"What?" Torra said. "He didn't leave with the others? You saw them leave?"

Osprey reached up and touched his amulet, then gingerly touched the burn underneath, wincing. "They did some sort of ritual just before … before the fires. Something came to that hilltop after they left. Something evil. Something besides the dragon. It roared."

"You're not making sense," Darilos said to Osprey, leading the woodsman down the hillside. "You are obviously in shock."

The woodsman turned and faced Torra, his hand gripping the .

"By Okun," Osprey said, "those robed ones summoned something—some beast not of this world! But I was in pain from the fires, and smoke clouded my vision. I … I only heard a roar that … "

Torra glanced at Darilos, but the mage seemed lost in thought, face taut. He noticed her gaze then turned away. Osprey seemed too distraught to say more.

"Come," she said to Osprey, "Let's go talk to the other mages. They need to hear your story." She and Osprey walked several feet down the hillside. She looked back and saw Darilos had not moved. "Are you coming?" she asked.

Darilos didn't answer or move at first, brooding. When Torra and Osprey moved on, he followed slowly and at a distance.

CHAPTER EIGHT
General Feng

Far south of the blasted waste of Caranamere, at the southern tip of Taxia, the air in General Feng Tong Lu's tent was thick with the pungent scent of *tangoluc* incense. The smoke was thick enough to make his eyes water, yet he inhaled deeply, taking the rich vapors into his lungs to purify him for the next step in his meditation. Long had he sat there, conquering his emotions against the excitement to come, and opening his chakras.

His senses were heightened. A breeze, chilled from the snowy mountaintops just to the north, ruffled the canvas of the tent around him. He felt the hardness of the soil beneath his meditation rug. Outside, the movements and quiet banter of his soldiers joined with the clop and neigh of their horses. But beneath these sensations, there was the crisp scent of snow and evergreen trees carried by the breeze, the sharp edges of pebbles in the soil beneath the rug, and the words of the soldiers as they passed a platter of food between them by the crackling of a fire.

A slave entered through the tent flap but immediately turned and retreated. Feng knew his appearance would be imposing to the slave: slim and gaunt, bald head sweating, stripped to the waist and cross-legged, covered with scars, and obscured in a darkened tent by a lavender haze of smoke. Normally such insolence would be punished. This time, Feng let the thought go, along with any other thought that came to him.

He focused on his third eye, the chakra that the So-Chai masters called the *Noc Chan*. He cleared his mind. He became the wind that rustled the tent. He melded with the rocks beneath the rug. The smell of the *tangoluc* incense became his scent. And in every way, he let his senses merge with the environment around him, becoming him, until his identity disappeared completely.

For fifteen long years he and his soldiers had searched for the Convergence. Feng had all but given up his long and storied career in the Emperor's Army, dedicating everything to finding the artifact. Starting with an obscure line of characters painted on a flaking mural in an ancient So-Chai monastery, he had followed the clues and omens. Those characters had promised absolute control of magic. Through this "Convergence," a person could rule as a god, manipulating both terrestrial magic flowing through the world, made by the Triumvirate gods and regulated by the Towers of Magic and their Heartstones, and Celestial magic, the energies created by the Outer Gods that flow outside, and sometimes into, Irikara. No one, not even the most powerful mages in the world, could control both forms.

Feng wasn't a mage, nor did he intend to be. He who had a power that strong could get anything he wished: money, fame, and, as Feng desired, control of nations. At last, after three generations, he could wrench his family's throne back from the Quisha emperor. The "Lord of Silk and Steel," as his soldiers referred to him, would become the emperor of the oldest continuous nation in the world of Irikara.

So he followed the trail of crumbs left by the Ancients in search of the Convergence. Through legends older than the monastery at Wei Jing. Into crumbling bamboo tablet scrolls hoarded by the ascetic scholars of Kunokain in the foothills of Chonutsa. Even deep into the abandoned dwarf warrens of Golnobonum, where giant worms hunted the endless tight, dank tunnels for hot flesh and the walls were etched with languages long forgotten. Yes, and after all that searching, after the maimed and wasted lives of hundreds of his men, after nearly bleeding, starving, or drowning, and alienating himself from the Quisha military and noble families and risking banishment, General Feng had finally found a relic in a dark and shattered corner of the ruins of Torta Bane, at the edges of the Ruined Lands. That single item, a tarnished hoop of pure silver, twenty feet wide and created by the Citrine Dragon, had finally been used to command the demon dragon, Azartial, to appear and give him the answer he needed.

"Masters," Feng muttered in his native language, Quishan. "My three lords. Emperors to my emperor. I beckon you. Grant me your mind, lords. Hear my thoughts. I relinquish myself to your dominion."

He had purified his body. He had opened all channels to his soul. And yet, the three emperor gods, the Triumvirate, would not always answer. Sometimes they demanded blood. And the pain would help him focus.

Without hesitation, and with minimal disturbance to his meditative state, Feng reached to his side and grasped the teak handle of a flail, the knotted leather lashes rolling softly from their folded state to brush against the rug. Feng held the flail upright before him, clenching his iron-hard fist around the handle until he was sure there would be no slippage. Then, with a sudden exertion, he whipped the flail around his right shoulder, then his left, then back again in an uninterrupted cycle. Each lash seared his back, opened old scars, laid bare skin and muscle. Each slap of the knots made him grit his teeth, but no cry left his lips. The pain exhilarated him, left him more alive than before, and he funneled all of it through him to his *Noc Chan* chakra.

In moments, Feng felt hot blood dribbling down his back, soaking into the silk of his cummerbund.

"Masters," he repeated. "My three lords. Emperors to my emperor. I beckon you. Grant me your mind. Hear my thoughts. I relinquish myself to your dominion."

Still no response. He increased his exertions, sweating, grunting with every excruciating stroke. He wondered, would he have to sacrifice a slave again to get their attention? He repeated his chant once more.

This time the Triumvirate came. Their tendrils of control wormed into his mind. And outside of his being, in the tent around him, he felt their presence. Their power surpassed the chill of the breeze, the hardness of the stone, the aroma of the incense. Theirs was an energy that was at once intense and subtle, coming from every particle of air and soil around him. Irrefutable.

"I have found it, my lords," Feng said aloud, still whipping himself, increasing the strength of the lashes in an ecstasy of excitement, beating with each sentence he uttered. "I found the Convergence! After all these years of searching, I knew it was here in Taxia. So many men lost along the way! But I finally beat the information out of that alchemist in Totinol, and his scrolls confirmed what the demon dragon had hinted. I found it!"

And through those tendrils of thought came a single, overpowering word, bellowing up from the unfathomable depths of the world below him: *Where?*

"Pendoni," Feng blurted, his voice shaking with emotion. "The Convergence is at the convent of Pendoni, in the Calnuria region of Taxia!"

Each wet slap of the flail rent his skin and still he whipped himself. He laughed long and unrestrained into the lavender smoke. "Pendoni!"

CHAPTER NINE
Thaumaturge

Darilos was disappointed they found a living witness to
the destruction of Caranamere, other than himself and
the Brotherhood of Blood. He had found a few others just
after the explosion: a badly burned woman who had begged
for her death, an ash-covered man wearing a scorched baker's
hat and whose arm had been severed, and a teenaged boy, his
clothes and hair burned off of him, running through the ruins
shrieking in mindless sorrow and pain. Darilos had killed them
all, quick and painless, a few "loose ends" before the mages had
appeared. He couldn't have any witnesses to his role in the event.
The Expeditionary Mages had found a few other, badly burnt
witnesses, near death and babbling incoherently, but they offered
no new insights, and they all died within minutes of being found.
Osprey, on the other hand … this forester had seen too much.

Darilos would have killed Osprey, too, if he had found that
ignorant woodsman first, but he needed Torra's favor and she
seemed an acquaintance of this man. A complication. Darilos
made a mental note to consult the Nexus to see how this
forester's future and past lined up with Torra.

After the mages had tended to the few survivors they'd
found, they gathered together and made their introductions to
each other. Most of the mages knew each other, having been
dispatched as Expeditionary Mages by the Great Towers for
prior investigations of magical matters.

Now Darilos sat on a charred roof beam near the crater,
watching a few feet away from the others as the mages gathered

around Osprey and listened to the woodcutter's story. Besides Torra and Kai, a third white-robed mage from the Tower of Light was the fat and balding Master Kuno, who sported a thick beard the same color as his white robes. Darilos found him to be a pathetic, bleeding heart sort who spent more time comforting the forester than questioning him. Mistress Kai, on the other hand, Torra's tower mentor, asked questions about the nature of the people on the hill. Darilos didn't like the shrew, always glancing over at him with a distrustful eye. Her line of questioning was joined by the tall, stern Lord Preneval, one of two black-robed mages from the Tower of Darkness. Darilos had heard of this one—known as the Transformer. He was the only mage allowed by the towers to investigate the ancient art of transmutation of living beings, an art normally considered renegade magic.

For her part, Torra remained silent. She listened with bated breath as Osprey related the violence of the explosion, and her eyes took on an even more haunted look as he described the resulting firestorm. As he finished describing the interaction between the Emerald Dragon and the robed figures, Torra's face reddened, making fists of her inflamed, chapped hands.

Her raw emotion excited Darilos. He tried not to let it show.

"Osprey," asked Mistress Lolund, a black-robed female with an aquiline nose and silver hair pulled back in a bun. Her voice was as sharp as her eyes. "You said the Emerald Dragon flew off with a huge crate or chest. Did you see any markings on the chest? Could you see anything inside it?"

Osprey shook his head. "No markings. It was very big, and I could tell by the way the dragon hefted it that it was very heavy, even for him. One odd thing, though. I think light was shining from under the lid."

A moment passed while the group considered the implications.

"How do you pay a dragon?" asked a red-robed mage, his robes indicating he was from the Tower of Balance. He lounged against a broken foundation a few feet away, smoking a long, thin cheroot of Sandovan tobacco. The sweet, pungent odor occasionally wafted over to Darilos, at odds with the sulfurous vapors of smoke still blowing in thick curtains over the ruins. Others had called him Master del Titccio. "Gold, sure, but more importantly with items of magic or antiquity. Relics which would create light of their own, if powerful enough, light enough to stream from the lid opening?"

Master Donovan, a short, slim, black-haired man, had introduced himself as being from the Tower of Balance. He had a large feline following him. Some sort of half-wild pet? A thin sword hung from his waist on one side, and a parrying dagger on the other. Donovan added with a strong Northman's accent, "We have not found any items of magic in debris—none of great power. It is strange. This is center of magic and energy vortex."

"The Guild has a large inventory of items in its archives," Torra said. "Even a blast of this size would not have destroyed them all. You haven't looked hard enough."

Kai gave Torra an austere look. "Apprentice, if anyone could locate them it would be Master Donovan." Kai turned back toward masters del Titccio and Donovan. "There wouldn't have been time to collect the items from the debris and put them in a chest for the dragon, in the time frame the woodsman describes, if that's what you're suggesting. Mordan's payment could not have been the magical items thrown out from the blast."

"Then stolen before blast," said the last of the red-robed mages, Master Gral, also from the Tower of Balance, a young man with a piggish upturned nose and a blue tattoo of waving lines that covered the left side of his face. When he spoke, his native language had chirps and clicks and odd inflections from high to low, even for such a short sentence. His exotic accent was so strong that Darilos barely understood him despite magical translation. Master Gral was conspicuously armed with a massive, curved machete-like blade that hung from his waist. The only other mage who was visibly armed with a weapon was Master Donovan.

"Impossible!" Torra blurted. "Stolen? The archives were in the cellar, magically shielded against teleport entry and encased in a room that was lined with lead and with bedrock walls. The only entry was narrow, accessible only by making your way through the entire complex and two reinforced doors and past the chambers of the First Astronomer. The mages would have brought the house down before they relinquished those items."

"And yet they are gone, nonetheless, and bringing the house down is exactly what happened," said Master Donovan in an emotionless tone.

Darilos rolled his eyes. "You people bicker like children!" He stood and brushed ash off his robes. "Isn't it obvious? The Guild was betrayed." He laughed inwardly at the bone he had just tossed these dogs.

All faces turned to look at him.

"Don't look at *me*," Darilos said, remembering his pretense as a short-term member of the Guild. "I'm no traitor. But I *am* suggesting others are." He gestured toward Donovan. "You didn't find any magical items. And now this simple woodsman claims supernatural light coming from the chest that was payment to the dragon. In the few weeks I was with the Guild, I heard murmuring amongst its members. Murmuring about cabals.

Murmuring about a new cult called the Brotherhood of Blood."
It was a prepared lie, of course. He had never stepped foot in
that building.

"Impossible!" Mistress Lolund responded. "You are
suggesting members of the Guild would pay to destroy
themselves, and even side with the Triumvirate? This, after the
Triumvirate used their elves to attack the Tower of Light and
murder hundreds of Tower mages? Some of the mages they
killed came from this very institution!"

This crone has spirit! Darilos thought. He shrugged his
shoulders. "I only know what I heard. It was a dark atmosphere
in that compound. And the conspirators up on that hill *did* wear
robes."

Torra shook her head and muttered under her breath,
"Unbelievable."

A moment passed. Kai and Lord Preneval both stared at
Darilos intently. *Yes*, Darilos thought, *you sense that I'm different,
don't you?*

"Whew! That's intense." Master del Titccio puffed on
his cheroot, then added, "We must find out more about this
Brotherhood of Blood. If they could arrange to pay a dragon,
no matter if the items were from the Guild or not, and destroy
Caranamere and the Astronomer's Guild, then they are now the
predominant power in this region. Perhaps even more so than
the King of Taxia or the Taxin Trade Guilds."

Mistress Lolund gathered her black robes in a bunch and
stepped over a pile of splintered boards away from the cluster of
mages. "And what of this … what did you call it?" she glanced at
Osprey. "This 'evil thing' the robed ones summoned? What did it
look like?"

Osprey sputtered, apparently having problems remembering. "It, um, it had … " He rubbed a hand across his face. "I didn't see it clearly. I was trying to recover from the blast. The thing roared, and I saw it flying over the destruction. But, well it wasn't flapping wings. The color of it, I thought I caught a flash of blue … "

"Come on," Darilos said. "A blue flying thing? Another dragon?"

Osprey shook his head. "I … I don't know. It's not like I seen dragons before the green one."

"It's not likely the Sapphire Dragon," Mistress Lolund said. "She is known to be in the Azure Sea area right now."

"And how large was this creature?" asked Master Kuno, stroking his white beard.

Osprey shook his head again. "I don't know. Not as big as the Emerald Dragon, I think."

"And exactly what role did this creature have to play in all this destruction?" Darilos asked.

Osprey looked down and pounded the haft of his axe. "I don't know. It only appeared after everything happened, as far as I can reckon."

"What did it do after it flew over town?" asked the pig-nosed Gral.

"I lost sight of it. Haven't seen it since." Osprey looked around, as if expecting the beast to fly out of the burning hillsides.

"Well," Darilos said aloud to the group, "whatever the thing was, we should keep it in mind. Meanwhile, it seems to me that your attention should turn to the motives of the Brotherhood of Blood."

"Wait," said Kai. "We haven't determined that this Brotherhood is at fault, or were the ones on the hill. So far our only evidence that this group is involved at all is your report of rumors in the Guild and Osprey's report that robed figures were seen. In fact," she added, stepping closer to Darilos, the leather of her pants and vest sliding softly, "we haven't ruled out that *you* were one of those robed figures."

Darilos leaned back, relaxing his body instead of tightening at the accusation. *Here we go,* he thought. *What took you so long?* "Ask your witness, Kai. Did the woodsman see anyone with brown robes up on that hill?"

Osprey started to answer, but Kai interrupted. "It doesn't matter," she said, stiffly, "robes can be changed. And distance deceives the eye. Where did you say you were when the blast happened?"

"As I told you when we first met, I was returning from the capital, Axim, and was near the town of Gaes, about half a day's ride northwest of here, when I saw the explosion."

"And who were you traveling with? Anyone?" Kai demanded. When Darilos nonchalantly shook his head, she continued, "And why were you at the capital at all? Would anyone there be able to vouch for you?"

Darilos chuckled. "Well, aren't you boorish, Kai." Kai bridled at the remark, which Darilos enjoyed immensely, so he continued, "I was in Axim on behalf of Second Astronomer Cortanal, conveying an ancient text to a magical antiquarian from the nation of Maldurb. I delivered it at the agreed upon time and place, and then returned here."

Kai placed a hand on her hip. "What book was it? What was the antiquarian's name?"

"It was more of a collection of crumbling writings than a book, a 'codex,' really. I did not presume to investigate what was writ in it. None of my business. The antiquarian's name is Hozor of Crancoff."

"There is such an antiquarian," Torra said, her voice low. "A collector of magical devices and tomes. The Astronomer's Guild has done business with him in the past."

The expressions on many of the mages' faces seemed to relax, but Kai pressed forward. "Where did you say you were from, prior to coming to Caranamere?"

"I didn't say. I've had enough of your insinuations, Kai," Darilos chided. "Perhaps instead of throwing your suspicions on willing witnesses, you should spend your energy on true investigations."

"You don't seem such a willing witness to me, Darilos!" Kai responded. She turned suddenly to the other mages. "Del Titccio. Lolund. Preneval. Do you sense his energies? Try hard. Do you sense anything at all?" She turned back. "I sense nothing! Go ahead, Darilos, cast a spell, any spell. Just cast a *Light* spell. Open up your mind for us to test."

This was an alarming and offensive change in tactic. Darilos consciously worked to keep from losing his smile. "I don't catch your meaning." A lie. Of course he knew she was on to him. His was an energy not of this world. He would be a void to them. "Are you suggesting I am masking my magical abilities or energies?"

"I sense it," Lord Preneval said dryly. He took a step forward and cocked his head to study Darilos. "He lacks a magical aura."

Darilos chuckled.

"Look how he scoffs at us!" Kai said.

Darilos dropped the smile and let his face take on a serious demeanor. "It is time I told you the truth."

Torra stepped back, eyes wide. The others grew quiet, and even Kai's scowl momentarily disappeared.

"I am a thaumaturge—a devotee of celestial magic."

The group was speechless. Torra blinked in confusion. Kai shook her head and started to say something, but stopped before the syllable found life. The only sound was the far-off collapse of a ruined building.

"What's celestial magic?" Osprey asked. "How's that different from any other wizard magic?"

Torra explained, "Normal magic is 'terrestrial magic,' derived from the energy of this world. But a very rare number of mages study the use of energy derived from outside of the world. 'Celestial magic' is terribly difficult to learn and dangerous to cast, requiring supreme ability, but the spells that come from it are nearly as powerful as renegade magic. This makes thaumaturges feared and ostracized." She cast a quick *orb* spell, creating a small sphere of lavender light in her hand. "Celestial energy is so powerful, in fact, that they can't even cast small spells like this one." She let the orb disappear. "Because thaumaturges bathe themselves in celestial energy, they don't have the aura of normal mages."

"And they're banned in most institutes of magic," Mistress Lolund said, an angular brow raised in interest. "Thus the reason you are an itinerant mage and reticent to admit your craft. But what an ally you would make in a fight against the Triumvirate gods! You are invisible to them. It's no wonder First Astronomer Com Dimb wanted you here. And the Tower of Darkness is actively seeking your kind."

"It was the Second Astronomer who asked me to stay," Darilos replied. "Com Dimb was opposed to it. In fact, the two were locked into a feud of some sort and disagreed on most things." Darilos sat back down and returned to his previous, lounging position, feeling very satisfied with this prepared lie. "So, Kai, my dear leather-clad doubter, does this satisfy your concerns or do you still think me the enemy?"

"Yes, I do. In fact, I think you need to explain why— "

"Enough." It was Master Kuno, the white-robed altruist. "Have temperance, Mistress Kai. We don't have reason to believe this man to be anything more than he claims. As a mage from the Astronomer's Guild, however brief his recent association was, he is our best lead at understanding what happened, along with Osprey." He gestured to the woodsman. "We should ask Darilos further about the 'cabals' he mentioned and the Guild's reason for having him here. But I suggest we now plan our next steps." He paused to cough against the smoke. "We must work fast. It is now late afternoon, and already a crowd is gathering at the entrance to the valley."

Others turned to look. Caranamere was situated in the floor of a roughly bowl-shaped vale, the outlet of which opened up past a series of mounds to the plains below. At that point, at the edge of the blast damage, perhaps fifty or sixty peasants and low noblemen from the surrounding countryside and towns had gathered to witness the destruction and mourn the dead, wailing loudly or milling about, afraid to come nearer.

Darilos let himself relax a little, satisfied with his cover. Let that witch, Kai, try and reveal him! He turned his attention to Torra and tried to read her expression. She didn't seem afraid. She seemed to study him, like a piece of art. Yes, *art*. The analogy pleased him. And he wondered if he saw a gleam of recognition somewhere in the depths of those intoxicating azure eyes.

"That's them!" Osprey shouted, pointing the blade of his axe toward the crowd of mourners. "The robed ones from the hill. I'm certain of it."

Amongst the crowd were two crimson-robed figures, raising their hands and chanting.

Well, Darilos thought, *I knew the disciples couldn't stay away from the fun. They're as stupid as I thought.* "There's your enemy, returning to the scene of the crime. Allow me to introduce the Brotherhood of Blood!"

CHAPTER TEN
Conversion

A mist of thoughts coalesced in Torra's mind as she listened to Darilos' claim of being a thaumaturge. The rational part of her believed him, but in his blue eyes, somehow, lay the glimmer of some other truth.

The mist evaporated, though, when Osprey pointed out the robed figures. Instantly, a deep hatred surged through her. She found herself stumbling across the ruins, eyes locked on the killers, the destroyers of her home and loved ones. An emotional fever rose in her. She'd activated her magic center and started thinking of offensive spells when a hand gripped her shoulder.

"Let go of me!" she snapped, without looking.

"Calm yourself, apprentice!" Kai said. "Only a fool rushes at the enemy."

Torra shrugged off Kai's hand. "Killers! Look at … look at Caranamere! They … they … !"

Again Kai's hand grasped Torra and wouldn't let go. But Kai didn't hold her back. Instead, the mistress controlled the pace of their advance, as the other mages caught up and, as a group, moved forward toward the valley and peasants, leaving Darilos behind.

"Observe your opponents first, Torra," Kai cautioned, close to Torra's ear. "We must have evidence that they are who we think they are, and that they are responsible. We must learn their strengths and weaknesses. Do not reveal that we suspect them."

Torra reluctantly obeyed, but her anger grew. Every broken corpse along the way, every shattered wall, reinforced her ire.

Soon the group passed by a destroyed mill and was within earshot of the peasants and robed ones. Torra recognized a handful of the peasants as citizens of Caranamere who, it seemed, had been away from town when the explosion happened, perhaps in the fields, hunting in the woods, or visiting neighboring towns. Sadly, she didn't know any of them personally.

There were a half dozen robed figures. One of them was standing on a stump, his head and face concealed in the shadow of his cowl and facing sidelong to the mages to address the crowd.

" … and I tell you, before your eyes, you see the acts of the evil ones, those who would twist energies to create corruption. For too long have they been here, tucked away in a forgotten corner of our kingdom, disobeying the holy law against such witchcraft, while you good folk have toiled away to build your land!"

"By the gods!" shouted someone in the crowd. The peasants pulled closer to the speaker.

The Brother on the stump pointed at the group of mages. "See there! They have brought this destruction upon themselves. They have toyed with dragons and gods. They have corrupted the highest levels of your government to turn a blind eye and meddled in the affairs of good men! And what did we get for their meddling?"

"Ruin!" shouted a peasant. "They destroyed our town!" said another. "Say it, Disciple!" said a third.

"They destroyed themselves!" the disciple said. "They brought dragonfire upon themselves! Now their bodies burn in the hells, but they took the lives of our people with them!"

Torra gritted her teeth, pulling against the iron grip of Kai.

"Magic!" shouted the disciple. "Magic, they call it! But *we*—" he swept a finger over the crowd, "—we call it *witchcraft*!" He pointed again at the mages. "And they have brought ruin to *your* sturdy homes, and *your* families, and *your* precious children!"

"They dare to blame *us* for this?" Torra growled. But no one reacted.

"Destruction!" shouted a third Brother, a young man with shaved head.

"We are the Brotherhood of Blood!" said the disciple to the crowd, "and we are here to show you the path back to righteousness, the path away from evil magic! Purify yourselves, from your mind to the blood in your veins, and we will fight them together, and all of their minions. Minions who serve as magistrates of your good towns, as merchant leaders, as members of the King's court! Cast aside their false gods who never answer your prayers. Yes! False, for the wizards created them long ago to appease you!"

At this point, some of the peasants turned, eyes averted or shaking their heads, devout to the gods of the Taxin pantheon. One drew the holy symbol of Okun in the air in front of her.

"Do you doubt me? Do you believe in the old, false gods? Who amongst you is a true believer in them? Show yourself and I will prove my point!"

"I will prove it!" declared Osprey. He stepped from the group of mages and stormed toward the disciple.

"Oh no," muttered Master Kuno from the depths of his beard. "The fool took the bait."

"Excellent!" the disciple said, turning back to the crowd. "See how this witch lover comes to their aid? See how he is burned by his own sin?" He looked over at Osprey. "I issue you this challenge. Let us each pray to our gods of choice to rebuild this town, and we will let these good folk decide who are the true gods! You may even go first. Tell us, to which old false god will you pray?"

"My gods are not false!" Osprey shouted, brandishing his axe. "I will pray to Okun, as my father did, and his fathers before him."

"Go ahead, soothsayer of falsehood! For your forefathers were betrayed by the witches' magic."

Osprey immediately bent to one knee, his head bowed and arms upward toward the sun, axe laid in front. "Oh, Okun, father of the gods, blessed are we who bathe in your knowledge and protection. We thank thee for our survival. I pray to thee to bring back that which was destroyed, to rebuild Caranamere, and prove false those who would cast doubt upon thee. Show us your ways so that we may understand that every destruction is the beginning of a new creation." He ended by drawing the circle of Okun in the air before him.

The crowd of peasants watched the ruins, completely silent, waiting for a manifestation. Even some of the Expeditionary Mages turned to look back at Caranamere, though their eyes held no sign of hope. There was only ash and smoke swirling over fragmented buildings.

"Well?" asked the disciple, his voice dripping with contempt. "Where is your miracle, false prophet? Your amulet did not glow. No arm reached down from the heavens to rebuild so much as a chicken coop."

"It takes time!" Osprey explained. "Okun's ways are subtle, his work slow and steady."

The disciple turned back to the peasants, mockingly raising a hand to his ear. "I don't hear any building going on!" He lowered his arms. "It is now our turn!"

Torra groaned. *These pathetic fools*, she thought, *praying to the empty air as if gods cared at all.*

The disciple bowed his head followed by the other disciple and the young man with the bald head, apparently an acolyte. The disciple on the stump pulled out a knife and slit the palm of his right hand, then squeezed, allowing the blood to coat his hand and drop to the ashy ground.

"Oh, great Triumvirate," the disciple chanted, "to you I give the promise of the future. Take from us the shreds of our jaded past. Correct our ignorance. Deliver us to your great powers. Before us lies the destruction of your foes who seek to corrupt your people. Bring back some of what they lost. Rebuild a portion of their town so that they may see the triple glory that is you. We beseech you!"

Torra felt a movement of energy—the stirring of magical forces, like a breeze at first, then a stronger wind, swirling and penetrating soil and rock and ash. She looked around but could not pinpoint the source.

The other mages felt it too. They turned to look, backing slowly away from the disciple and the crowd.

Torra looked at the disciples and saw the slightest glimpse of their chins from the darkness of their hoods. Their mouths moved in synchrony in some shared prayer. No! A *spell.* Their words were indistinct at first, then rose in syllables unfamiliar to her. Though the air was charged with magical energy, some small part came directly from the disciples. These were no priests! These were mages who preached against magic! But the magic they commanded …

The ground shuddered, scattering the mages. The peasants gasped in unison as a large stone suddenly lifted upright, then another, then another, stacking upon each other, forming the walls of a small house that had fallen. Then smaller stones. Then wooden supports. Broken rock fused together. Splintered wood rejoined. Crushed roof tiles flipped through the air, falling into place, one by one.

Torra watched in amazement. She knew of no one spell that could do all of these things at once. It would take a dozen mages to perform such a feat in such a short time. It was only when the door to the house tumbled across the ground past her, as if pushed by a mighty wind, that Torra remembered to breathe. The door slammed onto the hinges of the house with a bang.

The magical energy washed away, like a wave rolling back into the ocean, leaving a completed house and a stunned audience gaping at it. The house was not quite as it had been in her memory, and stood slightly out of kilter, still burnt and cracked, but it was a marvel to behold among the remains of Caranamere. The disciples lowered their arms and slouched.

The peasants exclaimed in shared awe. "It's a miracle!" some yelled, "These are true gods!" One dropped to her knees and prayed, "Rebuild my home, Triumvirate, I beg you!" Another joined the sudden cacophony, shouting, "Me as well! Make *my* home!" One woman with a faded yellow scarf, tears streaming down her face, wailed, "My daughter! Can your Triumvirate bring back my daughter, too?"

Tiredly, the disciple on the stump turned to his audience and stated, "You, too, may possess the power and understanding of the Triumvirate by becoming an acolyte. See here, this young fellow," he gestured to the bald young man in lighter robes. "He has given up his life and possessions to follow our true path. And just in time! For his family was among those who were murdered by the witches of Caranamere. Be as he is, renounce all possessions and titles to follow the path, and take on a new name, and we shall deliver you to truth."

The young man smiled, his face becoming serene.

Torra took a closer look at the acolyte, stepping toward him. Then she drew in a sharp breath. His red hair had been shaved off, his muscular frame was hidden by the robes, but his eyes and slim face gave him away, a face she had looked into with endearment for so many years.

Her old lover! "Taenos!" she shouted.

Taenos turned to see who had called out his name. It was him, she thought, no doubt about it.

"I am not of that name anymore, witch!" he replied. "I am now Stonecaller." And then he seemed to recognize her. His eyes grew wide as his mouth formed her name. Then he seemed to shake himself out of his thoughts and rushed back into the crowd, shouting, "Keep her away from me!" before fading into the crowd of peasants.

"Taenos!" Torra shouted, running toward him. "Wait!" But the peasants were swarming around the Brothers, begging to know more about the Triumvirate, and blocking her path.

"Be gone, witches!" the disciple on the stump shouted to the mages. "Flee. Your time has passed!"

"You are fake," shouted Master Donovan, his voice thick with a Corrusian accent. A couple Brothers turned to look. "You use magic to make yourself seem holy, while at same time saying we are evil."

"Look here!" the disciple called out to the peasants. "Listen to the witches as they attempt to repaint angels as demons!" His voice sounded so familiar to Torra, smooth and noble.

Torra started to mutter a spell, and the disciple did the same in response, but Lord Preneval quickly interposed from behind her. "No, Torra! You must stop! It is not the time, for it would only seem to prove the disciple true to the naïve peasantry."

The disciple sneered at them from beneath his cowl. For a brief moment Torra got a glimpse at him. His face seemed familiar, with high, pockmarked cheekbones, but she needed a better look.

The disciple backed away, joining the crowd. "Come, my children! Come away from this evil place! Come, lead us to your towns, to Aranom and Harvinel and Gidel, to pray and to mourn, and I shall tell you the way of the Triumvirate. No more lies! No more of their false gods and witchcraft!"

And most of the peasants followed them, walking back down the road and surrounding the Brothers. Torra and the mages watched as they went. For a fleeting moment, Torra spied Taenos looking back, his eyes wide with wonder and meeting hers. There was pain there, she thought, and … something else. Longing? Guilt?

And then he was gone into the crowd and around a turn in the road.

"Why are we just standing here!" Torra shouted, gesticulating toward the retreating disciples. "We should stop them! They're lying to my people!"

"And what would you have us do, apprentice?" Mistress Lolund asked, her face steely. "Run after them, casting fireballs and scaring the peasants even more? Go invisible and hope the Brothers don't use their magic to reveal us, then call us demons? No. I know this was your home, but you must separate yourself from the tragedy and think strategically about … "

"Damn you!" Torra shouted. She ignored Lolund's shock and backed away from the group. "It's obvious they are responsible!"

She shot a beseeching look toward Osprey. "It's our *home!* We have to do *something!*"

Osprey took a deep breath, then turned to look at the reconstructed house. "By Okun," was all he said, flatly, and shook his head.

The mages were silent, seeming to avoid looking each other in the eyes. Far back toward the smoldering crater, the shadows of the surrounding hills had grown long and covered the cremated remains of the town like a shroud, with the lone figure of Darilos still reclining where they had left him.

CHAPTER ELEVEN
The Observatory

Torra seethed with rage. When conversation led to where they would stay the night, Torra barked that she knew where. Without further explanation, she grabbed her pack and led the mages up the eastern hillside of the valley, ostensibly following an ages-worn path which was now covered by fallen trees and half-obscured with debris and cinders. They found themselves constantly climbing over fallen trunks. Master Kuno, the old master from the Tower of Light, had to stop repeatedly, huffing and puffing, as he hauled his girth up the hillside and over debris, stopping often or using a shoulder from Master del Titccio. Everyone was coughing and raw-eyed from the smoke. The red-robed Master Donovan, too, walked with an odd, bow-legged gait that suggested some traumatic injury in his past, and appeared to have difficulty with the climb, but he didn't complain. He was closely followed by a large cat with lynx-like features and a swirling pattern on its sides that changed color to match the drab surroundings. Torra was briefly curious about the cat, but she refused to ask. She was too angry for trivialities, and the tender soles of her bare feet throbbed from treading on debris and hot ash.

Partway up the hillside Torra, came upon Darilos sitting on a rock and holding a pair of sandals. He smiled at her, untroubled and unfatigued, and held out the sandals to her, as if he had read her mind. Torra paused a moment in front of him, thinking Darilos must have teleported himself to get up to that location unseen—not a trivial spell!—and wondering where the sandals had come from. They showed no signs of wear or damage and seemed her size. He gestured for her to take them, so she did. They fit perfectly. Neither said a word, and she was too angry about everything that had transpired to say anything without sounding rude, so she simply gave him a look that she hoped would convey a sense of thanks and trudged on up the hillside. He remained seated, still smiling, as she turned her head back to the business of getting uphill.

The mages were covered with ash and soot by the time they reached the ridgeline, faces tracked by beads of sweat, and had to cast *Clean* spells on themselves to repair their dignity. All of their robes had been singed by embers. Sunset had come, leaving a disconsolate dusk in the failing light. But despite the effort and trouble, none dared to ask Torra where they were going, or bother her at all.

At the top of the hillside was the Observatory, a squat but highly-decorated round, granite tower with a domed roof and a single door at the bottom. The walls facing the valley were decorated with relief carvings in the likeness of esteemed mages, but the ash and scorch marks made the faces seem ominous and dreadful. Between these mage carvings were slit-like windows with thick glass which, luckily, did not seem to be shattered.

"Dwarvish glass!" Mistress Lolund said.

Her anger exhausted by the climb, Torra leaned against the building and explained. "The dwarves of Sarsa call it 'metal glass,' forged in great secrecy with valuable metals like palladium and silver, gifts from the Under King to the First Astronomer in exchange for enchanted items."

They found that the doorway was blocked by debris, including a massive tree trunk. With a start, Torra realized it was possible that surviving Guild members could have been trapped in there, and said as much. The group immediately set to removing the debris, including the use of magic to move the trunk, but upon finally gaining entry through the wide, double doors, and quickly searching the two rooms, no one was found. It had been empty when the explosion happened. The lack of survivors only served to reinforce the despair she felt.

The two-story interior was untouched by the destruction below other than a few loose objects that had tumbled to the floor when the valley quaked. The lower floor was nicely appointed with furniture and even a couple of daybeds. A spiral stairway led up to the sparsely decorated top floor where the Astronomer's Guild had performed their stargazing. When the mages came upstairs with Torra, she explained in a monotone how the observatory doubled as a watchtower to overlook the valley below.

Torra demonstrated how the roof of the building could be opened by manipulating clever bronze mechanisms embedded in the granite wall. Using only a touch on a bronze knob, Torra set in motion the clicking and turning of the mechanism. The overlapping bronze plates of the roof slid open, unfolding like the bloom of a flower from the middle outward until the entire roof was open to the gloaming sky. The process was smooth and nearly soundless, with no more grating of metal-on-metal than a sword pulled from a scabbard. A snowstorm of ash and small debris that had rested on the roof now drifted down around them.

"Such amazing workmanship," Master del Titccio remarked, running his hand over the metal rods that extended into the room. He then stepped over to a telescope mounted on a tripod in the center of the room, accompanied by a simple wooden chair. The only other furnishings on the top floor were an ornate divan and a small table covered with scrolls. "And what of this telescope?" del Titccio asked. "Never in my long life have I seen such fine workmanship." Bending closer, he blew away ash from the lenses and examining them, he added, "And the glass looks so pure and finely ground."

"The roof is dwarvish," Torra stated. "As is the telescope, though the glass was imported from Maldurb."

"Ah! I should have known!" he said. "Only the dwarves of Sofon could work such a metallurgical feat."

Torra shrugged. "Sarsa, actually. Not Sofon." In happier times she might have told the tale of breaking it in her youth while showing off to her friends, and how her master, Morikal, took her with him to the dwarf warrens of Sarsa to replace it. She had been indentured for months in those hot, steamy warrens, working off the cost of the telescope and helping the dwarves make a new one, all the while learning the dwarvish culture and important skills that went into making it. It was an adventure worth telling.

But this was no time for tales, she thought. Master Morikal was vaporized. Her friends and family cremated. Nothing left of that old life but rubble and an ex-paramour turned traitor. Torra reached out and gently rotated the telescope that she had used so many times. Looking at the stars seemed unimportant now. She stepped back to the roof mechanism and manipulated it to close.

The mages descended the stairs to the bottom floor to eat whatever provisions they had brought. Torra had two meals-worth of cheese, bread, and dried meat with her, but she didn't eat or go down the stairs. Instead, she slumped on a wooden chair next to the telescope she helped build. She ran a hand over its surface, evoking memories.

In her mind's eye she went back to those days when she had broken the telescope. Upon returning from Sarsa, Torra had triumphantly placed the new telescope back on its tripod and celebrated with the other mages. She had just turned sixteen, before the first symptoms of her Brimstone Disease. That night, eight years ago, after the celebration was over and the mages had all gone back to the guild compound, Torra had sneaked over to Taenos' home, stealthily creeping up to his window shutters and rapping on them with their secret knock. Seventeen-year-old Taenos had come to the window, overjoyed by the sight of her return, and together they sneaked away into the night and up the long path to the observatory, fearful that his father, the town constable, would discover him absent.

Torra took Taenos up to the second floor of the observatory. There, only feet from where she now sat, the two of them had made a nest out of blankets and cushions and, from there, looked up into the sky with the telescope. After so much time underground, it was a pleasure for her to see the stars again and smell the sweet air, and she eagerly showed Taenos all the constellations in view.

Hours had passed as she related her dwarvish adventure to him. He drew closer to her as she talked, put his arm around her, leaned against her. Torra remembered his body warmth, the roll of his bicep against her shoulder, the gentle look in his eyes. Taenos kissed her then—not for the first time—but with a passion she had never known before, and she had gently laid back against the floor, reveling in the embrace. Murmurs of love. Warm, then frantic caresses. Then they were lost in the moment, disrobing, hungry to satisfy young urges.

It was the first time for both of them. Afterward, they laid there, naked and wrapped together under a blanket, until the magenta light of sunrise slanted through the open roof. They quickly dressed, then ran back down the hillside path, laughing and leaping like sprites, until they got into town. They parted at the doors to the Guild compound with one last kiss.

Torra wiped away tears as her memory went forward in time, to her twenty-first year and the day she left for the White Lands Federation, almost two years before now, to warn the Gold Dragon about the Stone of Lethori and the threat of the gods. Taenos was Under-Constable by then, subservient to his father's will, and deeply suspicious of Torra's training as a mage. By then he had grown jealous of the time her training took her away from him, displacing his jealousy to dislike magic in general. They were estranged by the time she left. She had passed him on her way out of town, given him a wave and smile. He had only watched her, lips tight, a mix of sadness and anger in his eyes, shadowed by the helm of his guardsman's armor.

Back in this moment, she asked quietly, "Taenos, what happened to us?"

"Taenos? Do you mean the Constable's son?"

The voice jarred Torra from her thoughts, and she struggled to compose herself. She hadn't meant to say that out loud. Osprey stood at the top of the stairs. His tattered shirt had been cleaned and mended, doubtless by a mage downstairs, but was open in front to reveal the large and angry red burn on his chest.

"Never mind," she blurted. She cleared her throat and wiped her eyes again, then pretended to inspect the telescope at her side. Osprey stepped forward into the room.

From downstairs came the sound of raised voices, Mistress Lolund and Lord Preneval. She caught snippets of their argument. " ... can't possibly be serious!" Lolund said. "You'll never find the beast!" Then, after undecipherable statements,

Preneval retorted, "Only then can we determine their motivations, Emerald Dragon be damned!"

"They're arguing over what to do next," Osprey said. "I don't figure I'm any use down there. It isn't as if I know anything about dragons and magic."

Torra shook her head and said gravely, "Given what's happened, I'd say you know more than most would ever wish."

Osprey nodded and sat down across from her on a divan. The sinewy woodsman, with his woolen and deerskin hide clothing, seemed out of place on a fine piece of furniture painstakingly carved from mahogany harvested in distant Koba, wrought by craftsmen in Maldurb, and topped with a pillow woven of Almanian angora. The Guild compound had been filled with this sort of imported furniture and fine art. Now this lonely divan was the only remaining piece of such craftsmanship in the town.

"Your friend Darilos is gone. No one has seen him since coming up here."

"He's not my friend," Torra muttered. But Osprey's statement didn't surprise her. Somehow she had known he wasn't in the observatory. She had ... *felt* it? Or was it that, for the first time since they met, he didn't seem to be hovering near or watching her? She wondered why that thought didn't disturb her. "He'll be back."

Again Torra heard shouts from below. "The King?" Kai shrieked. "What good could that possibly accomplish? From all accounts he's a pompous lackey of the trade guilds. Torra was right, *now* is the time to attack ... "

Torra blinked in surprise. Had Kai actually agreed with her? She strained, but couldn't make out the response from other mages. She flexed to stand, intending to go downstairs, but Osprey interrupted.

"I know why you're up here alone," Osprey said. "I know what you're thinking."

Torra settled back into the chair. "You do?"

Osprey scratched at his jet black, singed hair and shook his head, eyes down. "How could they defile our beliefs like that? It's blasphemy!" He suddenly stood and stepped over toward the far end of the room. Torra started to reply, but Osprey continued, "They call our gods false. *False!* After all this 'Brotherhood' did to destroy our town, now they try to destroy our beliefs! Without Okun we are nothing! No morals to ground us. No shared culture to hold us together."

Torra couldn't hold her tongue. She turned to face the woodsman. "No morals, eh?" she spat. "I don't believe in any gods. Does that make me a horrible person, Osprey?"

Osprey sputtered, seemingly unable to comprehend. "You? But, you're one of us, from Caranamere!"

"So? Am I so alien because I refuse to believe?"

"How? How can you fail to believe in our gods? The evidence is all around us, every day!"

"What evidence?"

"Birth! Hope! Love! The rebirth of spring. The growth of crops and the coming of rain after drought. All we have to do is pray and believe."

"Birth is a natural process. So are spring and rain and the growth of plants. You can predict the weather, control birth and crops. Hope and love are feelings, at the whim of those who act them out and their mental state. No matter who you worship, the feelings are the same.

"Are there entities beyond our understanding?" Torra continued, standing now, shouting. "Of course there are. But they don't read our minds. They don't respond to our prayers.

They don't walk the earth and manipulate things with invisible hands. They are entities with vastly greater powers, but only that. People worship the Gold Dragon, but only because he has powers they do not understand. Does this make him a *god?* He tolerates their worship only because it soothes them and gives them faith in themselves and their nation, but he cannot hear or answer their prayers any more than I can if he isn't physically there with them. There are primitive tribes of people in parts of this world who would even worship *me* if I merely show them the magic I know! Does this make me a god?"

"Blasphemy!" Osprey choked, eyes wide, body trembling. He stood suddenly and pointed at her. "I knew your parents. I know they were believers. How *shamed* they would be to hear you! Does the study of magic make you all such unbelievers?"

Torra paced, running a hand through her hair. "I've seen more and studied more than you, Osprey. I've seen what the Triumvirate gods can do. Seen them exercise power that far exceeds the rebuilding of that little house by the Brotherhood. It was through the Triumvirate's power that our town was destroyed, but this only proves that they are powerful. Worshiping them with rituals and sacrifices changes nothing. And your god, Okun, if he exists at all, resides on a plane of existence beyond our own, with a feeble grasp on a few priests, able to grant them some powers and abilities. But not to you, Osprey. All the prayers you could muster, all the sacrifices you could make, would change nothing. Meanwhile, the Brotherhood of Blood takes their energy directly from the Triumvirate, who reside here, trapped in our world, making each Brother both priest and mage. You cannot compete against that!"

"Shame on you!" Osprey said. "Okun is not 'feeble!' I know the power of the gods because they saved my life and spoke to me directly!" He traced a circle in the air at Torra, a silent blessing. He took a deep breath and closed his eyes a moment, seeming to calm himself, then said, "You are upset, and rightly so, but do not cast your anger toward me or our gods. I will pray that you see Okun's light. May he destroy the ignorance that clouds your mind and bring forth a new world of understanding." Then he abruptly stood up and turned to leave.

You just can't argue with the superstitious, she thought. *By the stars, why did I have to go and say anything? Just let him have his comfort and keep my mouth closed.* Torra frowned. Here she was, feeling like an orphan in the wasteland of her home. How must he feel?

"Osprey!" she said. The woodsman had already started down the stairs, but he stopped and half-turned. "I'm sorry," she continued. "Please come back. I … I have something for you."

He hesitated, but then he came back and sat down again. Torra rummaged through her bag and pulled out a small glass jar of salve. "I have a condition called 'brimstone disease.' One of the symptoms is that I get rashes and cracking skin, so I use this cream to help it. It helps with burn wounds, too." She pointed to Osprey's chest, at the bronze of Okun and the inflammation underneath and around it. He opened his tattered shirt and exposed the wound.

She opened the lid and went to apply the salve, but then thought twice. She didn't really know the man, so she handed the jar to him. "Just rub it over anywhere that was burnt. Try not to use too much. It's all I've got, and it's hard to make."

He gave a quick smile. "Bless you." Then he started rubbing the herb-scented salve on his chest, wincing as he did so.

Mistress Kai shouted up at her, "Torra! Come down! Stop moping up there and come here, now!"

Torra narrowed her eyes toward the stairs and remained seated. For a brief and puzzling moment, she wondered what the stranger, Darilos, would say to Kai if commanded that way. Something biting, no doubt.

"Torra!" Kai shrieked.

Osprey met eyes with her—a look of sympathy. Torra said, "Just leave the jar in my pack when you are done, all right?" Then with a sigh, she obeyed her mentor and stepped slowly down the stairs.

CHAPTER TWELVE
Domis-Alta-Calla

Darilos was far, far away from the ruins of Caranamere and the party of mages. So far, in fact, that it was still gloaming where he was, a sullen sun pushing through hazy clouds, whereas it was now fully dark back at the observatory.

In every direction stretched foreboding wastes: the "Great Wasteland," as it was typically called in various languages, or sometimes "The Poisoned Lands." He had teleported to the heart of it. A drab overcast always blanketed this land. Nothing grew. Nothing moved, save for poisonous, gray dust blown by a never-ending wind. Not a drop of rain had fallen here for tens of thousands of years. The fumes and dust of the Great Wasteland would sicken any normal human or animal in minutes and kill them within days. The handful of entities that inhabited this land were dangerous, long-lived, and avoided humanity.

Darilos quickly shed his human form. Blue flames burned away the flesh and cloth. Amber wings jutted out like daggers, but nowhere near as long as this world's dragons. The pain was fleeting, replaced with a sense of freedom. He roared at the joyous feeling of being Azartial again, demon dragon. He stood for a moment, reveling in the sensation, and took in his surroundings, losing himself in the memory of what this place had been, so long ago.

Directly in front of Azartial stood a broad, wind-eroded altar with a shallow basin on top, ten feet across, upon which lay the gleaming Key of Otemus. The sword's platinum blade and chain-wrapped, two-handed hilt shone in stark contrast to the gray, scorched earth and structures. The light blue shimmer of a *Protection* spell covered the altar and the key. Remote and inaccessible as this location was, he couldn't take the chance of anything happening to the artifact. If triggered, the *Protection* spell would explode with enough force to kill an ice giant and penetrate even the strongest of *Shield* spells.

Surrounding the altar was a circle of fallen and shattered pillars. Only a lone pillar still stood, wind-sculpted by the ages from a cylinder to an oddly beautiful, organic, undulating shape. Beyond the pillars was a rolling, somber landscape of blowing dust dotted by jumbled outcroppings formed of fallen stone buildings, buildings built in a time older than legend and forgotten by nearly all of mankind.

Before the gods destroyed it, this had been a harmonious sanctuary of gleaming white structures and verdant gardens, with waterfalls and wild horses, populated by priestesses in flowing white garments. Called Domis-Alta-Calla, or "Heart of the Dominion" in the ancient Occultian tongue, it once lay at the center of the vast Western Dominion of the Empire of Occultii. Pilgrimages were made from hundreds of miles to reach this point and make sacrifices of fruits, vegetables, and small livestock upon this altar. He had visited Domis-Alta-Calla before the Great Destruction and seen the beauty for himself, the last time he came to this world, forty-five millennia ago.

When the suzerain of the Western Dominion decided to go along with the Triumvirate's wishes and march a massive army into a portal to attack the Outer Gods, those Outer Gods unleashed the Great Destruction, raining fire upon the land. They turned the Western Dominion into the Great Wasteland, drained the beautiful Emni Sea to form the Meril Desert, and raised up the Meril Mountains around the sea, causing earthquakes that rocked the world and destroyed all of the major cities of Occultii.

Azartial chuckled. *One shouldn't piss off the gods!*

Domis-Alta-Calla was the most secure location Azartial could think to keep the key. Not only was it impossible for any human to travel across the poisoned vastness of the Great Wasteland, but Domis-Alta-Calla was forgotten by the world. Furthermore, it lay in an "energy void" for terrestrial magic, a place where most of the energies of the world were absent, making it impossible for anyone other than a thaumaturge or extra-dimensional entity such as himself to magically travel to or cast spells in. There were energy voids for celestial magic energy as well, where his magic wouldn't work. Luckily, Domis-Alta-Calla was not one of those. *But Pendoni is*, he thought.

Azartial had come to Domis-Alta-Calla just after the destruction of Caranamere to leave the key—one of his "loose ends"—before going back. Now he had returned to consider what to do with the sword and to ruminate on his options.

He sat against a pillar, his tail swishing in agitation and disturbing the layer of dust, and went through his mental checklist. He had destroyed Caranamere, cast suspicion upon the Brotherhood of Blood, and collected the Key of Otemus. All was going as planned. Now, as he had hoped, Torra Com Gidel was at Caranamere, and he, as Darilos, would be with her.

Azartial closed his eyes, took several deep breaths, and focused. His mind's eye drifted through fluorescent clouds into the Ether, then into a deeper portion, folding away into a region filled with a chaotic web of energy flows, or life lines, of a myriad of colors—the Nexus. He guided himself to the lines for the current time and found Torra's. It was easy to locate hers, blinding and swift, running alongside that of her tower mentor, that shrew, Kai.

Azartial looked for changes since his arrival, and changes since the run-in with the Brotherhood of Blood. There was the Brotherhood's line, a woven rope of intertwined lines. After the destruction of Caranamere, and the mages' run-in with them at the entrance to the blasted town, Azartial saw that the "rope" of the Brotherhood quickly expanded, with lines coming from every direction. It seemed they had gotten a lot of converts.

Azartial then looked around and found lines he didn't recognize at first. Most were the expeditionary mages, for following them back in time they went to the Towers of Magic. But another shimmered and ran closely with Torra's after the destruction of the town. He huffed in annoyance. This was that bumpkin woodsman, Osprey. But the shimmering quality was particularly troublesome. It meant that he was blessed by the Outer Gods, almost like a priest. Killing him would anger the gods, causing "issues" later, and he didn't need that kind of interference in his mission.

And his own blue-flaming line was there as well, running parallel to Torra's, but never quite touching.

Azartial propelled himself forward in time, following the lines of Torra and the key. He wanted his line and Torra's to touch. So far no luck. But he also wanted to see if Torra and the key would make it to Pendoni. At one point an event erupted, where many lines came together and wavered dramatically, some ending in a pop and flash, and there was some sort of energy disturbance. *Is this Pendoni?* he wondered. *Is this when the key opens the lock?*

And among those other lines that come crashing together was one that Azartial recognized immediately. It was the apricot-colored line of the southern general, Feng.

Azartial focused more closely on the general's line. It shot like a ray of light straight to Pendoni, closely followed by hordes of other lines, many ending in dramatic struggles. Feng would fight his way to Pendoni, every mile. This was a man who was driven to succeed!

Two very important facts jumped out at him at once. First, the core of General Feng's line shimmered slightly, a sign of being touched by the Outer Gods. Second, his line vibrated with the attention of the Triumvirate Gods, like some unleashed war dog wearing a collar. Being touched by Outer Gods meant one of two possibilities: either he was a priest to them—highly unlikely given his apparent service to the Triumvirate—or as Azartial suspected, Feng had been saved by them at some point in the distant past. He had either been healed in some major way by a priest or had died and been resurrected. *How* he was touched didn't matter. But he intended to find out, anyhow.

It would seem that stern human is seeking Pendoni as well, he thought, *and will arrive when Torra does. Good. The seed I planted in Feng's thoughts, years ago, has blossomed just as planned. It's time to pluck that little flower. Power-hungry humans are so easy to manipulate.*

The entire time Azartial consulted the Nexus, he felt the watchful eyes of the Outer Gods and the Triumvirate. He knew most of them couldn't see what he could see. Few entities could enter the Nexus. But they had an idea. They could see faint glows, like spying through fogged glass into a home.

He unfocused his mind, flew back away from the Nexus, through the colored clouds of the Ether, and back to the present time and dimension, where his corporeal body now sat.

Azartial grunted and shook his head. The whistle of the wind and the sharp, acidic scent of the air of the Great Wasteland returned to his senses.

The demon went to the altar and picked up the Key of Otemus, turning it in his talons. His blue flames danced and flashed off the silvery blade.

He thought back to his visits to Hozor of Crancoff, the collector of magical antiquities who had first alerted him to the location of the key and the Convergence's location. Disguised as Darilos nearly a year and a half ago, Azartial had persuaded the old man to share what he knew, at the cost of a dozen extremely rare books Azartial had to kill for or steal from around the world. Only then did the old man lead him to his expansive library and, pulling open a hidden chamber, reveal the Codex of Otemus and the secrets it contained. And it was Hozor who informed him that the Key of Otemus was kept at the Astronomer's Guild.

From the Codex, Azartial had learned a trove of information: that the key fits a lock at the convent of Pendoni, in modern-day Taxia, where the Convergence would be revealed, that the key could only be wielded by two people, cooperating at the same time: one person who had been touched by the power of the Outer Gods yet fought against them, and one person touched by the power of the Triumvirate yet fought against them, and that the one who wielded it could control both terrestrial magic and celestial magic.

Torra Com Gidel and the southern general fit those descriptions.

Now all he had to do was lead them both to the door—and convince them to cooperate.

Easy, he thought, placing the key back on the altar. He would return for it erelong. But first, it was time to pay a visit to a couple of men to keep his machinations moving.

CHAPTER THIRTEEN
Strategy Session

General Feng stared down at a series of large maps unrolled on a low, wide table. The lambent orange flicker of beeswax candles lent the drawings of mountain ridges and winding paths a mystical quality. In the center of the largest of the maps was written, "Khosoon Pass: beyond is Calnuria," in Totinese. A second map was labeled "Khunti Territory," also in Totinese. At the top of the third map, written in flowing Taxin calligraphy, was, "Here be the great nation of Taxia, may the gods favor his majesty, King Halis III and his Winter Queen, Esebel of Totinol."

To either side of the table, standing with arms behind their backs, waited Feng's two commanders. The first was an older man with a long, shaggy white beard, stooped back, and three deep scars grown dull with age, running across his face. He was dressed in the green and blue military coat of a Quisha army officer and the blue silk cummerbund of a commander. Across the table from the old commander stood a tall, muscular man with dark brown skin and bald head. Though he also wore the blue silk cummerbund, his scarred chest was bare and around his thick neck sat a twisted bronze torc—the sign of a slave of high standing. The two ends of the torc each featured the head of a Tsian'sina'ku, a mythical "lion-snake," the symbol of House Feng.

The men only wore their military outfits in the privacy of the tent. At no time during the troop's excursion into Taxia had they been seen wearing them outside, for the troop was posing as merchants.

A stiff evening wind buffeted the tent around them. All was quiet save for the flapping of tent walls and flutter of the candles. An orange pendant hung on the inside, back wall of the tent. The image of a Tsian'sina'ku twisted in the center of it. The pendant would normally hang outside Feng's tent, but as with the military outfits, it had to be hidden from passing eyes and kept inside.

At last, Feng gave a grunt. Without looking up, he said, "Ming'ai. Analysis!"

The old commander gave a quick bow. "Lord Feng, it is with great humility I offer my expert opinion." His voice was gruff, but his Quishan inflections were that of high aristocracy of the imperial court. "Though the main road to the pass is wider and easier to travel, our true nature will certainly be discovered at Dodonor Citadel. We have sixty footmen and thirty slave warriors, my lord, not nearly enough to take Dodonor by force. We have posed as a merchant caravan successfully, through your wisdom and excellent leadership, but at Dodonor we will be searched and discovered."

Feng interrupted. "We fooled the guards at Shangang Pass when we crossed over to Taxia from Quisha."

"Yes, my lord, but Dodonor has less traffic and a stronger garrison. The Khunti Lionriders raid Calnuria daily, so Dodonor is vigilant against arms crossing over." Commander Ming'ai pointed to one side of the middle map. "Instead, I offer another solution. We must take the east path, revealed to us by our scouts. Shepherds told of a winding route away to the northeast of the pass, often taken by the Khunti, which will circumvent Dodonor. I estimate the route will be slower, and steeper, and we cannot take the wagons. But if we miss the worst of the weather we can cross over into Calnuria within a week, undetected."

Feng gave a slight huff. The huff was enough, though, to cause Ming'ai to step back and wait. Ming'ai was of House Sung, vassals of House Feng and the Feng emperors going back at least five generations, loyally. So it wouldn't do to dress him down in more severe style, at least not in front of another commander, particularly a slave. Sternness was certainly the best approach. But first … .

"Tonang. Analysis!"

The slave warrior gave a deep bow. "You honor me, Master." His Quishan was crude and strongly accented with the more guttural language of his homeland, Inlai'chi'a. "Dodonor will not suspect us to be anything other than a merchant caravan, as we have posed for the past several weeks. With heavy march, we will arrive at Dodonor Citadel late tomorrow night. They will receive us in the bailey of their citadel. If they search us, we will present them with the cotton and silk rolls that we claim to carry to Axim in the north. If necessary, we will bribe them with the gems we carry."

"And if they find our weapons?" Feng asked.

"We attack, Master. Our Shadow Guard will climb the walls of the bailey to take their archers and lower ropes for us. Sources say that they garrison two hundred soldiers when at full capacity, but we have the element of surprise and can quickly take them."

Feng gave another huff. Tonang lowered his head and stepped back, silent. Tonang was a good strategist, Feng had to admit, and he tried to treat the slave warrior well, particularly given his rank. Still, if Feng didn't hold Tonang's family hostage back in Quisha, on pain of death if anything should happen to him, then he didn't doubt for a moment that Tonang would abandon the army and spring for home.

Minutes passed as he considered, then Feng spoke, still looking down at the maps. "Ming'ai, you are correct that our force cannot directly conquer theirs. But we will not take the east path. You have served my family well, so I am surprised you would suggest something so stupid. It will take too long, and a force as large as ours would be detected. The Khunti we run into would not be silent about our approach and we would have little to offer them to allow our passage. And though your plan would avoid conflict with Taxia, it also would do nothing to draw away troops from the area of our target. We would have to fight them anyhow, only now it would be deep within their territory. Your plan is shortsighted." The old commander only bowed in response, eyes downcast. He knew when to hold his tongue.

Feng mulled his thoughts for a moment, weighing his options as he rubbed a hand over his stubbly face. It was time for a surprise. "Tonang," the general continued, "how many casks of rice wine do we yet carry?"

Tonang thought for a moment, then replied, "At last count, five barrels and eight firkins remain, my master."

"Bring me Chiang'wu."

Tonang gave a quick bow, then exited the tent. Feng continued studying the map. Ming'ai pointedly cleared his throat.

"Yes, Commander?" Feng said, annoyed.

"My lord, if I may speak freely, is it your intention to start a war with Taxia? If you go with Tonang's plan, the hostility would not be taken lightly. The Quisha imperial court already considers you heterodox. We have endangered the Silk Treaty by bringing a force of this size into Taxin lands. An attack on a Taxin citadel would be … "

Scowling, Feng cut him off with a raise of his hand. Ming'ai gave a cautious bow and growled but spoke no further.

In moments Tonang reentered the tent followed by a hobbling old man with wild, wispy gray hair and a long beard to match. His faded, purple-patterned tunic and blue pantaloons seemed at odds with the military outfits of the officers in the tent. Crisscrossing his chest were two straps, each with a dozen leather pouches sewn onto them, and at the bottom of each strap were larger leather packs. Chiang'wu was a renowned herbalist and supernaturalist from the Charinzon region of northern Quisha, though he was not of high birth, nor a mage. His knowledge of herbology, both to heal and to kill, was legendary, but he was also practiced in demonology and astral lore.

"Yes? You called for me?" the old man said, his voice high and shrill. His eyes twinkled with the flash of madness.

"Chiang'wu, how much dried Zinwo weed do you have in your collection? Enough for ten casks of rice wine?"

Chiang'wu drew in a sharp breath, his face lighting up like a child given sweets. "Ha! Do you mean what I believe, Lord Feng?"

General Feng flashed a sidelong look. "You know what I want it for."

The old herbalist gave a little jig of excitement and a quick whistle. "Yes, Lord Feng, I do believe we have just enough. Just enough, indeed! Ha!"

Ming'ai's gaze darted between Feng and the herbalist. "My lord, what plan is this? What is Zinwo weed?"

Chiang'wu burst in with an answer. "Oh, it is wonderful, Commander. Ha! Such a plant can be found nowhere but in the western highlands of Quisha. Zinwo has no scent or taste, but when dried and mixed with alcohol, then drunk, it dissolves a man's brain until his mind is gone, but his body yet lives. Ohhh, it doesn't do so immediately, on no, it starts as a headache and blurred vision, then nausea, and then the victim passes out before his mind is gone altogether. It appears at first as if he drank too much alcohol. Ha!"

"My lord!" Ming'ai exclaimed, eyes wide with alarm. "Poisoning is so … dishonorable. I do not see your wisdom in this action."

"That is because you lack hardness! Have all your battles failed to temper your steel? We will win this battle with whatever tools are available to us."

Feng turned to the herbalist. "Chiang'wu, add the Zinwo weed to the casks. Tonang, as we near the Khosoon Pass, have our forward scouts leak to the garrison at Dodonor, and at any inn, that we carry casks of delicious sweet rice wine amongst our trade goods, enough for a garrison, bound for Axim in the north, and that the guards at Shangang Pass demanded and received many casks." Feng turned to the old commander. "Commander Ming'ai, tell the men we will push forward on the main road to Dodonor, and not to drink the rice wine, of course. Make sure we arrive at Dodonor just after sunset, when they will keep us in their bailey until the morning, but I suspect they will still demand the wine."

"How can you be sure they will drink it?" Tonang asked.

Feng's blood rushed to his face as he gritted his teeth. "Taxin soldiers are weak. They are away from home, on a cold pass high in the mountains, with few chances for strong drink. Are you really that *stupid?*"

Ming'ai persisted, sweat beads on his wrinkled brow. "My lord, you must understand that Taxia will consider this an act of war!"

"Then we must ensure no one in Dodonor lives to tell the tale. Besides, I have a plan. I already dispatched two of our scouts into Khunti territory with a message to meet us at Dodonor Citadel the morning after next." He waved his hand. "You are dismissed."

The three men bowed, turned, and walked out the entrance of the command tent. Ming'ai paused a moment at the flap, his eyes clouded with mixed emotions, but then he grunted and continued out without voicing his concerns. For this, General Feng was thankful. He would hate to have to make a bloody example of him. Ming'ai was, after all, the closest thing to a friend he had.

CHAPTER FOURTEEN
Departing by Night

It was midnight at Palal Jehai, the palace of the Gold Dragon. The sky was overcast, but one of the twin moons was full, the other half, lending an apparitional light through the thin layer of clouds and giving the sheer cliffs over the palace a burnished glow. The first snowflakes of the season were falling, light and diffuse, through the crisp, still air—a gift of serenity from the heavens.

Someone tugged on Ingal's travel vest, pulling him out of his reflections. He stood in the rarely used Rear Court of the palace, a simple, circular courtyard in the back with walls that were high enough to prevent anyone from outside seeing if he was inside. Two hefty servants were attempting to buckle the last strap of his tanned elephant-hide garment trimmed with gold studs.

"Allow us," Ingal said, and took over from the servants, cinching a bronze buckle. He had packed light, with only a few books—oversized, of course—and a couple of potions stowed away in the six pockets. He chuckled to himself as he tightened the top left pocket, remembering that in this pocket the young Taxin mage, Torra Com Gidel, had once ridden in on a journey to the elvish lands of Peshilaree, two years before. He wondered how she was faring at the Tower of Light. It had been nearly half a year since last they had seen each other, and with the tower still refusing to communicate directly with him except for state business, updates on her status were lacking.

Now the pocket held four precious tomes he had borrowed two decades ago from the Astronomer's Guild in Caranamere. Now he would be visiting again, unannounced as it was, and return them in person. *What was the First Astronomer's name again?* he thought. *Ah, yes, Colnos Com Dimb.*

The excitement of taking this journey, thinking about Torra, and the crisp air all gave him a joyous feeling.

But Ingal's joy quickly faltered. The shock from that morning's "incident" still stung. It was clear that a great surge of magical energy had occurred in the direction of Taxia, and the Triumvirate was behind it. And though the Triumvirate was willing him somehow to go, perhaps straight into a trap, he could not resist. He had to know what happened. Perhaps the Towers of Magic had sensed it as well, but they weren't about to tell him what was going on. He had to see it for himself.

"Fleeing?" The voice was Rethuud's, from behind the dragon, speaking in Peshilarn.

Ingal turned. Rethuud stood in the doorway to the interior of the palace, half in shadow, leaning against the door jamb.

Ingal's chamberlain interjected, moving in front of the elf. "I'm sorry, sir, but the master is not to be disturbed!"

"It's all right, Baliniq. Let him through." As Rethuud stepped into the courtyard, Ingal dismissed the servants with his thanks.

Naturally, Rethuud didn't bother bowing. "First you reveal you are seeking a truce with the Hall of Emeralds, now you are secretly fleeing the palace in the dead of night."

Ingal replied to the elf in Peshilarn. "Careful with your words, Rethuud. We are not *fleeing*."

"Out for a midnight flight, then? Just another flurry in the moonlight?"

Ingal smiled despite himself; no one had ever tried to compare him to a snowflake! He stretched his wings and gave them a quick flap, getting a secret pleasure in how the rush of air bothered the elf, but wincing at the tightness of his wing muscles. He hadn't flown any real distance in weeks. "We are not accountable to you, Rethuud. But now is a good time for us to attend to a quick investigation. It may be nothing. We may be gone for as much as a week, but things are calm enough on the war fronts."

"I doubt your viziers and generals will see it that way. Most weren't pleased by today's audience."

"It isn't their pleasure I seek." Too late to stop himself, Ingal cringed at his use of first person, the continuing evidence of the brief link he had shared with the Triumvirate's energies when he cast the renegade spell during the battle for the Tower of Light. Somehow talking to Rethuud kept him from watching his words.

Rethuud toyed with the leatherine-wrapped grip of his sword. "Well, I hope your investigation is worth it. A lot can change in a week. For all you know, Ocrin's ogres will come screaming over the border tomorrow, and you won't be here to lead the charge against them."

Ingal tried not to show his surprise that Rethuud knew about the ogres and other beasts. Ingal had learned about this "secret weapon" of the Doom Empress from spies deep in Ocrin territory. How had Rethuud learned? But he didn't want to give away his hand. "Ogres, Rethuud?"

"You aren't the only one with spies, Jehai." He half-turned to go back inside, then seemed to remember something and turned back. "Oh, do be careful. A report from the north of Peshilaree included a sighting of the Pearl Dragon, Slivice. She was seen flying down from the Northern Triad nations into Oiya Inoi, possibly to Ocrin."

Ingal figured Rethuud was fishing for hints, as a show of concern would suggest he was headed in that direction himself. "Noted," was all he replied.

"Fair journey, whatever your investigation may be," Rethuud said, then he disappeared back into the shadows of the corridor as quietly as he had come. Rethuud was the only person in the palace who could sneak up on Ingal. *Or perhaps*, thought the dragon, *I'm just too old to hear an elf anymore.*

As always, Rethuud had a good point to make. Why *did* he feel the need to leave at midnight, from the rear court, instead of at dawn from the front courtyard as usual? Why so secretive? Ingal grunted. He couldn't shake the thought that the energy surge was something malevolent and dangerous. Best not to alarm his ministers or the viziers. Nor did he wish to alarm the pilgrims to his palace, whose numbers had swelled in the last year, populated more by starving farmers begging miracles to save their crops than admiring worshipers. And with the war …

Moments after his departure, the chamberlain would have the cloth-of-gold flag taken down from the entryway—a signal that the Gold Dragon had gone—not to be raised again until his return. There would be no hiding that he had left. Servants talk. Pilgrims search him out. People in the countryside see him flying overhead.

Ingal turned to Baliniq, the only person remaining in the courtyard. "Remember, if anyone should ask our whereabouts, tell them we are surveying the land and the battle fronts. We expect to be back within a week."

"Yes, my lord." Baliniq bowed.

And with that, Ingal again stretched out his wings, leapt into the sky, and ascended with powerful wingbeats to the chilly firmament, turning southwest over the rolling, snowcapped mountaintops.

CHAPTER FIFTEEN
Three Conditions

Shortly after Feng ended his strategy session in the late evening, a commotion in the quartermaster's area broke out, with a crash among the supply wagons and soldiers running to investigate. Word soon came to Feng that the load on one of Feng's personal supply wagons had been upended, perhaps by a beast or a hill giant, but none could be found. The perimeter guards had seen no animal nor any strangers. The camp was searched from top to bottom, but nothing out of the ordinary was discovered. Feng suspected it must be some of the slaves getting bold and robbing his personal stores, but all was accounted for, and interrogation of slaves yielded no results. He had extra guards posted around the camp, then wearily wound his way back to his personal tent, well after midnight.

Opening the flap to his tent, Feng found one of his pleasure slaves, Shana, lying on the furs of his sleeping pallet, clad only in a silk loincloth and the slave's torc around her neck. Upon seeing him, she smiled and writhed her body like a snake, caressing her ample breasts and thighs as she did, accentuated by the flickering light of a lone candle.

It wasn't odd for him to summon Shana at this hour. He often relieved himself of stress with her, as the scars on her body attested. Yet he had not called for her. Nonetheless, her movements excited him, his breathing quickened, and so he stepped in.

But he stopped just inside. Something wasn't right. There was no guard outside the flap, but more concerning was Shana's attitude. She normally recoiled at his appearance, fearful of his torments. Any desire she showed was always feigned to please him.

"Slave, I did not bid you come."

Shana didn't answer. Instead, she sat up, then went on all fours and crawled over to his feet, kissing his knees and running her hand up his thighs.

Feng kicked her, sending the woman flying backward to the pallet. How dare she touch him without permission!

But instead of cowering, she sat up with a look of amusement, her smile turning from sultry desire to a leer.

It was time to teach this slave a lesson in humility.

Feng stepped across the tent, reached over to a post and grabbed his flail, gripping the teak handle tightly and letting the lashes uncoil. "I don't know what you're smiling at, but this will cure you of your humor."

He let fly his wrath. The knotted leather lashes whipped out. They slapped hard against Shana's exposed breasts. Shana parted her mouth in surprise, emitting a quick gasp.

Her eyes flared bright blue, glowing out of the darkness, and she took a step toward him.

Feng stepped back, his heart skipping a beat. He transferred the flail to his left hand and then reached to the pommel of his sword with his right. "What are you?"

He took another step back. His foot hit something soft. He dared to look down.

A woman's leg. Following it up and behind a lacquered trunk, he saw the unmistakable form of Shana lying in the shadows, her head turned completely around her shattered neck, mouth gaping, lifeless eyes staring up at him.

He dropped the flail then drew his sword and pointed it at the thing walking toward him. It was laughing now, but this wasn't a woman's laugh. It was guttural, deep, changing in tone. Its eyes flared again, blue flames in the pupils.

"What are you?" he asked again. "What do you seek?"

It stopped walking toward him, now at the tip of his sword, but didn't answer.

At once Feng thrust forward, the sword piercing the imposter's breast and plunging deep into its torso.

The impostor remained standing and alive, its leering smile growing broader. Feng pulled his sword out. The wound, unbleeding, incredibly healed back up as he watched.

"Guards!" Feng cried, then tried to dash around to the door, but the imposter simply grabbed his arm and flung him across the sleeping pallet to crash into a small chest, knocking it open, sending incense cones flying.

Feng quickly got to his feet, turned, and saw the creature transform. The blue flames of its eyes spread, burning across its face and then down its body until its entire form was aflame. And then the fiery body erupted in a shower of blue sparks, causing Feng to throw an arm in front of his eyes. When he looked back he gasped in surprise. It was a demon, burning bright blue with a long muzzle of sharp teeth and thin amber wings that scraped against the canvas roof of the tent. It laughed again, deep and echoing.

"By the Three Emperors!" Feng shouted. "The Demon Dragon!" Despite his military training, he froze up, unable to attack.

"Yes," the demon said, tapping his fingertips together. His talons clacked as they struck each other. "Call me Azartial. Forgive my little game, but we can't have you turning and running at the first glimpse of me. How many years has it been since first you summoned me? Do tell. I have no sense of the passage of time in your world since then." Despite the beastly form, the demon's voice was smooth and human. He spoke in Feng's native language, Quishan, in a perfect noble dialect.

Feng at first had difficulty finding his own voice, his mind racing between awe, fear, and thoughts of either trying to get around the beast or attempting to escape under the canvas of the tent. But the demon would quickly overtake him. "It has been at least a decade, demon! How is it you are here?" Then, trying to add some command to his voice, "I did not summon you! This is not your dimension!"

The beast smiled. "Indeed. But, you see, I am on a hiatus of sorts, visiting your fine world for a bit of an errand. I won't go into details, but suffice it to say that the Citrine Dragon's silver summoning ring you used last time won't be necessary anymore—though it certainly did prove useful to find you. I figured you would keep it. But imagine my surprise when I materialized next to it at the bottom of a supply wagon!" The beast's eyes lit up with humor. Its smile revealed a double row of sharp points and a bright blue, serpentine tongue. "Such an immeasurably fine, magical artifact to be stored next to sacks of provender!"

While the demon spoke, Feng had formulated a quick plan of escape. He pointed to the body of Shana and feigned sorrow. "She was my beloved!" he lied. "How dare you!" When the demon turned to look at the body, Feng tackled the center pole of the tent, lifting it and pushing it aside. Immediately the tent collapsed onto them, and Feng lurched away from the demon and to the edge of the canvas to slip under and out.

The demon's flaming body ignited the tent canvas.

As Feng crawled on his belly out of the tent, he heard cries of alarm from his soldiers and slave warriors, who came running from every direction.

They stopped short in horror when, from the burning canvas, emerged the demon dragon, roaring in anger, ripping apart the canvas with sharp talons and throwing the flaming shreds aside. It turned, sneering, to watch as Feng stood and backed away.

"If you wish to kill me," Feng shouted, "then you'll have to fight my army too!"

"*Kill* you?" the beast laughed. "Why, you pitiful mortal! If I wished you dead, I could have annihilated you in a hundred different ways! *And* your army!"

Soldiers quickly encircled the burning tent and demon. They drew their swords. They lowered spears and various pole arms until, at last, the dragon stood in a ring of iron teeth all pointed at him. At a signal from Feng, the soldiers stabbed forward, delivering gashes that would kill any mortal creature.

The demon dragon roared in pain. "That's enough play. We must talk in private." It pointed at Feng, and at once the world spun around Feng until all was a blur.

And then he was falling.

Feng tumbled head over heels into a dark void, frigid wind rushing past his ears. He was falling, falling. Wind rushed past his ears. He gradually became aware that the demon was descending alongside, but upright, controlling his angle with his slim wings.

Snowcapped mountaintops were below. *Far* below. He realized with a shock that they were at a great height in the atmosphere. Plunging fast. Moonlit clouds were level with him. He gasped in fright.

The demon laughed, hearty and jovial. He had a relaxed posture as he fell with Feng. "What's the matter, General?" It shouted over the wind. "Not so haughty now, eh?"

"Take me back!" Feng demanded, barely able to find his voice amongst his panic.

"Now, now, son of emperors, is that any way to ask? How about a 'please?'"

Feng drew in a deep breath, trying to calm himself. The mountains were rushing up at him. The end was near. "Please!" he shouted.

"Fine, but let's go where we can talk in greater comfort."

The world spun again. Feng closed his eyes against the vertigo, then he hit the ground. Impossibly, the impact was soft, as if falling from only a few inches, but enough to knock the wind out of him.

When Feng opened his eyes, he saw before him a sandy shelf of land. The air was dry and warm, not at all the chilly mountainside of the encampment. They were on the edge of stark, brown hills covered in scrub. The shelf looked eastward over an endless desert of low dunes. Dawn was breaking, which threw off his sense of time; it had been the dead of night only moments before, back at his encampment.

Feng stood on shaking legs.

The demon dragon sat on its haunches to his left, staring off over the desert.

Feng asked. "Where are we?"

"It's beautiful, isn't it? The desert? The nomads of this land call it *Tanash'tina*, meaning 'riches abound.' Where your people would see only a wasteland of dunes, they see this as a utopia, full of minerals and incense, gleaming oases, and sparkling sands that shift with the sigh of their gods. Every grain is a jewel to them. Why, just to walk on the dunes is a joy and an honor to them, even as they bake in the sun."

The demon turned to look at Feng, the salmon light of dawn glimmering on the white of his talons. "We are very far to the east of where your troops are encamped. Why, it would take you the better part of a year to travel back there by ship and horse, if you could find your way. Though you won't find any horses here. Camels, yes, and these amazing beasts that look like horses but with elephant-like trunks and tails, and tan stripes. I think they call them 'dromangu.'"

Feng looked about in panic, sweat breaking out on his bald head. There was no sign of habitations, nor roads, nor even trails. He felt for his sword, but the scabbard was empty. He must have dropped the weapon when he was falling. "What is it …" He realized his voice was shaking, so Feng took a deep breath and started again, with command. "What is it you want, demon? Why have you sought me out?"

"Ah, now we come to it!" The demon stood and stepped closer. It was bipedal and over seven feet tall. His reptilian tail swished back and forth in excitement. "You see, when you summoned me all those years ago, in search of the Convergence, you unintentionally sparked a bit of a revival amongst the gods I serve. It set into motion a series of schemes to track down the artifact. With such power, one could easily rule a nation, a continent, or even all of Irikara." The demon ran its forked tongue over its teeth and stared deeply into Feng's eyes, as if to read his thoughts. "That is, if the ravings of a madman named Otemus could be believed —a madman who had been in contact with the Overgods, the gods that the Outer Gods pray to! Yes, such entities exist! They created *me*.

"And as I talked with you then, I and the gods around me sensed the attention of the Triumvirate and the power they emitted around you. Alarmed, they made plans. If the Triumvirate gods were so close to you, and you sought this mythical object of power, then we knew that now was the time to act. And so I was—how should I say it?—*dispatched* to investigate. The Triumvirate gods became aware of this, and so they turned their attention to other movements, such as the attack on the Tower of Light. Their plans were accelerated."

"Why should I care about your plans, or your gods?"

The demon chuckled. "When I consulted the Nexus, where I see the combined fates of all individuals, I found something useful in your time line." The demon dragon drew near to Feng, within touching distance. Feng felt the heat of the blue flames. Smelled the beast's surprisingly saccharine breath. "Tell me, my dear general, how did the Outer Gods touch you? There is something in your past, isn't there?"

"I'm not telling you a thing!"

"Hmm." Azartial swept his claws, and then the world swirled again. There was a mighty splash, and when the spinning stopped, Feng stood ankle deep in warm water, slowly sinking in mud, and it was night again. Hot and steamy. He and Azartial stood side by side in a swamp surrounded on all sides by dense jungle. Thin trees crowded on all sides, their vine-covered trunks breaking into innumerable roots just above the surface of the water. The flapping of birds' wings sounded through the branches, and dark things slithered through the black water. Dawn had not yet come, but a thin light managed to pierce through the canopy. The glow from the demon's flames cast a blue, wavering, supernatural light on the vegetation.

"Perhaps I should leave you here until you decide to be more cooperative!" Azartial scolded. "Good luck, though. Many call this heart of the jungle the 'Engulfment.' Dark elves are said to stalk here, and many strange beasts. Even the insects are deadly. We are far to the south of your troops, by the way." Azartial leaned forward. "Now, tell me, how were you touched by the Outer Gods?"

Feng growled, gritting his teeth. What choice did he have but to comply? "Then I shall tell you, if I must." He thought back to his youth, when he'd seen his eighth summer. The ride on the royal barge down the Emperor River. They hit submerged rocks. The barge came apart and sunk in the swirling, muddy water. His six-year-old sister called out to him as she was pulled under, reaching toward him, desperately calling his name, before he went under too. Feng scowled. "As a child I drowned. A priest of the Lotus God was found and revived me. I had been dead for half an afternoon at that point. My sister was never found." Feng closed his eyes at the memory of his mother wailing.

The demon's eyes lit up, and a smile crept over its muzzle. "Ah. So it's fair to say that you have been touched by the Outer Gods, but now fight against them for the Triumvirate, yes?"

Feng knew what the demon was getting at. Such was the requirement for one to open the doors to access the Convergence. "Yes. What of it? I owe nothing to the Lotus God!"

"He might think differently."

Something slithered over Feng's right foot. He jumped back, his boots sucking out of the mud, but the movement startled something in the trees behind him and it skittered away through the limbs, jabbering. Feng pointed at the demon. "I demand you take me back to my camp!"

"I rather like it here," Azartial said. "There is *life* here, life like nowhere else in Irikara. Dozens of species in every square cubit, so much so that every organism fights for that space, with fang or claw or stinger. To survive here is to balance on the edge of the dagger, and that deadly balancing act is like an art, full of *passion* and *energy*." It said those last words with reverence. But then the demon looked over at Feng, waved his arm, and made the world spin again.

When they rematerialized, Feng and the demon were back on the sandy shelf overlooking the Tanash'tina desert. Feng's head ached from the teleporting, and he bent over and retched. When the vomiting ended, he felt none the better for it. Azartial seemed to wait patiently for the general to finish.

"I have a deal for you, dear general."

Feng wiped his mouth with the back of a sleeve. "I serve the Triumvirate, not you, *or* your gods."

Azartial ignored this. "You aren't the only one searching for the Convergence. Surely you realize this. No one seems to know what form this object takes, but its function is known. It has the power to combine both terrestrial magic—the energies of the Triumvirate gods—and celestial magic—the energies of the Outer Gods."

"This I know," Feng replied. "But doubtless you seek it too. Clearly I cannot stop you. Why don't you just take it for yourself?"

"I don't seek it for myself," Azartial replied. "My job is to find out what it is and report back. If you have it in the meantime, what does it matter to me? But I know something you don't. Tell me, General, do you know where to find it?"

"Yes, but I shan't tell you."

Azartial smiled. "Oh, I know already. The convent at Pendoni. Do you forget that when you summoned me all those years ago, I pointed you in the direction of an alchemist named Shanti Tolec? Don't you think I knew by then?"

Feng nodded. "I found Tolec, after much searching, in Totinol. He had ancient scrolls on the Convergence. He proved useful."

"You're welcome," Azartial said.

"I am not beholden to you."

"You will be in a moment. You see, I have an object you need. Without it, you can't get the Convergence."

Feng tried not to show his surprise. After a brutal interrogation, the old alchemist had revealed where the crumbling scrolls of Otemus were kept and what he knew of the Convergence. There had been no mention of any 'object.' But then, many of the scrolls were damaged beyond legibility, and they were written in an extinct language that Tolec had to read to him—under force, of course, before he died of his wounds. Had Tolec omitted a crucial part? Or was the demon dragon bluffing?

"Explain," Feng said.

The demon threw back its head and laughed, the sound echoing off the scrubby hillside and out over the desert. "My dear general, were you just going to show up at Pendoni and demand the Convergence from the nuns? Just march your troops through another nation and take it by force?"

In fact, that was very close to the plan, but Feng sidestepped. "I shan't share my plans with you."

The demon grinned. "The nuns can't access it. Didn't Otemus's scrolls say so? It takes two people, General Feng. One who has been touched by the Outer Gods but fights against them. That's *you*. And it takes another person, but I'll choose right now to keep their requirement to myself. I have such a person, and I will send her to Pendoni. And there is a third requirement. A key, which I also possess, that you must use to unlock the door to the Convergence chamber. Only you, or someone like you, can use it for its purpose at the same time as the other person. Only when all three requirements are met will the door open and reveal the Convergence to you, and then you will possess the most powerful artifact in the world."

Feng knew about the other person required but had figured that one of the Pendoni nuns met that requirement. After all, they guarded the door, according to the old scrolls. They must be able to enter, right? "So what do you want for this 'key?'" *Everyone has a price*, he thought, *even demons. Or, perhaps*, especially *demons*.

The demon paused, seeming to savor the moment, as the dawn grew in intensity to an aureate yellow, illuminating the land with a promise to burn away those who were unprepared.

"As I mentioned," the demon said, "I am only here to investigate for the Outer Gods. But Pendoni is in an energy void, a powerful one, where magical energy of any sort, including both terrestrial and celestial energy, cannot work. Otemus surely chose the location for that reason. Thus, without magic, I cannot be there unless I choose to go in my native, magnificent form, as I stand before you," the demon held his arms out as if to display himself, "which for reasons of my own is, shall we say, not preferred." The demon slowly circled Feng, its heavy feet crunching on the loose mix of sand and gravel.

"So what I ask of you are three small conditions, and you will be able to keep the prize all for yourself. The first condition is that you use the Convergence to perform specific actions that I demand, at least once a year. Otherwise it will remain in your possession to do with as you please, to keep until the day you die, at which point I will take it."

"And how do I know *you* won't kill me for it? It would be easy enough, with your powers."

The demon grinned. "I am immortal, as are the gods. The lifespan of a mortal human is but the batting of an eye for us. Take it. Use it to reconquer your nation … or the world, for that matter, if you can manage it. Be an emperor and die of old age in a golden palace, with the Convergence by your side. I don't care. Just don't use it to trifle with the gods, for their wrath is great."

The thought of allowing someone else to dictate how he used one of the world's most powerful objects, even for a moment, seemed like a deal-breaker. But he was in no position to refuse. "And the other conditions?"

"Second condition: the other human who opens the door with you, Torra Com Gidel, is not to be harmed, even though your instinct will be to kill her on the spot. She is, after all, an enemy of the Triumvirate."

Feng grimaced. How could he protect an enemy of his gods? "I shall kill whomever I please, demon!"

The demon narrowed its eyes and flared its nostrils. "And so shall I, General. I have half a mind to do so right now!"

Feng knew he was powerless against this beast. He averted his eyes. "Go on."

"Third: you are to kill a man, or have him killed, the moment you first meet him. It will go against the only principle you hold dear."

"What principle is that?" Feng asked, nearly spitting the words. He had killed countless men—thousands, if including soldiers killed at his orders. He had laid waste to entire villages, like the fishing village of Lok Tan in Inlai'chi'a, mostly women and children, ordered the babies thrown into the river as their mothers wailed at the docks, just to make an example of their village. But the other villages on the River Tan fell in line after that, with no bloodshed. Over a thousand lives had been saved because a dozen babies were drowned by his men. He knew peace always comes at the end of a blade. "As I said, I shall kill whomever I please."

"Then you will please yourself to kill an apostle of the Triumvirate."

Feng's eyes widened. The demon was right. To go against the wishes of the Triumvirate was a line he would never cross. To kill their apostle? "Unthinkable!"

The demon emitted a horrible, echoing laugh. At last, as the echoes died away, it asked, "Unthinkable, my sweet general?"

The demon took a talon and ran the sharp tip across its own arm, slicing open the scales and flesh, seeming to savor the pain, its tongue coiling out and over its muzzle, quivering in a shudder of exhilaration, eyes closed in ecstasy. Feng was no stranger to this sensation.

"Sometimes, General, you must cut yourself to know you are alive." It opened its sapphire eyes and stared into Feng's as if to study his soul. "The death of a mortal—any mortal—is the slightest of cuts, but some are more stimulating than others. Would it help you to know that this servant of the Triumvirate, Apostle Agnon, is a traitor to his own people?" The beast again moved its head close to Feng's. "Tell me, General, haven't you employed traitors to get an edge on the enemy? What do you do to those who are traitors, even as their treachery works to further your own goals? Can you trust them when you've finished with them? No? Do you keep them alive, certain that they won't turn their perfidy against you as well? Do you mourn their passing after you've disposed of them?"

The demon was right again. Feng collected his thoughts, turning to look over the desert. Already, heat waves were starting to warp the air over dune ridges. Dare he make a deal with a demon? If the Convergence were worth everything he thought, power of that nature deserved the will of immortals and demanded compromise. He wished he could summon the Triumvirate first, to get their approval. "Can you give me a day to think it over?"

"No," the demon responded bluntly. "But I can leave you here and go find another to satisfy my need."

"If I comply with your three conditions, then the Convergence is mine to have and control, with no other interference from you?" The demon nodded, its eyes alight with blue flame. "Very well," Feng said, sighing, still looking eastward to the sunrise. "It's agreed, demon dragon."

The demon's flaming blue eyes flared. "Swear an oath to it!"

Feng growled, then replied, "By the three emperors, I swear to uphold your three conditions in return for you helping me possess the Convergence!" He pointed a finger at the demon. "Now you swear an oath as well."

Azartial responded by stating, "I swear to honor my three conditions, by power of the Overgods." It licked its lips, the long, thin, red tongue snaking up and along the muzzle as its eyes flashed. "It is done!" the demon announced. "I will track your movements and deliver the Key of Otemus in due time. And, my good general, as I said before, do call me by my name: *Azartial.*"

Feng started to turn back, but he found himself spinning, once again teleporting, reappearing on the muddy ground next to his smoldering tent in the encampment and darkness. He retched, raising himself with shaking arms, nothing but strings of saliva coming out of his quivering mouth.

Azartial was nowhere in sight.

A cry went up, and Feng's soldiers and slaves ran to his side to attend him. "The general's alive!" one shouted. "He's defeated the beast!" said another. Feng pulled himself to his feet on unsteady legs and pushed the men away, until his commanders, Ming'ai and Tonang, appeared.

"Your sword, Master," Tonang said, handing the weapon over in ceremonial fashion, head bowed. "It fell from the heavens after you disappeared. We feared for your well-being."

Feng took the sword and sheathed it, coughing against the bile in his throat and staggering from vertigo. For a moment he wondered if he had imagined the whole episode, but his boots and clothes were coated with the sand and mud of three very different parts of the world.

Feng grabbed Tonang by the shoulder and pulled him close. "Find Chiang'wu at once! I must discuss demons with him."

CHAPTER SIXTEEN
Trouble Sleeping

Torra was in Caranamere, at the corner shared by the blacksmith and the Dancing Mage Inn at dawn. The quaint wood and stone buildings of the town stood strong and firm over streets that were clean and paved with blue flagstone. The air was redolent with the scent of fresh baked bread, the embers of the smithy's forge, and the earthy essence of fall oaks.

The air exploded. Blinding white. Buildings blew apart. Screams filled the air. Everywhere was flame.

Torra wailed in horror and ran. Ran through the streets of Caranamere. Surrounded by walls of fire. Ran past friends and family with their hair and clothing engulfed. They were burning, burning, burning.

She tried to find her parents' home, but no matter how fast she ran, she never got closer.

At the town square, a victim crawled toward her, reached toward her, screamed for her. Torra recognized her as her mother. But her hair was burned off. Her face melting. "Help me, Torra!" she croaked. "You did this! You can stop it!"

"I can't!" Torra yelled, reaching for her mother, but they couldn't touch.

"You can!! You must!!" Then her mother collapsed, gasping. "Why did you do this?" Torra moved to help, but her mother clawed at her own burning face, screaming, as her eyes rolled back in her head, her mouth froze into a mask of horror, and she lay still.

Laughter erupted, deep and powerful, high over the roaring flames. Torra looked up, expecting to see the Emerald Dragon, but instead there were three massive shadowy figures—the Triumvirate gods—laughing down at her. They each raised an arm, pointing. Torra turned to look in that direction. Through a tunnel of flame she saw the gates of the Guild complex.

She ran to the gates. Grabbed the handles. The iron burned her palms with a sizzle and Torra screamed in pain. The gates wouldn't budge.

"Without our gods, we are nothing!" said a voice from somewhere behind her, the voice of Osprey. Torra noticed a massive keyhole in the gate, which confused her, as there was no keyhole before. "I don't have the key!" she yelled.

She turned to look for a key but instead saw a horde of townspeople, all of them on fire, shambling toward her. Her younger brother, Nickos. Her strong, broad-shouldered father, Raenos. The many people she had known. They begged her to open the door to let them in. Before her eyes, their skin was melting away to charred skeletons.

"No!" Torra cried, turned, and banged on the gate again. "I'm sorry!"

"Torra," said a new voice, deep and wise. It was the voice of the Gold Dragon, Ingal Jehai, though she could not see him. A gust of cold wind rushed past her, the beats of his wings extinguishing the flames and blowing away the burning townspeople.

Then Torra found herself floating in a haze of gray-blue clouds. As she slowly awakened, Ingal's words came echoing to her. "Perhaps we are all gods in our own right. With each action we bring forth the birth of a new reality, however small or large it may seem." His voice faded away.

"Ingal!" she said. "Don't leave!"

And then Torra realized she was awake and had said the words aloud.

For a panicked moment Torra didn't know where she was, thinking the stone beneath her was the cobblestone streets of Caranamere. But she forced herself to breathe and live in the moment. She lay on the flagstone floor of the observatory, her pack rolled up as a pillow beneath her damp brow.

Torra had awakened repeatedly during the night, each time in a fevered sweat, and then, upon closing her eyes, found herself reentering the same horrible dream.

She opened her eyes. The room was still dark save for a small lit candle near the top of the stairs. Its dim, flickering glow cast shadows on the walls, shifting like the Triumvirate gods in her dream. She sat up, fearful of falling back into the dream again, rubbed her eyes with the palms of her hands, then stopped herself, remembering how her palms had been burned by the gate handles. *It's just a dream*, she thought to herself.

Torra fumbled for her waterskin, pulled the stopper with a shaking hand, and eagerly gulped. Her throat was dry, her skin itching, her fingertips numb. The brimstone disease always got worse in times of stress. She absentmindedly scratched at her forearm.

On unsteady legs, Torra made her way downstairs to the water closet, winding past the slumbering forms of fellow mages. Mistress Lolund, as senior member, had been given one of the two daybeds. Master Kuno was given the other. Kuno lay there, a rotund mass, snoring, and was still snoring when she came back out of the water closet. She spied the form of Mistress Kai propped against a cabinet, her robes used as a blanket over her. Kai was still the only mage in the group who wasn't dressed in mage's robes. Master Gral was bundled nearby, but when she passed him, he opened his eyes and stared at her, the whites of his eyes standing out from the darkness. She hurried away.

Torra thought back to the evening before. Gathered together in the entry room downstairs, the Expeditionary Mages had reviewed and critiqued all evidence, including Osprey's account as well as what Darilos had shared, though the thaumaturge had not been found by Master Gral or Master del Titccio when they had gone out to search. Darilos's disappearance was, to Kai, more fodder for her suspicion.

A cordial review of the facts had crumbled into argument when it came time to make assumptions about what had happened and how best to investigate. Two factions had emerged.

One, led by the stiff and proper Lord Preneval from the Tower of Darkness, argued that they should investigate the Emerald Dragon first, as it seemed Mordan was the one who cast the renegade spell and, by the strictest law of the Council of Magic, should be held accountable for the crime.

But this was vociferously argued against by Master del Titccio from the Tower of Balance, who held that the Brotherhood of Blood should be investigated first, since tracking down the Emerald Dragon would be very difficult. Mordan could be a nation away by that point, and the Brotherhood might be responsible for hiring the dragon in the first place.

It didn't help that Preneval and del Titccio clearly harbored rancorous animosity toward each other from the beginning, the origins of which Torra could only guess at. All she gathered was that both were from noble families of Azure Sea nations. Mistress Lolund sided with Lord Preneval, while Mistress Kai sided with del Titccio. Voice volumes increased until they were shouting over each other.

Torra had chosen to remain silent other than answering questions about the nature of the town, the Astronomer's Guild, and the immediate region and culture, accompanied by similar remarks from Osprey, who sat across the room from her. The heavy discussion she had had with him about atheism and blasphemy still hung in the air between them. Masters Gral and Donovan chose not to get involved in the arguments beyond stating certain facts they had determined, seeming to yield investigative decisions to the senior members. And Master Kuno, the most senior of all, tried his best to calm both sides and reorient the discussion.

In the end, no one knew where the Brotherhood was based or where the Emerald Dragon had gone, making both plans difficult to follow. Nor did anyone know what to make of the "beast" that Osprey had seen on the hilltop or the chest full of glowing items given to the dragon in apparent payment. The only thing the group really agreed on was that the magical energies were clearly that of a renegade spell.

Master Kuno interceded, suggesting that everyone get some rest and start fresh in the morning. Truly, everyone was exhausted by that point. A watch was set through the night outside the only door to the observatory.

Now, in the wee hours, things seemed peaceful enough, though she wasn't sure how much time had passed. Rather than heading back upstairs and to the dream that tormented her, Torra decided to quietly open the observatory door and step outside. A breath of fresh air would do her good.

Thoughts of fresh air evaporated, though, as she inhaled sulfurous char in the chilly predawn atmosphere outside. The twin moons shone upon an ashy landscape to create an eerie pale glow, like the skin of a corpse, pockmarked by the embers of still-burning debris around the hillsides and in piles down in the crater. Banks of smoke crept through the trees like wraiths.

… they were burning …

Torra jumped as someone cleared his throat to her right. She turned and saw the northerner, Master Donovan, seated on a chair, his back to the wall of the observatory. His red robes blended surprisingly well in the darkness.

"My pardons," he said, "I do not mean to disturb." His voice was low and rolled with his thick Corrusian accent.

"It's all right," Torra said, and hugged herself against the cold. "I couldn't sleep." Trying to think of something nice to say, she added weakly, "Thanks for staying up for the watch."

She saw him fingering an item in his lap, then realized it was a rod of translation. Without it, Torra surely wouldn't have been able to understand him. "There is no movement down there," he said, his thick black mustache bobbing. He turned to her and put his right hand to his chest in a formal salute. "We have not been introduced properly. I am Annorov, of the Donovans of city Oskalinsk."

Torra put her hand on her chest, as he had done, and replied, "Torra Com Gidel." Lowering her hand, she added, "My last name means 'from the town of Gidel,' which is a couple days' ride north of here, though I grew up here in Caranamere. My parents realized my magical talents and moved us away from those who considered magic 'evil.'" She looked back down to the crater, and wondered, for the first time, if maybe they were right. For a moment she thought back to her parents and their sacrifice to move to Caranamere and away from family, but a snap vision of her mother burning in the dream threw her mind into disarray.

… You did this! You can stop it! …

Master Donovan's reply came to her as if from a distant tunnel. "Magic is illegal in Magnus Regnum, as well, where I am from." He paused. "But, like here, it is tolerated by nobles."

As her eyes adjusted to the pale light, Torra realized that something stirred beneath Master Donovan's chair. Eager to turn the conversation to something pleasant, she asked, "Your cat. Is it a pet?"

He gave a quick grunt, almost like a laugh. "Yaggu is 'guise cat.' You know, yes?" Torra shook her head. Donovan continued, "Sometimes, they are called 'ghost lynxes.' They have patterns on fur which change color like what is colors around it. They blend into surroundings." He stopped to give a quick chuckle. "You see him now only because he lets you. He watches you right now. He knows I trust you and does not hide."

Master Donovan turned back toward the crater, his sword and scabbard clanking against a chair leg. "Yaggu is no pet. He is my 'familiar.'"

Torra blinked in surprise. Familiars were very rare, as they required a mage to bond with a wild animal in a very specific and spontaneous way when the terrestrial energies were just right. Their spirits merge to become one person, where the mage and the animal shared all senses and emotions. "I've only ever seen two mages who had familiars," she said, thinking of two high masters at the Tower of Light. "One has a ferret, the other a svelte dog."

He chuckled again. "Svelte dog! Wild dogs of grasslands in far south. That is new one for me."

Torra shivered from the crisp air, but she wasn't ready to return back inside to the darkness and dreams. She scratched at her itchy wrists. "How did you come to have Yaggu as a familiar?"

He tilted his head in a gesture Torra couldn't quite translate. Was he reluctant to discuss it? But he answered. "I was soldier in Magnus Regnum, forced to fight." He shook his scabbard for effect. "Trained in war against nation of Oiya Inoi. Fought many battles. At castle of Tornogensk, all fellow soldiers were killed, and I was wounded and captured. They already knew I had magic, and tortured me. Broke legs in many places. Broke many bones. Cut me many places. Left me in high tower cell to die. But I had strong hands and fingers, thin body. Just enough movement in legs. Squeezed out window and climbed down on night much like tonight." He pointed up at the twin moons. "I crawled through forest, hiding from soldiers, for many days. Was near death, but found place of great magic energy near a stream. There was a den in stream bank, so I crawled inside. That was Yaggu's home, and when he came home he found me. I thought I was dead man."

At that moment, Yaggu started purring under the chair, and opened his eyes wide to stare at Torra, his eyes reflecting the moonlight with a greenish tint. Annorov continued, "Yaggu did not attack. Instead, energy of place worked inside us both, made us one. He sensed my wounds and pain, and I sensed his energy and health. He healed me with his strength, and he brought me food. We learned from each other. Communicate in mind." He tapped his head with a finger. "I set my legs with sticks and vines. Very much pain. But with Yaggu's help, in only a month I was able to stand and make way slowly back home. He came with me. We cannot separate now."

"That's really ... incredible," Torra said, wishing she had something more profound to say about it, standing there on the ashes of her valley. The ashes of her people.

... eyes melted in a blackening face ...

Torra let out an involuntary gasp of horror at the memory, then put a hand on her mouth.

Master Donovan watched her for a moment, a glint of the moonlight playing in his concerned eyes. He looked back again toward the ruins. "In the war, my people, and theirs, razed entire towns. Displaced thousands of common people. But that was warfare. This ... " He gestured toward the crater. "This is crime that will haunt the hearts of all people." He turned once again toward her. "I am sorry for your loss, Torra Com Gidel."

Torra blinked, realizing this was the first time any of them had expressed sorrow for her loss, including Kai. "Thank you." She reached to her wrist and rotated the copper bracelet she had found—her mother's bracelet. Tears came again. She wiped her eyes and turned away from him. "They'll pay with their lives for what they've done!" Her jaw quivered. She shook with sudden rage at the memory of the burned corpses still lying in the rubble in the valley. "They'll *all* pay!"

... their skin was melting away to charred skeletons ...

She gritted her teeth and made a fist. "The Brotherhood, the Emerald Dragon, anyone else responsible ... I'll make them *burn!*"

CHAPTER SEVENTEEN
No Rest

Azartial teleported to the top of a wooded hill. There he found himself surrounded by the rocky foundation and fallen stones of an ancient watchtower, now home to a copse of thin oaks with contorted trunks. A herd of deer scattered at his demonic appearance, rustling through dried leaves and loose stone in their haste.

He was tired. It had been a long day and night with many teleportations and transformations, far more than he was used to, and his reserve of energy was drained. He could not imagine a more satisfying day. *Where does all that energy go when you're having so much fun?* he thought. So many of his plans were coming together, he didn't want to lose momentum. But he admitted to himself that he needed rest.

Azartial crouched at the edge of the hill. Below him, two rivers joined to make one, sparkling in the light of the moons. The people here called these rivers the Hill Fork, tumbling down from the hills to the east, and the Plains Fork, meandering in from the fields to the west. Once joined, they became the Maldurbia River, which flowed southward in wide, lazy loops bordered by fields and marshes until it reached the immense and stately Axim, the "king" of rivers, as people in this part of the world called it.

All of the scene was quiet and still in the early morning moonlight. The city of Crancoff, capital of the nation of Maldurb, sat at the junction of those two forks, nestled up against a steep hill which the common folk call the Sentinel, at the top of which, like a crown, sat Farren's Fortress.

In olden times the castle had been a proper fortress, but in the last hundred years it had transformed into a palace within the fortress walls, home to the fat king of Maldurb, Aleran III. He was a man so obese that his bed frame was rumored to be made of stone to hold his immensity, and transporting him down the hill to the city was an all-day affair.

Azartial absentmindedly plucked at the tall grasses at his feet. He envied humans of one thing. Well, he thought, *two*, really: they sleep, and they dream. They live out their fantasies in abstract images as their bodies recuperate from the toils of the day. And when they awake, their bodies are ready for a new day and their minds are cleared of mental clutter.

Demon dragons could not sleep nor dream. A part of him badly wanted both.

He weighed his waning energy against the job at hand and considered resting for a few hours. But time was of the essence. Torra and those annoying tower mages back in Caranamere would soon be waking, eager to continue stumbling through their investigation. If he waited too long to get back, they might go and do something that would throw themselves off the path he wanted. There were still important pieces to put into play.

Azartial took a deep breath, then sat on the ground and crossed his legs, a dilapidated stone wall at his back. Meditation would be helpful to absorb more celestial energy, at least what little he could get of it. The same magic that trapped the Triumvirate in the world of Irikara also limited the amount of celestial energy that could filter in from the heavens.

He joined the citizens of Crancoff, hopefully including a certain elderly antiquarian named Hozor, in silent relaxation.

The last thought on Azartial's mind before he let his mind go blank was an ancient legend of the town of Crancoff: the hill that lorded over it, the Sentinel, was believed to hide a stone giant by the same name—a giant in perpetual dormancy until the city was threatened, at which point it would awaken, break out of the mountain, and protect the city.

~~~

It seemed like hardly any time had passed when a scarlet dawn peeked over the hills to the east. Below, a cock crowed in the countryside near the Hill Fork Bridge, and then another answered from the streets of Crancoff. Azartial knew he had run out of time. The moment to act had come.

He stood on cramped legs, took a deep breath, then transformed to his human appearance, once again as Darilos Velar. This was usually a simple transformation, but being so low on energy, he felt it draw down his reserves as if he'd run for miles.

The plan was simple. In his prior visit to Hozor, years before, he had seen where the old academic kept the Codex of Otemus in a secret chamber in his library. Azartial's task was an easy matter of teleporting to that library, taking the Codex, and teleporting out. At that hour the library would certainly be dark and empty. Hozor wouldn't know he'd been there, nor even wake from his slumber. No need for fuss. And no need to kill an old man who might yet prove valuable in the years to come.

With a last glance at the glowing horizon, he drew forth more of that precious energy and disappeared from the hillside.

He rematerialized in a room full of light. Before his eyes had even adjusted, he heard an old man gasp in surprise. Papers flew.

Darilos stepped back and tripped, falling backward over a pile of books and landing in an awkward lump onto a woven rug. He tried to look around, but a series of thrown books pummeled his head, one after another.

"Get out!" Hozor bellowed. Darilos was finally able to look the old man in the eyes.

Darilos tried to stand on his cramped legs. He reached over to a bookcase to steady himself, knocking off books and magical knickknacks, but a combination of his cramps and another book hitting him full in the face made him stumble, tipping over a candelabrum. Red-wax candles fell from their sconces, touched on a pile of papers, and immediately combusted the dry papers into a small bonfire.

"No! My research!" Hozor yelled, and rushed forward, suddenly ignoring the intruder.

Darilos reached out, grabbed the old man by the throat and bushy gray beard, then pushed him against the bookcase, Hozor's blue dressing robes fluttering open to reveal a chest full of white hair. "Be still!" Darilos commanded. And yet the old man's panicked eyes went to the burning pile of papers, tongue lolling as he struggled for breath, right arm reaching toward the flames.

"Put it out … " Hozor gasped. "Give you … what you want … "

Darilos frowned. His goal wasn't to torture the man or ruin his "research," and he still needed his cooperation. He pushed the old man away, then looked over and stomped out the flames on what was left of the papers.

"There," he said, turning back. "Now, settle down." He expected to see the old man leaning against his busy desk, holding his throat and panting. Instead, the man stood staring intently at him, a small black sphere in his outstretched hand. Darilos realized the sphere had been on the bookcase a moment before.

Darilos started to cast a *Shove* spell, but the old man slammed a palm onto the top of the sphere. Darilos drew a shocked breath as his remaining power was ripped from him, the energy flitting from him to the sphere in a greenish haze. The form of Darilos disappeared in a shower of blue sparks and Azartial burst forth in a shimmer of blue flame and flash of amber wings. Devoid of even enough energy to stand, he fell to his knees with a roar of frustration and anger, tail whipping in agitation and knocking books from shelves.

Hozor, took a step back, eyes wide, mouth open. "I … I dared to dream it true. A demon dragon! You *are* Azartial!"

"Yes!" Azartial grunted, now on all fours, arms shaking. Still the sphere absorbed energy from him. "What is this thing?"

Hozor made the briefest of glances downward. "As you know, I collect items of magical power. This is an 'absorber.' More specifically, a 'celestial absorber.' Incredibly rare; the only one currently accounted for. Only a handful were ever known to be made, created by the archmage Serentilus, over a thousand years ago. It absorbs celestial energy from any item within line of sight, including from celestial entities such as yourself. I never guessed it could work so thoroughly!"

"It's been a busy night." Azartial's arms shook. He didn't know how much longer he could remain standing. "But you know you cannot kill me. On this plane of existence, I am immortal." *The sphere just happened to be sitting within reach of him? He was waiting for me!* "You were expecting me, weren't you?"

Hozor placed the sphere on his desk. The infernal stream of energy continued draining from Azartial's body. "Yes," the old man said, voice wavering. Then, with a touch of pride, he added, "I have an extensive network of contacts. They shared telltale signs over the years. Your arrival during the Battle of the Tower of Light. The sightings of you, from various lands. Rumors of actions you'd taken, perhaps in human form as someone called 'Outlander?' When you inquired about the Codex of Otemus, and arrived in the guise of 'Darilos,' I conducted a little test." Hozor pointed at a green sphere, sitting on a rack near the door to the room. "Do you see that sphere? It, too, is an absorber, but one for terrestrial energy. Not as rare an artifact, to be sure, but still worth its weight in platinum. I activated it in your presence, as you read through the Codex of Otemus, and though it absorbed the energy of a number of magical items in the room, it did nothing at all to you, nor did you notice. Any normal mage would have been weakened, which meant … "

"Which meant that I was either a thaumaturge or a celestial entity."

Hozor nodded. "I know what you're after. You can't have it. The Codex is the key to the Convergence."

"And I have already read it, if you recall." Still, the energy was draining. Azartial was having difficulty keeping his eyes open. He felt like lying down. "The Codex is not for me. My intention is to give it to the Expeditionary Mages from the Great Towers."

"You lie," Hozor said. "Why wouldn't they come for it themselves?"

An arm buckled, and Azartial slumped to the ground. "Haven't you heard?" His eyes fluttered. "You pride yourself on your network of contacts. How can you miss … the destruction of the Astronomer's Guild?"

Hozor blinked in surprise. "What?"

"Yes. It's gone. Blasted by fire." His other arm went limp and he laid down fully upon Hozor's multihued Ongoran rug. "Along with the entire town … of Caranamere … destroyed by the Emerald Dragon and the Brotherhood of Blood." Azartial's eyes closed a moment, but he forced them open again. He fought to stay alert. "We suspect the Brotherhood wants the Convergence … for the Triumvirate. I must … I must get the Codex to the mages … right away."

"You're a liar," Hozor said, absentmindedly playing with his long beard. "How do I know you tell the truth?"

"You don't." The demon gasped. He had so little energy left. "Consult your network … by the time you get your answer … the Brotherhood may have … Convergence … all will be lost."

He took a deep breath. His muscles relaxed. His wings drooped and folded.

"I have my sources," the old man said. "I will know soon enough. Sooner than you think. Then I will decide if I wish to help you." He looked down at the absorber, then back to Azartial. "You may be immortal on this plane of existence, demon, but soon your energy will be drained completely. By the time you get it back, I'll be long gone."

Azartial knew he couldn't stop him. For the first time, a human had gotten the best of him—a feeble old man with a palm-sized sphere!

"You will see," Azartial said, "and I will get … vengeance … if you … do not relinquish … Codex." With a great effort, Azartial moved his head to make a show of looking around the room. "All your collection of magical objects … I will destroy it all … Then I come for you."

"I have more than this to protect me!" Hozor said.

Azartial tried to laugh, but it just came out as a pained wheeze. "I'm sure you do." Behind the antiquarian was a window, and through it he saw the hill known as the Sentinel, bathed in early morning light, and thought again about the myth of the giant. "Even the Sentinel … won't be able … to protect you."

At last, he took a deep breath and closed his eyes as the final shred of energy was sucked out of him. *Is this what it's like to sleep?* he thought, and then the world went black.

~~~

Azartial opened his eyes. He found himself lying in the same position as when he passed out. Bright sunlight streamed through the window. He blinked and covered his eyes from it. Hozor and the sphere were gone.

Rising up, Azartial quickly scanned the room. Many items were missing, Hozor's magical treasures, including both absorbers as well as many of the books and papers. But when he turned to look at the desk, it had been cleared off save for a tome of vellum sheets loosely bound with catgut, pages crudely cut to different sizes, and placed on top of a modern leather satchel. He didn't need to look closely to know what it was, but he stood on shaking legs and stepped over to it. The Codex of Otemus. Next to it was a note, hastily written, the ink smeared in places for lack of proper drying:

I consulted several sources, and they all confirmed your story. Caranamere and the Astronomer's Guild are destroyed. Mordan flies north with a reward. I have no inroads to the Brotherhood of Blood, so I cannot confirm your assertion that they are partially to blame. But if they were to deny it, I would not believe them, for they have walked the streets of Crancoff and I have heard their lies myself. I know which gods they serve.

Do not think that I trust you, demon. I do not know your game. We are not allies. But I have done you your favor. Now do me one as well. Bother me no more. Be gone, to whatever foul plot you are weaving!

— H.

Azartial wadded up the note. Running his long tongue over rows of sharp teeth, he reached down and opened the Codex to the last page. The ancient vellum was dry, threatening to flake, but he found the passage he was looking for, written in a language long-dead and nearly forgotten, by a man so insane that he could barely remember his own name.

In Pendoni, there shall be found, upon the Ledge presided over by the Altar of the Blind Sisters, a Door of Stone that may be openeth by none but two Persons. The first of these Persons wieldeth the Key, be he touched by the Gods of the Cosmos, yet fighteth against them. The second of these Persons must also wield the Key, be he touched by the Three Gods of Origins, yet fighteth against them. Only these two should be, their Hands both upon the Key and touching each other, elsewise the Door remaineth shut. Inside shall be found the greatest Power in all the World, for its name is Convergence, and in that shall be controlled the powers of both World and Cosmos, unlimited.

Beneath that was scrawled in different ink:

May all of Humanity forgive me.

"We shall see, Otemus," Azartial said. He transformed back to the guise of Darilos, closed the Codex and placed it in the satchel.

He stretched, joints popping. He was incredibly well-rested! And he was fully energized again.

"Hozor, you wily old man," he said aloud, "you have done me a greater favor than you think! Sleep truly *is* rejuvenating. No wonder humans do it. Now, if only I could dream!"

Without further ado, he put the satchel under his arm and teleported away.

CHAPTER EIGHTEEN
Noble Visitors

A pale red dawn filtered through the narrow windows of the observatory, the light diffusing through fine ash in the air to reach inside like ghostly fingers. It found Torra slumped over a table in the back of the first floor, her eyes tired from a sleepless night. A candle had burned down and guttered, but it no longer mattered. Even though she now had enough light from the sunrise, she could no longer pretend to concentrate on the materials there.

Before her lay a loose stack of star charts arranged by calendar and "moon dates," the means of keeping track of the twin moons and their movement, each sheet wide enough that she couldn't reach the other end unless she stretched. She ran her hand over the lower right corner of the top chart and sighed at the signature there.

Around her, the other mages had been waking and going about their morning business. Lolund and Kuno were eating, talking in low tones. Preneval was shaving. Master Gral was praying, his hanat knife laid in front of his bowed head. Master Donovan was eating with del Titccio while taking watch at the entrance.

It was Osprey, though, who stepped over to her and looked down at the charts with their geometric shapes and radiating lines, neatly printed labels, and mathematical equations. He seemed fresh and alert from a night of good sleep.

"That looks important," he said. "What is it?"

Torra wiped her eyes. "Star charts. To be more exact, this one is what we call a 'geometric lunar event projection.'" Osprey was quiet, and when she glanced up, he just shook his head. Taking into account his background, she explained, "The Astronomer's Guild isn't just magic. We actually *are* astronomers—the best in all the land. This …" She gestured to the star chart. "This is a masterpiece. It's breathtaking. For centuries, astronomers have tried to predict solar eclipses. Some, like Dolos Thack of Askrena, or Tsen Tao'tsi of Quisha, have been able to predict with reasonable accuracy the eclipses of the sun, Claris, with either of the twin moons, Isa or Tollus, but none have been able to predict when and where all three celestial bodies would be in perfect alignment. A double eclipse. Until now!" She felt thankful that such a masterpiece had survived the explosion.

She turned to see Osprey's reaction, but he just stood there looking at her blankly, so she added, "Don't you see? A triple alignment is so extremely rare that it happens only once in nearly a thousand years!" She looked back down at the map. "If this prediction is correct, in just fourteen years the double eclipse will be seen in the morning hours …" She shuffled the papers. " … here!" She pointed to a different parchment, a map showing the nations of Quisha and Inlai'chi'a, and the Veldtlands plains with a streak of shadow slashing across them "Across the Southlands. In our lifetime!"

She looked back to him, her eyes wide with excitement. He watched her with a look of mild confusion, then, nodding, said, "In the Holy Writ of Okun, it is written, 'And lo, but the moons combined to throw shadow on all the land, and the sun became black, and all that was holy was thrown into chaos, for nigh had come the demons of Hek'or. Great prayer was made, and warriors of Okun came forth to battle the deadly shadows, striking spear and sword into the darkness. With great merriment and calls to the Gods, they chased away the shadows, and the sun became unshadowed, and all was healed.'"

Torra closed her eyes. She wanted to wail against his ignorance. The same sort of superstitious mumbo-jumbo was what was powering the Brotherhood of Blood and their followers. But she tightened her lips, took a deep breath, and simply turned from him to look at the charts.

"I will pray for the light," Osprey added. "It was good of your guild to predict when Hek'or's darkness will come again." Then he walked away. Torra couldn't have been more thankful he was gone.

After his steps faded, she opened her eyes again and ran her hand once more over the signature at the corner of the star chart. There, in his neat, spidery script, her old master, Morikal, had signed his name and put claim to this masterpiece. The date next to it indicated he had finished only two nights before.

Other than the little dagger she had found, and her memory of him, this was all that remained of Morikal and his legacy.

"We have visitors!" Master Donovan called up from the entrance. Immediately the mages went to look, with Torra filing out last. By the time she emerged, the mages were already discussing how to proceed.

" … go down and make introductions." Master Kuno was saying. "Perhaps they may prove helpful." The others were nodding.

"We must be cautious," Mistress Lolund said. "They may mistake us as the enemy."

Kai turned and looked at Torra. "You will come with us. You speak Taxin naturally and know their ways."

"Whose?" Torra asked, then finally shouldered past the others to look down into the valley. The crater was still smoldering, but through the fumes, at the far end where the main road exited to the fields beyond, was a line of horsemen. The morning light glinted off of steel plate armor. They stood, surveying the destruction, at almost the exact spot where the Brotherhood of Blood had stood the evening before. The house the Brotherhood "rebuilt" was still standing, not far from them.

Torra squinted to see details. "They are flying rainbow pennants from lances. And I see plate armor. These are knights from Gaes, the seat of power in this region."

"Get your things," Kai said. "We will go to meet them at once."

~~~

Torra was in a rush to get down to the visitors, but white-robed Master Kuno insisted that they all travel together, even though he was by far the slowest. He wisely decided they go on foot rather than by magical means so as not to disturb these newcomers with magic, since it was outlawed in the land. Despite the slow speed, the ash and the constant climbing over downed trees and debris left them all wheezing and coughing. By the time the mages arrived at the crater, most of the contingent from Gaes had dismounted and were swarmed by the few outlying townsfolk and families of victims begging for help, some of whom she recognized.

Torra was now close enough to make out the faces of the nobility. Leading the visitors was a man she recognized as the Chamberlain of Gaes, Timbrook Taegus, the right-hand man of Lord Nonis Gaes, the "Crystal Lord." Taegus had served that role for as long as Torra could remember. Many times a year, Taegus would visit with First Astronomer Colnos Com Dimb at the Astronomer's Guild to discuss trade with the Guild and impose the King's wishes on behalf of the Lord of Gaes. In Torra's role as Third Astronomer, prior to leaving the Guild, it had fallen to her to greet Taegus and his guard. Taegus would only look down his long, twisted nose at her, mutter that she was to get him tea, like some common servant, then ignore her further. When she offered to lead them to the First Astronomer, he would state loudly, "I do not follow women. They follow me."

By Tower tradition, the eldest of the Expeditionary Mages is to be the first to address notables, so the responsibility fell to Master Kuno. Torra informed Kuno about Taegus, then continued, "Lord Gaes rules over this region for the king, but he is old and senile. It is Taegus who truly rules. Taegus is joined here by the grown children of Lord Gaes, Elbin Gaes ..." She pointed at a strapping young man around thirty with long, untamed locks that fell across his armored shoulders. His ornamented plate mail clanked as he paced back and forth, glancing toward the crater. " ... and his younger sister, Sassala Gaes," Torra continued, directing Kuno's gaze toward a young woman clad entirely in oiled leather and ring mail instead of the frilly garments most Taxin noblewomen wore. Sassala's eyes burned with anger and frustration beneath unruly red-tinged bangs at the destruction before her. It was only Taegus who seemed unfazed by what lay before them, his face expressing the usual scowl. Torra added, "It is said that the children long for their father to die so that they may seize control and be rid of Taegus. Though the son by rights expects to rule after his father's passing, his sister is said to have aspirations. They are a dangerous family—to each other."

"And how was their relationship with the Astronomer's Guild?" Kuno asked, gingerly balancing to step over a pile of rubble.

"As you know, magic is technically outlawed in Taxia, though nobility tolerate it, including the king." She lent her arm to Kuno to help him off the debris. "And mages who travel the Bronze Trail trade route, to the north, are ignored as long as it is profitable to do so. Thus, communications with Caranamere were always coded or hidden. Court 'astronomers' are common, including at Gaes. It was common, too, for the Astronomer's Guild to supply charmed weaponry and armor in return for necessary sundry items and supplies. I assure you that the armor worn by the prince, there, is charmed."

The entourage from Gaes had watched the mages as they made their way across the destruction and waited for them to approach. At last, the mages made a loose line in front of the contingent. Timbrook Taegus sat upon a black courser. His thin face was as hard as stone and he wore a cloth-of-gold brocaded surcoat over a gleaming set of ring mail.

Just as Master Kuno, wheezing, bent his girth in obeisance, the Lord's daughter interrupted. "What the hell happened here? Explain yourselves!"

Taegus raised an eyebrow at Sassala's outburst, but looked to Kuno for his explanation.

Kuno seemed unintimidated. "Good Lord Taegus, we represent the three Great Towers of Magic. It falls to us to investi—"

"You have an echo when you speak," Taegus said, referring to Kuno's rod of translation. "Do not use your magic to talk to me. This is Taxia. Speak Taxin or do not speak at all."

Taegus is trying to take control, Torra thought. The mages all turned to look at her, the only native speaker in the group. She stepped forward and accepted Kuno's rod from him, so she could understand Kuno's native Lakarthian language, then translate his words to speak her own native Taxin to Taegus. She saw Taegus's eyebrow raise as he seemed to recognize her.

Torra relayed who they were and when they arrived, about the villagers who had died, and how only one survivor and witness, Osprey, was found. Kuno told of the Emerald Dragon, but wisely only hinted that others may have been involved, not mentioning the Brotherhood of Blood or the mysterious "beast." Taegus remained unmoving upon his mount, still looking down his nose at her.

"We implore you," Torra finished, still translating Kuno's words, "to please share with us what you know of … "

Taegus cut her off. "You were Third Astronomer, were you not? I heard about how you left our beloved nation to become one of *them* at the Tower of Light. Fighting a far-off war, they said, and cavorting with elves and dragons. Yes, word reached all the way back here! Well, what do you think of your dragons, now?"

Torra hesitated. She knew her words could change the course of the investigation, to win or lose Taegus as an ally. And she knew full well that Taegus didn't tolerate pleasantries or half-truths. She decided to be blunt. "I'll make the Emerald Dragon burn, like he burned our people. And anyone who aided him. When we find them, they will know pain and suffering. And if you don't help us find them, then you can go to the seven hells."

The other mages gasped.

"Torra!" Kai chided.

Taegus at first raised an eyebrow, then, beyond probability, he laughed. But the sound of it chilled her. It was at first a surprised chuckle, then deeper, resonating with dark tones that promised revenge. His eyes resumed their steely ice.

"Then my aid you will have, and the aid of the Lord Gaes." Taegus wheeled his courser around to face the lord's children. "Sassala, take a third of the guard and search the ruins for whatever you can find of import. Enlist these peasants and have them pile and cremate the corpses." Immediately the young woman shot the chamberlain a dark look, and then transferred it to the mages. She ordered a few of the guards to join her and stepped into the ruins.

Taegus then turned to the prince. "Elbin, if you would, see to the comfort and protection of the mages, and find them mounts." Elbin nodded and turned his dark eyes to the mages. Torra saw a mix of fear and awe in them. Doubtless he was wondering how much power they wielded, if magic could reduce a town to ash and debris.

Taegus turned back to the mages, once again addressing Kuno. "You will all accompany me back to Gaes, there to give your account to Lord Gaes himself. It will ultimately be up to him to determine how best to offer help to you in your investigation or to share the information we have."

Elbin instructed his men to give their mounts to the three eldest of the mages, Masters Kuno and Preneval, and Mistress Lolund, even though Lord Preneval was clearly more able to walk than Master Donovan with his limp. Neither Taegus nor Elbin offered their own horses. The others would have to walk until new steeds could be found, and they set off at once.

Mistress Kai stepped next to Torra and looked her in the eyes. "'Go to the seven hells?' You have all the negotiating skills of a pig in heat, apprentice! You are lucky you did not just ruin this for us. And," she raised a finger at Torra, "we are not here to exact revenge on the dragon or anyone else. We are only here to investigate on behalf of the Tower. Do you understand?" Kai didn't wait for a response and kept walking.

Master del Titccio, on the other hand, flicked back his long salt-and-pepper hair and said to Torra, "Don't listen to her, love. You were marvelous!" and winked at her.

For her part, Torra didn't give a damn what Kai thought about it, or any of the others, for that matter. They disappeared around the bend, leaving her to mourn alone and take one long, last look at the town she'd called home. The burnt hillsides with their trees felled in angles away from the epicenter. The ruins of buildings. The crater at the center, in which there was no sign of the great edifice that was the Astronomer's Guild. And everywhere, fine, swirling ash depositing gray on everything, like wisps of ghosts, the angry spirits of a thousand people.

Already, Sassala and her guards had rounded up the peasants and started picking up corpses. One guard had picked up the body of a child, burned beyond recognition, and tossed it to the ground near the crater.

Always before, as she came home and rounded the curve to come to this first sight of the town, at the spot where she now stood, her heart would fill with jubilance to see it before her—to view the sturdy Astronomer's Guild compound surrounded by stone-and-timber houses and businesses, hear the roll of the miller's wheel as it plunged in and out of the creek, smell the scent of fresh-baked bread, wood fires, and oak forest, and listen to the bustle of a busy town. For many minutes she tried, and failed, to match the vision in her head with the desolation before her now. It was all gone—the buildings blown to rubble, the forests burned to cinders, the corpses heaped in a pile by soldiers and locals. And when she and the remaining survivors died, none would remember the town as it had been.

With a pang of sadness, tears threatening to come again, Torra wondered if she would ever return. Or if anyone would, for that matter. In the centuries to come, would Caranamere be forgotten, another dark legend passed down to scare children?

Torra turned her back to Caranamere and slowly walked down the road.

CHAPTER NINETEEN
Leaving the Past Behind

Torra lagged far behind the others as she walked away from Caranamere. She glimpsed the mages and the contingent from Gaes as they rounded a turn in the rutted road. Mistress Kai, who was near the rear, glanced back as if to say "catch up" before she was lost to sight. Master Donovan, by Kai's side, looked back as well, though appearing more concerned. Torra was in no mood to catch up to them. She really hadn't been alone for any time since she'd discovered the catastrophe, and she needed to collect her thoughts.

Stately oaks grew along the roadside, their canopies red and yellow with the autumn chill, thick enough to shade the road most of the way. The lively chirps of auburn sparrows and warbles of wrens were occasionally interrupted with the kuk-kuk-kuk of king squirrels, darting through the canopy in flashes of red to be lost in the fall foliage—all punctuated by the occasional, piercing cry of an elusive griffin hawk, far above. Torra stepped as if in a dream, for how could such an idyllic scene exist within a few minutes' walk of the horror and still-burning landscape that was now Caranamere?

As if in answer to her thoughts, a gentle breeze brought with it a waft of smoke. She shivered, imagining the ghosts of the dead traveled with it.

The road meandered generally northwest, gently descending in the valleys between low hills. Torra passed a meadow where she and her family would often go on summer days, sometimes with other families, to picnic and relax after the work had been done. The old, gnarled maple tree still stood at the far end where she and her brother Nickos would chase each other while playing Mages and Dragons, or if other children had joined, link arms and play Send-Me-Your-Princess, or just climb the tree and dangle bare feet. In her teen years, she and Taenos would sneak off into the woods behind that tree to kiss and caress, free from prying eyes.

The woods were interspersed with small crop fields. Rye waved in the wind, tan and ready for reaping. Other fields held green-leafed turnips, potatoes, or bright orange pumpkins, also ripe for harvest before the first hard frost. Yet not one peasant could be seen working the fields. *They're dead*, she realized. *These crops may rot in the fields.*

She picked up her pace, not wanting to be alone anymore. Perhaps it was the thought of ghosts, but she perceived an odd energy in the air, familiar somehow.

Just as she reached the next bend in the road, a man and woman stepped out of a thicket of woods, ten paces ahead. The man was balding, perhaps in his forties. He was dressed in the homespun clothing of a laborer, sleeves too tight for his muscular physique, his worn boots splashed with mud. The other, a woman with arms and hands smeared with ash, wore an equally stained dress that was shredded along the lower hem. Her hair fell in tangles around a sooty, tear-stained face, deeply etched with worry lines. A faded yellow scarf was wrapped around her neck. Torra recognized her from the group of peasants who had listened to the Brotherhood and witnessed the "rebuilding" of the house, the day before. She was an occasional visitor to town from one of the surrounding villages, likely a family member of a citizen of Caranamere.

"Well, well," said the muscleman in the local Taxin dialect, looking up and down at her robes. "Looks like one o' the witches is tailin' behind."

Torra started to back up, then turned as she heard a rustling in the leaves. Two teens stepped out from the woods, fifteen paces behind her, dressed similarly to the muscleman. One was lean and pock-marked with greasy blond hair. The other, fat and pimply, resembled the strongman in the face. Both held rusty daggers. Their eyes burned with hatred.

"I know you've been through a lot," Torra said, holding her hands out, palms open, in a way she hoped was nonthreatening. She activated her magic center and started thinking of defensive spells. She didn't want to hurt them. "I don't want any trouble."

The woman started sobbing, her face contorted. "*You* don't want any trouble? You? And what about us? *We* lost our families, our friends!"

Torra shook her head. "You don't understand. I lost … "

"You lost *nothing!*" the woman shouted, pointing at Torra, then held out her arms. "Do you see these ashes? *Do you?* I dug through burning rubble looking for my precious granddaughter. I told my daughter not to move to that witch-town! All I found was blackened bones!"

"I lost too!" Torra shouted. "I lost my family! I remember you. I lived there, too."

"That just makes you a traitor!" shouted one of the teens behind her. Torra cautiously turned. The blond youth pointed his dagger at her, edging toward her. "The Brotherhood told us about you! That it was you *witches* who brought the dragon. It was your own curse upon Caranamere! And our town will be next!"

The pimply-faced youth at his side nodded. "You disobeyed the holy law against witchcraft, while we toiled away to build our land!"

"The Brotherhood lies to you," Torra said.

"They don't lie!" the blond youth said, now only a few feet away. "I was there when they rebuilt that house. Seen it with my own eyes! If we believe, they may rebuild the whole town."

The woman stalked forward as well. "But won't be no more wizards to kill us all!"

The muscleman glanced to the woman. "Want me to grab 'er, Rula?"

"He said we could do whatever we wanted," Rula replied.

Torra shouted "Help!" as loud as she could toward the turn in the road where she'd last seen the other mages. "Mistress Kai! Master Donovan!"

The muscleman turned to see if the mages might come running back, but Rula just leered at Torra. "Go get her," she said.

The man advanced.

"Gag her, you fool!" Rula shouted. "Don't want her casting—"

"*Chasanti al!*" Torra shouted, hand stretched toward the muscleman. Her *Force Strike* spell sent a wave of energy that hit the man, knocking him off his feet. He landed on his back, gasping for air.

Torra whirled, hearing the youths running up behind her, and chanted, "*Accorae sint bosidona!*" A ray of light shot from her pointed finger, hit the blond youth. The *Neural Fire* ray crackled with electricity, jumping between the teens. They both fell to the ground with spastic seizures, their bodies jumping like fish out of water. Daggers jigged around in hands that couldn't let go. She hoped the spell hadn't been too powerful. She didn't want to kill them.

A yellow scarf flashed over her head and into her mouth. She was pulled to the ground. Kneed in the back. Pain shot up and down her spine. She cried out against the gag.

"Witch!" Rula wailed. "Witch!" Then she kicked Torra again, this time in the torso. Torra grasped the woman's arm, digging her nails into the woman's skin. She tried to cast a *Paralysis* spell, but she couldn't form the words against the scarf. "You'll die!" Rula screamed. "Gunos! Get up, you lout! Help me!"

Then suddenly the strongman was at her side and trying to grab Torra's arms. Dust flew as Torra kicked at him, twisting against the scarf and the woman to keep her feet toward him. But he was too strong. He caught hold of one leg, and then the other. Torra screamed, beating at the woman's arms, writhing in an attempt to get free.

"A blade," Gunos grunted, and pulled Torra closer to the unconscious youths, letting go of one leg and reaching out as far as he could for one of the daggers that now lay by their sides.

Torra squeezed her eyes shut, trying to get control of her mind. *What would Morikal do?* she asked herself, thinking of her former mentor. Then her eyes shot open. *The dagger!* She reached for her travel bag hanging from her shoulder and fumbled for Morikal's dagger—the one she'd found in the ruins.

With Gunos only inches away from the youth's dagger, Torra's hands groped past rations and a spell book. A sharp pain shot through her finger as it sliced across the exposed blade of Morikal's dagger.

Rula pulled harder. Yanked Torra's head back. Her fingers fell away from the dagger.

Torra pulled against the scarf. Clasped her fingers around the chain-wrapped handle. Extracting Morikal's dagger from the bag, she plunged it into the woman's arm.

Rula screamed in pain. Let go of the scarf. Swung to hit Torra. Torra stabbed the knife into the woman's leg.

Rula screamed again and fell back. "You bitch!" she shouted.

The muscleman, Gunos, turned back to see what was going on and found Morikal's blade slashing through his forearm. He pulled back with a growl of pain.

Torra pushed herself backward. "*Gorain tatalba doos!*" she shouted, and pointed at Gunos. The man instantly froze in position, his face a sneer of pain, his bleeding arm cradled to his chest. The *Paralysis* spell had worked, for now.

Torra stood and turned toward the woman. Rula stepped back, fear showing in her eyes. She mumbled, "Don't … don't … Witch!" She took two tentative steps backward, then turned and ran into the woods, limping from the stabbed leg. "Help! Brother!"

Brother? Torra thought. She watched Rula go, then gasped as a cloaked figure dressed in the crimson vestments of the Brotherhood of Blood stepped out through the undergrowth. Rula ran past him, slowed, then shot Torra a smile full of malice.

The Brother's face hid under a thick cowl, his hands crossed in their sleeves. He stepped with purpose down into the road.

Still holding Morikal's bloodied dagger, Torra sidestepped past the prostrate figures of the youths and the muscleman's frozen body. *If I can get back to Caranamere,* she thought, *the guards from Lord Gaes can protect me.* But she knew she wouldn't make it that far. A tingle in her mind told her that the Brother was preparing to cast a spell.

Torra tried not to let her fear show. "What are your intentions?" she demanded.

The Brother stopped advancing. "You have an opportunity, Torra."

His voice was very familiar. She recognized the grammar and inflections of a nobleman from the west of Taxia. This was the same man who addressed the crowd at the entrance to Caranamere. "Who are you?" she asked. "Show yourself."

"I am Disciple Immolatos, but that is the name given to me by Apostle Agnon when I was reborn in the view of the Triumvirate." He lowered his hood, revealing a shaved pate and a cherubic face set with strikingly blue eyes.

"Master Feros?" Torra couldn't believe it. Feros was a respected master and pyromancer ... at the Astronomer's Guild! He had been named as Third Astronomer after Torra left the position. Though he no longer had the blond curls or the quick laughter that defined him, there was no mistaking him. "You ... you betrayed us?" *Darilos was right!* she thought. *Traitors in their ranks!*

"No, Torra. No one was betrayed. But some were not ready to make the change."

"Change? *Change?*" Torra felt her face flush with anger. "You destroyed an entire town! *Our* town! Our guild! Women and children! My *family!*"

"We called to the Triumvirate. Prayed for them to take away our jaded past and correct our ignorance. They did that. They delivered unto us the Emerald Dragon, and through him, they burned the past away, removing the obstacles to our wisdom and future. Don't you *see it*, Torra? A mother bleeds with every birth. We are at a birth, here, for the entire world. The blood of innocents is a sacrifice for a thousand years of prosperity." His blue eyes began to water. "I feel every one of those deaths. I wept for hours. But you have to realize, each of those who died will be saints in the next iteration of Irikara."

Torra shook her head. "You're monsters."

"No, Torra. We are mages, just like you—but also clerics to the Triumvirate." Feros held out a hand toward Torra. "Join us, Torra. The power we wield is beyond anything the Guild could have provided us. Power to do good. Power to change the world. I know you feel it. You've seen what it can do. Imagine what *you* could do with it!" He held his hand out further, his eyes sincere. "Please. I know you, Torra. You have great potential. It's time to take the power and make a difference."

Torra gritted her teeth so hard she thought they might break, then shouted, "Never!"

The mage now known as Immolatos sighed, withdrew his hand, and raised his cowl back over his head. "Then, I'm afraid, you must meet the same fate as the rest of the Guild."

CHAPTER TWENTY
Hidden

Darilos watched. In human form and hidden in the woods, he spied through the foliage as the troop of Expeditionary Mages passed, just as he expected they would, surrounded by a retinue of guards from the local minor lord. *Pitiful*, he thought. *Like lambs to the slaughter. So eager for answers, they'll trust anyone.* Immediately he noticed that Torra wasn't among them. No others seemed missing. All his plans revolved around her. *She's not a follower*, he thought. *Torra's stronger than they are, even if she doesn't know it. Perhaps she finally realized it and went her own way?*

He started to move out of the woods to go look for her, but stopped as he noticed movement across the road. A trio of humans. One was of the Brotherhood of Blood, wearing crimson robes. The others, a man and a woman, were commoners. They turned to look down the road toward Caranamere, and one made a quick bird whistle—a sign to someone in that direction.

And then Torra came into view, stepping down the road, a troubled look on her brow.

For a moment he considered rushing out to warn her, but he stopped himself. There was opportunity here. *She can handle the commoners easily enough*, he thought. *As for the Brother, let's see what she can do. And then, if things seem bleak, she might need a hero to swoop in—someone she could trust.*

Darilos turned and, looking down the road, reached out a hand and extended his energy outward, from side to side. Some fifty paces away, an invisible barrier formed. Not a physical wall, but a barrier to sound. *Wouldn't want the mages and the soldiers to hear the coming encounter, now would we? They would spoil the moment. Generated with celestial magic, the Brother won't notice it.*

He watched as the commoners, joined by two youths on the other side of Torra, closed in. The woman was muttering some sort of sympathetic nonsense about Caranamere.

And still the Brother had waited in the woods, off to the side, watching the event unfold, just as Darilos did. Torra seemed unaware.

Torra was much too kind to the peons. They threatened her, then attacked her, and still she didn't kill them. The bleeding hearts at the Tower of Light had ingrained sympathy into her. But it was only when the peasant woman wrapped a scarf in Torra's mouth that Darilos began to worry. And when the man reached for a dagger, Darilos considered getting involved—until Torra finally found her inner strength and stabbed her attackers. *No one takes you seriously until the blood flows*, he'd thought. She then paralyzed the man. *I hope his heart stops*, he thought.

Then the woman retreated … and the Brother advanced.

You're winded, Torra, Darilos thought. *Stall. Catch your breath.* Darilos made a fist. *Then annihilate him. You can do it!*

And stall she did, engaging in conversation suffused with outrage. When the Brother pulled down his hood, Darilos recognized him as one of the disciples who'd been with Apostle Agnon on the hilltop, a lieutenant of sorts. Darilos couldn't hear everything they said, but it was clear from his demeanor and gestures that the disciple was trying to make some sort of request—perhaps to recruit her.

Stupid fool. You destroyed everything dear to her, and you expect her to cooperate?

Darilos couldn't feel magical energies from the Brother, as typical with terrestrial magic, yet he felt Torra as she activated her "magical center." What was it about her that made him feel her and no others? Being a creature of celestial magic, he shouldn't be able to feel terrestrial energy from her. Could she feel *him* in the same way?

Then she shouted "Never!" and the two mages started casting spells at each other.

Darilos thrilled with each expulsion of energy from her. Each flash, each formation of magic, touched him, tumbled through him, filled him with a moment of exhilaration. He wanted their battle to go on forever. He wanted to be linked forever with her, *in* her. And the more powerful the spell, the more orgasmic the experience. It was more than he'd suspected. So enraptured was he that he almost let down his guise as Darilos, blue flames starting to flare around him, until he brought back his concentration.

"Yes. Yes!" he muttered, jerking in excitement as she cast another spell. "Again!"

CHAPTER TWENTY-ONE
Duel with a Disciple

Torra dodged a ball of flame thrown by Master Feros. The sphere of orange fire flashed past her head, hot upon her cheeks, and exploded somewhere behind her. He cast another *Firefling* spell, but she cast a one-word *Deflect* spell and knocked the sphere aside. It hit an oak, instantly engulfing the trunk with flame.

She stepped back, tripping on the prone body of one of the teens. The pimply boy groaned, opened his eyes wide, and struggled to roll aside. Torra ignored him, for Feros was attacking again, chanting. Realizing she still held Master Morikal's little dagger, she threw it at Feros.

The enchanted blade tumbled end over end and struck Feros in the shoulder, sinking into the flesh up to the hilt. Feros yelped in pain, disrupting his spell, and fell to his knees as the air around him erupted in a sonic boom—the result of the interrupted spell casting. This gave Torra enough time to retaliate. "*Oris anatal!*" she chanted, and reached out toward the dagger, then pulled downward, willing the dagger to move. The blade ripped down several inches through the flesh and robes of Feros, still deeply embedded.

Feros howled in pain and yanked out the bloody dagger. His crimson robes instantly darkened with blood around the wound. His eyes flared with anger.

Torra cast a *Lightning* spell, but Feros stopped it with a *Negate* spell before it had even started, then, chanting, stomped the ground. The road shook, and Torra was flung upward a foot before landing awkwardly, stumbling away from Feros. The strongman landed with a thud, becoming unparalyzed and gasping, and the two youths crawled off the road.

Feros pressed on his shoulder wound. The cheery face that had smiled down at her so many times in the past was now twisted with pain and anger. Blood dribbled down from his ears as he chanted again. "*Raystonea mesendai!*" A beam of blinding white plasma expelled from his mouth at Torra. She leapt to the side, but Feros sustained the powerful spell.

Torra cast a *Shield* spell. An invisible wall in front of her caught the *Plasma Beam* spell, fire flying out to all sides in front of her. She knew she couldn't keep up the *Shield* spell much longer, and thought to herself that Feros must surely be exhausted as well. And then she remembered her own, feeble *Beam* spell, back at the Tower of Light, and how Mistress Kai had dealt with her. Torra steeled herself, then, dropping the shield and leaping to the side, she chanted, "*Bene gontai!*" and pointed at Feros, using as much of her remaining energy as she could.

Her *Continuity* spell froze Feros in his incantation, the beam now emitting from him without his will, continuing to drain his energy and making it impossible for him to close his mouth or stop the spell. He raised his eyebrows in realization of what had happened, the beam arcing across the road in a jig-jag of burning death, cutting through branches and burning the trees. Flaming branches fell around them.

He refocused on her. Torra was ready, again throwing her *Shield* spell before her. But the flaming blast prevented her from moving from her spot. It would be a contest to see whose spell would end first, and who would die. The last bit of energy she had was rapidly being used up.

A quick movement to her right caught her eye: a figure in brown robes dashed from the woods. A scream. An explosion.

Feros's plasma beam shot up into the sky as Darilos slashed at the man with an ethereal blade he had conjured. The shimmering energy blade cut through Feros with no effort at all. Plasma coursed through Feros's body and exploded outward. Blood and burning flesh flew from the body, hitting Torra's shield and coating the road around her.

A rush of energy from Darilos's spell spilled over into her mind.

"No!" a woman screamed. It was the peasant woman, Rula, standing in the woods beyond the road. "Brother Immolatos!"

Darilos turned and slashed his arm toward her. The ethereal blade flashed across the woods and cut through trees and woman alike, slicing her in half at the torso. Three trees around her, including a stout elm ablaze, were cut cleanly through the trunk, crashing to the ground in a flurry of leaves and cracking limbs, shaking the earth around them.

Again Torra felt the rush of energy from his effort. Her heart beat quicker. Her breath shallow. It was orgasmic, like lightning shooting through her nerves. She didn't understand.

Darilos then turned to the man and boys who were stumbling away toward Caranamere, and raised his blade to strike again.

"Stop!" Torra commanded, dropping her *Shield* spell. Darilos turned. His azure eyes met hers, and he let the ethereal sword dissipate. There was only care in his expression, as if the violence of the last minutes had failed to affect him.

He wasn't even breathing heavily.

"They're just peasants, Torra. And they tried to kill you!"

"They're grieving and confused. Leave them be."

Torra looked around at the blood and gore, Feros's disembodied legs in the middle of the road, his burning flesh draped over branches above, mingled with strips of shredded and smoking crimson robes, and the body of the woman, cut in half, her entrails slumping out of her torso.

Torra doubled over and retched. Fell to her hands and knees on the blood-spattered leaf litter, palms pressing into dozens of little acorns. Struggled to catch her breath. Head pounding from the effort of casting so many spells in such a short period. She vomited again.

Darilos leaned over her and put a hand on her back, rubbing slowly across to her shoulder.

"You're exhausted," he said, his voice soft and fluid. "You're lucky I came when I did."

Torra nodded, wiping her mouth. She gazed up at him, consciously avoiding the direction of the bodies.

"You are strong," Darilos said, "stronger than any of those other mages." He reached out a hand and helped her stand, then put an arm around her, guided her down the road away from the carnage and fire. The canopy overhead was alight with burning leaves, crackling, as she walked on shaky legs.

"I don't feel so strong," she said, voice hoarse.

She winced and stumbled, recalling the moment that Feros exploded in a rain of flesh. It would be burned into her memory forever.

"It's all right," Darilos said, pulling her back to the present. "You'll be fine." He used his other hand to gently turn her head to look at him. His unruly blond bangs hung down over deep blue eyes.

"Where were you last night?" she asked. She kept her eyes on Darilos, stepping purposely, avoiding looking at the bloody scene around her.

"I have something. Something that will change everything about your investigation." He shook a leather satchel hanging at his side. "An ancient tome. Do you remember, when we first met, that I had escaped the blast because I had been away on an errand for Second Astronomer Cortanal?"

Torra stretched her memory as she wiped sweat from her brow. "Yes. I recall. You called it a 'codex.' Said you had taken it to an antiquarian named Hozor. Kai didn't believe you."

He stopped walking. His eyes grew wide with excitement. "Well, I went back for it. What I found in it changes everything." He paused, turning and looking down the road. Torra followed his gaze and saw two figures coming at a run around the bend. *Oh no!* she thought, her heartbeat quickening. *More of the Brotherhood!* But then she recognized Mistress Kai and Master Donovan. Relief washed over her.

"Have you ever heard of a place called Pendoni?" Darilos asked. "There's something there. Something the Brotherhood is seeking. An artifact of great power called the 'Convergence.' I think that's what this was all about!"

Pendoni? she thought. She had heard of it, years ago when she traveled south on an excursion. She nodded. *Artifact?* It was all so confusing right now. She just wanted to leave this place.

"I have found that the Brotherhood is stronger than we thought," Darilos continued, "and more widespread. But if they get the Convergence, they won't stop at destroying one town. They will set fire to whole nations, whole cultures. Genocide!"

"Torra!" Kai called out. Torra raised her hand in acknowledgment.

Darilos eyed Kai with obvious suspicion, then looking back at Torra said, "You cannot tell them. You cannot trust them."

"You were right," Torra said, now standing on her own without his help. "That Brother was a traitor to the Guild. He had been one of us." Darilos started to say something, but Torra cut him off. "But Kai and the others aren't like them. Kai is beholden to my welfare. And the Expeditionary Mages are probed carefully by the towermasters to ensure loyalty. I need to tell them what you found."

"Torra!" Master Donovan yelled, his guise cat familiar, Yaggu, trotting alongside him, colored in swirls of mottled brown like fall leaves. They were only paces away. "Are you all right?" he called.

"Don't tell them about the Codex," Darilos warned, voice low. There was a finality in the word, urgent with command. "You must surely know the magnitude of power we are dealing with. Power corrupts, Torra. Don't trust *anyone* with this."

Torra looked him in the eyes, saw the intensity there.

"Just read it," he said, and handed her the satchel. He spoke in a whisper as the others approached. "Judge for yourself. But be fast about it. If the Brotherhood reaches the Convergence before we do, all will be lost ... "

Her head was still spinning. Too tired. Too hard to focus on his words.

Kai and Donovan reached the pair, looking at the destruction around them with clear alarm. Donovan pulled a cutlass from the scabbard at his side.

Kai gave Darilos a dark look, then leaned in to Torra and embraced her.

Torra didn't quite know how to react, slow to return the gesture. Affection wasn't something Kai showed often, unless it was to woo some young man.

Kai unwrapped herself. "What happened here, apprentice? You lagged behind for too long, so we came back. Are you harmed?"

"I'm well enough," Torra answered, glancing over at Darilos. "I was ambushed by one of the Brotherhood mages. If it weren't for Darilos, I'm not sure I would have survived." She put a hand on Kai's shoulder. "The mage was a master at the Astronomer's Guild. A traitor. I knew him well … or thought I did. How many others of the Brotherhood of Blood were members of the Guild?"

"Come," Master Donovan said, still surveying for enemies. "Let us be away from here. We can discuss more, later."

Torra nodded. Spotting Master Morikal's blood-covered dagger on the ground, she bent to pick it up. She wiped it with a handful of leaves, then placed it back into her bag, wrapping it as best she could with the handkerchief. She figured she would clean it more thoroughly later. The party then moved quickly back down the road, Darilos followed a few steps behind.

"Why didn't you call for us?" Kai asked. "We were just down the road."

"I tried. I yelled for you. And the noise of the fighting … "

"We heard nothing at all," Master Donovan said.

She shook her head. "I … I don't know how that is possible."

Torra looked back. Darilos followed closely. And behind him the woods were on fire, burning leaves and debris falling to the blood-soaked path.

Darilos nodded to her, knowingly. She turned her attention back to the road. A cloud of doubt crossed her mind, but she was too exhausted to examine her thoughts more closely. *Just read it,* she thought, echoing what he had said to her. *Judge for yourself.*

And there was an energy still resonating through her, like a fond memory. The energy from Darilos's spell. It was like nothing else she'd ever felt before.

CHAPTER TWENTY-TWO
Discovery

Ingal flew through the frigid night air of the high mountains, nonstop, even when ice started coating the edges of his wings. There were no thermals in the wintry atmosphere to help keep him aloft. He cast a *Levitation* spell on himself, which worked to reduce his weight and make the flight easier. As difficult as these conditions were, it was necessary to scale the high mountains. Going around them would have taken at least another day and a half.

Despite his altitude, white mountain peaks still towered over him here, at the highest mountain range in the world. Old Drogo, the tallest of all peaks in the Sarsan Range, and possibly the world, stood lonely and desolate as Ingal swung wide around it, turning from a southwestern to western course.

He remembered back through forty generations of his lineage. In every one he found an enduring love of the mountain the dwarves call Drogonomocorran, "King of Mountains," among the diversity of other names it had. Many times over the eons he had flown to the top of it, challenging even his mighty abilities, for the air was so thin at the top that any lesser being would suffocate. He had seen from that great height unfathomable distances and the undeniable curve of the world.

His ancient muscles ached. Numerous healed wounds still reminded him of his last battle with the Iron Dragon, Gogonith. Despite the hardship, there was an immutable drive that kept him going, and he knew not its source.

As he reached the divide of the range, in the wee hours of the morning, he questioned himself for the dozenth time why he was in such a rush. Why did he abandon his duties to the White Lands Federation in a time of war for this? What could possibly be so important? It was as if a far-off clarion had echoed off the valleys, high and shrill, calling him to it. But no such trumpeting could be heard. He felt only the rush of the empty, chilly wind across his ears.

At long last, as dawn suffused the eastern horizon with shades of salmon and cyan, and the mountains grew slowly lower in elevation until they were no longer snow-topped, Ingal allowed himself to rest. He settled on a ridgeline dotted with clumps of low-growing perennials and lichen and folded his wings around himself for warmth, his breath forming clouds of steam. Even here, above the tree line and far away from human settlement, Ingal spied a boulder to his right with weathered but unmistakable carvings of figures on it: a half-circle with rays projecting from it, and the stick figures of two humans with spears. He would likely have missed them save for the early dawn luminance casting the carvings in an oblique light. He wondered, for a moment, what could have drawn the ancient artist to this location and led him to carve in the rock. Had there been an unexplained "clarion call" for him, too? The petroglyph was eroded almost to the point of eradication, and it surely predated the Shintori tribesmen of this region by thousands of years.

By the time the sun was fully risen, Ingal's heartbeat returned to normal and his wings lost some of their ache. He stretched and leapt into the air again. From here it was all downward, and much of it was spent gliding with a gentle tailwind. Within an hour, the mountain ridges gave way to foothills and he crossed over into lands claimed by Taxia. He was growing near, now.

His eyes searched for the valley of Caranamere. But even before he found the dim plume of smoke, he *felt* the wrongness there. Caranamere was a natural energy vortex—a place of great magical power—but the energy radiating from it was far stronger than usual, pulsing with primordial dominion. Ingal had felt it before, at the Battle of the Tower of Light, when the resurrected elvish lord, Peshiluud, cast a renegade spell to destroy the bonerock Heartstone, and then again when Ingal had cast a renegade spell of his own to open a portal for the Celestials to enter the world and protect the Tower.

Ingal pushed himself to fly as fast as he could.

To Ingal, it seemed like forever before, panting from his exertions, he at last flew over the final ridge, whereupon sat the dome of the Guild's observatory. He looked down into the bowl of hillsides that formed the Caranamere valley. What he saw below nearly stopped his wingbeats. He bellowed in sorrow, the roar of it echoing off the hillsides.

Not one building was left standing. All had been leveled. And where the imposing Astronomer's Guild had once dominated at the center of the town, there was now little more than a deep impact crater covered in rubble. All else was angled away from the center, charred and ashen. Hardly a stone was left stacked one on the other. The smoke of burnt timber mixed with an underlying odor of burned bodies.

The Gold Dragon circled, barely believing his eyes, trying to convince himself that this wasn't just a bad dream. His thoughts flashed to the faces of the mages he had known from there, the great masters who had learned at the Guild through the eons, and even his dear friend Torra Com Gidel who had come of age here but, luckily, was safe at the Tower of Light.

Questions spun through his mind. Did any mages survive? Colnos Com Dimb, the First Astronomer? The emeritus master, Morikal? Doran the Gray, eldest of all and bent with age, who had lent him the books he had in the pocket of his vest at this very moment? And what of the townspeople, most of whom were related to the mages? Did many escape? Only a renegade spell could have wrought such destruction. Who could have cast it? Was the Triumvirate behind this one, too?

Seeing his appearance overhead, figures of men and women scurried for cover through the debris of what had once been a thriving town. *Survivors?* he wondered. A pile of burnt corpses and body parts was mounded up near the crater.

Ingal had to inquire about what happened. He dove down into the valley and alighted at the edge of the crater, his strong wingbeats throwing up a vast cloud of ash as he landed.

When the cloud dissipated, he looked about for the survivors. What he found instead was a half dozen soldiers and an armored noblewoman with long reddish hair. Some held spears decorated with rainbow pennants, a symbol of the local lord. All had sword and spear pointed at him, as if any of those weapons could truly damage him. All but the woman showed fear in their eyes. The group was warily sidestepping through the rubble toward the entrance to the town. A handful of peasants peered fearfully from around distant cover.

Ingal stood up straight, put out his wings, and held a forefoot up in blessing. "I am Ingal Jehai, Gold Dragon and ruler of the White Lands Federation," he said in Taxin. "Who is in charge here?" At ninety feet in length and nearly as wide in wingspan, morning sun blazing off his golden scales, he knew he was an imposing sight.

Five of the soldiers dropped their weapons and ran for the entrance.

"Cravens!" the woman shouted over her shoulder at them, then turned back to Ingal. "*I am in charge,*" she said, not bothering to identify herself. Ingal guessed she was a lordling. Wasn't the local lord advanced in age? "We have had enough destruction by dragons!" she shouted. "Be gone! You are not welcome in our domain, Aximdrac!" She used the nickname by which he was known in Taxia.

"Destruction by *dragons?*" Ingal huffed. "Are you saying dragons did this?" *More than one, even?*

His heart sank, remembering how the Iron Dragon, Gogonith, had been turned to the Triumvirate. Gogonith had destroyed Alneri Keep with a single spell, likely a renegade *Earthquake* spell, and helped a traitor attempt to betray the White Lands Federation. Both Gogonith and the Triumvirate god, Draq, had tried to recruit Ingal to the Triumvirate's side, too.

How many other dragons had been turned to their side? He recalled how Rethuud warned him that the Pearl Dragon, Slivice, had been spotted flying southward. *Did Slivice, do this? Or perhaps the Emerald Dragon, Mordan? Both have committed atrocities in the past. Or what about the Citrine Dragon? He has been missing for centuries.*

The woman gestured for her guard to retreat faster, now that they had circled to the north side of Ingal, closer to the entrance to the valley.

"It was the Emerald Dragon." She spat on the ground. "See *him* if you want the details, and when you see the infernal beast, tell him we won't rest until justice is done and his heart is rent by my lance!"

The other guards broke and ran, along with the commoners who had been hiding. The woman followed. Ingal called out to her, "And the mages? Do any yet survive?"

The young woman turned and yelled, "None from here. Cremated, every last one, unless they are there." She pointed her weapon at the pile of bodies. "The others who came afterward are in our custody lest you should finish them yourself. Dare not come for them!" And then she turned the corner out of the ruins of the town.

"Where did they go?" he called after her. She did not come back or answer. But he thought he knew where: likely the seat of the local lord, the town of Gaes.

The 'others who came afterward?' he thought. Does she mean Expeditionary Mages? Certainly the Great Towers would send them quickly. He knew better than to try to hail the Towers, for they hadn't answered his hails since before the Battle of the Tower of Light, believing he was somehow an ally to the Triumvirate, despite all that he had done to the contrary.

Ingal was left to himself in the desolation. There was no sound beyond the distant crackle of fire still burning on a hillside. There was only the slightest breeze, enough to move the fine ash in phantasmal patterns.

He searched the Memory—the recollections inherited from the last nineteen generations of Gold Dragon dating back thirty-six thousand years—trying in vain to recollect another instance like this one. There were natural disasters, like the volcanic eruption that destroyed half a dozen villages in Hamal over two thousand years before, in his youth, or the Battle of Terin Talba in what is now southern Ongo, where four armies converged and, in their months-long battle, laid waste to the entire region over eight-thousand years ago in the time of his forebear, Tosem.

Or there were genocides, like the slaughter of the Corinuza peoples of what is now the nation of Oculnuuz by citizen soldiers of the Charinin, in the youth of his immediate forebear, Rambonor Jehai, five thousand years before. He saw again the Oculn marshlands colored crimson with their blood and the thousands of bodies of men, women, and children hacked to pieces, rotting in every direction.

But the destruction of Caranamere was altogether different. This was not an act of nature, nor did it seem an act of war, at least not between armies of men. And genocide was a cultural horror perpetrated by thousands. Renegade magic of this type could only be cast by an individual mage of great power—or a dragon. No, the destruction of Caranamere was different than all those other events. Something more sinister. Something more focused. A show of power. A message to an enemy. It was …

"It was an act of terror," he said out loud.

His words melted into the air, lost to the pile of corpses.

Then he saw movement out of the corner of his vision. Ingal turned, expecting to see another peasant or guard, but there was no one. The air grew pregnant with magical energy, pulling at his senses like a thousand pins prodding his head.

And then he caught another movement, back the other way. He turned and saw a humanoid shadow rise from the pile of bodies.

Ingal blinked, wondering if this was a trick of the smoke, but the shadow figure was still there, defying the filtered sunlight. It rose as if it had lain amongst the corpses, then stepped down from the piles and strode toward him.

Ingal knew what this was. Not a ghost. It was a Shadow Emissary—a projection of thought and energy used by powerful entities to communicate across vast distances, but seen only in his mind—a form of psychic spell. He could feel it, even through the well of energy left from the explosion.

The Shadow Emissary stepped to within twenty feet, then stopped and bowed.

"Identify yourself!" Ingal demanded.

The shadow stood upright again, then slowly took on color. The featureless charcoal shades transformed to a bearded face with olive skin, a tunic made of a single bear hide pulled over one shoulder and held at the waist with a cincture made of entwined leather straps, and moccasins on his feet. On his head was the head of the bear, still attached to the bear hide tunic, its teeth resting upon the brow of the man who wore it. Black hair tumbled out from underneath to frame his face. The man held a long spear with a broad copper spearpoint at the end, decorated by a clutch of colorful feathers hanging from the shaft. A small, ceremonial mirror of highly polished copper hung from the cincture. Swirls of blue tattoos decorated his arms and the exposed shoulder and chest below his neck. Heavily muscled and blocky in appearance, the man was short in stature.

The primitive just stood there, watching Ingal with piercing black eyes.

Ingal was wise to this game, though. This wasn't the first time he had been visited by a Shadow Emissary-turned-real. It had happened in his palace in the White Lands, and again in the Elvish "Glen of Peace," Tegora'Seima. The Triumvirate God, Draq, had appeared to him in the form of an ancient leader, Noc Ang Soon, and had even transformed into a small child. All of these figures were from Ingal's distant memory.

"I said identify yourself!"

The man spoke, his voice shrill and accented strangely. "You know who I am, Gold Dragon. I am your creator! I am so pleased you came."

"Draq! I know this ruse. Why do you take such a form as this?"

"The better to educate you, my child."

"You dare show yourself after what you've done here? Why did you destroy Caranamere?"

The primitive stepped lithely across the destruction to the edge of the crater, leaving no footsteps in the ash and soil, and looked down into the epicenter.

"Answer me!" Ingal said.

"*I* did not destroy Caranamere, my child. Your brother, the Emerald Dragon, did this, though we enabled him."

"Why?"

The primitive turned to look at Ingal again. "You are ancient compared to the fleeting life of a human, yet you are but an infant to me." He gestured with his spear out over the crater. "Perhaps you would remember the last time this place was destroyed, yes? But not the time before that. Nor the time before *that.*"

The last time it was destroyed?

"Think hard, Gold Dragon. Deep into the memory I blessed you with."

And then Ingal remembered. It was, indeed, far back into the Memory. Before the Astronomer's Guild, there had been another structure made of wood. A building of tiers and fluted eaves. Flags of brown and red fluttered from the tips of each corner. And a village around it. A center of magic and mages, but without the pretense of astronomy.

"Yes," said Draq. "You remember, don't you? And what became of that place?"

"Destroyed," Ingal said. "An invading army from the north—the Torineen Empire, with its squads of pyromancers."

The primitive drew an arc in the air. "Caranamere was known as Carna Cameer. But it had risen from the ashes of an older place, destroyed by a different army, centuries before."

He raised his arms. Everything took on a golden halo, then the halos coalesced into forms that melded and swirled, finally settling into a ghostly vision of structures around them, superimposed upon the destruction, a semblance of a half dozen longhouses made of poles and bark surrounding an altar in the middle of the field. The glowing vision of the altar was suspended over the center of the crater.

The primitive raised his arms again, and Ingal's magical senses tingled once more. The vision of the altar and longhouses disappeared, followed by a deep rumble that shook the earth beneath him. The few remaining trees at the edges of the town shook and fell. From three different sides of the hills around the town, earth exploded in a shower of flying chunks. Great stone forms rose from the bosom of the hills, tilting upward, rotating. The soil clinging to them fell away. Each of the three forms stood upright and stabilized.

Each of the stone forms was a massive thirty-foot statue, long-buried in the hillsides. The details were eroded away, but one was masculine, a second feminine, and the third … The wings were broken off, but it was clear what had been there. The third was a dragon, forefeet raised in anger, maw gaping and lined with stone teeth.

"The Triumvirate," Ingal said.

The primitive smiled. "Long have we been worshiped. Long have the peoples of this world refused to forget us, though calling us by different names. But even that wasn't the earliest habitation here, by far.

The primitive stepped back to his original position in front of Ingal. "You asked me to identify myself. Yes, I am Draq, but the form I show you is their first human leader, Dorthas son of Dorni, who conquered this location from the elves, far back into the dream-time of humanity. They called this place Qurna'an, meaning 'sacrifice place.' To here their people made pilgrimage. Here they learned magic for the first time. Here they worshiped us. Here they brought slaves and made sacrifice. More sacrifices were made yesterday …

"If you joined with us, your vast Memory would be made whole again and you would recall ALL, back to the very origin of the world. You would remember meeting Dorthas son of Dorni and all that was said. And you would remember your visits here before then."

The primitive raised its arms, the spear jutting up toward the sky. "Behold!" Again the ground shook, centered within the crater.

Ingal stepped back as soil and rock flew from the crater floor, pelting him and crashing into the ruins around him.

When the dust settled, Ingal saw that the floor of the crater had been dug away, deeper still, to reveal massive granite blocks arranged in a circle around a center stone.

The primitive waved the spear in the air, and the blocks stacked, one upon the other, to reveal a megalithism of standing stones and arches with the center stone as an altar.

Ingal's eyes grew wide. "This place has always been an energy vortex, hasn't it?"

"As you call it, yes, ever since the Outer Gods stole our world and capped our energies with the Heartstones. But Dorthas son of Dorni understood, as the elves did before him, that the energies here were of *us*, the Triumvirate gods, to use in our glory, to commune with us, and to use against their foes as magic."

The primitive changed again, dissolving in form, growing, darkening, rising higher and higher, and wider, until it took on the rough form of a dragon. It towered over Ingal, eyes ablaze in blinding white orbs of electricity. Its body was a mass of cold darkness popping with constellations of stars and sapphirine lightning. This was Draq's true form, first revealed to Ingal in the elvish lands two years ago.

Ingal stepped back, wings out and ready to take flight. He activated his magical centers, but what spell could harm a god?

"I shouldn't have to tell you," said Draq, his voice deep and echoing, "but everything is built from a foundation that stems from the Triumvirate. For we created the world and everything in it!"

"And you can destroy it," Ingal added. "You very nearly did, with the ancient land of Occultii."

"The *humans* did," Draq said. "In our name. The Outer Gods destroyed their land for it."

"Do not pass on blame, Draq. You put the humans up to the act, just as you put the elves up to the act of attacking the Tower of Light. Do you also claim no responsibility for what happened here? Mordan is strong in magic, but to our knowledge, he had no reason for this destruction. Did the Triumvirate convince him to do this?"

"You have been an unruly child, Gold Dragon. It is why we punish your lands with fires and droughts and blizzards. But others are not so disobedient. Gogonith would have been our first choice, but you murdered your brother."

"It was self-defense, Draq. Answer my question!"

Tendrils of dark energy shot from Draq and wrapped around Ingal's frame. Ingal fought it, but the coldness burned into him, pushed him to the ground and held him there. The god bent over him and pulled close to him. The burning white eyes came close to Ingal's face. "It is not your place to command me," the god said. The air was chilled near the god's face.

Draq continued, "In time, you will come around. It is your *nature* to do so. Why continue to resist? The Emerald Dragon understands. He needed … other motivation, but he came around. And as for the humans … Well, they fight against each other, as confused infants do. You care for them, rule them as a shepherd keeps his flock, keep them with you like pets. But they come and go, don't they? They are born. They procreate. They die. Their little accomplishments fade and are forgotten, their shrines and statues erode and get buried, their buildings crumble, rot or burn. Not like you. Not like any of my creations, the dragons. You live on. Your memory holds it all."

"You underestimate humanity, Draq." Ingal squirmed against the strength of the god, but it was no use. He had to find a way to weaken him. *How do you harm a god?* And then he came to a realization. He had to test it. He closed his eyes and focused on his mental center of magic, concentrating his energy. He would need everything he could muster.

"And you overestimate them, Gold Dragon."

Draq lessened his grip on Ingal and pulled away. "Soon, much of the world will be as this place. The process has begun. And it is here, in this land, where our champions will find our secret weapon to control the energies of the Outer Gods. It is foretold!

You can choose to be part of the process, or we will push you to the side, helpless."

As Draq's frigid tendrils unwrapped from Ingal's frame, he knew it was time for his test. He sat up, pointed a forefoot at Draq, and chanted a spell. "*Tocoro donotus fundi!*" The *Absorb* spell was stronger than he had thought, intensified by the residual energy from Caranamere's destruction.

At once, a dark cloud of Draq's energy flowed from the god into Ingal. The rush of power shook Ingal's body, infused his blood, threatened to burst forth from every cell. He was blinded, and for a moment he feared he might lose control. His head reared back and he roared from the power of it.

Draq slapped the Gold Dragon in the chest, breaking the spell and throwing him high into the sky in an arc across the town. Too late to catch flight, he instinctively pulled his wings tight against himself to keep from breaking them and shouted a *Shield* spell. Then he slammed into the far hillside, hitting something hard and rocky, and fell to the ground with a rumbling crash.

Ingal shook his head and gasped. He tried to sit up but yelped in pain from his ribs.

He looked around. Through the cloud of dust and ash, Ingal saw Draq advancing toward him, gliding across the town, a moving void of darkness, until he once again towered over Ingal.

"You disappoint me," Draq said. "In punishment, I shall rain fire upon your palace and turn your rivers into steam."

Ingal started to laugh.

Draq tilted his head. "You find it funny that your people suffer for your misdeeds?"

"No." Ingal winced and groaned as he gingerly sat up. "I laugh at your pettiness." He looked into the god's blazing eyes, and quoted the ancient Charuzin poet, Ahn Tel, a master of So-Chai elemental magic:

> I have looked into the Eyes of my Creator.
> Shake with Dread.
> Blood on Lips.
> Pain and Fire.
> Rending of Flesh.
> Yet I laugh.
> And in laughing I betray a simple Truth.
> In his Eyes I see Myself, small and simple.
> A Leaf upon the Hurricane …

Draq's massive form shrunk back down, took on the shadow emissary form, and once again colored and morphed into the diminutive form of Dorthas son of Dorni. He pointed the spear at Ingal. In Dorthas's shrill voice, he said, "Do you see yourself as a leaf, my child? You can be so much more. You *are* so much more! The coming storm will transform this world, and everyone in it will share in our power and our glory, able to partake in our energies and live in comfort, once we are rid of the Outer Gods and their control. A new golden age for Irikara. Join with us and be part of the solution. It is in your *nature* to do so. As with this place, the world as you know it has been destroyed and rebuilt many times, each time better than before. It is the nature of things. Do not fight against the hurricane, my child."

The primitive discolored back to shades of charcoal, then the Shadow Emissary dissolved and disappeared. Ingal felt the energy of Draq fade away, and he was alone again.

Ingal grabbed his chest, felt a broken rib, carefully flexed his wings. Another sharp spasm stabbed him in the back just above his hips. But the pain had been worth it. *What spell can harm a god?* he asked himself again. A smile played at the edge of his mouth. His test had been worthwhile. *A spell that siphons off its energy*, he answered.

He looked down at the object that had broken his fall. It was one of the newly unearthed statues—the one of the dragon. He hit so hard that the monolith had fallen and broken in two, cracking apart where the head met the body. The roaring maw now stared up at the morning sky, askew from the torso.

Ingal thought back to Ahn Tel's poem. He hadn't quoted the last lines to Draq, but now he said the end out loud:

> … In his Eyes I see Myself, small and simple.
> A Leaf upon the Hurricane.
> I become the Wind.
> I become the Creator.

CHAPTER TWENTY-THREE
Traveling to Gaes

Torra moved as if in a fog. The mix of emotions from the past day and the duel with the Brother had left her mind clouded, her body aching, and her concentration wavering. Her magical energy was a reflection of her internal chaos, flaring and ebbing like a smelter's furnace pumped by bellows.

Mistress Kai urged Torra forward along the road but offered words of support and recommendations on how she could calm her mind. That, too, was confusing, as it was so contrary to her usual sternness. Master Donovan, too, walked alongside, his sword in his hand the whole time and scanning the roadsides to see if any more Brothers or angry peasants hid behind the oaks and maples. Yaggu had disappeared again into the woods, though Master Donovan explained that he tracked parallel to them, camouflaged. Darilos stepped silently a few dusty paces behind, his presence betrayed only by the swish of his robes and Torra's feeling of being watched. *No*, she thought, *not watched — guarded*. Given what had happened, she was pleased to have him there.

The sunny sky turned overcast as ominous clouds moved in from the east. A breeze picked up, bringing chilly gusts that made the rash on Torra's shaking hands ache. She had the special salve she had earlier loaned to Osprey, but it was now packed away in her bag and she didn't want to stop to rummage for the little jar.

When they caught up with the rest of the party, Mistress Lolund kindly offered Torra her horse, but Torra refused. She wasn't about to be seen as weak, even if she felt it. She scratched at the flaky skin on her arms and neck, ignored the pain of her cracking fingers, and tried not to think about the blood spilled everywhere after the battle. After everything she had been through in the past day, it was time to be strong again.

The other mages were aghast when Torra and Darilos explained what had happened. Darilos described how he had teleported nearby, noticed the battle between Torra and Feros, and interceded, and how bravely and skillfully Torra had fought. It was a rare compliment that she appreciated, even if she didn't share his glowing sentiment. Mistress Kai gave a surprised and satisfied nod when Torra told how she had used a *Continuity* spell on Feros to keep him from ending his *Plasma Beam* spell, as Kai had so aggressively taught her back at the Tower of Light.

Reactions to Darilos's *Ethereal Blade* spell, and the gruesome manner in which he ended the lives of Master Feros and the peasant woman, were mixed. "Well done," Master Preneval stated, eyebrow raised, to which Master del Titccio responded, "I disagree. Subduing him would have been better, as we could have interrogated him."

Master Gral grunted in agreement, thick arms crossed on his barrel chest.

The mages shook their heads in disbelief when they heard that Feros had once been a trusted member of the Astronomer's Guild.

"Why would he turn on his own people?" Master Kuno asked, shifting on the horse he'd been loaned, the narrow saddle under him nearly hidden by his girth. "He had everything available to him at the Guild, even access to the Great Towers. And he was of noble background. He wanted for nothing."

Red-robed Master Gral spoke, his mouth forming syllables, clicks, and chirps that were difficult for his Rod of Translation to translate, lending him what Torra felt was an unjustly brutish tone. "Better question it is to ask—what gain come of treason?" He put a hand on the hilt of the thick, curved hanat knife hanging at his waist. "What do Brotherhood give that not Guild give? Do Triumvirate to him give favor of great magic energy? Much dishonor it is to treason."

"Clearly," Torra replied, "the Brotherhood's power is great enough to hire a dragon and destroy a town." She looked at the blue-tattooed Gral. "You are correct, I think. Feros tried to lure me to their side by saying, 'The power we wield is beyond anything the Guild could have provided us. Power to do good. Power to change the world.'"

"I don't think doing 'good' is what he had in mind," Master Kuno said, as he cast a *Clean* spell on Torra, removing the blood and grime from her skin and clothes, prompting Master del Titccio to cast *Mend* on Torra's singed and ripped robe. Torra gave her thanks, even though she knew how to do these spells herself.

"I'm not surprised about Feros," Osprey said, leaning upon his axe.

"Why not?" Torra asked.

Osprey rubbed at the burn on his chest where the amulet of Okun had branded him. "I seen him, the fat one with the false smiles and gleaming eyes. Many nights he'd mosey through the streets from the Guild to the Dancing Mage Inn and proceed to drink til he could hardly stand." He shook his head. "Cavorting with the painted ladies and taking part in the sort of behaviors that Okun warns us about, all the while boasting about his own virtue, laughing, his eyes shifting back and forth, but dropping tiny lies hither and thither about this mage or that. Lies the ladies would repeat to others. Lies that passed like ripples on a pond until they went through the whole town and back to the Guild." Osprey nodded knowingly. "His worst sin wasn't the lies, though. It was his false representation. He was a schemer."

Master del Titccio smiled, pulling a thin cheroot of rolled tobacco from a red pouch that matched his robes. "And, dear man, how did you hear these lies if you weren't also taking part in his escapades?"

Osprey smiled guiltily. "Well, Okun permits a drink or two in an inn."

"He'd be a poor 'father' not to!" del Titccio chuckled. He lit the tip of his cheroot with a quick *Combust* spell, blew out the flame, and took a drag on the other end, inhaling the bluish smoke and, after a moment, exhaling it with a sigh of contentment. He offered it to Osprey, but the woodsman shook his head, eyeing it suspiciously. Only pipes were smoked in Taxia, and not the strange, sweet-scented herb that del Titccio was puffing on.

Throughout the reunion, Elbin Gaes, the young lordling, listened and watched from his brown and white Screenan charger, circling back to the mages. His steel plate mail had a chest plate enameled with the rainbow stripes of his family crest. He looked at Torra. "Your town has been destroyed. Your enemies abound. And we are beset by powers greater than your kind has been able to control. You were stupid to wander from our protection."

Sitting stolidly in his saddle, the stern Chamberlain of Gaes, Timbrook Taegus, looked down his angular nose in annoyance. "Wolves always attack the stray lambs first. Now, if you are done visiting and primping our stray, perhaps we can continue on our way? Lord Gaes awaits."

Mistress Kai put a hand on Torra to urge control, but Torra wasn't in a fighting mood anyhow. Darilos, though, spoke up.

"Beware the wolf in sheep's clothing, Torra." Darilos then looked up at Taegus, chin high. "Particularly if that clothing is spun in cloth of gold or covered with enameled armor."

Taegus turned without answering and spurred his courser into a trot. Elbin, though, sneered at Darilos. "We protect our people, mage."

"Not very well, apparently."

Elbin started to pull his sword, but seemed to rethink it and sheathed it again. Gritting his teeth, he wheeled his charger around and caught up with the chamberlain. Darilos never lost his grin.

Osprey traced a circle in the air—the sign of Okun—and closed his eyes. "It falls to Okun to protect the people. What has happened is part of his plan. We must have faith in that plan."

"Says the only survivor," Darilos scoffed. When Osprey shot him an angry look, Darilos added, "I assure you, no one person figures into the plans of any god."

The party of mages and guards followed Taegus, but Mistress Kai and a number of other mages walked slower, gathering around Darilos as they walked.

Kai said to Darilos, "You'd best keep your mouth shut, thaumaturge, before you endanger our investigation." Darilos just shrugged at her. She continued, "I suspect there may be another wolf in sheep's clothing—or robes. Where did you go last night?" Her lips were tight, eyes narrow. "What have you been up to?"

"I had errands to run," he said. "You know … Delivering babies, feeding the poor, plotting to take over the world. It's the little things that matter."

Master del Titccio guffawed, but Kai wasn't laughing. She turned to Torra. "What is in the bag he handed you?" She stepped over to Torra. "Here, let me look in there."

Torra drew in a sharp breath and glanced at Darilos as Kai reached for the satchel. Darilos made a small sweep of his hand, and Torra felt that queer sensation again, the electrical energy she had felt when he cast his *Ethereal Sword* spell against Feros, though this was fainter and less stimulating.

Torra didn't stop Kai as she opened the satchel. Kai was, after all, her tower mentor. And shouldn't she know about the Codex, anyway?

Kai reached in, triumphant, grabbing what was inside and pulling it out with a jerk. Torra looked away in shame for hiding the Codex from her.

"I felt she could use a bite to eat," Darilos said, "and another bag for her travels."

Torra turned and saw that Mistress Kai held a stack of *brolis*, or Taxin hardtack, tied with twine. Torra blinked, realizing the illusion. If she had felt him cast the spell, why didn't the other mages? She shouldn't feel his magic, either.

Kai looked again in the satchel, but it was empty. With a harrumph, she shoved the *brolis* back into the bag, then turned again to Darilos, pointing a finger at him. "You're hiding something, and I'm going to find out what it is."

Master Preneval cleared his throat, then said in his very proper voice, "Just tell us where you went, Darilos, and allay our suspicions, before Mistress Kai decides to go through *all* of our belongings."

Kai shot her black-robed colleague a poisonous look.

"Fine," Darilos said smoothly, his voice now serious. "I teleported to Harvinel, the city to the west of here, to inquire about the Brotherhood of Blood."

"And what did you discover?" Master Donovan asked.

"Their leader is called Apostle Agnon. He is powerful with the magic of the Triumvirate. And, my sources said, the Brotherhood has tendrils in every court this side of Axim. Some say even in the King's court. The only thing holding them in check was the Astronomer's Guild. And," he added, glancing at Torra, "they now seek an ancient artifact of great power. What it is, they could not say."

Torra threw him a dangerous look. *He is lying by omission. What about the Convergence?*

"An ancient artifact from the Astronomer's Guild, perhaps?" Mistress Lolund asked.

"No, not the Astronomer's Guild," Kuno answered. "Clearly they had insiders who could have gotten that."

Master del Titccio nodded, stroking his ragged goatee. "It would stand to reason that Feros was not the only one of the Guild allied with the Brotherhood. Could they have argued whether to have the Guild support the Triumvirate rather than the Great Towers?"

Mistress Lolund pursed her lips, making the wrinkles around her mouth deepen. "And when they couldn't win that argument, they decided to go rogue and destroy the Guild." She looked over to Darilos. "What was it you said yesterday? 'Murmuring about cabals among their rank and file?' A 'dark atmosphere' in the Guild? I couldn't believe you then, but what Master Feros revealed to Torra seems to confirm your suspicions."

"Thank you." Darilos shot a smug look at Kai.

Master Kuno looked down from his horse, his normally jovial face now darkly serious. "We must consider, dare I say, that if there was a conspiracy amongst masters at the Guild, that it could even extend to masters of the Great Towers or other institutes of magic."

Master Donovan stroked his thick mustache and nodded at Kuno. "We must keep this ... how do you say? ... close to the chest. When we are settled tonight at Gaes, we must make our reports to the towermasters directly."

"Aye," del Titccio agreed.

Torra remained silent. She thought back to all her colleagues at the Guild. The masters, the students, the visiting scholars. Master Morikal. First Astronomer Com Dimb. Their faces flashed past her memory. Some she liked, some not so much. But she had trusted all of them with her life. Master Feros had been trusted— loved, even—like a favorite uncle. She wondered, how many more could have turned to the Brotherhood of Blood?

"Mages!" Taegus shouted down the road. "We must move!"

They complied, turning quiet and pensive as they continued down the road.

~~~

After many miles, the vibrant, oaken foothills fell away and the curving route straightened and opened up into a broad valley of rolling hillocks with a narrow river, the Harvin, meandering to the northwest. Two other roads soon joined, one from the northeast and another from the south, turning the rutted lane into a well-pounded road.

At the far end of the valley, where the river turned westward through a gap in the valley, Torra could just make out the town of Gaes and its central citadel. She thought back to her childhood. Several times a year, Torra's father would team up with their neighbor, Ordan the cobbler, to drive Ordan's wagon to Gaes to collect supplies. She and Nickos would always jump onto the wagon at the last moment so their father couldn't say no, and ride with him to the Gaes market. A gentle man, her father had come to expect it, always scolding them half-heartedly and then giving in. The sight of the valley, and the exciting town at the end, would bring thoughts of sweet candies sold there and exotic items from far away countries brought to the town by way of the Bronze Trail trade route: sparkling jewelry of emeralds and silver from Ongo to the north, soft angora fur mittens and shawls from Alman to the west, pungent spices and silk from Quisha to the south, and argent weapons and armor from Sarsa and Sofon to the east.

But something was wrong. A plume of black smoke rose from the town, sparking concern from some of the guards. An order was given for four of the guard to split off and ride ahead to discern what had happened. She heard speculative muttering from the other mages about whether the Emerald Dragon may have attacked Gaes, as well.

A hand touched Torra's shoulder. She turned, and Darilos was close at her side. He bent slightly so that his blue eyes were level with hers. "Look there," he whispered, nodding up toward Timbrook Taegus. The chamberlain sat upon his mount, looking toward the distant town. "Look at his eyes. He isn't surprised by the smoke, is he?"

The chamberlain had stopped at the head of the mages and turned to discuss matters with Elbin. Taegus was as stoic as ever.

"He's always that way," she whispered back.

"And the boy?" His eyes moved toward the lordling. "What do you make of Elbin Gaes?"

Elbin's face betrayed an inner struggle. Eyes downward, looking anywhere but toward the town of his namesake, lips frowning, brow tight, hands fidgeting with his reins.

"I don't know him well," Torra answered.

"Then tell me this: Is Taegus the sort of man who doesn't know what's going on in his own realm? If there were a cabal of mages planning the destruction of Caranamere and infiltrating royal courts, don't you think he would know?"

"*I* didn't even know, and I'm from here!"

Darilos nodded. "Yes, and how many years ago did you leave here?"

Three, she thought. She saw his point. A lot could change in that time. "Taegus is no one's friend, but he is loyal to the kingdom. If you're suggesting … "

"Loyalties change, Torra." Darilos turned his head, seeming to hear something, but he continued, "Watch their reaction when the scouts return from Gaes to report on the fire." He turned back to look her in the eyes again, and murmured, "For that matter, watch the faces of your fellow mages, too. You delude yourself if you think the Brotherhood has limited their efforts to Caranamere or the local courts. Mordan upended more than a town. The power has shifted, and those who seek power will move to follow it."

Annoyed at his paranoid accusation, Torra was about to retort, but they were interrupted by noises from back up the road toward Caranamere—feet pounding in near-unison from a rapid march and the jingle of metal armor and weapons. The mages took a defensive posture. Masters Donovan and Gral pulled their weapons, as did the guards.

The other lordling and sister to Elbin, Sassala Gaes, came around a bend in the road, followed closely by the guards who had remained with her in Caranamere. They were all breathing hard and sweating profusely after a hard march.

Chamberlain Taegus stepped his horse toward them. "Sassala, what is the meaning of this? You were to remain and dispose of the dead."

Sassala called a halt, and the soldiers stopped in formation. Her red-tinged hair was matted with sweat. "We may well have joined them, Taegus, had we not fled. A dragon flew in."

The mages erupted in excitement.

Mistress Kai stepped toward her. "Which dragon?" she asked.

"Was it the Emerald?" del Titccio asked.

"If so, we must return and confront him," Preneval said.

For her part, Torra's eyes widened. She felt her face flush with anger. Her first thought was vengeance upon the Emerald Dragon.

"No," Sassala replied. "It was the gold one: *Aximdrac.*"

Torra gasped in surprise. "Ingal!" Her anger instantly washed away, and for a moment she wanted to run back to Caranamere and see him again. Her gaze fell on Darilos, but the thaumaturge had a bemused look on his face.

"The Gold Dragon!" Lord Preneval exclaimed, his dark eyes flashing. "Of course the destruction would draw his attention."

Master Donovan made a sweeping gesture with a muscular arm. "A strong ally, he could be." He looked around at the others. "Was it not the Gold Dragon who turned the attack on the Tower of Light?"

Eyes turned to Torra. The mages all knew her relationship with the Gold Dragon and how she had fought side by side with him at the battle. She felt she had to respond. "We must go to him," she said. "Master Donovan is correct. He is an ally. We must at least signal him."

Taegus harrumphed. "We've had enough of dragons! You mages buzz like bees, but have you stopped to consider that he may be in league with the Emerald Dragon?" He pulled his broadsword and pointed toward Gaes. "Do you wish another city destroyed?" He pulled on the reins and turned his steed. "We must double our speed and proceed to the citadel immediately."

Torra was unfazed. "He wouldn't do that!" She wheeled on Sassala. "What did he say to you?"

"He pleaded ignorance," Sassala responded. "But I didn't engage in idle chitchat with the beast."

"We have to signal him," Torra said again to the group. She looked to Kai, pleading for backup.

Kai nodded but remained silent.

"You've all taken leave of your senses!" Taegus said, sheathing his broadsword. "I should leave you here to burn in the beast's fires. But I have my orders. Come! Do not make me command the guards to bring you!"

The soldiers tensed, hands going to their sword hilts or clenching spear hafts.

Master Kuno interceded. "My good chamberlain, we go willingly to your lord."

Taegus half-turned toward him, eyes narrowed. "I said I didn't want you to address me in your foreign tongue!"

Kuno sighed in annoyance, but gestured to Torra. She took the hint and addressed Taegus in Taxin. "We agree to go with you willingly."

"Good!" Taegus barked. "Then keep up!" He whipped the reins and his horse trotted down the road at a fast clip. Everyone turned and followed as fast as they could walk. But Master Kuno leaned down from his saddle and muttered something in

Kai's ear, then Kai joined Torra, eyeing Darilos with a look of suspicion.

Kai grabbed Torra's arm and leaned in to her. "You know how to signal Ingal, yes?" Torra nodded. "Then do so, in as quiet a manner as possible. Perhaps go to the woods to 'relieve yourself' if you need an excuse."

Torra didn't need to excuse herself. A few minutes down the road, she cast an *Energy Burst* spell, chanting "*Hakam matosi.*" She put a great deal of magical energy into it, for Ingal would need to sense it from miles away. She knew the other mages felt it as well, and surely recognized the spell. Several glanced around at her, but most seemed to purposely ignore it, going along with the plan. She cast a mischievous glance toward Darilos.

The mage eyed her inquisitively and seemed to shiver. *Thaumaturge. He's not supposed to be able to sense my magic.* But she wondered. Every time she cast a spell, he seemed to get a little quiver of excitement. This time was no different. She continued looking at him, and he didn't flinch away. Then his eyes went down to the leather satchel containing the Codex and back to meet her gaze.

CHAPTER TWENTY-FOUR
Interception

The signal was unmistakable, but not a surprise. When Ingal sensed the *Energy Burst* spell, he was already aloft and heading downrange toward Gaes and the Harvin River valley, winging over another patch of burning oak along the roadway below. There was something familiar about the energy of the spell that he couldn't place, like a whisper from a friend.

But he couldn't concentrate on it through the pain that came with every wingbeat. Lifting off had been the worst part. After Draq had attacked him, Ingal cast a *Harden* spell on his chest to tighten it, but it wasn't enough to completely immobilize the broken rib. There was also an injury to his lower back, making the jump into the air an exercise in pain tolerance. His sternum burned, and many muscles in his back and chest ached with every movement. The healing potion he had so carefully stowed in the upper right pocket of his travel vest had been shattered by Draq's blow, slathering the pocket's contents with fluorescent green liquid, and an expensive loss.

So he allowed himself to glide as much as he could, turning slightly to make a beeline toward the source of the spell, flying low enough over the rolling hills to catch thermals to lessen his heft. He had a good tailwind from the storm moving in from the mountains in the east, redolent with the scent of mountaintop snow. It would be much colder here, soon.

From what the pugnacious young lordling woman had said, Ingal expected Expeditionary Mages in the area, probably traveling to Gaes. Thus he was already nearing the location of the signal by the time it was given. If she and her soldiers had made good time, then most likely they delivered the news of his arrival, he figured, and the mages signaled him in response.

He soon swooped into Gaes Valley. The land widened into a flat basin with the Harvin River streaming through the middle, edged with willows and cattails. Tall mountain ridges fringed both sides, gaily colored with fall foliage. On the road ahead he spotted the party of soldiers and mages traveling toward the small city of Gaes and its ancient stone citadel, with the mounted nobility in front, mages in the middle, and footmen in formation behind, the sparkling river flowing to their left. The mages wore different robe colors—red, black, and white—suggesting these were indeed Expeditionary Mages, and one wore brown. *A survivor of the Astronomer's Guild?* he wondered. Beyond were fields of crops and then the town itself.

A thick plume of smoke rose from the town. He hoped no one had been hurt in the fire, and considered helping, but he had to focus on the mages.

Ingal swung around and broadly circled the party. A masked heron and a flock of ducks startled from the neighboring wetland and took flight, squawking and alerting the guards. A leader called a halt, shouting commands to his men. Immediately the guards formed a ring around the mages and nobility, spears outward. The soldiers looked up, wide eyed and fumbling in fear. The mages, though, pointed up, eyes alight in excitement.

Ingal took his time, circling thrice before landing on the road a stone's throw behind the party. In a tense situation such as this one, it was best to keep them from feeling trapped, so he chose to land on the side farthest from the town. He spread out his wings, raised his right forefoot in customary salute, and announced in

Taxin, "I am Ingal Jehai, Gold Dragon and ruler of the White Lands Federation."

"Aximdrac!" one soldier shouted and dropped his halberd to the ground. Two of the soldiers broke and ran, despite the lordling woman shouting, "Hold the line!" The break was enough for the mages to shoulder through them. The horses spooked, and one reared up so suddenly that the rider, a young nobleman in plate mail, was nearly thrown.

The first mage Ingal recognized was a potbellied, white-bearded man on horseback whom he recognized as Master Drokil Kuno, a Lakarthian from the far west, though as rumor has it he'd spent so much of his life at the Tower of Light that he'd nearly forgotten his homeland. Behind him stood a mustached mage in the red robes of the Tower of Balance with the dark and serious look of a Northman. Beside stood a black-robed master of the Tower of Darkness with oil-slicked hair whom Ingal knew as Master Garinos Preneval, Prince and brother of the King of Gaicalk. Ingal had not met him in person, but they had shared dispatches and *Counsel* spells regarding the art of transmutation. Preneval was the only mage sanctioned by the Council of Mages to engage in that renegade magic, forbidden for millennia due to the excesses of ancient masters who, through the dark art, created monstrosities that still haunted the land. The mage's interest had earned him the nickname "The Transformer."

Then, just as Ingal was about to speak, he heard an excited "Ingal!" from a smiling figure behind them. He immediately recognized his young friend, Torra Com Gidel. *Of course,* he thought, *she must have sent the* Energy Burst *signal!* That explained the "familiar energy" he'd felt.

Ingal returned the smile, but before he could respond, Kuno made a semblance of a bow from his saddle, hand on his chest in Lakarthian style. "Lord Jehai!" Kuno said, "We, the Expeditionary Mages, representing the Towers of Magic, do bid you welcome."

"This is not your land to offer welcome, mage," countered a slim man astride a black horse. His fine cloth-of-gold surcoat marked him as nobility, and his air was of one in charge. Ingal wondered if this was the Lord Gaes, but he seemed too young and lacked the thin coronet that lords in this region wore on such travels. The nobleman trotted his courser forward to the side of Kuno and eyed the dragon with unintimidated resolve, as steely as a general. "You are not welcome here, dragon, ruler or not. Your kind has attacked our land in an act of unprovoked warfare."

Ingal tilted his head. "It is only warfare if it is between nations, sir. The White Lands Federation is not involved, nor do we speak for other dragons. We come here seeking answers, as ally of Taxia and as grandmaster mage. To whom do we speak?"

"I am Timbrook Taegus, chamberlain and representative of Lord Gaes, ruler of the Harvin headlands by the will of the King. I am accompanied by his heir, Elbin Gaes," he gestured toward his left to the young man in plate mail decorated in rainbow colors of Gaes, "and his sister, Sassala Gaes." He gestured to his right at the young woman Ingal had met in Caranamere, sword drawn and face tight.

Ingal nodded to each. "We mean no disrespect, Chamberlain, nor are we waging an invasion. If you wish to combat a dragon, sir, may we advise you to choose another?"

The woman, Sassala, shouted, "Be gone, dragon! Or we will be forced to drive you away!"

Ingal almost let out a laugh as he witnessed the look the mages flashed at her, a mix of annoyance and hilarity, for even if all of the soldiers attacked him at once, their spears and swords would do little against his scales.

"Such boldness is to be commended, my lady!" Ingal stated, then took a weighty step toward them, wings flaring. The line of guards shook and rippled in a combined flinch. "If you will not abide our presence as dragon, then perhaps you will tolerate us as mage—one who has lost good friends in the destruction of the Astronomer's Guild. We will confer with our colleagues from the Towers, my lords and lady, and decide from there how best to proceed."

Taegus shifted his eyes across the line of quivering soldiers, then back to the dragon. "You may confer, Lord Jehai, but then you must take leave of our lands."

Ingal nodded. But he knew as well as Taegus that there was little the chamberlain or his lord could do if he were to tarry overlong or, for that matter, decide to camp on the doorstep of their citadel and make a feast of their livestock.

Taegus stepped aside and ordered his men to allow the mages to step through the ring, much to the vexation of Sassala Gaes. They pulled back into a formation farther down the road.

At last Ingal could see the full contingent. Besides Kuno and Preneval, he also knew the red-robed Master Truey del Titccio, bastard grandson of King Granus the Bold of the Azure Sea nation of Esse (and thus a prince, though he shunned the title), a potionmaster of the Tower of Balance, and a virtuoso lyrist. Upon meeting eyes, del Titccio gave a quick half-bow. When once del Titccio had visited the Tower of Light, a decade before, Ingal had played the game of Navalis with the mage in the verdant gardens around the tower, to the delight of hundreds of onlookers, mages and city folk included, with a servant moving the pieces for the dragon. To his chagrin, Ingal had lost the naval strategy game to del Titccio who was, by all rights, a reigning champion of the game in his land, so Ingal had made a gift of fine wines to the long-haired mage.

Ingal also recognized Torra's mentor, Mistress Kai Ninga'ai, who bowed to the dragon but remained silent, glancing toward Torra with a look that he couldn't quite interpret. He had only once talked to her, at a rendezvous between Ingal and Torra a year ago. Ingal had inquired about Torra's progress. Kai had been very forthright, trying to hide the awe that he had seen a million times on those who addressed him for the first time, but mincing no words in describing Torra's weaknesses.

Ingal did not know the others: the mustached Northman in red robes, his Tower of Balance colleague with the blue tattooed face, nor a slim, black-robed elder woman from the Tower of Darkness, her silver hair pulled in a tight bun.

Of great interest to Ingal was a fresh-looking, blond-haired mage in the brown robes of the Astronomer's Guild watching him with clever blue eyes. He stood beside what looked to be a common peasant, his skin reddened and hair singed, carrying a woodsman's axe. These were most certainly survivors. The woodcutter, however, seemed afraid and hid behind the protection of the others.

The mages stepped forward, many talking at once, with Torra practically running. "Ingal!" Torra shouted again, "You came!"

Ingal focused on the young mage and grinned, then he remembered her origin and softened his expression into one of consolation. "Torra, it is good to see you again. Our heart leaps to see such a good friend, but we are saddened by the occasion. We assume you lost many loved ones. Please accept our condolences."

She looked up at him, her face a mix of emotions. "It's good to see you too, my lord. And thank you. Much and more has happened in the last day. We were betrayed!"

"Betrayed?" Ingal looked to Kuno. "By whom?"

"My lord," Master Kuno said, pausing to collect his thoughts, "it is good you have come. No stronger ally could we have in these dark times!"

He does not answer the question, Ingal thought. *Is he fearful to admit to us, or to himself?*

"And yet, Kuno, the towermasters and the Council of Mages continue to refuse our hails, unless it is through emissaries." Ingal tapped the ivory tip of his tail in irritation. "They presume that we side with the Triumvirate, despite our defense of the Tower of Light from the elves."

"Um, yes," Kuno responded, "I was aware. And yet, I must beg your forbearance, for your aid is much needed in the current investigation, and I am not privy to the council's thoughts on that matter."

"Perhaps you can tell the council, then, that we just battled with one of the Triumvirate gods at the ruins of Caranamere." He paused a moment as a wave of surprise washed over the mages. All of them, that is, except the brown-robed mage in the back, who merely raised an eyebrow in what looked like mild amusement. "It is not the first time we have refused the Triumvirate's demand to join them, nor, I suspect, will it likely be the last." The pain in Ingal's sternum flared, and he reached a forefoot up to touch the wound. "Draq confirmed to us that the Triumvirate is behind this attack, conferring upon the Emerald Dragon the energies needed for a renegade spell. But what is their motivation? We do not know. The most we were able to ascertain is that they have allies here who seek some sort of 'secret weapon' to 'control the energies of the Outer Gods' and fight their fight for them."

At the last comment, Ingal noticed Torra widen her eyes in surprise, then turn and look back at the blond-haired mage from the Astronomer's Guild. *They know something about this.*

Preneval cleared his throat. Then, in his very proper way of speaking, hands clasped behind his back, he said, "Lord Jehai, it is an honor to finally meet you in person." He gave a bow accompanied by a flourish of the arm. "Perhaps we know who the Triumvirate 'allies' may be. Have you ever heard of a cult called the Brotherhood of Blood?"

Ingal had not. "No doubt these are the 'betrayers' of whom you speak."

"Indeed, Lord Jehai, for at least some of them were mages of the Astronomer's Guild itself!"

Ingal reared back, eyes growing wide. "Traitors, indeed, if they were part of Caranamere's destruction!"

Kuno and the mages updated Ingal on the events of the past day and a half, from the discovery of the destruction of Caranamere up through their introduction to the Brotherhood of Blood. Kuno also introduced the thaumaturge, Darilos Velar. Ingal was particularly interested in finding out more about him.

The mages fanned out into a semicircle around Ingal, the better to quench their curiosity. Ingal espied, through his peripheral vision, the stocky, tattooed mage reach out and touch the scales of his left foot, glancing up to see if he'd been detected. Ingal swished his tail at him, causing the mage to jump back in surprise.

At one point, in relating what Osprey had told them, Preneval whispered into the ear of Kuno, and Kuno nodded before continuing. Ingal got the impression that he was leaving out some important detail of what the woodsman had witnessed, something he'd seen after the Emerald Dragon had fled. There had been a time when Ingal's hearing would have picked it up, but in his old age he could not make out the words.

Ingal found the story intriguing about how the Brotherhood rebuilt the house. Such a spell was not without precedent; indeed, it was said that the great master Worvus the Blue of Hamal had rebuilt much of the city of Hubani after an earthquake, by harmonizing with lesser masters. But a group of mages preaching against magic as "evil" while at the same time casting advanced spells? *That* was unheard of!

Kuno deferred to Torra to relate her story of the duel with Master Feros, a mage Ingal had met on his last visit to the Astronomer's Guild, over two decades before. The tale was harrowing, but for all the danger of the incident, it was the reveal of his treachery that was most alarming. The implications were clear: Feros, or "Disciple Immolatos" as he was known to the Brotherhood, wasn't alone in his perfidy; there were others who had been from the Guild. How many others, and their role in the Brotherhood, was unknown.

When she finished, Ingal gave a thoughtful sigh. "We are relieved you survived unscathed, Torra. It would sadden us greatly if any ill were to come to you." He paused a moment as Torra thanked him, then he added, "We well know your strength and bravery from our prior adventure. But it is a tribute to your skill that you bested a master!"

He then turned his eyes toward the blond-haired Guildsman, who had remained silent throughout the tale. "We commend you for coming to her rescue, Darilos Velar. You have proven to be an asset to the expedition. And it is a surprise to come upon a thaumaturge. How exceedingly rare! It is strange that we have never heard of you, particularly since you are associated with an institute of magic!"

Darilos shrugged. "I was new to the Guild, Jehai."

Ingal tilted his head. There was something familiar about this man, but he couldn't quite place it. His mannerisms or voice, perhaps? Addressing him as "Jehai" was odd. Ingal was certain they had never met, and yet … He had no magical aura—less so even than an average person—though this would make sense if he were a thaumaturge. "And with whom did you study, prior to joining? Avos of Mikinos? The elusive Ongoan known as the White Mouse? Chaes Novek, of Hamal? You are fluent in Taxin, yet your mannerisms seem foreign to this region."

Torra's mentor, Kai, turned and gave a self-satisfied smile at Torra.

Darilos was slow to answer, but his face did not change. "I'm certain it was no one you know, Jehai, for my master practiced in secret. Because of our art and the power we wield, we rarely divulge our identities."

"And yet you have, at least in regard to yourself. So much so that you joined an institute of magic. Or, at least, you have given *an* identity. What led you to join the Guild?"

"A temporary member, to be sure. I was itinerant, traveling, seeking knowledge. And as such I visited the Guild. I joined at the behest of the Second Astronomer, Master Cortanal. He felt we could exchange knowledge with each other about our crafts." He paused, a gleam in his blue eyes, then added, "And, I think, he wanted an outsider to trust."

Ingal remembered Master Jas Cortanal, a tall, lanky man with a long auburn beard, skilled in the way of magic, but quiet and pensive, unlike the First Astronomer, Colnos Com Dimb, who took charge and had control of everything in the Guild. "Are you suggesting that Cortanal did not trust others in the Guild, Darilos? Did he know of the Brotherhood or suspect treachery among their ranks?"

Darilos smiled. "I suspected, yes, Jehai, but he died before he revealed his thoughts to me."

"We see," Ingal said, but he didn't think Darilos was being truthful. His demeanor was too controlled, his movements too relaxed, his voice too smooth. Once again, Darilos reminded him of someone. "And what do you know of this 'secret weapon' that Draq mentioned?"

"This is the first I have heard of such a weapon, Jehai."

Ingal kept an eye on Torra during this interaction. At Darilos's last remark, she glanced away, looked down, licked her lips.

He abruptly turned his gaze to Torra. "And did *you* know of this 'secret weapon,' Torra?"

Torra drew in a breath, a little too sharply, paused as if to consider her words, glanced around her, then said, "I don't know either, my lord. But I suspect we will learn soon."

She was holding something back. That last glance seemed to suggest she didn't completely trust the others. Perhaps that was not surprising, given that one of her former masters had turned against her.

"Gold Dragon!" shouted Taegus from his group of soldiers. "You try my patience! We have allowed you your discussions. It is time to take your leave!"

Ingal made no move to acknowledge the chamberlain's rudeness, though to stay overlong *did* risk an incident. He had no measure of the man and wondered just how far he would go with his threats. Ingal had no concern for his own safety, nor even of the mages', but Taegus could easily sour their investigation, and his men would die needlessly in a fight.

Ingal looked to Kuno. "May we propose that you continue your investigation of this Brotherhood of Blood, but leave to us the pursuit of Mordan. We have dealt with him many a time in our past, and can do so again."

With a seeking glance toward his colleagues, Kuno cleared his throat and put on a smile. "Lord Jehai, with all due respect of course, the Great Towers have entrusted *us* with the full investigation, as the Expeditionary Mages. While we welcome your inquiry, I must insist that we interrogate him ourselves."

Ingal harrumphed. *Duty before common sense.* "Mordan has just laid waste to an entire town with nothing more than a spoken word. He is larger and physically stronger than we are. He is armored, and lustful for power. It is a folly for you to seek him. As we told Taegus, let a dragon take on a dragon, good mage."

But it wasn't just Mordan's strength and magical ability, Ingal thought. Those who cast renegade spells had been known to lose their minds, regardless of species. He suspected the Citrine Dragon had once cast such a spell, leading to his insanity. The Iron Dragon, Gogonith, had remained sane but stopped referring to himself in the plural—a first sign of mental instability—at least until Ingal killed him. Ingal himself had felt his mind tearing after casting *Rift Widening* at the Tower of Light, making it difficult to refer to himself in the plural as well, and on rare occasions that he kept to himself, he had awakened confused about which lifetime he was in. Would Mordan suffer mental issues after *his* renegade spell?

Kuno shook his head. "We canno … " The last word was cut off, though, as elder mages gathered around him, led by the woman in black robes and the red-robed mage with the heavy mustache. After a moment of discussion, Kuno nodded and addressed Ingal again. "Perhaps there is a compromise, Lord Jehai. Mistress Lolund and Master Donovan have suggested that you go forward, find Mordan and confront him, and then use totems to pull some of us to you so that we may interrogate."

"Totems?" asked the woodsman, leaning toward Torra. Ingal suspected the two knew each other from Caranamere. Torra was about to answer him, but Ingal broke in.

"Good man, I see you wear the bronze sun of Okun. What is your name?"

The man's eyes went wide, but he stammered a reply. "O … Osprey." He blinked and made a quick, hesitant bow of his head. "Okun be praised."

"May the father of gods shine his light on thee in your time of sorrow," Ingal said—a common benison for Okun's lay followers. He saw Osprey relax his stance, the fear in his eyes softening.

Ingal continued, "Osprey, upon reaching the rank of 'master,' a mage makes for himself or herself a token object imbued with a small part of their magical spirit. It is not a religious symbol, like your pendant, but it does hold power and is dangerous to make, for if it is done wrongly, it could trap the mage's 'magic center' in the object, rendering them unable to perform magic again. To offer this to another person is a great honor and sign of trust, for only one may be made at a time, and it may be misused if it falls into the wrong hands—even to the point of controlling the mage's mind. What these mages have suggested is that some of them give us their totems, and when we find the Emerald Dragon and confront him, we cast a spell called *Totem Pull*, which will teleport them to that location. Thus, they would join me in questioning or confronting Mordan."

Ingal winced, realizing he had referred to himself as 'me' instead of 'us.' After all this time, he still suffered from the effects of the renegade spell. Thankfully, none of the mages seemed to notice.

He turned back to address Kuno. "But we will not know where you are or what you are doing at the time we find him and cast the spell. It may not be convenient, and we may not be able to signal you."

"We understand," Kuno said. He pulled out a small bag from his pack, emptied what looked like strips of dried meat from it, and turned to the other mages. "After our discussions last night, I feel it would be best if one of us from each tower joined Lord Jehai. I offer myself on behalf of the Tower of Light." He reached into a pocket of his robes, pulled out a small pyramidal token, and dropped it in the bag. "I propose Mistress Lolund represent the Tower of Darkness and Master Gral the Tower of Balance."

Both of the volunteers nodded in agreement. Lolund walked forward, paused a moment, then dropped in an obsidian shard. Gral made a grunt, then placed what appeared to be a red, spiked seed pod into the bag.

Kuno tied the bag shut, then offered it up to Ingal. "My lord," Kuno said. Gral looked up with grim, tight lips, and Lolund shifted her eyes away. *Perhaps they are having second thoughts?* Ingal thought. He sensed the magical energy from the totems, like shining lights.

Ingal held out his forefoot, palm up and, after Kuno dropped the bag into his massive palm, tipped the bag into a voluminous pocket of his travel vest. "We will keep them safe and summon you as soon as it is reasonable to do so."

"My Lord," Kuno said, "Do you know where he has gone?"

"Mordan?" Ingal shook his head. "No, but we have a suspicion. The Emerald Dragon has many lairs, but there are only a couple where he would keep a treasure of such magnitude, safely guarded." *And*, he thought, *only one of those would be restful enough for an increasingly troubled mind.*

Lolund asked, "And how much time do you think it will take you to travel there?"

"It shan't be more than two or three days before we find him."

Taegus pulled his sword, and his men formed up, drawing their swords and readying their spears. "Last warning, Gold Dragon! Leave now. There is no reason for bloodshed!"

The mages moved in irritation, activating their magic centers.

"There is no reason, indeed, Taegus," Ingal said. "We shall take our leave now." He spread his wings and raised a forefoot again in blessing. "Travel with ease, my friends, and may we find the cause of this sorrow."

"Goodbye, Ingal!" Torra called, and bowed. The other mages bowed as well.

"Farewell, Torra. We will meet again soon."

And then, making an effort not to cry out at the pain in his back and ribs, Ingal leapt up into the air and beat his wings, lifting upward and catching a cold eastern breeze to quickly rise over the party.

As he circled around, he gazed down upon the faces of the mages, the soldiers, the chamberlain, the nobility. Taegus he didn't trust, but at least the chamberlain was open in his hostility.

Kuno and the other Expeditionary Mages seemed trustworthy, though reserved.

And of the Guild member, Darilos Velar, there was something unsettling. Untrustworthy. He had saved Torra's life, and he seemed knowledgeable about the Brotherhood of Blood, that much was clear. And yet …

But he couldn't dwell upon it. He had to trust the mages to do their part.

The pain had intensified with that last leap. With a last glance backward to make sure he'd gone far enough that the mages wouldn't detect it, Ingal cast a *Levitation* spell on himself, this time to lighten the load on his sore rib and other injuries.

Ingal winged over the yellow-and-orange oak canopies then crested the rocky ridgeline and headed northward out of the Gaes Valley. His thoughts went before him, seeing in his mind the path he would take. It had been many centuries since last he had confronted Mordan at one of his lairs. How much had changed? How powerful had he become?

Mordan always favored armor and weaponry to augment his brute strength and lesser magical skills. But clearly his magical skills had vastly improved. Ingal decided he would need to even those odds. So he had one stop to make before continuing to the Emerald Dragon: the cavern of Sologothu, and the arsenal he kept there.

CHAPTER TWENTY-FIVE

Gaes

Torra was giddy after having seen the Gold Dragon again, as she was every time they met. Watching him fly away was hard. She imagined herself in his vest pocket again, flying high above the world, off to a shared adventure. Oh, if only she could go with him again!

She sighed as he disappeared over the ridge and the soldiers got everyone back in order. She couldn't go winging off with Ingal again. She had a mission, and a very important one at that. He had his job to do, and she had hers.

Then her thoughts turned to worry. Ingal was clearly wounded after his fight with the Triumvirate god. He had tried to hide it, but she could tell—from the way he held his chest, the odd stance he took, the wince upon landing and taking off. But none of that physical discomfort seemed to mar his wits.

She knew how perceptive Ingal was. Torra worried that he knew she was hiding something: the "secret weapon" that the Brotherhood sought, this "Convergence" that Darilos had mentioned, or the Codex that he had brought back. But her deception was justified, right? Well, more of an omission than a deception. And she wasn't about to spread alarm without taking care to examine the Codex herself.

Timbrook Taegus and Sassala Gaes got the soldiers back in formation around the mages. No sooner had they started off when the mounted scouts came galloping back from town, their horses in a lather. They called out to Taegus, then pulled up next to him to whisper with alarmed faces. Torra couldn't make out what they said, but she watched Taegus's eyes as he leaned down to talk to them, as Darilos had suggested.

The chamberlain *didn't* show surprise at what he'd heard.

Torra glanced back at Darilos. He simply nodded knowingly at her.

Without explanation, Taegus ordered a faster march and sent more soldiers forward.

It didn't take long before word spread through the group. The Temple of Okun was burning.

Osprey cried out, "The temple!" and tried to run forward, but Torra put a hand on his shoulder.

"Stay with us," she said. "We will be there soon, and with us you are protected." He nodded, but soon he was near the front of the group, urging them forward.

As the sky darkened with storm clouds blown in from the east, the winding dirt road left the side of the Harvin River and its marshes and straightened through fields of grains, squashes, and root vegetables. Field workers, ending their day, stood in somber groups, leaning on their tools and watching with wide eyes, whispering and pointing as the mages went past. Some made warding signs toward them—the circle of Okun, or pointing their middle and index fingers of their left hand at them in a more ancient gesture. It was strange to see, since the citizens of Gaes had always tolerated the mages of Caranamere, even if magic was technically outlawed in Taxia. Soon a loose procession of peasants followed the mages and soldiers at a distance, curious about the odd group of mages, no doubt, and at the end of their work for the day.

At last, nearing the gloaming of the day, the mages came to the town of Gaes, passing through an outer ring of hovels, then to the east gate of the dilapidated outer walls. There were usually only a couple guards posted, at least when she had lived in the region, but today a dozen stood ready in chain mail hauberks and armed with pikes as Timbrook led the group inside. The gates hadn't been closed for nearly a century, not since the Two-Seasons War with Sofon, yet now the cobblestones showed sign of the gates having recently been scraped over them to be shut.

Beyond the wall, a wide thoroughfare led uphill to the citadel. Two-story stone buildings lined it, crowded together but stately in appearance. Balconies were normally decorated this time of year with corn stalks and pumpkins, an honor to Flores, Goddess of the harvest and fertility, but few were decorated this year despite the fields being bountiful on the way into town.

A crowd of townsfolk stood to either side of the cobble thoroughfare that led through the town to the inner citadel, which loomed on a hill with a far more imposing wall. Some of the townsfolk held fire buckets. They watched with wide, accusing eyes, hissed and made more warding signs, then fell in behind the mages and soldiers. Torra sensed some of her fellow mages activating their magic centers. She did too.

The wind shifted, and gray smoke blew into the thoroughfare, acrid with the smell of sulfur and char. Osprey cried out and burst from the protection of the soldiers, running through the crowd toward the Temple of Okun. Torra ran after him.

"Torra, stop!" Kai screamed, but Torra didn't look back. She wasn't going to leave Osprey to his fate alone.

They ran between two buildings, then up and over a lawn and onto the ruined terrace of the temple. The fire had mostly subsided, leaving behind scorched stone walls and blackened timbers. The building had once been the most beautiful in the town, domed and imposing with fluted pillars. The pillars still stood, but the dome had collapsed and brought down a wall and the front portico with it. A thick black plume of smoke rose from the interior.

Osprey ran to the broad stone steps of the temple. "No, no, no, no!" he shouted, hands outstretched.

Two figures lay there in burnt priest's robes, draped across the steps, a handful of townspeople trying to aide them by supporting their heads and giving them water. A slim priest was severely burned, his robes in blackened tatters and his exposed skin charred in places, his hair completely burned off. He had already died. The other priest, though burnt bright red, lay coughing weakly. His hair was burnt as well, but wisps of it remained—enough to show his head had been shaved into a tonsure. Around his neck hung a high priest's amulet—the circle of Okun, made of silver and gold—a much richer version of the layman's amulet that Osprey wore.

Torra stopped and stared, shaking. The destruction of Caranamere was still too raw. Seeing yet another stately building reduced to ruin and the burnt bodies froze her in place. She almost turned and ran back to the safety of the mages.

"Father Alim!" Osprey cried. He fell to his knees next to the priest. "Who did this?"

The priest turned to him and looked at him with clouded eyes, then reached up and felt Osprey's face with shaking hands.

"It's Osprey, Father, from Caranamere," the woodsman said, his voice going tender.

"My son," he said, then he grimaced. "Such horror. Such horror."

Osprey asked, "Who did this, Father?"

Torra pulled herself out of her shock and looked around. A cluster of townsfolk had come with them and had formed a circle. Mistress Kai and Master del Titccio burst through them, accompanied by three guards. Then Darilos stepped through as well.

"The Bro—" the priest was stopped by a coughing fit, then his head lolled. Osprey gently cupped his hand around the priest's head to help steady him. "The Brotherhood," Father Alim said again. "They … burned the Temple of Flores yesterday … then came for us." He was wracked again by coughing, then gasped for breath. "Magistrates … turned against us. Townspeople …"

Then Father Alim's eyes grew wide and he reached again for Osprey's face. "A vision, my son. You … you are …" Another spell of coughing. "You must now …" He closed his eyes and chanted. The words were of the "old tongue," an ancient form of Taxin once called Taxidi, but Torra recognized it as an Okun benediction. The priest shouted a final word, and his hands glowed a golden luminance, penetrating Osprey's cheeks where they touched him. Then the priest placed his right hand upon Osprey's forehead.

Osprey fell backward onto the steps in a seizure, his legs and arms quivering, mouth agape and eyes staring up at the smoke. The crowd of onlookers gasped and fell back.

"Osprey!" Torra said, and bent to help him. But it was over in moments. Osprey's eyes refocused. He took in a deep, shuddering breath, then rose up slowly into a sitting position. He looked around at the ruined temple and the crowd as if seeing it all for the first time.

"Osprey," Torra said, "what happened to you?"

He didn't answer. Instead, he moved forward again to Father Alim and took his hand. The priest was barely conscious, but he placed his golden into Osprey's hand, then his arm moved and he pointed toward the body of the other priest. "Take it … the

Writ …'" he muttered, then took a last, shuddering breath and died.

"So much loss," Osprey said, tears welling in his eyes. He and Torra both looked over at the other priest. Clutched to his side was a large, bound copy of the Writ of Okun, the gold leaf on its cover mostly melted. "Heretics have corrupted the people of this town. We must show them the light again."

Osprey made the sign of his god at the priests, stating, "Be in the light of Okun." He then bent and picked up the Writ and took Father Alim's holy amulet, leaving his own bronze amulet on Father Alim's chest. Torra, Osprey, and the other mages were escorted back to the others on the thoroughfare by the soldiers. The crowd had become more hostile. They were now shouting at the mages. "Get you out of our town!" one yelled. "Killers!" another shouted. "Dragon kin!"

Darilos laughed out loud at that last insult.

Elbin's eyes were wide and darting back and forth, his face a mask of fear, hand on the hilt of his sword. But his sister, Sassala, shouted back at the masses. "You!" she said, pointing at one of them. "Cobbler Harkent! How dare you accost us after all the days you spent in the stocks last month for public indecency! Go back to your cups. It's the only thing you're good at!"

They passed through the Market Square, where once Torra had delighted at exotic gifts. Gone were the wares, replaced by a hail of stones and vegetables thrown by the mob. Master Gral was hit in the back by a large cobblestone. He turned, growling, and brandished his massive, curved hanat knife. Master Donovan, too, had pulled his sword, muttering to himself in his native Corrusian. His guise cat familiar, Yaggu, stalked close to his side, his eyes and ears darting back and forth and tail bristling. A rotten squash hit the rump of Master Kuno's horse and burst apart, seeds and slime flying across the faces of two guards next to him, and the horse bolting forward until caught by Elbin Gaes. Darilos, on the other hand, seemed mildly amused, deftly dodging a pumpkin, then catching an apple and throwing it back at the peasant.

"Guards!" Sassala shouted. "Defend!"

The soldiers tightened their ring, with halberds pointed outward. But the mob didn't relent.

"Villains!" one man shouted. "You'll pay for Caranamere!"

"Murderers! They'll send the dragon for *us* next time!"

"Go back to yer so-called Guild and burn with the rest of 'em!"

Two men bolted forward at Lord Preneval, but a soldier put his dagger into one's gut. The other was kicked to the ground and stabbed through with a halberd.

Torra turned, casting a *Shield* spell just as a stone would have smashed her head.

"Such rabble," Lord Preneval said after casting a *Shield* spell as well. "The lord of Gaes must be weak to allow the peasantry to act with such impunity."

Annoyed, Torra was about to retort that these peasants were her people, but then, through a momentary gap in the angry crowd, Torra spotted two crimson-robed figures standing in the shadows. She started to point them out, but then …

Someone in the crowd threw an axe. It flipped end over end, narrowly missing Master Donovan, and buried itself in the shoulder of one of Taegus's guards, who cried out and fell to a knee.

"Enough!" Darilos shouted. He raised his arms outward, then spun in a circle. A thunderous boom issued from him. Everyone outside of the group of mages and guards were pushed backward in a sonic blast. Most were thrown completely off their feet. Men and women slammed into walls. Wooden stalls burst apart.

Everything grew suddenly quiet as the crowd recovered.

Electricity ran up and down Torra's body. Somehow, Darilos's spell sent waves of heat through her, just like when he defeated Master Feros. For a moment, she forgot about the chaos around her.

"Run now!" Taegus shouted. "It's your chance!"

But Torra was transfixed, staring at Darilos. He noticed, then grabbed her hand and pulled her with him, breaking her out of the rush of ecstasy.

The group ran as fast as they could, still ringed by guards, until, at last, they passed across a drawbridge over a deep and wide ravine. Glancing down, Torra saw large spikes at the bottom. Once through, the drawbridge was raised and an iron portcullis fell shut behind them.

They were inside the citadel, standing, panting, in a wide bailey. Master Kuno, sweating profusely, nearly fell as he dismounted, had it not been for a helping hand from Master Gral. Lolund and del Titccio were doubled over, holding their sides. Master Donovan was bleeding from the back of his head.

"By the stars!" Torra exclaimed, looking again at Darilos.

Outside, the shouts had picked up again. Stones rained down sporadically into the bailey around them.

Taegus, cursing, ordered the horses stabled, then ushered the mages toward a set of thick, oaken doors at the entrance to the great hall built to the side of the keep. The doors were sided with massive standing stones. The mantle over the doors was likewise made of thick stone, but was topped with a row of very large crystals and shimmering tourmaline of many different colors.

"What in the hells is wrong with them?" Sassala Gaes shouted, sheathing her sword. "The whole damned town has lost its mind!"

"They're confused by the Brotherhood and the destruction of Caranamere," Torra said.

"Oh, don't go justifying them!" Sassala replied. "Any of them attack me, and I'll put my sword through them easy enough! I quite nearly did!"

Mistress Kai shouldered past Darilos and roughly put a hand on Torra's shoulder, squeezing. "What did you think, running off like that, apprentice? Do you *want* to die?"

Torra threw off Kai's hand. "I was defending Osprey!"

Kai flashed an irritated glance toward Osprey, who stood off to the side, eyes downward, clutching the gilded Writ of Okun as if it were a baby.

"Osprey is not our concern, apprentice," Kai continued. "We are here on behalf of the Towers to investigate. You must *separate* yourself from these people, even though you may have known them all your life. We must not pass judgment! We must not become attached. Do you understand? Your duty is here— she made a circling motion, indicating the group of mages, "—with *us.*"

"Well, pardon *me* for passing judgment, Mistress!" Torra said, staring her down. "But my entire town is gone. And now *my people* are misled about the culprits! I will not see *my land* torn apart!" Torra pushed past Kai toward the hall's oaken doors, refusing to look back at her mentor. Darilos followed, an eyebrow raised in response to the outburst, smirking.

Kai's look of shock turned immediately to anger. "It was a mistake to bring you here!" Kai shouted after her.

CHAPTER TWENTY-SIX
Choosing Sides

Darilos lounged in a corner of the Great Hall where fluttering torches did little to dispel the shadows. The better to observe without seeming obvious. A wind had picked up outside, sending whistling drafts down the chimneys of the two hearths in the room. Unfortunately, the draft wasn't enough to blow away the acrid scent of sweat and mildew.

The Great Hall was awkwardly large for such a small band, their voices echoing off the soot-covered walls and vaulted ceiling. A long, scarred table with benches ran down the middle of the hall, and another row of benches lined both walls. An imposing granite throne stood on a flagstone dais at the far end of the room, festooned with tourmaline and quartz crystals in a garish display of the domain's chief export. The country bumpkin, Osprey, had called it the "Crystal Throne" with a bit of awe on his simpleton face.

Osprey now sat at the far end of the table, one hand on the newly acquired Writ of Okun, the other fondling the religious amulet he'd taken off the dead priest. He was muttering a fervent prayer with his eyes closed as if his god was going to suddenly appear before him. Servants had fetched fresh clothes for him, finally replacing the burnt and tattered bits that he'd been wearing all this time. They were brightly colored and finely cut, unlike the clothes a woodsman would normally wear, and he seemed out of place in them.

The mages, too, had taken time to magically clean and mend their garments.

All but four of the guards had left. Those four now stood in pairs at the front and back entrances with spears crossed. Before he left, Taegus had ordered servants to attend to the mages, bringing in stewed potatoes, platters of roasted duck on beds of herbed squash, and glass bottles filled with ruby-red Maldurbian wine. The food was merely picked at. The wine, on the other hand, went quickly, and servants rushed out for more.

One of the servants, a black-haired old hag with a hooked nose, recognized Torra and showered her with attention, proclaiming, "Oh, you poor thing!" and "I 'member when you was this big!" holding a hand to her waist. Torra returned the affection with a wan smile.

Darilos shifted his attention to two mages, the haughty black-robed one called Preneval, and the waspish Mistress Kai. They stood across the Hall, heads close together, whispering, their eyes darting toward him. They were far enough away that their gossip wouldn't be overheard by any human, but Darilos was hardly human. He could just make out what they were saying.

" … didn't use an incantation when he cast the spell," muttered Preneval.

Kai nodded. "Is that typical of thaumaturges? I've never seen one cast a spell."

Preneval gave the slightest of shrugs. "Not from what I've been taught, but I am no expert in that sort of magic."

"We should ask Kuno."

Thankless bitch, he thought. *Yes, you ask Kuno. The bleeding heart will give me the benefit of the doubt. I did, after all, save your petulant lives from an angry mob and rescue Torra from a traitorous master mage.*

Thinking of Master Kuno, Darilos glanced over at the fat, white-robed mage, who stood away from the others, his back to them. Kuno had cast a *Counsel* spell and now had a glowing, ovoid window in the air in front of him, the edges flickering in a thin row of crackling electricity. Darilos couldn't see past Kuno, but he knew the portal would allow sight and sound to pass and that some Tower of Light high-level mage would be on the other side as Kuno gave a report.

Master Donovan stood across the hall from Kuno with a *Counsel* window of his own, giving his report to the Tower of Balance, toying with his long mustache as he did so. From his angle, Darilos saw the form of a person through the magical window. As he talked, Donovan leaned heavily against a wooden pillar. A trail of blood was crusted down the back of the mage's neck from a small head wound, left uncleaned.

Mistress Lolund was also in the process of casting her own *Counsel* spell over near the Crystal Throne, to give her report to the Tower of Darkness.

A metallic note twanged through the room. Master del Titccio, the mage with the long salt-and-pepper hair, had produced a lyre in some magical way that Darilos hadn't witnessed. But instead of being made of wood, it was composed of a silvery metal and was rather boxy looking instead of the typical roundness.

Master del Titccio sat on the corner of the table and struck the strings again. Using a little square pick of metal instead of his fingers, he produced different notes. The sound was of a sort Darilos had never heard before. Exotic and reverberating.

del Titccio smiled at Master Gral, sitting next to him on the bench. "The strings are of fine, twisted wire," del Titccio explained, without being asked. "I picked it up last time I visited the dwarven warrens of Sofon." Gral only responded with a grunt and rubbed at his back where he had been struck by a thrown object during the mob attack. del Titccio struck the lyre again, this time strumming across the strings, and the room came alive with a scale of closely spaced notes. The atmosphere in the room lightened, both figuratively and in reality, with the torches seeming to grow brighter.

He smiled again, settled the lyre against his shoulder, and played a peasant's ditty. As he played, colored orbs formed in the air around him. At first the lights were dim and fuzzy, moving slowly outward and orbiting him at head height, but then they came into focus. They coalesced, formed humanoid shapes about a foot high, and were soon blue men and green women dressed in finery and stepping to the beat as one, perfectly choreographed.

In a tenor voice, he sang:

I once kissed a maiden with hair so fair,
A blushing young girl with barely a care.
I took her hand and she proclaimed to me,
Johnae, my love, I give my heart to thee.

To thee, to thee, I give my heart to thee.
Stay here, my love, and give your life to me.

del Titccio smiled broadly as if he'd just told a witty joke, and Torra smiled, delighted by the performance. "Delight" was not a look Darilos was used to seeing on her. The emotion had so little of her energy compared to her despair or anger.

The glowing dancers paired up, dancing a ballroom dance, circling each other, hand in hand, as they continued to orbit

Master del Titccio. Torra clapped in joy and leaned against a pillar.

Master Gral just looked at the goateed mage in a blank way that suggested he only understood part of what was sung, but otherwise was fascinated. Preneval and Kai scowled at the singer with annoyance. And the others continued with their *Counsel* spells, ignoring him completely. del Titccio continued:

Kareen, my love, it is to war I go.
The lord of the realm doth proclaim it so.
My heart stays with you, but my sword will sing.
My life is not mine, for it is the king's.

The king's, the king's, for my life is the king's.
I'm away to war. My life is the king's.

"Aw!" Torra said, in mock sadness at the song's message, but then laughed and applauded. The dancers gave a bow then, as the song ended, they faded away.

del Titccio gave a little laugh. "I didn't hear you cast a spell!" Torra said. "Is the lyre enchanted?"

"The lyre is not enchanted," del Titccio replied. "Just as you can conjure spells with words or singing, like the harmonizers around the Heartstone at the Tower of light, so too can you by playing music. All you need is to activate the magic center in your mind. I know only a handful of musical spells. Such spell casters are called 'instrumancers,' though some just call them 'bard mages.' They are as rare as thaumaturges." He glanced over to Darilos, sitting across the room, then looked back to Torra. "Sadly, my instrumancer mentor died soon after starting to train me."

245

del Titccio gave a carefree shrug. He offered the lyre and pick to Gral. "Want to try?" Gral took only the pick, seeming to want del Titccio to continue holding the lyre, then scraped the pick upward along the strings. The instrument immediately issued a strong metallic screeching sound, filling the room with an ear-splitting discordance that caused everyone to stop and look over at them.

"Oh!" Torra exclaimed and covered her ears, but she giggled, too.

Gral immediately dropped the pick and stepped away from the table, leaving del Titccio sitting there and looking around in amused embarrassment. Darilos laughed aloud. He liked this mage.

Torra turned her attention to a servant who had brought in more wine and filled a goblet for her. With all others preoccupied, Darilos seized the moment and stepped out of the shadows to Torra. He picked up a goblet of wine for himself, though he had no interest in drinking it, and looked Torra in the eye.

"I heard what Mistress Kai said to you as we entered."

Torra's face soured as she played with a copper bracelet she was wearing.

Darilos continued, "I don't know why you let her talk to you like that. Just because she's your mentor doesn't mean you should be disrespected. And what did the others say when they overheard? Nothing?" He paused, and her eyes darted away. "As I thought." He pretended to take a drink, then set the mug down. "They don't understand. Coldhearted. Dry like a desiccated leaf. The death of a thousand innocent people is but an 'investigation' to them."

Torra glanced back to where Kai still stood with Preneval, then nodded her head. "She isn't known for caring."

"She's a lot like the Towers of Magic, isn't she?"

Torra raised an incredulous eyebrow. "I don't follow."

Darilos waved a hand. "Oh, I'm sure they talk about what to do with the Triumvirate. But what do they actually *do*? A host of resurrected elves attacked the Tower of Light. How did the Great Towers respond? Did the Towers raise an army and enter Peshilaree to eradicate the threat?" Torra shook her head. "No," Darilos continued. "Did the Council of Mages appeal to the Outer Gods for help against the Triumvirate?" Torra just looked away. "And what about the towermasters and high masters? Did they leave the safety of their top floors and seek out allies?"

Torra shook her head, her lips tightened. "Not that I know of."

"No," Darilos answered, his voice dropping to a conspiratorial whisper. "No, they didn't. You helped defeat the elves, and from what I hear, if it hadn't been for you courageously retrieving a book of magic and fighting the elves from Griffinback, the tower would have been lost!"

She nodded, looking down, but said, "The Gold Dragon saved them, not me."

"Don't be so humble! Accept the respect you are due! Respect that the towers didn't earn. Meanwhile, forces have gathered. Cults like the Brotherhood of Blood have come to power. The Emerald Dragon bargained. Plans were put into motion. The Triumvirate has unleashed natural disasters on the White Lands Federation, killing thousands. And that's just what we know about. What's going on in the rest of the world? And all the while, the Council of Mages *talked*, too uncaring about the deaths to take action. The Great Towers are impotent, reserving their power until too late. And who pays the price?"

Darilos saw Kai break off her conversation with Preneval, noticing Darilos with Torra, and step toward them.

Torra creased her brow. "Look, the elder members are consulting with the towers now. Let's see what they say. It'll be time for action, I'm certain."

"And if they don't take action, Torra?" He put his hand on her shoulder, squeezed, put his face closer to hers. "*We* aren't beholden to them. *We* aren't Expeditionary Mages." He pointedly looked down at the satchel with the Codex. "We know what the Brotherhood is after, and it will make them far more powerful if they get it. We, *you and I*, have the chance to *do* something. Let us go retrieve the Convergence before they do! Then we can use it against them. Our side will have the power, Torra …" He gently squeezed her shoulder again. "*I* care, and there won't be another tragedy like Caranamere."

"What's that about Caranamere?" Kai said, having stepped within earshot and peered at Darilos.

Darilos removed his hand from Torra's shoulder. "Do tower mages always interrupt private conversations, Kai, or just you?"

"He was just comforting me," Torra interjected.

Darilos smiled inwardly. *She lied for me.*

"He doesn't seem like the comforting type," Kai replied.

Darilos picked up his mug of wine again. "Well, it's a better effort than yours, *mentor*." He spat the last word. "What was it you said to her? Oh yes. 'We must not become attached.'" Seeing Kai's eyes narrow, he added, "And wasn't it you who said to Torra, 'It was a mistake to bring you here?'"

Kai growled. But before she could retort, the guards at the rear entrance uncrossed their spears and tapped the shafts on the flagstone floor. One announced, "Enter the lord's steward, Grendaen Com Harvinel!"

A slender, gray-haired man in a crisp red uniform entered with two servants and tapped the bronze butt of his staff against the floor. "We are looking for those named Torra and Osprey."

Torra took a step forward as Osprey concluded his prayer. "Yes?" she said.

"Lord Gaes commands that all native Taxins are to be given their own chamber for the night, for comfort."

Kai raised her hand. "No, Torra needs to … "

"I accept," Torra interrupted, and gathered her things, ignoring the glare from Mistress Kai. Mistress Lolund also raised an eyebrow and shook her head, but Torra ignored her, too.

Darilos nodded to Torra as Osprey stepped past, and the two went with the steward.

Kai crossed her arms. "What are you doing?" she asked.

"I'm sure I don't know what you mean, Kai."

She raised a finger at him. "Don't think I don't know what you're up to. You're cozying up with Torra, and I doubt you have good intentions. I don't know where you *really* come from, but we need to be working on the same side, here."

Darilos harrumphed. "There are many sides to this polygon, Kai. But one thing is clear: *your* side isn't *hers*."

"More than yours," Kai retorted, and returned to the other side of the hall.

CHAPTER TWENTY-SEVEN
Dodonor

General Feng Tong Lu had waited patiently for hours, arms crossed as tiny snowflakes dusted the ancient stone battlements of Dodonor Citadel in a thin shroud of white— the color of death. In the drab light of a gray dusk, the citadel had appeared like a monumental wall spanning the whole of a narrow pass, with naught but an imposing gate in its center. Impassable sheer cliffs stood to either side of the citadel and a treacherous drop-off fell behind Feng's "trade caravan." The timberline was far below and rocky crags all around them.

Men walked the top of the citadel. From reports he had heard, Feng knew that behind the south wall the citadel was composed of a center bailey between two square towers, then a matching wall and gate on the north side. He could see the towers looming over the walls to either side.

As he had hoped, their arrival at dusk had been anticipated by the guards. A dozen Taxin officers dressed in yellow and green uniforms waved their "trade" wagons through the raised portcullis and massive amberwood doors of the South Gate, beyond the murder holes, and into a secure bailey. The rectangular bailey had a closed gate in each wall. The North Gate would provide access to the other side of the pass and the Calnuria region of Taxia. The East and West gates would allow access into the two towers of the citadel.

The east and west sides of the bailey had thirty-foot walls with crossbowmen standing guard at the top while soldiers and trade inspectors proceeded to rob them of all of their rice wine as a "tax." The forward scouts had done their job, seeding rumors that the caravan carried such an alcoholic treasure. After the wine was taken, the trade inspectors told them they had to wait until morning to pass through the North Gate to the other side of the pass.

It was clear that Chiang'wu could barely contain his excitement as the Taxin guards took the rice wine casks, each of which had a sprig of Zinwo weed floating inside. The old herbalist became so anxious, hopping from foot to foot and wringing his hands, that Feng feared he would give them away. He sent the old man back to his horse to wait, instructing him to continue studying the old texts taken from the alchemist back in Totinol for any mention of demon dragons.

As the hours passed, Feng watched as, one by one, the soldiers standing guard thinned. Cups had been passed between them, and they nodded their heads and licked their lips in approval as they drank. But those who drank of it soon dozed, then, stumbling or leaning against the battlements or their spears, vomited, and finally fell unconscious, snowflakes covering them like a veil. Chiang'wu's Zinwo weed had done its job. Feng knew that those inside the citadel were likely already dead by the time the bailey guards had succumbed.

The time had come. When the remaining guards finally realized what had happened, raising an alarm as they tried to rouse their comrades, Feng uncrossed his arms and flicked his hand as if waving off a fly. Immediately, Commander Tonang barked commands to the Shadow Guard. Two score warriors, dressed in black, peeled away from the cover of the wagons, threw grapples and rope, and expertly scaled the bailey walls to the battlements. The guards barely had time to release half a dozen crossbow bolts before the Shadow Guard was upon them, silently slitting their throats and disappearing through the tower doors. One of the guards cried out an alarm before he died. Feng was pleased that no one replied from deeper within the citadel.

The plan had been laid out and communicated well to Feng's troops: after the Shadow Guard gained entry, they were to open the east and west bailey gates from the inside. From there, the rest of Feng's troops would fan out through the citadel in squads, cutting down anyone they found, but only using weapons from the other Taxin soldiers. Whenever possible, they were to pose the fallen soldiers as if they had cut each other down—even impaling each other. If one of their own should die, the body should be returned back to the wagons. No trace of Feng's troops would be permitted to remain, and there was to be no looting.

It was a daunting plan. The entire expedition rested on how this night would turn. They were almost certainly outnumbered three to one, and there would be civilians to deal with as well: servants, scribes, and families of high-ranking Taxin officers. But the Zinwo weed should even the odds. Dodonor Citadel had guarded the pass for more than four hundred years—since before the treaty that merged Aximia in the north and Totina in the south to form Taxia—and had never been conquered. But where most would see its thick granite walls as impenetrable, Feng saw a symbol of overconfidence and arrogance. Taxins were, at their core, barbarians, given to weaknesses of the body, uncouth in behavior, and poor of spirit. Just as he knew they would steal and drink the wine, he also knew those who didn't die from the poison would die on their knees, begging in dishonor for their uninspired lives, stinking of unwashed bodies, and as mindless as the bland slop they ate with their hands. Even his slaves were better than these dogs.

There was a brief clash of metal upon metal beyond the East Gate, and Tonang gave orders to defend the gate if needed. But when the gate opened, his Shadow Guard were standing there unopposed. Moments later, the West Gate opened as well. Two of the Guard were lightly wounded, but there were only dead bodies of Taxins beyond.

Feng's soldiers instantly split into squads and funneled into the towers.

He caught Tonang's eye and gestured for him to lead the charge into the East Tower. Tonang gave a nod and did as directed. Arrows were now being shot sporadically from the upper arrow slits and battlements, but so far no one had been hit, and most had already taken cover. The attack had simply taken the citadel by surprise, unaccustomed as they were to assault by anyone other than small squads of Khunti Lionriders from the hills.

Feng turned to his other commander, the elder Ming'ai, and gestured to him to take the West Tower. "Yes, General," the scarred old man said, then turned and limped through the bailey gate. Feng followed close on his heels. Tonang was a loyal slave and Feng knew he would follow instructions. Ming'ai on the other hand …

Feng and Ming'ai passed into the West Tower. The herbalist, Chiang'wu, caught up to them. The many small leather pouches crisscrossing his chest bobbed up and down with every step. "My lord! My lord!" the wispy-haired old man shouted. He matched step with Feng. "Are you pleased my lord? With the Zinwo weed?"

Feng gave a short nod. "You have pleased me, Chiang'wu."

The wily old man gave a little jig in his purple patterned robes. "Then just wait until I tell you the next news!"

Two Taxin guards in boiled leather sat against the wall at the entrance, slumped against one another, a dribble of vomit from the mouth of the one on the left. Their chests moved with shallow breaths, but their eyes were fixed.

Feng bent over them and drew a dagger from one man's belt. "Tell me," he said to the herbalist. He figured the fighting had died down enough that the old man's excitement shouldn't be too distracting. Feng stabbed the blade into the heart of the guard's comrade then placed the dagger into the guard's hand. Blood pumped from the wound, spilling out onto the guard's lap and floor. The victim gasped, then he went still.

Ming'ai turned away, but Chiang'wu emitted a little titter. "It is the demon, my lord. I have been studying the scrolls we took from the alchemist in Totinol."

While listening, Feng pulled a short sword from a scabbard of the other dying guard and plunged it through the heart of the first. The guard jolted and gave a grunt, but otherwise did not react, dying in moments.

But Feng's thoughts were on that alchemist, Shanti Tolec. He saw again, in his memory, the old Totinese alchemist strapped to a chair, a scroll placed before him, forcing him to read aloud. Much of his left arm had had the skin peeled away in torture until he had relented and informed Feng of the location of the Convergence at Pendoni. Though, according to the demon dragon, the alchemist had neglected to mention the necessity of the Key of Otemus. Or did he not know? There were hundreds of scrolls in his library made of vellum, bamboo strips, or crumbling paper. Chiang'wu had taken all he could carry.

Feng continued onward into the tower. From a spiral stairwell down a corridor, he heard a woman screaming "No!" in Taxin.

"I'm listening," Feng said to Chiang'wu. "Continue."

"My lord, the language is very arcane, an ancient dialect of Yonulhz, but from what I understand, it states that a demon dragon cannot be killed in this dimension. It must be banished to its own dimension first—a magic that is nearly impossible except to the Ancients, and considered 'renegade.'"

They entered a great hall where a crowd of soldiers were slumped in various postures over a long wooden table and the floor next to it, some still with mugs of poisoned wine in their clenched fists. Feng's troops had already gone to work posing them as if they had fought each other, stabbing the men with their neighbor's swords, running them through with each others' spears, and putting their comrades' hands around their throats as if they had died while grappling. By the time Feng and his entourage had passed, the floor was slick with fresh blood and the room looked like a battle had taken place between opposing factions.

Ming'ai had gone pale by the time they passed. Chiang'wu, on the other hand, hardly seemed to notice, rummaging through a leather bag and finally producing an old, stained scroll. Bits of degraded bamboo flicked off as he unwound it.

"See here, my lord! See?" He pointed to a line of characters near the top. "It is so faint as to be almost illegible." He held it up to a wall lantern, and read aloud:

And in the waxing gibbous of the second moon of spring, in the tenth year of the rule of the Mulberry Emperor, the demon appeared again. But his Magnificence was prepared, for the Wizard of the Court had readied a trap.

The group had arrived at the foot of the spiral staircase, but stopped as the body of a teen boy came tumbling down the steps, his head bashed in and bleeding, thumping with each step until hitting the bottom in a heap. He was followed closely by one of Feng's troops and a screaming woman in a blue velveteen dress holding a babe in her arms. "Michal!" the woman cried to the teen.

Chiang'wu merely glanced up, then continued reading:

> No man-made shackles could hold the beast, and magical spells it could counter with ease. But thusly natural ligatures were thrown upon it, made of the thinnest limbs of Jade Hawthorn made pliant by working with the hands, and wherein the long hard thorns were thrust inward to the beast's skin. So-Chai energies of the Jade Hawthorn held fast the beast until a suitable cage could be fashioned …

The soldier on the stairs grabbed the woman by her long hair and pulled her head back, exposing her throat. She made a guttural shriek as the soldier pulled out his gleaming dao dagger and moved to slit her throat.

"Stop!" Feng shouted. The soldier immediately pulled the dao away from the woman's throat and gave a quick bow, still holding the woman by her hair. She looked over to Feng with pleading eyes, holding the baby tight to her breast.

Feng stepped over to the soldier. "What do you think you are doing?" he demanded. Before the soldier could answer, Feng cut him off. "Sheath your dao!"

The soldier did as told.

Commander Ming'ai nodded. "You should be ashamed of yourself," he said to the soldier.

Feng reached down and pulled a dagger from the waist of a dead guard at the foot of the stairs and placed it in the soldier's hand. "Here! Your commands were simple! Use no weapons other than those of the troops stationed here! It must look as if they did this to themselves in a mutiny!"

The soldier nodded curtly, and before the woman could scream again, he cut deep across her throat with the dagger, spraying blood across the wall. She fell to the steps, gurgling, clawing at the baby at her breast as it began to wail. Ming'ai's eyes went wide.

"And the child, my lord?" asked the soldier.

Ming'ai flashed a dangerous glance at his master. Feng ignored him. "Bash it against the wall."

"Wait!" Ming'ai said, but the soldier had already grabbed the crying baby by the ankles and, in one quick motion, slammed its head against the granite wall next to the steps, silencing it with a sickening crunch and dropping the body to the straw-covered flagstones. The soldier stood there, staring at what he had done, his mouth quivering.

The child's mother reached out to her baby, but her arm dropped and her eyes lost their glimmer of life, frozen on the sight of her dead children as she died.

"My lord!" Ming'ai said, his eyes wide with alarm.

Feng grabbed the old man by the lapel and roughly shoved him against the wall next to the blood smears from the child. "Commander, you forget yourself," Feng said, his voice steady but stern. "You are weak. Use your mind and think about this! No one can be left alive to bear witness to our presence here. This must be made to look like a mutiny of guards! And though the baby cannot talk, she would be left here, alone, to die of starvation with the corpse of her mother. Do you really think me that *cruel?*"

Ming'ai shook, his face beet-red, his lips tight with rage.

"Your service is near its end, Commander." He let go of Ming'ai's lapel. "After we have tidied up, you will return southward with the servants and the wounded and await me across the border into Quisha at the ford of Shangto. It will be your last mission. Upon my return, you will retire and live out the rest of your life at your estate in Tang'a, and your nephews will serve me in the imperial court upon my ascension to the Jade Throne."

"You cannot hope to hide our involvement, General!" Ming'ai said. "You've put Quisha at risk of war!"

How dare he speak out of turn! Feng thought. He pulled his jian sword and swung it, hitting the wall and nicking Ming'ai's left arm. The miss had been purposeful. Feng grabbed Ming'ai's collar and pulled the commander close, until their faces almost touched. "Commander Ming'ai Sung, yours has been an honorable service," he said in a tone that barely repressed his anger. "We have fought side by side in many battles across this part of the world. It would be such a pity if I had to end your life here, in the bowels of a barbarian citadel."

Ming'ai still shook, face flushed, looking at the handful of soldiers around them. Feng glanced at them as well. None dared look Feng in the eye.

"Now get back to the wagons and attend to the wounded!" Feng said to the commander, letting go of his collar. "If any of our troops should die, make sure their bodies are heaved over the cliffs. We don't want them found! And throw over the wagons, too. They will only slow you down. There is no need to pose as a caravan anymore."

Eyes downcast, the old commander nodded and limped back the way they'd come.

A moment passed as the soldiers returned to their duties. Then Chiang'wu cleared his throat and continued on as if there'd been no interruption to his reading of the scroll.

"My lord, jade hawthorn grows in the mountains here. Ha! Yes! We passed it on the way up. We can harvest it from the hillsides and prepare it to make bonds, should the demon return! Is it your wish, my lord?"

Chiang'wu was hopping slightly, like a child awaiting a bao filled with sweet meats from his grandmother.

Feng gave a wry smile. "You have done well, my mystic. When we have finished here, you may collect your jade hawthorn limbs and begin preparations. I will assign two swordsmen to help you."

Feng sheathed his sword and was starting up the staircase, stepping over the body of the woman, when Tonang came running to the foot of the stairs, breathless. He was sweating profusely, and there was a cut across his exposed left shoulder, seeping blood. The blade that made the cut had hit the bronze slave torc on his neck. The torc likely saved his life.

"Is the East Tower secured, Commander?"

Tonang gave a quick bow. "Almost, master. There is a pocket of resistance on the top floor, barricaded in what appears to be the Citadel Commander's apartments."

"Then why have you bothered me here, Tonang?"

"Your Shadow Guard took the upper guard towers and gate along the east ridge, my lord. Upon doing so, they espied a contingent of Khunti Lionriders at the ridgetop, conspicuously gathered. We have not initiated contact, nor have they approached the citadel fortifications."

Feng flashed a satisfied grin and stepped back down the stairs. "They are early, but all is going as planned, Commander.

Our scouts have apparently made contact and the Khunti
have followed through with a parley. It is my fervent hope
that they will cooperate with my machinations, knowing that
I have taken the citadel for them." Tonang's eyes widened in
apparent realization of the broader scheme. "Lead me to them,
Commander, so that I may negotiate."

Tonang gave a curt bow, turned on his heels, and led the way
back through the bloodbath of the great hall.

"Yours is a masterful plan, my lord!" gushed Chiang'wu, who
was busy trying to put the scroll back into his bags. "No citadel
can stand in your way, nor even a demon!"

Feng gave no outward acknowledgment, but he had to admit
that the plan had gone very smoothly. The Triumvirate would be
pleased.

As Feng and the others entered the bailey, a Taxin guard fell,
screaming, from the high northern wall and slammed the ground
with a metallic clank, his bloody helm bouncing off his head and
rolling across the flagstones. He landed by the North Gate—the
gate that led into the Calnurian valley.

Feng knew that other Taxin troops would soon be coming
to that gate to rotate fresh patrols from the valley. They would
receive no answer to their hails. They would investigate, climb
the treacherous cliffs, and enter the high ridgeline gates, only to
discover their comrades dead from an apparent mutiny. They
would raise alarms, send scouts across the valley. And by the
time Feng and his new Khunti allies arrived at Pendoni via the
foothills, any Taxin patrols would be called back to the Citadel
by the emergency, clearing the way for him and his troops to
retrieve the Convergence and fade into the mountains and back
southward with his smaller party of troops.

He just hoped the demon, Azartial, lived up to his part of the bargain and delivered both the Key of Otemus and the woman who was supposed to turn the key with him.

Servants were busy preparing to escape southward the way they came. Ming'ai, leaning over a wounded Shadow Guard, looked up briefly, made eye contact with Feng, then quickly averted his eyes.

Yes, Feng thought. *Look away, Ming'ai. For your glory has faded. But my glory is soon to blossom.* He stepped over the bodies of more Taxin guards at the East Gate and looked up at an increasing snowfall and the dull shine of the moons through the blanket of clouds. *Praise be to the Triumvirate. Emperors to my emperor. Grant me the power to wrest the Convergence in your name!*

CHAPTER TWENTY-EIGHT
May All of Humanity Forgive Me

The lord's steward led Torra and Osprey from the great hall and along an adjoining corridor to a small bedchamber. It was small but comfortable: a narrow bed with a down mattress and a clean quilt, a small table with a basin of water, a bottle of wine and a pewter goblet to drink it, and a tallow lantern burning low. It wasn't much different from her chamber at the Tower of Light, though the room lacked a door and there was no trunk for her personal items. It was colder than the Great Hall, but not intolerably so due to a small fireplace in the hall outside, and it didn't smell so musty.

Osprey was led to a neighboring chamber which, at a glance, seemed identical to hers. A third chamber was empty. The rooms shared a common hallway, at the end of which was a door that was shut, near the back entrance to the Great Hall, and she suspected guards were posted there.

Torra sat on the bed, still stewing about what Kai had said to her after they reached the safety of the castle. Darilos was right. Kai and the other Expeditionary Mages were aloof to the impact of the catastrophe, the suffering of the people—*her* people—and likely wouldn't take action even if the Brotherhood of Blood were to kill everyone before their eyes. Kai's reaction to the killing of the priests was a good example.

Torra laid down as anger simmered within her. She had to have justice! She remembered her conversation with Darilos. *The elder members are consulting with the Towers now*, she had said to Darilos. *Let's see what they say. It'll be time for action, I'm certain.*

As her eyes started drooping, his reply echoed in her mind. *And if they don't take action, Torra?*

She awoke with a start, a sharp scream echoing in her chamber. She didn't remember falling asleep, nor had meant to. But she realized she'd had a dream. It was the same dream as the night before. Once again there was a massive explosion with her in the center of it. But there was something different. *I caused the explosion*, she thought. Then she caught a glimpse in her mind's eye of that dream, where she had opened that magical "door" at the back of her mind, as she had during the Battle of the Tower of Light, unleashing a deep energy that overwhelmed her and exploded outward, blasting the flaming ruins and … what? An enemy. She couldn't remember who.

Torra sat up, rubbed her sore eyes, and pulled the quilt around her shoulders against a chill that had invaded the room. The lantern still burned. There was a small, glass window high up on the wall, and it was still dark outside. Rain and wind lashed against the little pane.

"Torra, are you all right?" she heard Osprey call out from his room. "I heard you scream."

Had that been me, out loud? she wondered. "Yes. Fine. Thank you. Just a bad dream."

There was a pause, then he replied, "I understand."

In the quiet of the moment she heard Osprey begin praying, muttering so low that she had almost missed it. She crept to her door and looked around, and in the dimness of the hall she saw his shadow upon a wall of his chamber, bent over something, and heard him turn a page of what was surely the Writ of Okun. Frankly, she was surprised he could read, given that he was just a woodcutter. But then, in Caranamere the literacy rate was very high, even outside of the mages.

Torra opened her travel pack, removed the little jar of salve, and rubbed the cool lotion over her raw, chapped hands and arms. The salve was difficult to make, so she had to be sparing with it, but still there was the temptation to lather it on for full relief. With reluctance, she put the cork stopper back on the jar and put it away.

Then she pulled out some strips of salted meat and chewed on one of them, more to distract herself from the pain of her skin than to satisfy any hunger. Soon her attention turned to her mother's copper bracelet, which she'd found in the remains of her family's home. *Darilos was right*, she thought. *None of the mages really cared about my loss. And what would the Great Towers do about the destruction of Caranamere? They hadn't even taken action after the elves attacked the Tower of Light. Why would they take action now?*

She turned and looked at the leather satchel that Darilos had given her, then sat again on the bed and pulled out the Codex of Otemus. For many minutes she just stared at the cover, running her fingers over the uneven sheets and crumbling binding. The smell of it could only be described as dry and animalic. Then she noticed something odd and held the cover up to the lantern light. Her eyes couldn't quite see it, but her fingers felt a subtle, raised pattern. Soon, eyes closed, she felt it out. A symbol embossed on the cover. As she ran her fingers over it, she tried to see it in her mind's eye. It was a straight horizontal line with a flattened half oval stretched across it. Three rays seemed to come from under the line and upward through the half oval.

She wasn't certain of its meaning, but it seemed somehow familiar. She let it go for the moment and opened the Codex, cringing as the binding crackled and bits of the vellum cover flaked off.

The characters, blocky and faded, were ancient in origin, scrawled in an unpracticed hand. This was an extinct language, so old that it took Torra a moment to recognize it as an early form of the Anurin language, from thousands of years before. Even after she cast a *Decipher* spell upon the pages, it was difficult to make out the letters. Normally, she would see the letters rearrange themselves to modern Taxin script, but the spell had limited ability with such an old language, leading to some words shifting as she looked at them. Still, she was able to piece it together.

It began with only one sentence on the first page: "May all of Humanity forgive me."

The next page was colored slightly different, as if written at a different time and source of ink and vellum. She spotted here and there small dark splatters that quickly turned to powder and wafted away if touched. It gave her the impression of ancient, dried blood. And between them, script so rushed that she thought for certain it was written while on the move, though likely the same author:

Be I mad or be I sane, 'tis the Priests only who can know. On the Seventh Night of the Feast of Groland, mine Eyes beheld a glorious Portal. On fire it was, but of cold Flame. And through it was I drawn, for I had no Will of mine own. And beyond, giant by the eyes of Giants, seven mighty Figures made of Stars bade me come near, and I obeyed, for I was great with Fear.

And they spake unto me, *Behold, for thine Eyes shall burn ever more with our Visage, as the Gods to whom thou prayest do pray to Us.* And when I made attempt to close mine Eyes, the attempt was Folly. They shewed me a great and terrible Thing, and its name was Convergence. Unto me was shewn the making of It and the Power It wielded. A horrible Thing it was, and not natural. Not alive, yet not dead, for it lay across the boundary of Worlds. All of Irikara, and all of the Cosmos, was under its Command. And into the Future I was taken. With Horror I beheld the shaking of the Mountains. The draining of the Seas. Plains were planted with the Bones and Blood of mine People. Dragons bowed and paid it Homage. And I could not turn away.

In the margins next to the line where "Convergence" was mentioned, was the same signal that had been embossed on the cover, though it was poorly scrawled and in an ink that was weak and barely visible.

Torra shook her head. The poor, miserable fool. Deluded by a blind belief in gods to the point of tormenting his mind. She had half a thought to toss the book aside, but sleep was worse for its nightmares, so she continued.

And they spake unto me, *We commandeth thee, inscribeth wheresoever thy Feet should trod and thine Hands should touch, to say unto the first of the Key Keepers, the Brotherhood is made of thine own, Traitors, and at their Command is laid waste thine Home and Father …*

Torra sat upright. "Brotherhood" made of "Traitors?" The coincidence was surprising. Words so ancient could not possibly be about Caranamere and the Brotherhood of Blood. She continued reading.

… And to the second of the Key Keepers, thine Homeland shall again be commanded at the wave of thy Scepter, for thy Rule shall be terrible to behold. But I shook mine head, for I understood not what they told me, a simple Herdsman. Scribing was not of mine Way. *None shall believe me,* I said unto them.

Thou shalt be disbelieved, they said, *for the Prophesy we place upon thee is a Burden too hard to affirm. Fool they shall declare thee. It matters not, for the Key Keepers shall recognize in your Words their Predestination and conceive of our Wisdom. The first, a Woman oppressed with Affliction of the Skin, shall know the Ways of the Wizards of the White Stone. The second, a Man, shall be of the Land of Jade, deadly in the Art of War and imperial of Mind.* So I obeyed and thusly have writ their Word upon every Corner I have come and dutifully into this tome.

Torra scratched at her cracking hands, a symptom of her own "affliction of the skin." She was one of the "Wizards of the White Stone," if by that he meant the Heartstone of the Tower of Light. The coincidences were surreal. To think that somehow this madman's crazed testimony, written two thousand years ago, could be in any way related to her was ridiculous. She didn't believe in prophecy. The man from the "Land of Jade" sounded horrible. Perhaps from one of the Southern Lands? The bizarre nature of all of this intrigued her, fiction or not, so she poured herself some wine, turned the page, and kept reading.

CHAPTER TWENTY-NINE
Incantations

Darilos had lain upon a bench in the corner ever since Torra was called to her own chamber. It was long into the night, but no one could sleep, with the exception of Master Gral, who was huddled up in a corner.

Master Donovan and Mistress Lolund conversed quietly at the table, picking at the remnants of food. del Titccio had pulled out his metal lyre again and quietly played another song, the odd, resonating chords echoing through the Great Hall in melodies that tended more toward peasant music rather than the high culture that the man had apparently been bred from. Every time he played another ditty, the long-haired mage gave a wry smile at the uppity Master Preneval. del Titccio played while smoking one of his little cheroots. The smoke filled the hall with an exotic, cloying flavor, which annoyed the other mages as they wrinkled their noses and shot the mage bothered looks—which made Darilos chuckle.

Darilos looked up at the rafters. Master Donovan's guise cat lay there draped over one of the beams, its fur having turned a swirly oak color that blended into the smoke-stained wood. It watched Darilos with eyes that rarely blinked as if the little beast were spying on him from up there.

"Mages shouldn't have pets," Darilos said to the cat. "Just another liability to tie your master down."

The guise cat merely gave a slow blink in response.

Darilos had half a mind to teleport out of there. The magical energy he continuously had to exert to keep this human form taxed him to the point of mental fatigue. But he couldn't risk leaving. He needed to be there playing the role of "mage" in order to sway Torra.

Mistress Kai had spent the last hour in conversation with Master Preneval, who stood by her side with his black-robed back as stiff as a lance and his nose up in the air, occasionally muttering back at her and fat Master Kuno. The old mage, Kuno, shuffled back and forth, gesturing with his hands at times and seeming to make meek shrugs to counter Kai's angry gesticulations. Though they often whispered, Darilos caught enough of their conversation to know that much of it was about him—the usual, conspiratorial grumblings from Kai, and Kuno making excuses for the mysterious "thaumaturge." Darilos smiled. It was a fun game he played, but it wasn't going to last.

Finally, the three of them came to some sort of decision, turned, and stepped over to him. *Here we go*, he thought.

Kuno led the three, then stopped a few feet away with the other two standing behind him. Darilos didn't sit up or look their way.

Kuno cleared his throat. "Darilos, I just wanted to say, on behalf of all of us, how very thankful we are for the way you repelled the mob in the plaza."

Darilos half-turned his head and merely gave a brief nod and an "mmphf" in acknowledgment, before returning to his previous position.

The old man looked positively apologetic. He scratched at his side, then added, "It's just that there is something—how should I say?—*odd* about the way you went about it."

Kai groaned, clearly impatient but seeming to hold herself back.

"Oh?" Darilos finally answered.

"Yes, well," Master Kuno continued. "You see, we noticed you didn't actually give an incantation of any sort. You just spun around with your arms out."

"Even high masters must speak incantations," Preneval said in the smooth, precise tone he always had.

When Darilos didn't speak, Kuno continued. "You see, I've known a thaumaturge. Are you acquainted with Avos of Mikinos? He has his own school in Askrena. He used a rather lengthy incantation for any spell he—"

Darilos jumped to his feet. Kuno gasped and stumbled back into the other two, who in turn barely seemed to catch themselves.

The other mages turned to look at Darilos from around the room.

"Well!" Darilos said to Master Kuno in a sarcastic tone. "I guess you know all about thaumaturges, eh?" He looked Kai in the eyes. "But tell me this, Mistress. Is every incantation the same for the same spell, for every mage? Let's say for a *Light* spell."

Kai narrowed her eyes. "Of course not."

"Of course not," Darilos repeated. "Because it's not a language. The *sound* a mage utters is merely a side effect of activating the mage's magical center. It is usually similar between mages, but because every mage thinks slightly differently, there can be slight differences in the incantation." He turned an accusing gaze to Preneval. "And is the length of the incantation of a *Light* spell the same for a high master as for an apprentice?"

"They still must utter—"

"Just answer my question, Preneval. Is it the same length for both?"

"No, certainly not."

"Certainly not!" he mimicked again. "A high master has cast a *Light* spell so many times that there is a mental memory for the process of casting. She need only utter a single 'Word of Command' to cast it."

"What is your point, Darilos?" Kai sneered.

He ignored her animus and turned to Kuno instead. "In fact, Master Kuno, some mages are so advanced that the simplest spells, like *Light*, require merely a grunt. Correct?"

Kuno nodded. "Yes, there are a few, under certain circumstances."

Darilos shrugged. "According to our new woodcutter friend, even the Emerald Dragon, upon casting the renegade spell and empowered by the Triumvirate, barked only a single word to cast his spell!"

Kuno looked down, brow tensed in sudden thought.

"Then consider this, dear mages," Darilos continued. "As you well know, the powers of a thaumaturge are formidable. If I wished, I could level this building—nay, this entire castle—if I chose. The spell I cast in the plaza was a trifle, a barest *fraction* of my energies! Comparable, in fact, to that of a high master casting a *Light* spell."

Darilos sat back upon the bench and turned his attention to picking at a loose thread of his robes.

"So," Kuno said, "you say you uttered a grunt for that spell, then, and we just didn't hear you?"

"No, my large friend," Darilos said. "I uttered nothing at all, for the spell is so simplistic compared to my powers that it required no more thought than picking at a loose thread." He stopped picking at the thread and looked past Kuno into the eyes of Kai again. "Imagine what I could do if I *did* say an incantation."

"Is that a threat?" Kai said, pushing past Kuno, but Preneval put a hand on her shoulder.

"Not here," Preneval said.

Kuno stepped between them and turned to Kai. "I think we've heard an explanation, Kai. Let it go. We have a mission to perform here, and we must be united."

"*We* are united, Drokil," Kai said to him. "But *he* is not one of *us!*"

"No," Darilos said. "But I am un-homed by a terrible tragedy. I am a *victim* of an unthinkable crime. You are here to help me, are you not?" He laughed inwardly at that.

"Caranamere was not your 'home.'" Kai's face flushed with anger and she gritted her teeth, but both Kuno and Preneval pulled her away back to the tables.

Darilos chuckled as he watched Preneval and Kai continue to react. This was, indeed, a fun game!

But Kuno sat on a bench at the table, ignoring the others, then glanced up at Darilos for a moment. In that moment, his eyes were glazed in concentration. It was a look pregnant with *knowing.*

Yes, Darilos thought, *this one is beginning to suspect my true identity. This game will not last for much longer.*

CHAPTER THIRTY
Sologothu

Ingal had flown throughout the previous day, gaining altitude as he crossed the Dobrinon River. Below, the rolling hills were like a carpet of red and gold, decorated by the season. Across those hills, to the northeast, lay the border with Sofon. Turning northwest, he passed over the broad Axinom River valley with its fields, its merchant boats, and the all-important Bronze Trail trade route. How many wars had been fought to control that stretch of river, he could hardly count.

At last he had reached a height where he could relax and glide. Already the pain in his chest and back, from his brawl with Draq, had made every wingbeat a test of endurance. But rest had to wait.

As the sun rode low in the west and colored the clouds with shades of pink and lavender, Ingal skirted the border of Taxia and its northern neighbor, Scroen. Below, the "Horseman Plains" stretched far to the northeast, amber and fruitful. Finally, as the evening passed into darkness, he crossed the border into Ongo and its foothills, building ever higher to the snow-capped wall of the Meril Mountains peeking over the northwestern horizon.

Now as he flew, the Gold Dragon's mind had been on the events of the morning. The blasted crater of Caranamere and his horror at finding it that way. The smell of burning bodies. The interaction with the mages. The distrust shown by the local lords. But, most of all, his thoughts kept coming back to the encounter with Draq.

the egg of his next forebear, Jehai (the first of his name and namesake of the current generation) had rested in the corpse of Nothos before hatching. The corpse and egg had once lain where the wyvern skeleton was now.

But the cavern was only an entrance. Such an uninviting place was hardly a sanctuary where one could rest peacefully.

Ingal stepped toward the back and, placing a forepaw upon a particular stalactite, barked a *Word of Opening* spell while pushing the bulk of the stalactite sideways, too heavy for any human to move. Immediately, dwarven mechanisms rumbled within the mountain. The rock wall separated with a crack, scraped backwards, then slid sideways, revealing a wide, square opening into darkness. The mechanism was a gift from one of the Under Kings of Sarsa in return for great deeds Ingal's forbears had performed for his kingdom.

He dispelled the *Light* spell on the cavern, then cast it again in front of him. He closed the door behind him by placing a forefoot upon a panel in the floor, reengaging the mechanism in the mountain.

Ahead, a smooth tunnel opened into a huge, domed chamber, in the center of which rose a mound of soft earth. Along the walls were benches carved into the rock. Ancient tomes and scrolls were stacked on one. On another were rows of glassware, oil burners, and phials of colored liquid—an alchemy set and elixirs that would be the envy of any potionmaster.

It was to that bench that Ingal headed, then grabbed a large jar of green liquid, removed the lid, and drank the fluid. In moments the healing potion soothed much of the pain in his back and ribs as the tissues healed themselves. It wasn't enough to completely heal him, he knew, but would be close enough to tolerate any further pain. As the magic worked through him, his blood flow increased, spreading warmth across his body and pumping blood into his head. His mind buzzed as if drunk.

Turning around, he spied his arsenal on the opposite wall over the entrance. Hanging on a massive hook high up in the wall, a gargantuan morning star dangled. Its spiked head was five feet wide, attached to a chain that was thirty feet long, with a handle so large that only a dragon or an ice giant could wield it. Next to that hung an ovoid shield as tall as three grown men, a steel spike projecting from the center. Both were masterpieces of dwarven workmanship.

Ingal slumped onto the earthen mound. He would need his rest before … what? He shook his broad head. For a moment, he couldn't remember why he was there. And then he recalled. Yes, he had been in Taxia. Queen Irana. How lovely she had been. Her long, auburn hair. She had been standing there on the palace grounds with a gown of Quisha silk and the intoxicating scent of magnolia blossoms in the air. The Amber Dragon was rampaging, destroying towns in northern Taxia. Ingal had to stop him. And thus he needed the weapons here in Sologothu.

He sighed. He would need help. He needed to seek out Tellonta. Only the Iron Dragon could be strong enough to help against the Amber.

Ingal squeezed his eyes and reopened them. Something seemed off. Something told him the Iron Dragon was dead, and that he'd killed him. But that couldn't be! Tellonta was an ally, if anyone could be!

He tried to stand, more out of a confused need to move, perhaps to pace, but only stood there, his left leg and forefoot shaking. But as he tried to focus, reaching for the reason why the Iron Dragon was dead, he instead had flashes of memory invade his mind. Of the Tower of Light and a pitched battle between mages. Of a dimensional portal opening in front of him in the air, ripping reality apart and beings flying forth from it. Of a smoking crater where Caranamere had once thrived. Of an ancient statue of a dragon thrust up through the earth. And then a massive figure, filled with pops of light and a pair of burning eyes. Tendrils of energy shot from it and flung him through the air.

But how could this be? The visions didn't make sense. Was he dreaming?

He wiped a forefoot across his face and down to the travel vest he wore. A tiny lump in the pocket sparked some familiarity. He reached in and withdrew a pouch. Inside were three objects: a pyramidal icon, a red seed pod, and a shard of obsidian, all heavy with magical energy. Why did he have these?

And then the memory returned. Creeping across his thoughts, as slow as molasses. These were mage tokens from Expeditionary Mages.

Caranamere had been destroyed—by the Emerald Dragon, Mordan—and it was Ingal's job to hunt him down.

Irana was long dead, thousands of years ago. And Tellonta, ally though he was, had been convinced by the Triumvirate to take his own life to save the land of Sofon, and his next generation, Gogonith, had been the Triumvirate's champion. Ingal had killed him after a pitched fight.

Now, he might have to kill another dragon because of the Triumvirate.

Ingal shook his head. Ever since he cast the *Dimensional Rift* renegade spell at the Battle of the Tower of Light he had increasing problems remembering the difference between generations in his memory. But this was the first time he'd been confused so badly. Or maybe it was a combination of tiredness and the healing potion? Or perhaps from absorbing Draq's energy? All of the above? Whatever was happening to him, he couldn't let it continue. Much and more depended upon his clarity of mind.

He feared dementia. His last forebear, Rambanor, had nearly lost his mind at the end of his life, grown so old. Could the same be happening to him?

The Amber Dragon had once gone insane, claiming he'd found "hidden knowledge" after casting a renegade spell. In the end, Ingal and Tellonta had to kill him to keep him from destroying innocent people—entire towns—in the Amber's attempt to resolve his inner demons. Could it be that he had glimpsed the Triumvirate? Had he lain in a sanctuary of his own, fighting erroneous memories, lost in his own past, as well? The next generation of Amber Dragon had disappeared a couple thousand years ago, with only occasional rumors that he had taken a guise as a human and wandered the lands as a monk. True or not, Ingal could use his wisdom now.

Ingal placed the mage tokens back in their bag and put the bag snugly back in its pocket. Soon enough, he'd be at Mordan's lair and confronting him about the destruction of Caranamere and his pact with the Triumvirate. Could he take on the dragon alone? With the tokens, Ingal could call those three mages to him to help. He wasn't sure that would be enough. Mordan was physically stronger than most any other dragon, much more than the Iron Dragon had been, though normally weak in magic. Under normal circumstances, the balance between the Emerald and Gold dragons would be about equal. But if the Triumvirate had given Mordan the ability to cast renegade spells, then the balance was now firmly on the Emerald Dragon's side.

"Rest, you old fool," Ingal said out loud. His words echoed off the domed chamber, and suddenly he felt very alone. With a word he extinguished the light and curled upon the earthen mound.

Sleep eluded him for some time. All he could see, upon shutting his eyes, were Draq's burning white eyes peering deep into him.

CHAPTER THIRTY-ONE
Rude Awakening

A sharp rap echoed though Torra's chamber, waking her with a start. A gasp caught in her throat as she realized a guard stood in her doorway, the butt of his spear having hit the flagstone floor to wake her. She took a shaky breath, straightened her tangled hair, and blinked, bleary-eyed, realizing she had fallen asleep sitting up in bed with her back against the wall, the Codex open in her lap.

"You are summoned back to the Great Hall," the guard proclaimed, looking down at the Codex in her lap and then back to her eyes. He stood in rigid attention, his hazel eyes narrowed behind his nasal helm as if suspicious of her activities.

Torra nodded. It was raining again, after having lulled during the night. Storm clouds would have blocked any morning light, but judging by her own weariness, she figured dawn must have only just broken.

She quickly readied herself, carefully placing the Codex back into the satchel and smoothing out her wrinkled robes. Long after the lamp died, Torra had stayed awake reading by way of a *Light* spell cast upon the palm of her left hand, even though doing it for so long taxed her magical energies.

She read the Codex cover-to-cover twice during the night. Otemus had been insane, yes, even paranoid, raving about how the world was out to get him, living a destitute life, and scrambling to achieve the goals that were demanded of him in his one supposed encounter with the "Gods of the Gods," as he'd referred to them. Yet, as he wrote in the Codex, he was driven to succeed in a way that no others could, haunted both day and night by the encounter as it played over and over in his mind, any time he closed his eyes. It was all he dreamed. It was all he could imagine. It drowned out nearly all other conscious thought. The Convergence was his world for decades until, at last, in the final scrawled pages, he stated that he had completed his great work of enshrining the Convergence in a cave in Pendoni, and then his visions had at last ended. Once again, as he had begun the book, he ended with "May all of Humanity forgive me." What became of him after that point, the Codex didn't say.

Pendoni, she thought. Darilos had mentioned that place when he first gave her the Codex, after the duel with … She blocked the fight out of her head. Had to focus! She had been on a learning excursion to the south, to find out more information about the elemental magic used by the hill people, the Dorsori. She had been at the ancient step pyramid known as Degrin Torkis, with two other mages, when local Dorsori tribesmen told her there was a place where their elemental magic did not work, nor any other magic. A place called Pendoni. A cult of blind nuns lived there. The Dorsori avoided the place, called it cursed. Though she and her companion mages did not go there, they discovered that every mile toward that direction reduced their magical ability. So powerful was this void, that even several days away they could feel its influence.

What better place to hide a magical artifact? she thought.

The guard stepped away as Torra collected her things, then reappeared in the doorway with Osprey by his side. Osprey looked like Torra felt, with bags under his reddened eyes. She knew from his constant prayers and muttering throughout the night that he hadn't slept any more than she had. He clutched the Writ of Okun under one arm and held his axe like a walking stick in the other. They didn't exchange greetings; rather, the look they shared with each other was enough to know how the night had gone.

"I'm coming," she said to the guard and stepped out of the chamber.

Nowhere in the entire Codex did Otemus actually physically describe the Convergence. It was a weapon—that much was clear—the most powerful the world would ever see, according to him. But what form did it take? Was it large or small? Made of metal, stone, or wood? A sword? A spear? Or was it a scroll or magic tome? Otemus was purposely evasive. All he had written about it was that it was the product of both "the terrestrial" and "the celestial" and that, after much hardship, he had placed it in a cave in Pendoni guarded over by the "blind sisters" and accessible only by use of a "Key" held by two specific people: one who had been "touched by the Gods of the Cosmos, yet fighteth against them," and one who had been "touched by the Three Gods of Origins, yet fighteth against them." He had been tasked with spreading the word and placing this Convergence in a safe location until it was "time," but it was his own touch to make the key, with the help of mages he had convinced, and enchant it with a spell that required the two special people who were least likely to cooperate with each other. It was his way of rebelling against the "Gods of the Gods" to try to prevent the apocalyptic war he had seen in his vision. The Convergence was hidden away and protected by a magical door.

Despite Otemus's ramblings and unstable mind, Torra believed the Convergence was real. Otemus, at least, had believed it enough to spend more than half of his life devoted to it.

She wished she could consult with Ingal right now, wherever he was. The wise old dragon would know what to do with this information.

As Torra and Osprey reached the back door to the Great Hall with their escort, passing by a pair of guards, she thought, *If Darilos is right, and the Brotherhood of Blood searches for the Convergence, then we must do everything in our power to stop them. Caranamere would be only the first town to be destroyed.*

CHAPTER THIRTY-TWO
Audience

At last there was activity. Darilos had pretended to sleep all night, interminably bored, until only about an hour before when there was a change of guards. As they came through the front doors from outside, Darilos estimated it was just after daybreak, though thick rain clouds gave little indication of the sun. It was raining heavily outside again, after a lull during the night, drumming against the roof and dripping down through leaks.

Servants brought in pots of venison broth, loaves of bread, and mead, along with basins of warm water and hand towels. Several of the mages were already awake, though Master Kuno was still snoring loudly until, at last, additional guards entered and announced that Lord Gaes would soon be attending.

Darilos perked up. It was always hard to be precise about timing, but when he last consulted the Nexus, it had predicted an explosive moment around this day. He needed to get Torra away from the danger that was to come.

Darilos blinked in confusion. For a moment, he was unsure where the confusion came from, but then he realized: he cared for Torra's safety. It wasn't just to get her to Pendoni and serve his purposes. He shook his head, unaccustomed to such empathy—a weakness, unbecoming of an immortal being. So fleeting was a human's life, it was hardly a trifle. And yet …

When he had come to Torra's rescue and killed the Brother attacking her, and then found her unharmed, he realized that he'd felt something for her. It was a sense of satisfaction more profound than when he'd received the Key of Otemus from the Brothers or when he recovered the Codex from Hozor. The look on her face—a mix of relief and thankfulness, and perhaps a sense of awe—it had meant something that still gave him a sense of warmth. He'd been so wrapped up in trying to give her the Codex, and concerned about the mages coming back, that he'd hardly given these odd emotions a moment's consideration.

So preoccupied was he with the thought that he barely noticed when Torra came through the back entrance, followed closely by the woodsman, Osprey. Seeing her changed his focus and shook him out of the strange sentiment. Both Torra and Osprey looked haggard, as if they'd hardly slept.

Mistress Kai eyed Torra coolly. "Did you enjoy your bedchamber?" she asked, a sarcastic tinge to her words.

Torra ignored her and stepped over to Darilos.

"Well?" he said when she was near. "Did you read it?"

She nodded and rubbed at the raw skin of her hands. "I see what you mean. If this 'Convergence' is real, then we must retrieve it before the Brotherhood does—assuming, of course, that they have this 'key' and the two people necessary to use it."

"Then you will go with me to Pendoni? We haven't a moment to lose. Let's leave right now."

"No. I still have a job to do."

Darilos huffed and rolled his eyes. Torra continued, "The other mages *must* come with us. They must be part of this. And we'll need their help if the Brotherhood shows up."

"We don't need them," he said, looking past her. Kai was watching them. He lowered his voice. "You don't know the extent of my power—or yours."

Torra tilted her head and puzzled over that statement, but then said, "Let them have their audience with Lord Gaes, then they will come with us, or I will without them. All right?"

This is pointless, he thought. It took a force of will not to simply teleport them both out of there without further ado, but he answered, "Fine." He couldn't lose her support now that he'd finally attained it.

"You seem to forget," she said. "*We* need the key and those two special people, too."

"I've got that taken care of. I just need you there."

"Why?" she asked. But there was a flicker in her eyes, and he knew she understood, even if she didn't want to admit it. He chose not to answer, but rather just to tilt his head a bit and hold her gaze, as he'd seen some humans do when something seemed obvious. She glanced away.

"Why do you smell of sulfur?" he asked instead.

She looked down and hid her rash, then raised her head and looked him in the eyes, whispering, "It's called 'brimstone disease.' It flares up in times of stress."

"I like the smell," he answered. She blushed, then looked away. "No, really," he answered, "Truly."

"Well ..." She didn't seem convinced. "Most people don't."

"You mean, like *her?*"

Torra turned and found herself face to face with Mistress Kai, who had been edging toward them.

"What are you whispering about?" Kai demanded.

"There is something I urgently need to tell you," Torra said, putting a hand on the satchel. "We need to go to a place called Pendoni. There's an artifact ..."

Darilos frowned. *Must she tell Kai?* But Torra's words were drowned out as guards at the door pounded the shafts of their spears on the flagstone floor and announced, "Enter the lord's steward, Grendaen Com Harvinel!"

In walked the gray-haired steward with the red uniform. In his left hand he held a ceremonial staff covered in golden filigree and topped with a cluster of clear quartz crystal points. Walking next to him was a valet with a small, red pillow upon which sat a palm-sized orb decorated with green jade on one side and rosewood on the other, representing the north and south of Taxia, the two hemispheres separated by a line of gold — a symbol of ascendancy bestowed upon Lord Gaes by the King of Taxia, Halis III.

The steward stood at attention, banged the butt of the staff on the floor, and announced, "All rise and recognize the Lord Gaes, King's Regent of Gaes Province and all of its riches and peoples, and enter the noble family with the lord chamberlain, Timbrook Taegus!"

Six knights entered, armored in ceremonial plate mail inlaid with crystal and tourmaline, and carrying swords and maces, joining the half dozen guards already in the room. They lined both sides of the hall, corralling the mages toward the center as Taegus took up a position off the right-hand side of the Crystal Throne. The chamberlain wore a rainbow surcoat over his ringed chain mail.

Next, the lord's offspring, Elbin and Sassala, entered and took up positions on either side just behind the throne. Each now wore a thin golden circlet upon their heads with a cut tourmaline on the front. Sassala looked every bit as tough as she had the day before, now wearing a studded leather jerkin. Elbin, though, glanced around, fiddled with the pommel of his sword and then adjusted his gem-encrusted breastplate. He threw a wary glance to the stern chamberlain at his side.

Lastly, the Lord Gaes doddered in, leaning heavily on the arm of a teenaged valet—likely some grand-nephew, if Darilos had to guess. Gaes was nearly bald beneath his tourmaline-studded, golden coronal crown, liver spots showing through the thin hair that remained. He was richly dressed in a robe of green velvet over a red tunic and a cloth-of-gold girdle with rubies, which hung loosely from his thin frame. Lord Gaes hobbled slowly to the throne, breathing heavily. His watery eyes gazed over the mages without seeming to see them, his lower eyelids drooping away from his eyes to show red flesh beneath.

From what Darilos had been told by his contacts in the Brotherhood, Lord Gaes had been predicted to die of ill health for decades. His son, Elbin, was expected to take the reins of leadership. They'd whispered that his sister, Sassala, longed for the crown herself, though she was the younger sibling, and women rulers were unusual in the culture.

As the valet lowered the lord onto his throne, a woman of around fifty years of age gracefully stepped just inside the door. She wore a silver circlet, green velvet robes and cloth-of-silver girdle and was attended by two ladies in waiting. This was the lord's wife, the Lady Gaes. Darilos's sources had told him that she was often the one brokering deals with the Astronomer's Guild, behind the scenes, for enchanted items. Darilos had heard that she was Lord Gaes's second wife, as the first was banished to a convent near Dosor Keep, far in the north of Taxia, for not bearing him children, and made a nun. It was because of the large age discrepancy that Elbin and Sassala were young enough to be mistaken as Lord Gaes's grandchildren. *It's surprising he'd been able to father them at all*, he thought.

Once the lord lowered himself onto the throne, the valet handed him the orb, which Lord Gaes held upright in his right hand.

Master Kuno approached the throne with a rod of translation in his hand, then gave an elaborate bow to Lord Gaes. "We, the Expeditionary Mages, representing the Great Towers of Magic, give our thanks to you, Lord Gaes, for your hospitality, and humbly beseech you for your help in our investigation of the destruction of Caranamere."

Lord Gaes squinted down at Kuno then grimaced. "You are not from the Astronomer's Guild. I was told there was a survivor." Though he had the gravelly voice of an elderly man, he spoke strongly and smoothly.

"There are survivors from Caranamere among us, my lord," Kuno explained, gesturing to Osprey. "A woodsman. Not a mage." Kuno glanced toward Master Preneval and Mistress Lolund. "But mages did survive, as we have discovered. One was a visitor to the Astronomer's Guild. And as for the others, they attacked …"

Taegus interrupted, "My lord, these are the only mages we found."

Kuno cleared his throat. "Yes, but as I was explaining, there are traitors…."

"There is no proof of traitors," Elbin exclaimed. "Allegations, based on a woman who was attacked by villagers."

"Not villagers!" Torra shouted.

"There weren't villagers?" Elbin said. "So you lied about that?"

Torra shook her head. "No! I meant in *addition* to villagers!"

Mistress Kai put a hand on Torra's shoulder. "Careful," Darilos heard her whisper.

Torra glanced over at Darilos, and in that glance was confirmation. His warning that Taegus was involved with the conspiracy had finally taken root.

Lord Gaes shook his head, seemingly overwhelmed by the outbursts. "A town destroyed! Dragons attack my realm. My townspeople in riot. A cult has supplanted our traditional gods. And now you, strange mages, show up at my threshold. Explain yourselves!"

Kuno gave a nod. "We realize this is a very shocking time for you and your brave people, Lord Gaes. Dark times have come to your lands."

Taegus bent down and spoke into Lord Gaes's ear, but he was too quiet even for Darilos to hear. Lord Gaes reacted by tilting his head. Sassala, seeming to overhear what was said, suddenly stiffened and shot an angry look toward the chamberlain.

Kuno continued. "We seek answers as you do, my lord, for the enemy of your people is the enemy of the Great Towers."

Lord Gaes narrowed his eyes. "Perhaps, as the rumors suggest, you are in league with the dragon who performed this unspeakable act?"

Torra's eyes widened as she and the other mages reacted to the accusation, a combined gasp issuing from their lips. *This is getting good*, Darilos thought. He watched the guards carefully. Things were likely to get heated very quickly now.

"No, my lord," Kuno said, arms wide in a gesture of supplication. "We would never … "

"Do you deny meeting with the Gold Dragon en route to Gaes?" Taegus asked.

Kuno was about to answer when Torra shouted, "The Gold Dragon had nothing to do with the destruction of our people!" She stepped forward, shrugging off Kai's hand. "My lord, you are truly my liege, for it is in your lands I grew and prospered. I would never betray you or my people!"

"Who is this?" Lord Gaes said, squinting.

"Torra Com Gidel, my lord," she answered for herself, "and I was Third Astronomer of the Astronomer's Guild prior to joining the Tower of Light."

Kai frowned and moved to grab Torra again, but Master Donovan stopped her. The Mistress scowled at him but didn't interfere.

Torra continued, "I saw the bones of my family, scorched among the ruins of my childhood home. I climbed the rubble of the Guild and stumbled, heartbroken, through the smoldering foundations of what had been my thriving town." She balled her fists. "I vow *revenge*, my lord! The suggestion that I and my fellow mages assembled before you had some role in this tragedy offends me, sire!"

Taegus pulled his sword as Torra approached. The two closest knights took defensive positions next to the throne and the lord's children. Darilos saw the other mages stiffen, no doubt activating their magic centers.

With his valet's help, Lord Gaes placed the royal orb in a concavity on the throne's arm, stood on shaking legs, and stepped to Torra. She responded by lowering her head in submission and kneeling.

Lord Gaes placed a hand on Torra's head. "My loyal subject, I know your name. And I doubt you no more. Your fealty is plain to see." He took his hand off and looked to Kuno. "I will aide you in your investigation, for there is information that we possess."

"My lord," Taegus said. "If I may lay some groundwork before we discuss." Though he spoke to Lord Gaes, his eyes shifted to look at the lord's son, Elbin.

Darilos took a step forward. *Yes, here it is!*

Lord Gaes sighed heavily. "Go ahead, Chamberlain."

Taegus gave a stiff nod and looked over at the elder mage. "Master Kuno, you are senior and speaker for your Expeditionary Mages, correct?"

"Yes," the portly mage replied.

"As I understand, it is your mission to investigate only, and not to meddle in the affairs of our Lord's dominion. Correct?"

Kuno raised an eyebrow. "This is correct. We seek answers, and have many questions for your lord. We wish to know—"

"And if you were to interfere in the business of the Lord Gaes, or seek to undermine his authority, then it would be a breach of diplomacy between Taxia and your Great Towers, or even an act of *war*. Remember, he who sits on the Crystal Throne speaks on behalf of the King of Taxia. Do you understand?"

Yes, Darilos thought, his eyes moving to Torra as she stood again. *Taegus asserts his power. Watch as the Towers stand by and do nothing.*

He heard Mistress Lolund mutter to Master del Titccio, "What is he going on about? What is he planning?"

Kuno tightened his brow. "I am confused, Chamberlain. Are you suggesting we are interfering in state business?"

Lord Gaes shifted to look back at Taegus with rheumy eyes. "Let me be concerned with that, my chamberlain."

Taegus nodded to Elbin, who nodded back.

"It is no longer your concern," the chamberlain said.

Then he thrust his sword up through the lord's torso.

The blade slipped through Gaes's body and the tip emerged, dripping with blood, through the red tunic of his chest. The elder's mouth and eyes opened wide in a soundless display of pain, then he dropped to the ground.

Darilos gasped in surprise. *The audacity!* he thought. The room erupted as everyone reacted. Shouts, defensive spells, swords pulled. Lady Gaes and her handmaidens screamed.

Torra stepped back, wide-eyed. The other mages chanted and activated a *Shield* spell around their party.

Sassala screamed, "Father! No!" Her arms were seized by the two knights by the throne, who had surely been ready for this moment.

The Lady Gaes screamed, high and loud, and dropped to her knees, hands covering her face.

Darilos turned to the chamberlain. Timbrook Taegus stood rigid on the dais, sword extracted and running red, scanning the mages for their reactions. Looking into his pale eyes, Darilos knew the plan had been to do this all along.

Face red, eyes burning with anger, Torra started to chant a *Lightning* spell.

"No!" Kai said, and shook Torra to make her stop.

Torra shoved Kai away, then turned to start casting again. But once more Kai stopped her, grabbing her arm. "*No*, apprentice! We cannot interfere. You would implicate the Tower of Light in this!"

Darilos wanted to laugh. Kai only emphasized how impotent the Towers were, echoing what he'd said to Torra.

Torra yanked her arm out of Kai's grasp and turned to Kuno. "We have to *do* something!"

Kuno, who was helping with the *Shield* spell, merely looked away.

A tight smile spread across the chamberlain's thin face. He turned to Darilos, the only member of the party not inside the *Shield* spell. Darilos, still calm, returned the smile. Taegus's faded.

Sassala struggled against the grip of the knights. Her sword had been taken away. "No!" she screamed again, her face bright red. "Taegus! How could you?"

With a shriek of anger, Sassala pulled an arm free. In one quick movement, she pulled a dagger from her boot and slammed it through a gap in the armor of the knight to her left. As that knight cried out, the other, still holding Sassala's other arm, smacked an armored arm into her face. She was knocked to the ground, dazed, blood streaming from her nose. The knights dragged her out of the room.

Elbin kept his back to his sister as he stared at his father's corpse and the pool of blood around it.

The teenaged valet rushed forward from the throne and punched Elbin in the side of his head, staggering the lordling. At Taegus's command, two guards grabbed the valet by the arms and dragged him out of the back of the Great Hall as well.

Elbin didn't even look back at him.

"This is an outrage!" Master del Titccio said.

Master Kuno nodded. "It is a coup."

"It's also patricide, as the lordling is part of it," Master Donovan added, the guise cat now at his feet. "No deed is more reprehensible!" His sword blade was glowing a dim blue.

"Truth!" Osprey shouted, his left hand around the amulet at his chest. "By Okun, it is one of the greatest of sins!"

Mistress Lolund stepped forward, her black robes fluttering. "Taegus, Elbin, explain yourselves! You could have done this at any time, yet you waited until we were here. Why?"

Darilos groaned. "Isn't it obvious, Lolund? They're putting on a show of power. A *puppet* show." Darilos turned his attention again to Taegus. "When are you going to reveal who the real puppetmasters are, Chamberlain?"

Taegus raised an eyebrow at Darilos without answering. He slowly turned, knelt, and took the crown off of Lord Gaes. Blood had pooled around the dead elder and dripped off the edge of the dais.

"My dear mages," Taegus said, standing again. "It is time for a change." He reached up and replaced Elbin's golden circlet with the Lord's tourmaline-studded crown. "All hail the Lord Gaes, King's Regent of Gaes Province and all of its riches and peoples!"

"Hail! Hail!" shouted the knights and guards, in unison.

"No!" Torra shouted. Kai was now fully restraining her, hands on Torra's forearms from behind. "Taegus! Your treachery will never be forgotten!"

The chamberlain ignored her and instead knelt toward Elbin. The young man's eyes shifted toward the door. His mother and her ladies had fled. Lifting his chin, Elbin turned, picked up the jade-and-rosewood orb, and took his seat on the Crystal Throne as lord of the realm.

CHAPTER THIRTY-THREE
Coup

Torra yanked her arms free from Kai's grip, then turned to Kuno, imploring "Do something!"

Master Preneval answered instead, his voice as steady as ever. "As the chamberlain pointed out, the Great Towers cannot interfere in matters of state, no matter how treacherous or violent, and we are the Towers' representatives."

Torra growled and looked over to Darilos. "You were right!" she shouted. "What did you say? The Towers are impotent, too uncaring of the deaths of innocents to take action?"

"Verily!" Darilos said, then looked at Kai and the mages around her. "They don't give a damn about your people, or even the bloody coup taking place before their eyes!"

The mages exchanged frustrated looks, but said nothing, save for Master Donovan. "We need to leave. *Now!*"

Taegus laughed then turned to the new Lord Gaes. "My lord, what is your first proclamation?"

Elbin appeared to snap out of his thoughts. "Yes," he gasped. "My proclamation." He gripped the orb tightly in his right palm. Then, as if reciting a prepared statement, he said, "Assassination of a sitting lord or nobility is a death sentence. Of this, I pronounce you guilty, Timbrook Taegus. But extenuating circumstances apply. I hereby pardon you of your crime."

Still wearing his leering smile, Taegus gave a bow. "I thank you humbly, my lord. I serve only the best interest of your realm."

"This is sick!" Torra spat.

"Yours is bold move," Master Gral said to Taegus, his words still crudely translated by his rod of translation. He held his massive hanat knife in his other hand. "Strongest mages of Irikara in room with you. We could strike you down!"

"You are *not* the strongest mages here, actually!" Taegus said, and motioned with his hand. At the command, guards opened the main doors to the great hall. It was raining heavily outside. Chanting figures moved in the downpour.

Torra felt a massive surge in the magical energy of the room, and it wasn't coming from her colleagues. It was a deep, thrumming energy—the same as at Caranamere. The other mages reacted as well. Still with the *Shield* spell raised, the rest of them turned as one—and saw hooded figures step into the room.

"The Brotherhood!" Lolund exclaimed.

Taegus gave the new lord another pointed look.

Glancing down to his murdered father, Elbin pronounced, "I hereby proclaim that worship of the Triumvirate is now the one, true religion of the realm of Gaes, and that I am their representative. All other religions are heresy punishable by whatever means necessary to impel conversion. I recognize the Brotherhood of Blood as the Triumvirate's priests, to be accorded full rights as clerics of the people."

"Heretic!" Osprey shouted. "How can you deny the providence of your gods? The religious heritage of our people!"

"The world is changing," Taegus said. "And it is now illegal for you, woodsman, to practice your religion here—unless you convert."

"Never!"

"Then you must be arrested."

"Osprey is under our protection as a witness and I grant him asylum," Kuno said. "We may not be able to fight you, but we can fight the Brotherhood!"

"Not if they are guests of the lord Gaes, as *you* are, and citizens of my realm," Elbin said. He stood, still holding the Orb of Rulership. "Welcome, Brothers."

A dozen Brothers filed in, six to each side of the room, and walked along the walls behind the guards. Their hoods were up, arms extended, hands glowing with a red energy. Beneath the glow, their palms dripped with fresh blood.

Torra gritted her teeth.

del Titccio took out a phial of blue liquid, uncorked it, and drank the entire draught. His hands glowed with a blue energy that slowly coalesced in a sphere between his palms, rolling with plasma, ready to throw as ball lightning.

"They have already attacked one of us," Master Donovan countered. "Guests or not, we are in our rights to defend ourselves."

"If answers you seek," Taegus said, "then you should ask those you are investigating, instead of attacking them. No?"

Kuno scowled. Then, to the Brothers, he asked, "Who amongst you speaks for your cult?"

"Ours is the oldest religion in the world, Kuno," said a Brother closest to the throne. "That hardly constitutes a *cult*."

His voice was very familiar to Torra. And then she placed it, eyes growing wide with realization. *It can't be!*

He continued, "I am Apostle Agnon, high priest of the Brotherhood of Blood." He lowered his hood, revealing a shaved head with stark, green eyes and an ashy, pockmarked face.

Torra drew in a ragged gasp. "First Astronomer Colnos Com Dimb!"

"I no longer go by that name, Torra," he said, flatly, "for I am reborn in the image of the Triumvirate. So it is for all of my disciples and our new initiates. You could be reborn, too."

The other Brothers lowered their hoods as well, each revealing bald pates. The full extent of their treachery hit home when Torra realized that the five disciples were all masters from the Astronomer's Guild. The other six, the 'initiates,' were townspeople she recognized. Then she saw the last one …

It was Taenos. Their eyes met. For a brief moment, Torra felt the old pang. But then her rage took over.

"Traitors!" she screamed. "How could you! Our people! You killed them! You killed them *all!* Taenos, how could you be with them?"

Taenos looked down and convulsed, holding his stomach as if about to retch. But she didn't care what his feelings were.

"Why did you do it?" Kuno asked Agnon. "You were the leader of the Astronomer's Guild! What could possibly drive you to commit genocide against your own people?"

"It was not our intention for the Emerald Dragon to destroy the entire town," Agnon replied, tensing his brow. Agnon pointedly gazed past Torra as he said this—toward Darilos. "But sacrifices have to be made." He opened his arms wide, the red energy surging over his hands and forearms. "*We* are now the predominant power in this region. Soon the entire world. Go to your Towers with that message. The destruction of Caranamere was but a taste of the Triumvirate's power. Because Gaes bent its knee to the Triumvirate, they will be spared further destruction when the world ignites in righteous fire."

"There is nothing 'righteous' about killing innocents!" del Titccio exclaimed, his hands still enveloped in balls of plasma, ready to strike.

"No one is innocent," said one of the disciples to the left of Agnon.

Osprey raised his axe. "Speak for yourself, murderer!"

"Sacrifices must be made," Agnon said, lowering his eyes with a sympathetic look. "I mourn for them. But we are born of the Triumvirate's energies. All who deny this must suffer until they demonstrate their allegiance to those who created them."

"So you hired the Emerald Dragon, Mordan, to perform this act of terror?" Kai asked. "With what did you pay him?"

Apostle Agnon smiled. "We paid him, yes, with a king's treasure, but we did not hire him."

"You talk in riddles," Mistress Lolund said.

Agnon was about to answer, but stopped as a guard stepped behind him and whispered into his ear. It was the guard with the hazel eyes—the one that had been sent to awaken her. The guard pointed toward Torra. Agnon turned to look at her, then down at her satchel.

"There are riddles within riddles, dear mage," Agnon replied, turning back to Kuno, "and we do not know all of the answers. For though we did not hire Mordan, the one who did is not *truly* known to us. An 'outlander' he is, in every sense. And he was paid as well."

"But why the Astronomer's Guild, Agnon?" Master Kuno asked. "Why turn traitor?

Mistress Kai added, "Did they know you were leading your so-called Brotherhood? Did they oppose you?"

"Their opinion was irrelevant," Agnon replied. "They chose death rather than to join us. And in their death, they became a statement of the Triumvirate's power." At that last word, Agnon flexed his hand, causing the red energies at his palm to spark and flash through his fingers. "Now you and the Great Towers have a choice: join us and the Triumvirate, or suffer the same fate as Caranamere!"

"No more!" Torra screamed, then chanted, "*Accorae sint bosidona!*" A ray of light shot from her outstretched finger toward Apostle Agnon. But he was ready. The red sparks from his hands arced up and met the ray of her *Neural Fire* spell and reflected it back. But not just from him. The reflection was mirrored from the hands of all of the Brothers, each now shooting back the ray toward Torra from their own hands. The rays hit the *Shield* spell surrounding the mages and exploded against the invisible barrier, flashing in a web of electricity.

"They have a *Mass Reflect* spell!" Master Donovan said.

"We must negate it!" Lolund said. "Harmonize!"

Except for Kuno, who continued with the *Shield* spell, the mages emitted a low hum from their throats, each concentrating on the magic centers of their minds. Torra joined as well, half-closing her eyes and focusing on the magical energies within her. Her emotional state created waves of chaos, but still it joined with the others. When they hit a crescendo, Torra opened her eyes and pointed at Lolund at the same time as the other mages. Lolund then stretched out her hand, chanting, "*Chorook haita!*" Immediately the red glow from the hands of the Brotherhood faded away.

del Titccio threw the plasma balls, one of which slammed into the disciple to Agnon's left, exploding in a shower of blue sparks, the man's body falling and flopping in a spasm. The other plasma ball narrowly missed Agnon as the apostle dodged, then returned the attack, chanting and creating a vortex of cold that descended on the mages. Torra's skin burned from the freezing air, her joints tightening.

Chaos erupted. A dozen voices called out different incantations at once. Colored lights of magical beams shot all around her. The *Shield* spell popped out of existence.

Torra fell to her side on the floor, shivering.

Mistress Kai jumped in front of her and deflected a ball of fire. The table exploded in a shower of flaming splinters Something whizzed past her head.

I need a defensive spell! she thought, but nothing came to her. Her mind had gone blank. *Shield.* What is the incantation?

Inches from her face appeared deep azure eyes. Pale skin. A wisp of blond bangs. Darilos. He was bent down and looking her in the eyes.

"Torra, we have to leave! You and me."

"Not … not without … "

"*They* can fight this battle. *We* have to leave! You know where we need to go!"

"I won't leave them!" Her wits collected, she stood on shaking legs.

Osprey ran forward, swinging his axe and yelling "Okun!" and cut deep into the shoulder of one of the Brothers.

To her left, Mistress Lolund started to cast a spell, but a disciple beat her to it. A club formed in the air next to him, shimmering purple. He swung hard. Hit Lolund in the head.

Lolund's skull burst with a loud *thwack!* Blood splattered across Torra. Shards of bone. Lolund fell.

Torra shouted, "No!" She reached her hands toward the ceiling. "*Gretum iack!*" she shouted, grabbed at the air with both hand, and yanked downward.

A rafter shattered in a rain of kindling at both ends. The disciple looked up—just as the rafter fell upon him.

She turned to look for Mistress Kai. Found her next to a burning pillar. An initiate of the Brotherhood, hulking in size, had his hands around her waist, trying to throw her to the ground. Torra watched her hit him in the head, to no effect.

Torra ducked as a table flew past her, split with a crack against the ceiling, opened a hole, fell in chunks to the floor along with shingles. A heavy downpour of rain fell through.

But the raindrops didn't fall straight. For a brief moment that seemed to stretch out, she was mesmerized by the weirdness of it. The flashing magic around her warped them, changed their trajectory. Affected gravity. And they spun out and around in odd swirls to fly in every direction.

She heard a clang of metal, bringing her back into focus, as Master Donovan swung his blue-glowing sword and parried an initiate who wielded a mace, then stabbed the Brother through his chest.

Taenos! she thought, but it wasn't him. Glancing around, she couldn't find him anywhere.

The bench to her right burst into green flames.

A chant to her left. She turned. Kuno cast an orb of light into Agnon's face, blinding him. Started to cast another spell, but was knocked to the ground by a *Repel* spell cast by another disciple, hitting his head against a table edge.

The guards had pulled back to the back entrance, protecting Taegus and Elbin with a ring of swords, wide-eyed in wonderment.

Master Gral was thrown into the air by a disciple's *Levitate* Spell, but del Titccio countered it and Gral dropped to his feet.

Then Agnon and the remaining disciples chanted in unison while their surviving initiates cast a *Shield* spell in front of them.

The energy of the room magnified. The shadows lengthened. All other energies were cast aside.

"The Triumvirate!" Master Preneval shouted. "They're summoning them!"

"We can't counter that!" Mistress Kai replied, helping Kuno to his feet. Blood flowed from a wound on his right temple.

"We have to leave. Now!" Darilos said to Torra, grabbing her by the arm.

Master Gral swung his knife at an initiate, chopping through the young man's arm. But two of the castle guards ran to the initiate's defense, pushing Gral back.

The Brothers' harmonized spell was nearing completion. Kuno threw another *Shield* spell around them, but Torra knew the strength of the Triumvirate energy would quickly overwhelm it.

Darilos shook Torra by the shoulder. "Torra! Now!"

Torra closed her eyes. Felt the thrum of the deep energy. Remembered back to the Battle of the Tower of Light, when that well of energy had burst forth.

And then she found it. That "door" in the back of her mind was thrown open. Raw energy pulsed forth into her, a geyser of pure power.

She threw her arms wide and started chanting the *Wayfaring* spell that Kai had cast to get them to Caranamere.

"Torra!" Mistress Kai shouted. "What are you doing?" She ignored her mentor.

"It's too dangerous!" Kai shouted, moving toward her. But it was too late to stop it. Too complicated. Dire consequences.

The brothers' spell was almost complete, their chant rising to a crescendo.

Torra allowed a moment to look at the room. Agnon pointed toward Torra, and at that command, the guard with the hazel eyes suddenly shot forth. Hacked past Masters Gral and Donovan. Lunged at Torra.

Torra felt a tug at her shoulder.

And then she was wayfaring.

The room spun. Grew cold. Disappeared. She was flung through emptiness.

Dimly she heard Darilos crying out, his voice growing gruff, shouting something. Other mages, too, were shouting. She sensed them, like fine tendrils linked to her mind.

But she had to concentrate. Wind whipped around her. Lights came and went, flashing past, blurring. A merging of random sounds—growls, whistles, and whooshing.

She wasn't sure she could hold it. None of the other mages had harmonized with her. None physically contacted her. And yet, she could feel the strings of energy between them and around them.

The site. Yes. The site. She saw it in her mind. The pyramid of Degrin Torkis. She could get no closer to Pendoni without being affected by the energy void there. She had to merge her memory of the place with the actuality. But it had been years since she'd been there. What if it had changed?

She couldn't afford to worry about it. The pyramid. It was there, in her mind, and merging with a blurring shape that had to be the place she intended. *Concentrate!* Everyone's lives depended on it. One misstep. Just one. And they could materialize inside the structure, or fifty feet over it, or …

And then she had it! The visions merged, blurred, merged again. With a final syllable, she stopped the incantation.

She fell three feet to the ground, slamming into hard packed soil and rolling to her side. The top of soil was wet and left a smear of clay on her cheek. There was a light, misty rain.

Kuno, del Titccio, Gral, and Kai emerged with her, hitting the ground with a thud. Osprey fell with his arms cradling his holy book, his eyes shut tight as he prayed. But he didn't hit the ground like the others. He fell and then ... paused ... just before hitting, as if he'd cast a spell to cushion his fall. *Another mage helped him*, she thought, looking toward them, but they were busy helping each other.

Masters Donovan and Preneval dropped onto the lowest level of the stepped pyramid rising to her right, nearly rolling off the crumbling edge. Donovan's guise cat leapt lightly from his shoulder. Even Mistress Lolund's corpse appeared with them and flopped to the ground with a thud.

Darilos appeared last, popping out of the air and landing lithely, then turning to look at her with wide eyes. Then he smiled, eyes wide with excitement, and turned in a circle as if celebrating.

Torra allowed herself to breathe. Everyone was accounted for.

"No!" Darilos said, blinking in realization of something. Then he roared—actually *roared*, low and resonating like a beast—then meeting her eyes again. For the first time, she saw panic there. His irises sparked with a bright blue light. "The Codex!" he yelled. "You fool!"

Torra felt her side for the satchel. It was gone!

Before she could quite register what had happened, Darilos gritted his teeth in anger and then disappeared. But in the moment of disappearing, he seemed to warp and stretch.

And was that a flash of blue flame?

I've seen that flame before ...

CHAPTER THIRTY-FOUR
Retrieval

It had all happened so suddenly. Before Darilos could react to the guard rushing at Torra, her spell had taken effect and he had been pulled into the gyre of her *Wayfaring* spell.

There was no escaping it. The power was raw, drawn from the heart of the world. Triumvirate energy. It flowed through him, thrilled him, shook his core. It was all he could do to keep the human form of Darilos as he roared in ecstasy. And it came from *her*. It was just like the power he felt back at the Battle at the Tower of Light, when their eyes had locked. She had the power he had longed for. The power he'd craved. The reason he had wanted her near.

And yet, because of the gyre, he couldn't move toward her. He was helpless, caught in the wake of her current, pulled through with the spell to wherever she was taking them. He thrilled at the shared energy. It burned through him like a seizure. He wanted it to go on forever.

And then it was over. They fell out of the gyre and arrived at the place she had picked.

For the briefest moment, their eyes met again. A shared fascination with what had been accomplished. What had been *felt*. He turned in a circle in a moment of celebration. But the energy was already dissipating.

And then he stopped as he realized what had happened. "No!" he yelled. The satchel was missing from her shoulder. And he knew—*the guard!* He'd seen the guard rush toward Torra. "The Codex! You fool!"

Darilos roared in anger and teleported back. He had to get there as fast as possible.

Everything had been falling in place, Darilos thought as his body dematerialized and the world swirled around him. He let the human form of Darilos burn away.

The Brotherhood showed their true colors to the mages and delivered their ultimatum. Torra agreed to go to Pendoni with me. And Torra seemed to be free of the will of her shrew of a mentor.

And then that damned guard grabbed the Codex of Otemus!

His body was at last free of the human form. Burning blue with flame. Back to his full height and strength. He gnashed his jaws in expectation of the fight to come.

He rematerialized in the Great Hall of Gaes, or what was left of it. The room was a mess of splintered and burning tables, gaping holes in the roof with rain pouring in. He roared at those he saw. Servants dropped the body of the old lord and ran. Azartial wasn't interested in them. Two guards armed with spear and crossbow, readied their weapons. Two Brothers ran from the room. Another lay dying in a pool of blood from a grievous shoulder wound.

Turning, Azartial saw three other Brothers with Taegus and Elbin, all gaping at his demon dragon form.

One had the satchel! It was Apostle Agnon.

"*Agnon!*" he roared.

Azartial thrust out his forefoot and cast a *Rigour* spell just as the Apostle started chanting.

Agnon's spell was just a *Word of Command*. He disappeared a fraction before Azartial's *Rigour* spell hit the others, locking their every muscle and freezing their faces in terror.

"No!" Azartial roared, looking around to see if Agnon might have just relocated in the building. But he was gone. Teleported. Could have gone anywhere in the world—with the Codex!

Chamberlain Taegus had his sword half-drawn from his scabbard as the new, young Lord Gaes, Elbin, was caught trying to take cover behind him. Then, off balance where he froze from the *Rigour* spell, Elbin fell face-first into the rubble.

Azartial roared again and leaped over the debris to his frozen targets.

A shout went up behind him. A spear flew past Azartial, missing his wings and head by inches.

He ignored it and grabbed one of the stiffened Brothers by the throat, sizzling his flesh. He released the *Rigour* spell on him. The disciple went limp and inhaled a ragged breath before Azartial let go of the neck and tightened his talons around the man's bald head.

"Cast a spell and I will crush your skull like a grape!"

The disciple gave a shake of his head, his eyes rolling in terror. His head grew bright red from the burning blue flames.

"Where did Agnon go?"

A crossbow bolt hit Azartial in the back. Then another.

He didn't bother turning. Instead, he reached his other forefoot out and grabbed the frozen chamberlain by the head. "Keep up the attacks and I crush him!" Azartial yelled at the guards. The attack stopped.

"Where is Agnon?" Azartial demanded. He tightened his grip on the man's head.

The Brother's lips moved. Barely a whisper. But Azartial just made out the words, like a prayer, "Deliver us to your great powers."

"What?" Azartial said, giving the mage a shake. "Where is he? I won't ask again!"

"*Ominum tessim teckard!*" the Brother chanted, even as Azartial began to crush his skull. The chant had hardly ended when the mage burst into flame, his body instantly overcome in an act of suicide. Screaming. Skin blackening from the sudden heat.

Azartial threw the burning corpse aside and growled. In seconds it was ash. He let go of Taegus and grabbed the other Brother, the hulking initiate, but thought twice about unfreezing him. Instead, he simply crushed the man's neck. Agnon wouldn't have shared his safe haven with an initiate.

"Agnon!" he yelled, then picked up the corpse of the other Brothers, turned, and threw it at the dozen guards who stood at the far end. The body flopped and rotated through the air, crashing into the group of armored men.

Azartial clenched his jaw so hard that his razor-sharp teeth sliced through his lips. Then he tensed, threw his arms over his head, and shouted "*Doctensa!*" as he clapped his hands as hard as he could.

A sonic blast detonated from his hands in all directions. Flames extinguished as a shock wave smashed through wall and pillar and roof. Wood, rock, and mortar exploded in a hail of debris that sliced through the air, embedded in walls, bludgeoned the bodies of guards, servants, and horses. The stable and forge across the bailey flew apart. Guards tumbled from the battlements. For a moment, the pouring rain stopped, forced upward and outward, before it resumed its deluge over the shattered debris and foundation of the building.

A corner tower of the Keep closest to the Great Hall shuddered and collapsed, toppling to the right in a thunderous crash and cloud of dust that billowed out across the yard.

He thought, *There's a verbal incantation for you, Kuno!*

Azartial regarded Taegus and Elbin and released the *Rigour* spell. They fell limp, gasping for air.

Elbin attempted to crawl away across the debris, looking back in terror at the demon dragon.

Taegus pulled at his sword, fumbling to free it in his panic.

"My dear Chamberlain," Azartial said, grabbing the man by the torso with one hand, his talons slicing into Taegus's chest. Taegus let out a gasp of pain. Blood soaked into his surcoat. "Tell me where Apostle Agnon went."

"Beast!" Taegus spat. "Those mages may have summoned you, but the Brotherhood will still reign!" He pulled and swung his sword. The blade bit deep into Azartial's left arm.

Azartial winced. But he laughed against the pain as the wound instantly healed. He grabbed the chamberlain's sword arm, twisted, forced Taegus to drop the weapon as something cracked in the man's arm. "No one summoned me."

From the corner of his eye, Azartial saw armored figures emerge from the ruins of the Keep's tower.

"Once again … Where is Agnon?" His flames flared. Taegus's surcoat burned where his talons entered.

Taegus writhed and gritted his teeth. "I don't know!"

"Really?" Azartial reached down and grabbed Elbin's leg. Elbin yelped in surprise as he was lifted upside down, the golden crown falling from his head to clatter on the debris and coming to rest in a bloody puddle. "His life if you don't."

Taegus grimaced. "I said I don't know! Somewhere to the south."

Azartial swatted his tail in aggravation. "That doesn't help me!"

He turned and stomped over to the Crystal Throne, swinging the chamberlain and Elbin with each step.

Through the rain, Azartial spied a half dozen guards at the collapsed tower, emerging from a floor below, gawking at the damage around them and the blue-blazing demon.

Azartial smiled at the irony. Reaching the throne, he raised Taegus higher. "Last chance, Taegus. Tell me where Agnon is. Now!"

"I have no idea, beast!"

Darilos believed him. These idiots knew nothing about the people they were in league with. They were mere power-hungry puppets, unaware of the true nature of the forces wielded by their new allies. But ridding the world of them would still weaken the Brotherhood of Blood.

"Then he has no life!" He looked down at Elbin as the young lord shook his head in terror, tears streaming down his face.

"I don't know either! It was all his idea!" Elbin shouted. He pointed at Taegus. "He said I could be Lord Gaes if I agreed! I … I didn't have a choice."

"Then you'd better sit your throne, Lord Gaes!" Azartial swung Elbin by the foot and slammed him against the throne as the young man screamed. Elbin's metal breastplate ripped against the stone with a metallic screech. His rib cage burst with a crunch as blood splattered across the gems and stone.

Taegus looked away as the body shivered then lay still, draped across the arm and back of the throne.

"Well, traitor," Azartial said. "Now the dominion is truly yours!" He bent down and picked up the jade-and-rosewood orb, then shoved Taegus into the seat, half-sitting on Elbin's bloody corpse. "Here's the Orb of Rulership you've desired!"

Azartial slammed the orb into the chamberlain's head, smashing it halfway into his skull. The chamberlain's eyes rolled up into his head as blood soaked his body.

Azartial heard the clang of metal upon metal. Sassala Gaes burst from the collapsed tower, sword in hand, parrying a guard and slicing through his neck. Screaming in exertion, she turned, ducked a swing, then stabbed her blade into the exposed armpit of another guard. The teenaged valet appeared behind her and slammed a rock into the side of another guard's head. The remaining guards ran from her to the front gate, glancing back toward Azartial as they fled.

Lightning flashed, immediately followed by booming thunder. It was only then that Sassala seemed to notice the devastation before her ... and the demon dragon. Her eyes widened as they met his through the rain.

"Oh, gods!" she exclaimed.

"Wrong celestial entity, Sassala!" Azartial quipped. "The rulership now falls to you! All hail the Lord Gaes, King's Regent of Gaes Province and all of its riches and peoples!"

The new ruler's gaze turned to the throne and the bodies there, then back to him. "What are you? Was it you who destroyed Caranamere?"

Azartial laughed. "No, Sassala. That was the Emerald Dragon, paid for by the Brotherhood."

"So you fight against them?"

Against them, yes. After enabling them. "They have served their purpose. Do you know where Agnon went?" *The Codex was never meant to fall into the hands of the Brotherhood.*

She shook her head. "No, but I wish to know."

315

Torra had taken her damned mages with her, and now the Brotherhood of Blood was sure to be close behind as soon as Agnon read the Codex.

His plan to get the Convergence was in danger. He had to hurry now and pull it all back together.

He addressed Sassala again. "You'd better rid your lands of the Brotherhood! I'd hate to have to come back and finish the job for you!"

And before she could respond, he teleported away. It was time to retrieve the Key of Otemus—the last game piece. And let the Brotherhood come to him.

CHAPTER THIRTY-FIVE
Lionriders

It had been only a night and a day since Feng's troops conquered Dodonor Citadel, but somehow it felt longer to the General. He was used to moving from one objective to another—it was the warrior's way, after all—yet this shift in approach had felt like the unrolling of a clean parchment where each character he wrote upon it was a new command of his destiny. He was this much closer to the Convergence … and the renewal of his family's rule upon the Jade Throne.

Feng shook his head. Such thoughts were vanity. He needed a clear mind or all could be lost.

As his troops had mopped up the last of the resistance at the citadel, Feng met with the Khunti Lionriders using a translator from among his guard who spoke Calnurian. Even though the Khunti had a language of their own, the tribesmen seemed to understand well enough. The six stout, gruff men had doubted his claim of conquering the citadel … until he took them and showed them himself, walking them past the bodies of the guards throughout the halls and chambers. He had achieved what generations of their primitive warriors had failed to do and then delivered it to them on a platter. With the citadel conquered, the Khunti could move in and control the southern pass for themselves, if they wished, and take back what they claimed as their ancestral lands.

But he knew the handful of warriors couldn't conceive what to do with this unexpected offering. Bewildered, they could only think to escort Feng and his three-score of Shadow Guard troops to their chieftain. Fine enough. As usual, it was all part of his plan. And he really didn't care if they ever took the citadel for themselves, as long as it pulled the Taxin army away from his true objective.

As Commander Ming'ai led the so-called "trade caravan" back south with the support troops, Feng and his Shadow Guard now rode eastward and higher into the mountains behind the Khunti, following high ridges and trails so narrow that a single slip of the mount would send them falling a thousand feet to their deaths. Commander Tonang rode at the rear to keep the men in check, and the old mystic, Chiang'wu, was in the middle of the column, the safest location for the only non-warrior in the party.

Soon after leaving Dodonor, the tiny flakes of snow falling from an ashen sky had grown larger and began blowing from the north. All day they had ridden with only short breaks along the winding trail. Feng and his men were prepared with heavy cloaks and balaclavas, but the chill still crept through clothing and left them shivering. The Khunti, on the other hand, seemed unperturbed and, at most, simply lifted fur hoods during the worst of it.

They were clearly a fearsome tribe and far more primitive than the Taxin barbarians. The Khunti were spread across the southern ranges of the Sarsan Mountains in small bands and were sometimes employed on the eastern slopes as guides, but here, on the western slopes, they were considered wild and unapproachable. These warriors were a short, stout people, dressed in furs and brandishing bronze-headed spears and traditional hand axes with short, curved wooden handles and triangular heads, also made of bronze, a symbol of manhood for them. Some also sported swords taken from Taxin soldiers they had defeated in battle. The men's weathered faces were characterized by purposely scarified lines incised at angles away from their eyes and running down into thick beards. But by far the most defining characteristic of these warriors were the massive Sarsan mountain lions they rode.

The beasts were easily thrice the size of a man. Muscles bulged with every movement under taut skin and short, gray hair that sported a variegated pattern of dark and light circles. Their eyes burned with a fierce light. The slightest move toward them resulted in a deep, rumbling growl that emitted past a pair of saber teeth longer than Feng's outstretched hand. Yet, despite the beasts' wildness, the Khunti warriors were paired with their cats in such a way that they could ride saddleless behind the lion's shoulders and command their movements. Even though the paws of these lions were as wide as a man's face, they padded along the trail with ease and near-silence compared to the relatively clumsy clomping of Feng's horse.

Jiknute, the leader of this squad of lionriders and head of the column, raised his spear twice as the trail broadened into a wide, flat, snow-covered meadow surrounded by cliffs that protected the meadow from the worst of the wind. It was as close to an ideal waypoint or camping area as any Feng had seen so far. At the signal, his men slowed their approach and spread out. He grunted commands to his subordinates, two of whom directed Feng and his troops into the middle of the meadow. Two others slapped the sides of their lions and, with no reins or obvious commands, guided their mounts up steep slopes to the top, the lions leaping from rock to rock and scrambling up sheer cliffs without losing their riders. No horse could ever make such a climb.

Jiknute came over to Feng, his lion padding softly in the snow. The lion snuffled at Feng's horse, then licked its chops as it seemed to consider the steed for a meal. The Khunti leader said a few brusque words to Feng's translator before riding off. "My lord," the translator said, bowing as far as his saddle would allow. "Jiknute states that we will stop here for a while to rest and eat. The next passage is very difficult, and we won't stop until after darkfall."

Feng nodded in reply. Time was of the essence, and he hated to stop for any length of time, but he had no choice but to take the Khunti squad leader's advice.

Chiang'wu dropped to the ground from his saddle, landing badly and crumpling into a heap. Several little bags of herbs fell from the straps across his chest, and he quickly collected them, then rose unsteadily. "My lord," he said, approaching Feng and bowing, "I am your humble servant, but I wonder about my fortitude. I fear I only slow your progress!"

"You are the only one here who isn't a warrior, Chiang'wu," Feng replied. "You've done an admirable job of riding."

The old mystic bowed again, nearly falling over. "I am unworthy of such praise from the Lord of Silk and Steel." He raised up and met Feng's eyes before respectfully lowering them again and then pointed to the edge of the clearing. "There, my lord, are jade hawthorn trees!"

Feng turned to look. The "trees" were little more than tortured shrubs, a bramble with thick trunks, only a little taller than a man, and one of only a handful of plants that dared to grow in such harsh conditions. It took a moment for Feng to remember their importance, but Chiang'wu quickly explained.

"It is as the ancient text had described, my lord. I shall collect the limbs at once!"

Feng gave a nod of approval, and the old mystic quickly hobbled over to the shrubs.

The general motioned to Commander Tonang, who had been ordering the guards to circle up in the middle of the meadow. The commander immediately came over and bowed, his face and bald pate hidden under the hood of his cloak, but the lion-snake heads of the bronze slave torc were exposed from under his collar. "Yes, my lord?"

"Have two of your men aid Chiang'wu with collecting tree limbs."

"For a fire, Master?"

"No. For entrapping a demon."

Tonang bolted upright, eyes wide with surprise. "Of … of course, Master, at once." Then he hurried away, barking orders to the guards.

Feng pulled back his hood and looked up at the blowing snow and the dim luminance of the sun filtering through gloomy gray clouds. All around him, his men busied themselves eating, drinking, and stretching. They dared not bother their steely general in his ruminations. None of them, not even Tonang or Chiang'wu, fully grasped the nature of the artifact they were marching toward or the promise of the power it would give him.

He thought back to the deal he had made with Azartial for attaining the Convergence. *What I ask of you are three small conditions, and you will be able to keep the prize all for yourself*, the demon had said. First, that the demon would be able to demand the weapon be used for a specific action of his choosing at least once a year. Second, that the other person who was to open the door to the Convergence, named Torra Com Gidel, would not be harmed, even though she was an enemy of the Triumvirate. And third, that he execute on sight someone called Apostle Agnon, beloved of the Triumvirate. The more he thought about this rotten deal, the less he liked it. But what choice had he? Azartial held the key to the door, and at a whim the demon could have teleported him high into the atmosphere or halfway around the world if he refused. Yet it was clear the demon needed him, too, and a jade hawthorn binding might just balance the power. At the very least, he could pry some answers from it.

Feng closed his eyes and quieted his mind. Took a deep breath. Opened his senses. Felt the chill of the wind against his cheek. The touch of snowflakes upon his skin. The powerful movement of the steed beneath him and the musky smell of its sweat. The sounds of his men. And though he wasn't in the comfort of a tent with his whip or incense, he did his best to open his chakras and reach his mind out to the world around him.

Quietly, he muttered a prayer to the Triumvirate for their guidance. "My three lords. Emperors to my emperor. I beckon you. Grant me your mind. Hear my thoughts. I relinquish myself to your dominion."

The gods didn't answer this time, but General Feng felt their gaze upon him. He placed a hand upon the pommel of his sword and tightened his jaw. Their glory would be his to share, or he would die trying.

CHAPTER THIRTY-SIX
Temple of the Dead

"Where in the hells are we?" Kai asked Torra, as she applied a makeshift bandage to Master Kuno's head. The group of seven surviving mages and Osprey had gathered together under a copse of trees to get out of the rain, but the canopy didn't block it all, so Master Gral cast a *Shield* spell over them to keep them dry. All of them showed signs of exhaustion, with Master Kuno slumped over, Mistress Kai attending to his wound. Master Donovan reclined against a tree, holding his head. Osprey leaned heavily on his axe.

Mistress Lolund's body was laid off to the side as respectfully as they could make it, given the circumstances, with her battered face covered by a white towel that Master Kuno had in his travel pack. The towel was stained red on the side that had been hit by a disciple's conjured hammer.

"This is Degrin Torkis," Torra answered, "near the city of Cordron, in Taxia, and about three day's ride south of Gaes, give or take."

A stepped pyramid loomed off to her left. Made of crumbling stone and festooned with weeds, it rose in five massive tiers to a flat top, with rainwater running down in rivulets through eon-eroded channels.

"It translates to 'temple of the dead,' or possibly 'dead temple,' in the old tongue. The pyramid is part of a lost city which was once the center of a vast civilization, until … "

"Save the history lesson," Kai snapped. "Why here? Why did you wayfare us here and not back to the Tower of Light, like a sensible person?"

"Ouch!" Kuno exclaimed, flinching under Kai's less-than-tender touch. The new bandage was already turning red, but the wound seemed minor despite the bleeding.

"Sorry," Kai apologized to him, and continued wrapping.

"It was the first place I thought of," Torra answered. *But it's on the way to Pendoni*, she continued thinking.

"Well we're damned lucky it worked! You could have killed us! What made you think you could try casting that alone, and for all of us, no less? It's yet another example of how you're acting impulsively and dangerously with your magic. It's the same lesson I've been trying to get through your thick skull for weeks!"

"*I* could have had us killed?" Torra shouted. "If it weren't for me and my 'thick skull' we'd all be fighting *gods* now!"

Kai tied off the bandage—which made Kuno wince—and then stood and pointed a finger at Torra. "One of these days your lack of control will wind up killing a *lot* of people! You don't know your own powers, apprentice!"

"We must calm ourselves," Master Donovan said, stepping between them and raising his hands. "What is done is done. Now we must move forward."

Torra grumbled and stepped back. But she knew Kai was right. She *had* been lucky. She didn't know how she managed to cast such a powerful spell alone, doing both roles of chanting and visualizing, and not even touching the others, and having only experienced it for the first time when traveling to Caranamere two days ago! The slightest misstep could have had them appear far higher off the ground, or merge into the stepped pyramid or trees, or even meld into each other.

"It's just like you to take her side, Annorov," Kai mumbled.

Master Donovan ignored her and put a hand on Torra's shoulder. Blood coated the sleeve of his robe, but Torra knew it wasn't his own. She shied away from it.

"Torra, I want to thank you," he said. "We *all* thank you. What you did may have been impulsive, but it likely saved our lives."

"Not all of your lives," Torra said, glancing over to the shrouded body of Mistress Lolund.

"Mistress Lolund's death was not your fault," Master del Titccio said. He was leaning against a tree and smoking a cheroot of his fragrant herbal mixture.

Master Gral nodded in agreement as he cleaned blood off his hanat knife. His robes were burned on one side. Half of his face was turning blue from bruising.

Kuno stood, grunting as he did so. Kai helped steady the old master. "Thank you, my dear," he said to her. Then to Torra, "Master Donovan is right. You should be thanked. But Mistress Kai is also correct. You have a lot of promise, Torra, but you have much training to pursue, and the power you wield is not to be trifled with."

Torra looked down. "Yes, Mistress Kai is right. It *was* foolish of me, in hindsight." Then looking to Kai, she added, "I guess I just didn't know what else to do." To Torra's surprise, Kai's visage softened.

"It is as I told you, back at the tower," Kai said. "*Casting magic is personal*. Your emotions ran high. You acted in a moment of crisis to save yourself and those you trusted. And it was in that moment that you accessed the deepest part of your magic center. Feel the passion that you pour into your spell. Learn to harness and control that. You must!"

"It truly was an accomplished feat," Lord Preneval said, standing next to Lolund's body. "We should save the argument for later." He turned to face Kuno. "Our mission is complete. We must return to the Towers to make our reports."

Kuno nodded. "Agreed, Garinos. The Brotherhood of Blood, made up of traitors from the Astronomer's Guild, is responsible for hiring the Emerald Dragon to destroy Caranamere ..."

"Not hiring," del Titccio corrected. "Their leader said they paid the Emerald Dragon but did not hire him. They didn't say who hired him."

"Right," Kuno said, "though perhaps it's a matter of semantics. As we saw, they conspired with others to stage a coup and take control of the Gaes region of Taxia."

"And you did nothing to stop them!" Torra spat.

"Torra, hold your tongue!" Kai commanded.

For several minutes the group erupted in argument, with Torra and Kai shouting at each other, and some vehemently defending their choices not to interfere in the coup, while others expressed doubts. But then Master Kuno clapped his hands for attention, and the copse slowly fell silent again.

"Ladies! Gentlemen! Please!" Kuno said. "Let's save our arguments for later. We cannot change the past. It will be up to the Council of Mages to determine how to deal with the Brotherhood of Blood now."

"Another matter is," Gral said in the stilted translation of his language. "Gold Dragon hunts Emerald."

"True," Kuno said. "Thank you, Master Gral. And he has your totem and mine, and ... He looked down at Lolund's corpse without saying that Ingal had her token, as well. "He will teleport you and me to his location to confront the Emerald Dragon with him. Perhaps we will learn who this 'hiring' party is."

The clouds flashed with lightning to the north, then thunder rumbled across the sullen clouds.

"There is one more matter," Kai added. She turned to look at Torra. "Darilos."

"What about him?" Torra said.

"Where did he go?"

del Titccio added, "He shouted something about a 'codex' and called you a 'fool' before he disappeared."

Torra's lips tightened as she considered what to do. She'd studied the Codex. She'd formed an opinion. And she knew what Darilos wanted her for. It was time to tell the mages. It was her duty, wasn't it?

"There's something I haven't told you. Something important." Torra looked into Kai's eyes. "I started to tell you back at Gaes Citadel, but we were interrupted." She took a deep breath and looked around to all of the mages. "There is a book that Darilos found, called the Codex of Otemus. He gave it to me just after he and I fought Master Feros ... " In her mind, she once again saw the master's disembodied legs. The peasant woman cut in half. The blood and gore mixed with smoke from the burning trees. She shook it off and continued. "The Codex was written by a man thousands of years ago, Otemus, at the behest of gods. He described an ancient artifact—called the *Convergence*—which allows the bearer to control both terrestrial and celestial magic at the same time."

"Such a thing is not possible," Lord Preneval said, raising an eyebrow. "It has never been successfully accomplished. Master mages have gone insane in their attempts to do so."

"And yet, according to the book, Otemus dedicated half of his life to creating this artifact and hiding it away in Pendoni," Torra continued.

"Pendoni?" del Titccio asked. "I've never heard of it."

"It's a convent in a remote mountain valley southeast of here," Torra explained. "I've never been there, but I know of the place. It is a strong energy void, known to the mages at the Astronomer's Guild."

"And where is this codex?" Master Donovan asked. His guise cat, Yaggu, sat at his feet, looking up at her as if he, too, were expecting an answer. His fur had turned darker as thunderheads rolled in.

Torra scratched at her itching hands. The skin was raw again. "Well … it was in a satchel that I was wearing during the battle at Gaes. Just as I cast *Wayfaring*, one of the guards yanked the satchel off my shoulder." She paused to see everyone's reactions, but they only watched in silence. "It's gone. I … I assume Darilos went back to retrieve it. I don't know. But … I read it through twice, last night. The language was of an ancient tongue, but I managed to translate it. I can remember it very well. And I'm convinced, as Darilos is, that the Triumvirate wants this Convergence, too."

"And now the Brotherhood of Blood has the book?" del Titccio added.

She nodded. "Or perhaps Timbrook Taegus and the new Lord of Gaes. If Darilos didn't get it back, that is."

"I have never heard of this," Kuno said. "One man, thousands of years ago. Only a mage of legendary power could fashion such an awesome device, and yet he is unknown to any of us. What makes you think it wasn't just mad ramblings? If such a powerful artifact exists, wouldn't you think others would have looked for it and found it by now? Wouldn't you think the Towers would have launched expeditions to find it?"

Suddenly Torra began doubting the account, but she pressed on. "It's hidden. Entombed. Protected by a magical door that requires a special 'key' that must be turned at the same time by two mortal enemies, as he described in the book: one who has been touched by the Outer Gods but fights against them, and one who has been touched by the Triumvirate but fights against them." She added, "Darilos says he has the key and has arranged to have these two people there …" Torra stopped short of adding, *and I might be one of them.*

"And where did Darilos get this key?" Lord Preneval asked. "Where did he get the Codex?" Seeing her shake her head, he added, "For just how long has he been planning this?"

Torra looked away from him. "I … I don't know."

"Do we even know the book isn't a fake, concocted by Darilos or others?" Kuno said.

"The writing was the old tongue. The pages extremely aged. Impossible to fake …" But she asked herself for the first time, *Could Darilos have faked it?*

As she had been talking, Kai's face had grown red, her lips tightening. "I knew it! How long have you been hiding this? Darilos isn't what he seems. If he has been in possession of this book and key, and is trying to conspire with you to …"

"He isn't conspiring!" Torra said, surprising herself with her outburst. She immediately looked away. *Why did I yell that?* she thought.

Kai took a step toward her. "Why didn't you tell us you had this book? Why didn't you share this information with us sooner? Did Darilos instruct you to keep it secret?"

del Titccio grabbed Kai by the shoulder. "Let her speak."

The Mistress threw off del Titccio's hand. "How dare you!"

"Please! Please!" Kuno said, raising his hands toward them. The two mages continued to glare at each other.

Torra broke the silence. "Look, I didn't know whether to believe it, either." She was scratching her wrist harder, drawing blood from the cracked skin. "I decided I would read it myself before I brought it to your attention. And we were dealing with more pressing issues, not the least of which was the destruction of my town and the riot in Gaes! So read it I did." She looked at Kai. "And that was when I tried to bring it to your attention. I admit I hid it from you all, at least for a day. And, yes, he wanted me to keep it from you. I'm not sure of his motive, but I believe he thought you would repudiate it. So, instead, he ... " She trailed off, wondering if she should add the next part, but it seemed too late to stop. "He wants to recruit me to seek out this artifact."

She expected more angry reprisals from her mentor, but Kai just stood there, her black eyes seeming to look through her. Kai closed her eyes and took a deep breath. Others looked to her, expecting her to speak. There was only another rumbling of thunder to punctuate the moment, and then Kai spoke.

"And you believe all of this to be true?" Kai asked, sincerity in her voice. "That this artifact is real? That it has the power to control both types of magic? That Darilos has the means to get possession of it?"

Torra nodded. "Enough to pursue it, yes." She paused, looking at their reactions. Kuno and Preneval frowned. Torra continued, "If there is any possibility that such an artifact is real, then shouldn't we retrieve it? Before the Brotherhood of Blood does?"

del Titccio whistled and looked away. Donovan raised an eyebrow and grunted.

"Is not our mission," Gral said.

"Truly," Kuno said. "We have achieved what we set out to do. We must return to the Great Towers. Let the Council of Mages make that decision."

"I am not an Expeditionary Mage," Torra pointed out. "I am not beholden to the same expectations."

"You are an apprentice to the Tower of Light," Kuno pointed out. "You are beholden to your mentor, and she to the Towermaster." Kuno looked over at Kai. "Kai, surely you object to this talk!"

Kai looked him in the eye for an uncomfortably long time. Around them, the rain pounded the magical shield as the wind picked up. Thunder continued rumbling. Lightning grew nearer, streaks of it just to the north.

"I trust her," Kai finally said, speaking louder to be heard over the gale. She turned to Torra. "If Torra wishes to pursue this, I will join her."

Torra nearly exclaimed out loud. All she could do was blink in disbelief as Kai turned her attention back to her. "Th … thank you," Torra finally said.

Kai added, "It is time for you to determine your own path, the next step in your training, and this seems like a worthy challenge. But you must command your emotions, just as I must in this moment. Too much is at stake not to. But Darilos is not to be trusted. It is clear to me he has other motives than just keeping an artifact from the Brotherhood."

Master Donovan rested his hand on the pommel of his sword. "If this Convergence is as powerful as you believe, then I will go, too. You could use my help. If there is energy void, my sword you will need."

A warm sensation of gratitude welled up in Torra at this sudden change in her mistress and the validation from Donovan.

When she looked over to Gral, the squat mage nodded at her too, seeming to agree to join them as well as he pulled out his hanat knife and touched his chest with the flat of his blade in a salute.

Kuno cleared his throat. "Well, before you commit to this quest of Darilos's, there's one more thing you should think about. Preneval and Kai have said that Darilos isn't what he seems. At least, that is their suspicion. Darilos carefully chooses his words to explain inconsistencies. He claims to be an itinerant thaumaturge, which is why we can't sense his magic, yet utters no incantations and performs no rites, which he says is because he is so powerful in the ways of his magic. If he is so powerful, why then have none of us heard of him? We are among the greatest mages in the world. He will not name his master. He claims he is associated with the Astronomer's Guild, and wears their robes, yet he mourns not for the dead and conveniently was not with them during the attack, then he showed up immediately afterward in clean robes. He comes and goes at a whim, unannounced, and is elusive about his actions. Even an interaction with the Gold Dragon fails to elicit even a trace of nervousness.

"Well, I may have an answer to this." Master Kuno looked around the copse, meeting everyone's eyes. Torra felt a shiver run through her body, and it wasn't from the chill in the air. "You see," Kuno continued, "I have a suspicion as well. I suspect he is not a thaumaturge. In fact, I suspect he is not human at all!"

The other mages looked to each other for reaction, clearly confused. Torra felt suddenly ill. In that moment, she remembered the power shed from Darilos when he'd cast his spells. Why had she felt it? But there was something familiar about that energy. Something that harkened back to the end of the battle of the Tower of Light. A part of her knew what Kuno would say, but she didn't want to hear it. She took a step back. Shook her head.

Kuno continued. "At the end of the Battle of the Tower of Light, just as the dimensional portal was closing, an entity entered into our world along with the Celestials. It was dragon-like in form, wreathed in blue flame, with thin amber wings. It flew away, not to be seen again. It took the better part of a year for us to identify this creature, consulting demonologists across the world and ancient, crumbling texts. In time, we came to find that the description fit a demon dragon known as Azartial. I believe Darilos is none other than this demon dragon."

The mages gasped as one, exchanging looks of astonishment. Kai's eyes went wide. Preneval bent his head in thought. Gral growled. And Osprey drew the holy symbol of Okun in the air in front of him.

Torra returned in her mind to that moment when she saw the demon dragon emerge from Ingal's dimensional portal. The creature had started toward Ingal, malevolence in its eyes. But when it locked eyes on Torra, it had softened and exclaimed, "You! You're the one! You're the one from the Nexus!" There had been energy there, which had shot straight into Torra like lightning. And its voice. Its voice had been smooth and deep.

del Titccio flicked away the stub of his cheroot and pulled his robes tighter against the cold. "Honestly, Drokil, that seems quite a stretch!"

Unperturbed, Master Kuno looked over at Osprey, who had been silent all this time. "Osprey, when we first questioned you at Caranamere, you said that an 'evil thing' flew over the wreckage of the town, immediately following the blast. That this thing roared and was blue in color. Do I state this correctly?"

Osprey clutched at the holy book in his arms. "That's as I recollect. The beast were large and dragon-like, but not nearly as large as the Emerald Dragon. Maybe twice as tall as a man. I think I saw blue. And it had wings, but they weren't big and flapping like the dragon."

"And you didn't see it again?"

"Yes," Osprey replied. "I mean, I didn't see it again."

Preneval scratching at the stubble on his face. "It would be celestial in magical energy, undetectable to our magic senses, and able to cast spells of great power with that energy, like a thaumaturge."

Kuno nodded. "According to the texts, demon dragons are footmen of the gods, made specifically to serve as a bridge between celestial dimensions, the terrestrial world we inhabit, and the 'ether' in between. It's been said that they can even squeeze between the cracks of time to an area called the 'Nexus,' inaccessible to many gods, where they can see the past and the future of people and manipulate it in subtle ways. In their natural form, they appear dragon-like. As such, they have powers similar to dragons, as described in the ancient texts. At least four dragons have been known to regularly take on the shape of humans or elves. It is therefore within reason that this demon dragon possesses the ability to shape-shift into the form we see as Darilos. The only other demon dragon known to have come into our world, a beast called Li'an'shi, was said to have deceived humans, elves, and dwarves by posing as one of them. So too it may be with this one."

"And there is another thing," Kuno continued. "Demon dragons can be summoned by dragons."

"Such as the Emerald Dragon, perhaps?" Preneval added. He then raised an eyebrow and looked toward Torra. "Or the Gold?"

"Ingal has nothing to do with it!" Torra shouted, surprising herself with her anger.

"And yet," Preneval shot back, "summon him, he did, at the Tower of Light. You should know. You were there."

She shook her head. "That wasn't intentional!"

"All of this is only supposition," Master Donovan stated. "Darilos may actually be as he says, and not some demon."

"Darilos has taken a special liking to you," Master Kuno said to Torra. "We have all seen it. And he has entrusted in you this secret about the Codex of Otemus. If Darilos is Azartial, then what do you think his motives are?"

Torra clutched at her stomach as bile rose in her throat. She managed to gather herself, though, and sputtered, "He can't be a demon dragon. I refuse to believe such nonsense! He helped us against the rioters. And he saved me from being killed by Master Feros, in case you've forgotten! Why would a demon do that?"

"Why indeed?" Kai replied. "Unless he needed you to serve a purpose. Why is it he wants *you*, specifically, to go retrieve this Convergence?"

Torra shook her head. This was all too much. She wasn't some 'chosen one'—a key wielder—foretold thousands of years before. Such was vanity. "He … he thinks I'm one of the two people who have to turn the Key of Otemus."

The mages were silent for a moment, considering what she had said.

Osprey spoke up at this point. "Demons are powerful and wicked. They are deceivers. So say the holy scriptures. If Darilos is a demon, he could have killed us over and over again by now, but hasn't. I just don't see how a man like that could be a demon."

"And yet, when we fought the Brotherhood at Gaes," Preneval said, "Darilos did not lift a finger to help, as far as I saw. Even with the power of a human thaumaturge, he could have leveled the whole building if he wished. Why would he protect us before, but not then?"

"Because," Kai said, "it wasn't *us* he was protecting." She looked to Torra. "It was *her*. And he wanted her to wayfare us out of there. Did he suggest it during the fight?"

Torra didn't know what to say. She couldn't remember. Maybe it was true.

"He want the artifact," Gral said, finally sheathing his hanat knife. "Delivers the Codex. Get the key. Find Torra as key turner. He guide Torra to Pendoni. It is obvious. But what he want with Convergence?"

"What any powerful entity would want," Kuno answered. "More power. A weapon like that, in the right hands, could conquer the world."

"Or for the gods it serves?" Kai added.

"Again," Master Donovan said, "this is supposition. Let us wait here and test him."

"We cannot wait here," Preneval said. "I must return to the Tower of Darkness. Kuno, del Titccio, you must return to your towers as well. We must tell the towermasters and the Council of Mages what has transpired. And," he added, "I must return Lolund's body."

"Agreed," Kuno added. "And we don't know if the Brotherhood of Blood, or the Triumvirate for that matter, may be coming for us here. Do the rest of you still wish to go to Pendoni to seek out this artifact, knowing that you may be doing the bidding of a demon dragon?"

"What choice do we have?" Torra asked. "If we don't pursue it, then the Brotherhood will. I refuse to believe that Darilos is a demon dragon, but even if he is, the artifact is better in our hands than in the hands of the Triumvirate!" Her eyes went to her mother's copper bracelet, still gracing her wrist. She had to make sure no one else would destroy lives like the Brotherhood of Blood had, and their mercenary dragon. If the Brotherhood found the Convergence first, how many more cities would fall? How many more mothers would be mourned?

Kuno called for a show of hands to determine who would be going to Pendoni. Kai gave a nod at Torra and raised her hand. Donovan and Gral raised theirs, as well. Osprey raised his hand and stated, "I haven't nowhere to go, anyhow. And if it's a demon you're with, then we've all been deceived, and by Okun's light I will do all I can to protect you and lead you back to the path of enlightenment."

Kuno, Preneval, and del Titccio did not raise their hands, for they were needed at their towers. But Preneval added, "I shall seek you out later, if able."

del Titccio eyed Preneval with suspicion. "Then so will I."

Torra seemed to move in a haze of exhaustion and bewilderment. So much had happened in the last three days. The thought of launching into such an expedition seemed inconceivable. And yet, the energy that Darilos released! She craved it. She wanted him near. She wanted him to cast his spells so she could feel that energy again. *It's wrong to want this, right?*

She felt her hand raising, the last one to do so, and committed herself to this quest … if only to be in his presence again, demon dragon or not.

CHAPTER THIRTY-SEVEN
Demon Dragon

What had been a lethargic shower when Azartial left the pyramid had changed to an inundating downpour by the time he returned. Sullen clouds had turned black, and lightning cracked in ragged streaks to the ground instead of playing in the firmament. Each strike sent a wave of energy that Azartial sensed, like a thousand hot needles piercing him at once. It was exhilarating.

Now back to human form as Darilos, he stood at a corner, peering at the mages huddled together in a copse of trees about forty yards away. Rain soaked him down to the human skin he wore, but he hardly felt it. Chill had no effect on him.

After Gaes, he'd teleported to Domis-Alta-Calla, in the Great Wasteland, and retrieved the Key of Otemus from the primeval altar where he'd stashed it, then he'd teleported back to the ancient pyramid. The thin, silvery sword, with its odd pits and extensions, leaned unceremoniously against a stone at the base of the pyramid. All of these exertions at Gaes, and the teleporting, had left him tired.

Azartial had been watching the mages, listening, long enough to get the gist of their conversation. He was too distant to hear details, but raised voices combined with his super-human hearing was enough to hear "Darilos," "demon dragon," and "Azartial" spoken in the same conversation and carried by the wind. "Fair enough," he muttered aloud. "Keeping up this human appearance is taxing." *Besides*, he thought, *once I get near Pendoni, even my magic won't work anymore.* He figured it wasn't really a surprise that they pieced it together, given their initial suspicion of him at Caranamere and the questions they were asking of him in the Great Hall of Gaes Keep. Still, he wished he could keep up the charade a while longer. "Humans only trust other humans … if anyone at all," he said out loud. He kept the form for the moment, simply because his natural form had blue flames which might draw attention to him.

At the end of the mages' conversation, he heard someone say "Pendoni" and then a number of them raised their hands as if voting, even the peasant woodsman, Osprey. Lastly, Torra raised her hand. He was mildly disappointed she couldn't keep the secret about Pendoni. *Well*, he thought, *at least she wants to follow the plan, despite what happened at Gaes. Or because of it? Shame these self-righteous mages want to tag along, particularly her shrewish mentor.*

Moments later, the group seemed to break up, saying their goodbyes with formal gestures. The prudish mage in black robes, Preneval, stood over the corpse of his fellow mage from the Tower of Darkness, Lolund, as the others stepped away from him. Preneval produced a small, hand-sized device, which he started swinging over his head. A cloud of dark energy radiated out from him, rolling like a miniature thunderstorm and defying the wind. When it was about five feet wide, it suddenly dropped over him and Lolund and they disappeared into it. The dark energy dissipated, and they were gone.

Next to go was the fat mage in white robes, Kuno, and the red-robed master with long hair, del Titccio. Other than Torra, del Titccio was the only mage Azartial felt he could tolerate. At least that one had a sense of humor and a love of music. Both of them cast spells and produced mirror-like portals that they stepped through before they and the portals disappeared.

The others dispelled the *Shield* spell over them, since spells like that attract lightning but don't block it. Then they pulled their robes and cloaks over themselves as much as they could and huddled together against the weather, five little field mice in a tempest. Poor Osprey didn't have a cloak or blanket of any sort and had to hand his holy book to the Northerner, Master Donovan, for safekeeping under his robes. Azartial chuckled. "Wouldn't want the ink to run or you'd never know what your god wants of you."

He pulled back around the corner of the pyramid, completely out of sight of the mages, and checked his surroundings. There was no sign of anyone else, so he sat on a dislodged foundation stone of the ruin and closed his eyes. He took several deep breaths and focused on the moment. Soon he found the bright spot of his consciousness and sent his mind into it.

Projecting astrally, Azartial was in the space between dimensions, the Ether. All around him were bright clouds of many different pastel colors. He willed himself through the folds of those clouds until he was in a place where the clouds came together, thick and wall-like. But they parted for him, as they did for few others, and he was inside, in the Nexus.

Before him, once again, flowed ribbons of light, each a different color or shade from the last: the ribbons of people's lives. He remembered the delicious surge of energy from Torra when she cast her *Wayfaring* spell—magic that he should not have been able to feel, for it was terrestrial magic. That feeling helped guide him until it was her energy line he found in the Nexus. Her ribbon was tight and sparkling, powerful, like liquid lightning, daring him to touch it. And around her, at this moment, were the lines of the Expeditionary Mages, rolling around each other. Osprey's ochre ribbon now glittered—a sign that he had been chosen by a god, the same as a priest might be. *No longer a country bumpkin*, Azartial thought.

Going back in time along the ribbons, he saw there had been a clash, with many lines coming together and exploding, as he'd predicted earlier. It was the battle at Gaes Keep. The dark lines of Apostle Agnon and his disciples. The lord of Gaes and his children. The other mages. Some, like Lolund's forest-green line, or the darker ones of some of the Brothers, simply came to an end in that battle as they died.

The little nudges he had given these lines earlier had worked: Torra was now on a path that coincided with the Key of Otemus. Feng's apricot-colored line came in from another direction and joined theirs, too, just as Azartial had planned.

But Apostle Agnon's ribbon came back around, as well, confirming Azartial's fears that the Codex would lead him to Pendoni. Azartial growled inwardly. He should have killed the pock-marked bastard when he'd had a chance.

And what's this? His own blue-burning line was there, but it now veered away from Torra's, growing slowly more distant from this point further, this moment at the pyramid! What had happened?

Azartial thought for a moment, then realized what had changed. Not only had the Codex been stolen, but the mages figured out his Darilos identity. Continuing an attempt to hide his identity would only lead to further distrust. Understanding human emotions was tricky, but it didn't take him being human to know that when caught in a lie, it's best to own it.

He pushed and prodded the lines further, forcing his blue-flaming line to cross this moment, while the mages were still there. A show of magic. A dramatic reveal! The demon smiled inwardly. Yes, that did it. His line grew more parallel to Torra's.

As with any manipulation of futures, unintended consequences came of it. Such was the danger of manipulating time lines in the Nexus. One small change in the past could cause larger changes in the future, and though he was very good at manipulations, sometimes there were unexpected complications.

For there, in the future, was another battle now, one that hadn't existed when he last manipulated the lines. It was a horribly strong, concussive, coming together of lines, with many ethereal pops and sizzles. Further, the bright golden line of the Gold Dragon came swooping in, as well! Azartial shook his head. Could he never rid himself of that interloper? This wasn't how it was supposed to be.

He could try nudging things again, but in this dimension, with its linear time lines, that could be very, very dangerous, and he'd already pushed things to the breaking point. It was best to let this play out. The goal of having Torra and Feng together with him at Pendoni had been achieved, it seemed.

The hazy influence of the Triumvirate gods was all over the place here. Azartial wondered if it was they who were interfering. Perhaps they had sensed what was to happen and somehow called the Gold Dragon into the mix? There were also lines of the other mages going along with Torra. This change in the time lines, this battle, could only be because the Gold Dragon or the other mages were now involved in Pendoni.

Yet the lines grew fuzzy at Pendoni. There wasn't a clear outcome as to who would live and who would die. The energy of that clash was going to be very strong. Powerful magic indeed. He asked himself, *How can such magic happen at the location of an energy void for both terrestrial and celestial magic?*

No outcome was guaranteed.

The gods would be watching.

Azartial let his mind exit the Nexus. In moments he had broken out of the meditation and returned his consciousness to this dimension.

Amazingly, the storm had intensified even more. The wind was a tempest. Rain blew sideways. Trees bent and swayed like dancers possessed of frenzied spirits.

He stood and peered around the corner. The mages had changed positions to huddle behind the largest of the trees in the copse, though it offered scant protection.

Lightning struck a tree only fifty feet away, issuing an ear-shattering crack and boom.

Azartial laughed. Since he'd been outed, and he'd grown bored of the subterfuge, it was time to end the charade. Time for that dramatic reveal! The human skin burned away in a flash of blue flame, melting and dissolving, and the demon emerged, his long, red tongue lolling in ecstasy.

He teleported to the crumbling top of the pyramid, far above the copse of mages. With a mighty roar, he raised his blue-flaming arms to the heavens and activated his magic center, broadcasting his energy to the world.

Attracted by his energy, lightning arced from the clouds in half a dozen streaks, striking Azartial's claws. The sky exploded in a barrage of thunder. Raw energy coursed through him. His blue flames radiated far around him like a sapphirine torch, for all to see.

Azartial roared in ecstatic pain and exhilaration.

"Mages! Dragons! Gods!" he exclaimed, laughing madly. "Hear me now! I am Azartial! Demon dragon! Footman of the Ether!"

WATCH for BOOK 3 of the
HEARTSTONE SERIES
COMING 2025
from GLADEYE PRESS

Book Three of the Heartstone Series

Lord of Silk and Steel

Jason A. Kilgore

The epic adventure in the mystical lands of
Irikara continues with powerful mage Torra
Com Gidel, the cruel General Feng, Golden
Dragon Ingal Jahai, and
Azartial, the Demon Dragon!

ABOUT THE AUTHOR

Jason A. Kilgore is a multigenre writer in speculative fiction, including horror, fantasy, and science fiction, as well as poetry, scientific publications, and essays. By day, he is a scientist with a global biotech company specializing in microscopy and cell biology. He lives in Oregon and when he isn't writing, he loves hiking and camping in the mountain wilderness areas and the Pacific coast.

If you enjoyed this story, recommend it to a friend or leave a review. Sign up for news about the Strange Worlds of Jason Kilgore: https://mailchi.mp/a9205da52dab/worldskilgore

Visit and follow the author's web and social media pages:

Author website: https://jason-kilgore.com/
Blog: https://jasonkilgore.blogspot.com
Twitter: https://twitter.com/WorldsKilgore
Facebook: https://facebook.com/WorldsKilgore
Instagram: https://instagram.com/WorldsKilgore

ACKNOWLEDGMENTS

A special thank you to my friend, Adam Breashears, whose generous patronage paid for the original cover art. And my everlasting thanks to my writer's group, the Peeps of Corvallis, Oregon, past and present, who critiqued every word and helped me take my writing to the next level.

MORE BOOKS FROM GLADEYE PRESS

The Time Tourists
The Yesterday Girl
Sharleen Nelson
Follow the adventures and missteps of time-traveling PI Imogen Oliver as she recovers lost items and unearths long-buried stories and secrets from the past in this exciting series!

The Fragile Blue Dot
Ross West
Veteran science-writer and journalist Ross West's collection of award-winning short fiction touches on the human aspect of living in a world on the brink of ecological disaster.

Dye. Run. Don't Die: A Love Story
K.G. Kolsen
Chased by shadowy figures, Winnie and Jimmy reunite somewhere between Oklahoma and Colorado and embark on a wild ride filled with disguises, stolen vehicles, murders, truck-stop perverts, a sex-cult, deadly shootouts, and rediscovered love.

The Risk of Being Ridiculous
Guy Maynard
Join 19-year-old Ben Tucker for a passionate, lyrical six-week ride through confrontation and confusion, courts and cops, parties and politics, school and the streets, Weathermen and women's liberation, acid and activism, revolution and reaction.

All GladEye titles are available for purchase at www.gladeyepress.com and your local bookstore.

Faith, Hope, Dying
Patricia Brown
Eleanor, Angus, Feathers, and the coffee club friends are back! When sisters Hope and Faith return to the small coastal village to settle their preacher father's estate, rumors swirl and the truth about a decades-old mystery leads to a fresh wave of murders.

Under A Dying Moon
Patricia Brown
When a young girl washes up on the beach, there is no doubt murder is once again the topic in town. Two more brutal murders bring the town to the edge of panic. Are the newly arrived young swingers involved or the cute retired couple? And what is the deal with the gnomes scattered around town?

Dying for Diamonds
Patricia Brown
When a mean-spirited mystery writer visiting her sleepy coastal town is murdered, Eleanor Penrose, her retired detective friend Angus, the coffee club ladies, and Feathers, the irascible African grey parrot, work to solve the puzzles without becoming the murderer's next victims.

A Recipe for Dying
Patricia Brown
The old people are dying in the small coastal town of Waterton, but no one seems to notice—after all, that's what old folk do, isn't it? Eleanor and her delightful assortment of friends, most whom are getting up in age, set out to discover what is going on. Is it a series of mercy killings, or murder, and is their investigation putting them in danger?

COMING 2024 *from*

 GladEye
Press

Trial
Guy Maynard
Facing serious criminal charges resulting from a 1970 demonstration, Ben Tucker navigates lawyers he doesn't trust, travels from the streets of Boston to the beaches of California through a country at war with itself, an improbable but passionate love affair, and budding communal ties with a group of college dropout freaks—with a date with a judge and jury in a solemn Massachusetts courtroom always looming in front of him.

Ash Valley
Guy Maynard
In this final installment in the trilogy, Ben Tucker, his soulmate Sarah, and a community of like-minded friends forge new bonds while seeking peace and tranquility far away from Boston at a commune in the rugged Pacific Northwest.

The End of Time
Sharleen Nelson
Book three in this exciting series follows the continuing adventures of time-traveling private investigator Imogen Oliver as she uncovers shocking new revelations about her family, faces more challenges in her rocky relationships, and the threat of a power-hungry villain who wants to shut down time travel for good.